POISONED

PATRICIA HARTMAN

Scripture quotations taken from the (NASB®) New American Standard Bible®,
Copyright © 2020 by The Lockman Foundation. Used by permission. All rights
reserved. www.lockman.org

ISBN: 978-1-953114-30-3
LCCN: 2021918915

Subjects:
1. Fiction/Christian/Suspense
2.Fiction/Romance/Suspense
3. Fiction/Thriller/Suspense

Published by EA Books Publishing, a division of
Living Parables of Central Florida, Inc. a 501c3

EABooksPublishing.com

PRAISE FOR POISONED

Imagine James Herriot fighting crime between treating patients. Now meet Doc Wheeler and get engrossed in her adventure as she cares for pets and livestock all while unraveling the life-threatening mystery that plagues her West Virginia town. The colorful characters and patients enrich the suspense and keep you guessing. I couldn't put it down. Hopefully, we'll be invited back to Hearthstone by Patricia Hartman for future adventures.

—Meg Taylor, WV animal lover and DVM at Highlands Vet Clinic

Poisoned, with its fast-paced dialogue, is a page-turner that constantly surprises the reader with unusual twists and turns. A true-crime story—human struggle, crime, corruption, political intrigue and even has a touch of romance. Hartman has a winner.

—James W. Geiger, Former FBI agent and prosecuting attorney and author of *The Gospel According to Relativity: Constant Value in a Changing World* and *Christianity and the Outsider: A Lawyer Looks at Justice and Justification*

POISONED Is Intoxicating! This suspenseful mystery is a must-read for anyone seeking a fresh thriller that captivates your imagination and keeps you guessing! *Poisoned,* a compelling mystery, excites and surprises as the story unveils a hidden darkness threatening the lovable characters in this peaceful town. Trust is challenged by a toxic force seeping through town while Dr. Julie Wheeler, veterinarian always on call, takes the reins. This story stimulates your mind and delights your heart, but be careful . . . you will not be able to put this book down!

Patricia Hartman, please give us more of these stories!

—Anne V. Alper, Attorney
Former Assistant State Attorney, Broward County, Florida

MANY THANKS TO . . .

RAMONA RICHARDS who set me on this path of writing novels through her deep-point-of-view course. I hadn't planned on writing fiction—I was just trying to develop better non-fiction. I have truly enjoyed the journey. Thank you for opening this world to me. I hope my work honors your teaching.

FAY LAMB who mentored me in the early stages of this new journey. Who knew characters could be flat? And thanks for the ideas that helped reshape this story.

EVA MARIE EVERSON, and all my fellow WORD WEAVERS who have guided and encouraged me in developing the craft. Thank you.

THE MOST AMAZING PEOPLE IN WEST VIRGINIA, including dedicated FBI special agents, DEA special agents, deputies, magistrates, prosecutors, veterinarians, mayors, waitresses, and so many other fascinating souls who humored me as I zigzagged the state from west to east, north to south, and everywhere in between. Thank you.

PATRICK HARTMAN, my incredible co-laborer and the lover of my soul who has traveled the roads of West Virginia and this awesome writing journey with me and listened to every word . . . how many times, honey? I love you.

OUR AWESOME GOD, who lovingly guides me on every step of this journey and makes this all possible. Praise Him!

Rescue me, Lord, from evil people;
Protect me from violent men
Who devise evil things in their hearts;
They continually stir up wars.
They sharpen their tongues like a snake;
The venom of a viper is under their lips. Selah
—Psalm 140:1-3 (NASB)

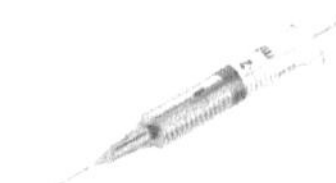

CHAPTER 1

Tuesday, October 24, 3:22 a.m.

No matter how delightful the ringtone—at 3:22 a.m. the phone call still violated her dreams. The alarm clock's red numbers glared at Julie Wheeler's one open eye. If her phone was so smart, why didn't it know how desperately she needed her sleep? As the town's only large-animal veterinarian, returning to her sweet dreams was not an option.

Richard nudged Julie and mumbled. "Hon. The phone."

"Uhhh ..."

The phone continued ringing. Julie *wanted* to move.

"Julie!" Richard nudged her shoulder.

"Okay. Okay." With a moan, she pushed herself upright. Wiping the crust from her eyes, Julie reached for her phone. Blurry letters came into focus exposing her perpetrator's name. "Sorry, Babe. It's the Olgrams."

"Again?" Turning away from her, Richard grumbled. "Maybe they should give up the dairy and move back to the city."

"Don't say that. They hardly call anymore."

"Your phone is ringing, isn't it?"

"You should talk. What time did you get home anyway?"

He didn't answer.

She touched the screen and tossed her hair back as she pressed the phone to her ear. Clearing her throat, she prepared her best professional voice. Instead, gravel-filled her throat as she said, "Morning, Harvey."

"Doc. Sorry to botter you at thees hour." His singsong Minnesotan accent could not contain his panic. "Petunia's trying to deliver. Only the tail's come out—no feet."

A full breech. Nights like this were rarely rewarding. Clearing her throat again, Julie asked, "How long has she been in labor?"

"I don't know. An hour?"

Too long.

"Have you done anything to turn the calf?" Julie asked.

"No. Shooldt I?"

"No. No. I'm on my way."

Julie tapped the end icon on her phone and bent over her knees. She rubbed her scalp. *Come on brain. Click in.* Richard's deep breathing assured her he wasn't losing sleep over this calf's plight.

Julie had to move quickly, but fatigue engulfed her. What was wrong with her? An image of her dying mother's frail thirty-eight-year-old body came to mind again—a regular remembrance since she turned the same age a few weeks earlier. She forced the memory away.

Julie turned on the bedside lamp. Her eyes struggled to adjust. Willing her numb body to move, she sunk her feet into the plush carpeting to stand. *Richard.* Shaking her head, she looked back. What time had he gotten home last night? Julie tried to think past the fog. He wasn't there when she dropped into bed at eleven. You would think the county's chief prosecuting attorney wouldn't have to work so late every night. It's not like Hearthstone was a metropolis—a fly could cover its name on the West Virginia map.

The calf.

She ran her fingers through her hair. *Come on, Julie. This isn't like you. Get a grip.* Another glance at the clock. 3:26. Four minutes. Good grief. That calf had no chance if she couldn't move any faster than this.

She hurried to the bathroom to gauge how badly she looked at this hour. Those wretched circles. What was she going to look like at forty . . . *if* she made it to forty.

Make it? *The calf.*

Hair … teeth … turtleneck … necklace … jeans … phone … light … Richard. She shouldn't have barked at him. She went to his side and took in his moonlit image. Even with his hints of gray, he was still the most handsome man in town. And, much to the chagrin of every woman in Hearthstone, Julie got to sleep with him every night.

She pulled up the last quilt her mother had made and gently kissed his forehead. "I love you."

"Mmm," was all he managed as he turned away.

Julie padded past the guest room, careful not to disturb her sister. What time had she gotten home? Not that coming home late was unusual for Heather. Julie had hoped her sister would have been more stable this time around. But Richard was right—her sister never changed. Feral cats were easier to domesticate and required less attention.

She raced down the back staircase that led to the kitchen and scurried from room to room to collect the necessities. Energy drink … boots … purse … keys … jacket. All in order, she headed out the never-locked front door to her new vet mobile.

Even covered in frost, the blue-jean-blue paint glowed in the moonlight. Julie entered her dream machine and started the defroster to clear the icy windows. If only she had parked in the three-car garage Richard had specially built to hold her supersized baby. But hide her beloved truck behind those doors? How silly was that? She wanted it out where everyone could see it.

Every detail signaled Julie was now a full-fledged rural vet—a 4x4 Super Cab Ford F-150 XLT outfitted with a coveted Bowie Platinum 8 Mobile Clinic. The paint job that boldly declared her love, HEARTHSTONE VETERINARY CLINIC. Nothing topped the feeling of climbing in—especially since she had paid off all her student loans before affording herself this luxury.

She checked her watch. 3:42. The de-icing was costing her patient precious minutes. But trying to drive with frosted windows had caused her only accident. She couldn't chance it again. It would be 3:52 when she got there—almost an hour and a half since Petunia went into labor. Defrost!

Julie popped the top of her energy drink and sucked down every drop.

Ooh. Her stomach rebelled. Was it the flavor? She checked the label. Green apple, her favorite. Another twinge. She couldn't get sick now. She was the calf's only hope.

The windshield was almost as hazy as her brain. Why was she so distracted this morning? Maybe Richard was right. Maybe she was working too much. But who was he to talk? Lately, all he did was work. Besides, what else could Julie do? People needed her. There was no one else.

Windshield clear enough, Julie flipped on the wipers and backed away from the garage on the right side of the two-story white-columned brick dream home. She crossed in front of the house and the privacy hedge that lined the driveway from the house to the main property drive. Out of habit, she stopped where the driveway pavement met the dirt road that led to the barn. She lowered the frosted passenger window to check for vehicles. Not that anyone would be coming out at this hour.

What on earth? Why were the barn lights on at this hour? A figure stood in front, looking her way. Jake? After only a couple of months of employment, Julie didn't yet know his habits. But there was no reason for a farmhand to get up before milking time. A chill shook her. Questions would have to wait.

Rolling up the window, she turned left down the drive and onto the road to the Olgrams' farm. In front of her, the moon shone through the barren trees, casting eerie shadows on a day that would never end.

———

As she reached the Olgrams' barn, Julie checked her watch. 3:52. Time was running out. She slid out of the leather seat, lowered the tailgate, and unlocked the door of the mobile clinic to retrieve her delivery kit.

The cold fall air assaulted her senses as she removed her jacket to don her vet bib-overalls. Hair pulled back, she slipped an elastic band on her ponytail, then retrieved the calf-puller kit from the back end.

Harvey hustled out of the barn. His patriotic suspenders accented his protruding red-flannel-covered belly. He never wore a coat, even in the dead of winter. Reaching out his hand, he said, "Thanks for coming at this hour, Doc."

"Only for you, Harvey," she said as she handed him the calf-puller kit, then motioned toward the barn and continued on mission.

Hurrying behind her, he said, "You say that to everyone. That's why you're everyone's favorite vet."

"I'm the *only* vet," Julie said over her shoulder.

Petunia waited in a well-lit stall where Harvey's petite wife comforted the pained heifer.

Mooo!

Gracie rubbed the heifer's face while speaking sweet nothings in her ear. Even Julie was soothed by Gracie's charming British accent.

The cow's head was tethered to the stall, a bucket of soapy water to her right, and plenty of hay for the calf's soft landing. Petunia's upright stance would make Julie's work easier.

"How's our patient doing?" Julie asked as she began arranging her tools.

The wrinkles in Gracie's face ran deep and the circles accentuated the night's trouble. "She's being a trooper, aren't you girl?"

Petunia turned her head back to give the new guest a once-over. The cow's eyes bulged. Julie ran her hand over the heifer's rump, patting her patient as she lifted her tail. "Look what we have here." Just as Harvey had said—tail, no feet.

Julie checked Harvey. His sunken eyes revealed his concern. Julie held his gaze. Speaking slowly to let her words sink in, she said, "Harvey, this is a full breech. The calf's legs are pointed forward, and I have to turn them carefully to keep the hooves from puncturing Petunia's uterus. And in the time all that takes . . ."

Harvey was tearing up. Julie put a hand on his shoulder. "You know I'll do my best, but we have to protect Petunia first because there's no guarantee with the calf. You understand that."

Harvey nodded. "I trust you, Doc."

Julie patted his shoulder as she released her grip. The frigid night air caught her breath as she pulled both sleeves all the way up her arms for this two-handed procedure. She tugged on her shoulder-length calving gloves and handed a bottle of lubricant to Harvey, mostly to keep him busy. Harvey squirted some gel on Julie's outstretched hand.

Petunia mooed and shifted.

"You're doing fine, girl. You're going to make a good mum," Gracie said.

Mum. Julie wanted that accent.

Refocusing, she said to Harvey, "Hold her tail up while I work to get this little one turned around."

Petunia lurched and mooed as Julie started her internal examination, but then settled as Julie determined the calf's position. It was indeed backward. "It's a classic presentation."

Harvey nodded as Julie strained to reach for the calf's first knee. She pulled it toward her, then covered the hoof in her hand to protect the uterus. She moved the hoof and positioned the leg into the birth canal. These workouts tired even the strongest of men, but Julie loved the challenge.

Mooo! Gracie shifted her burgeoning body.

Holding the first leg in place, Julie took a step back and pointed to the pulling kit. "I need the OB chain and a hook, then get the harness hooked up over Petunia's rear and put the ratchet together."

Harvey obliged.

Julie wrapped the chain around the first hoof. Reaching in again, she found the second knee, and then the hoof, turning it this way and that. Finally, she pulled out the second leg, joining it with the first in a delivery position inside the birth canal. The uterus—and Petunia—would be safe now. The calf's outcome, however, was still a question.

Julie took a step back to rest. A rush of nausea jolted her. She leaned forward and rested her hands on her knees. She had to concentrate. The clock was ticking. She couldn't be sick.

"Doc?" Harvey said.

Julie looked up at Harvey's pinched face.

"You okay? You don't look so good."

Forcing a grin, she straightened herself. Still fighting her discomfort, she said, "I'm fine. Just catching my breath."

Harvey's lips curved down. Julie needed to distract him. And herself, for that matter. She pointed to the ratchet pole. "Ready?"

Harvey picked up the assembled pole. Julie straightened and gently hooked the other end of the OB chain to the second hoof and said, "Okay, put that pole into the bracket and let's get busy. You know the drill."

He nodded.

She hooked both chains to the ratchet. Every several notches, Julie stopped to check the calf's presentation, added a little lubricant, and then proceeded again. Petunia was being ever so cooperative, staying upright for the duration.

The calf's hips cleared the pelvis. "We're just about done, girl," Julie said, mostly to encourage the couple. Julie motioned for Harvey to push the ratchet bar down while she gave one last pull and carefully lowered the calf to the pile of hay below. "It's a girl," Julie announced.

The calf wasn't moving. Julie cleared the newborn's nose and rubbed her with hay to bring her to life. "Come on, girl. Let's get going." Julie took a piece of straw and tickled her nose. Harvey bent over and joined the vigorous rubbing while Julie continued her efforts.

Still nothing. Julie's heart sank. It had been too long.

"Come on, girl. It's a goodt day to be born," Harvey said, a tinge of desperation in his voice. Rubbing harder, he said, "Dear Lord, brink her to life."

Julie scooped a handful of water into the calf's ear and she flinched. Life. After clearing her mouth, Julie tickled her nose again. She coughed up some phlegm and moved. With a wobble, the calf lifted her head and then lay back down.

Dragging the calf toward Gracie, Julie said, "Would you untie Petunia's head so she can meet her baby girl?"

Petunia began licking life into her baby. Julie stepped back, removing her gloves and pulling down her sleeves. She never tired of this scene. Gracie leaned down to relish the new life. The calf's head bobbed up.

"Welcome, little one." Gracie gazed upon Petunia as she continued her motherly bonding. "That's a good girl. Look at your new bundle of joy."

Harvey wiped his hands on his pants and pulled out his smartphone. He loved posting photos of his new calves on Facebook—which was great for Julie's business. Harvey centered the scene with Gracie, Petunia, and her baby on the screen. "Okay, Doc—get in the picture."

Julie moved in and squatted behind Gracie to hide her messy bibs. The best picture was not taken, however—the look on Harvey's face as he surveyed the miracle of life. He clicked several shots, checked the pictures, and then held out his phone. "Woodt you mind?"

Julie stood, accepting the phone as Harvey took Julie's spot. He beamed. She snapped several shots, then handed it back.

"What are you going to name her?" Julie asked.

Harvey looked at Gracie, who turned to Julie and said, "Micaela, I think. It's British. It means gift from God." Harvey shared a satisfied grin, then turned to kiss his love.

"Well, my work is done here," Julie said, then began to gather her tools.

"Won't you come up to the house? You can clean up and have a spot of coffee."

Julie started to agree, but nausea swept over her again. She might not be able to stop it this time. Heaving vets didn't make great house guests.

"As much as I'd like that, I need to get back to my office and get a couple hours' sleep." Julie struggled to hide her malaise. "I'll check in with you tomorrow."

"Suit yourself, but I hope you'll come back for a visit when you have some time. And please tell Richard thank you for letting us call you out like this," Gracie said.

"He's fine. Left him sleeping like a baby." Julie mustered a smile, leaving her questions about his late-night return unspoken. Why was it bothering her? Richard was as faithful as a golden retriever.

"Well, please let him know how much we appreciate him sharing you with us at this late hour."

Harvey picked up the kits, then walked Julie back to her truck. "We tank God for you," Harvey said as he shook her hand.

"I wish everyone cared for their animals the way you do." Julie collected her coat, not even stopping to take off her overalls. Closing the back end, she hurried, trying to ignore the pressure rising in her throat.

Harvey was still standing there. "I mean it, Doc." He held out his hand again, shaking hers slowly. When Julie made eye contact, Harvey said, "Doc, you don't know thees, but a few months after we got here, we were ready to pack it all in and move back to the city. It's only because of you, Hank at the feed 'n seed, and this whole community—but especially you—that we made it. We will forever be indebted to you."

Compliments made Julie uneasy, but she kept his gaze and nodded when he finished. She almost let out a tear, but then reconstituted herself. "You're welcome."

She released Harvey's gaze and hand and climbed into her truck. If she could just make it to the road before giving up her stomach's contents.

Julie backed her prized truck away from the Olgrams' barn, waving to Harvey and forcing a smile. She turned onto the road that led back to the highway. Once out of view she pulled off the road, got out, then raced to get around the truck before losing her energy drink. She braced herself on the truck as she forced herself straight. Another wave of nausea forced her back over, but there was nothing left to give up.

Julie shook it off. Erecting herself, she breathed in the cold morning air and exhaled a steamy cloud of relief. *Ahhh.* The feeling passed—for the moment.

She removed her bibs, pulled on her jacket, and opened the tailgate. Good. Heather had restocked the wipes.

Face—clean. Mouth—yuck. Julie located a half-full bottle of water in the console of her truck, swished the water in her mouth and spit it out, then drank down what was left. She searched her purse for a mint. An old throat lozenge would have to do. Anything to get that taste out of her mouth.

Julie climbed back in and checked herself in the mirror. What a sight. She pulled out her elastic band and shook her hair as if it would help her shed some years. She looked again. Still old. She flipped the visor up to make her age go away.

What now? Her smartphone stared at her from the console. She tapped it. 5:35 a.m. 32 degrees. No messages.

Julie hated to go home at this hour, afraid of disturbing what was left of Richard's sleep. However much that was. And what if she had a bug? She didn't want to give it to him. The sofa at the office would have to do. She could get in a nap and maybe get to the Dogwood Diner before her first patients arrived at nine.

Eww. Eat? Julie's stomach didn't like that idea.

She pulled her mother's gold horse-head pendant necklace from her turtleneck, clutched it between her fingers, and closed her eyes. "Momma, what's going on with me?"

Julie tried to suppress her fears but was not winning the war. Images of her mother lying in a hospital bed flashed. Her mother kissing the pendent, then willing herself to put it around Julie's neck. Just a few months before, her ever-effervescent mother had begun having stomach problems. Then fatigue. One day young and vibrant, the next day gone.

Julie tried to push the possibility away. Her age, her symptoms. There had to be another explanation. Flu? Exhaustion? Bad food?

Julie rested her head on her hands at the top of the steering wheel and again closed her eyes. Conjuring an image of her mother, Julie said, "Momma, where are you when I need you?"

Her mother smiled sweetly, and . . .

———

5:30 a.m.

SHERIFF MACK MCCONNELL STARED AT HIS COMPUTER SCREEN, his hands hovering over the keyboard. He sat back and looked at the ceiling. He leaned forward and rested his face in his cupped hands. How had it come to this?

Mack returned both hands to the keyboard and continued.

> *And so, my dear friend, when all is said and done, I just want you to know how highly I esteem you and how much you and Julie have meant in our lives. It was painful to push you away these last few years. We have missed you.*
>
> *Please don't blame Marge. Gambling is an awful disease that has poisoned her soul. It's my fault for not dealing with it at the time.*
>
> *I was supposed to be your best man. I regret letting you down.*
>
> *May God forgive me.*

He pushed the printer icon and watched his letter emerge. He reread each word, closed his eyes, and prayed.

Heart heavy, Mack picked up an expensive pen and signed what might be his last letter. He folded it and stuffed it in an envelope. He searched the top drawer, unable to find where Marge kept the stamps. Rifling through the other drawers, he found that sheet of Lincoln four-cent stamps from his collection. How ironic. Honest Abe.

He counted the appropriate number of stamps, licked and applied them, covering most of the upper right side of the envelope. Hopefully, Richard would appreciate their value and keep them.

He scribed Richard's address.

Staring at the finished envelope, he rose and took it to their mailbox. No, they might be watching. He looked around. Taking it to the post office would ensure Richard got it.

———

5:45 a.m.

"Hello?"

Tap. Tap. Tap.

"Dr. Wheeler?"

Who was that? Where was she? What day was it?

Opening her eyes, Julie lifted her head off the steering wheel.

It was still dark. How long had she been there?

A uniformed deputy was peering in her window. The rearview mirror flashed blue lights. What on earth?

Julie reached for the button on the door panel. The window did not respond. Of course. The truck was off.

Richard's stories of traffic stops gone awry came to mind. If she started the truck, it would look like she was going to flee, and if she opened the door, it would threaten the deputy. No win.

Julie turned again to make out this deputy in the dark. She didn't recognize him. He had a boyish look. She used to know all the deputies, from Richard's close work with the sheriff's office. Was he new? Would he know who she was and that she was married to the prosecuting attorney?

She opted for opening the door.

The deputy backed up as she slid out, setting a four-foot gap between them. He adjusted the belt on his newly pressed uniform and settled into an official stance.

What was he? Twenty-five? Why had Richard never mentioned him?

"What's going on, Deputy …" she said as she tried to read his badge.

"Cruz," he said as he shifted in his uniform. He checked his watch. Why was he in a hurry at this hour?

"I saw your truck by the road," he said in his Chicagoese, fidgeting again with his uniform, then standing on alert. "So—Doc Wheeler—ma'am …" he opened both palms toward her and tipped his chin up, begging for an answer to the unasked question.

This kid was the poster child for a tough guy. What was he doing in West Virginia?

"How'd you know my name?"

His reddened face froze as his eyes darted until they rested on the door of the truck. He straightened and pointed to the Hearthstone Veterinary Clinic sign on the door panel.

Why didn't she believe him? "Hmm," slipped out of her throat. The door of the truck only revealed the clinic name, not hers. Her neck hairs rose.

"Deputy, if you don't mind me asking, how long have you worked here?"

Cruz's face tightened. "Three months. Why'd ya ask?"

"It's just that my husband usually mentions new deputies he works with. He's never mentioned you. That's all."

Cruz's eyes squinted. After a long moment, his expression relaxed. "Sounds like you've learned the art of interrogation from your husband."

"Oh, so you know my husband?"

"Sure." He checked his watch again.

Where was the endearing respect that deputies usually had for Richard? Had Richard been hard on him for a screwed-up investigation? If so, why hadn't Julie heard about it?

"Well, Dr. Wheeler, if you're okay …" He took a step back.

"I'm fine, deputy. Just a long night—"

"Good." He turned for his car as if he had just been called to handle an emergency.

The deputy's car threw gravel as it pulled out, leaving Julie standing by her truck. The cruiser's taillights disappeared over the horizon.

Had he really just left her standing by the side of the road? Julie shook her head. She turned and ran her hand over the door sign, rerunning the mental tape of what had just occurred. She climbed back in and settled into the seat.

What happened to the days of sheriff's office barbeques, wedding invitations, holiday parties? There was never a month that went by without some sort of get-together. How long had it been since they had been to any sheriff functions?

Her body shook. She started her truck and headed to her office.

CHAPTER 2

6:00 a.m.

THE DARKNESS IN HER REARVIEW MIRROR reflected Julie's mood. What was different about today? Even in the predawn shadows of the Alleghenies, Julie loved this route to her clinic nestled in the foothills of West Virginia. Ribboning roads, white-fenced farmland, rippling creeks, ferned forests—everything she loved about living here.

But nothing about today's drive soothed her. It was as dark as her soul. She checked her mirror again, still envisioning the blue lights. Deputy Cruz. Why didn't she trust him? For someone who was supposed to "protect and serve," he sure didn't ensure her welfare.

The REDUCED SPEED AHEAD sign marked the border between the rural and residential, and alerted Julie to the entrance to her clinic. If they ever took that sign down, she would miss her driveway off WV 227 and find herself in the sprawling seven-block-long metropolis of Hearthstone.

Julie signaled her left turn to no one and turned just past the front patient parking lot into the staff parking. Eddie's car was snuggled in by the small barn that housed the large animals with her vet tech's upstairs apartment. The gravel crunched as it gave way to her mobile vet machine, inviting her tail-wagging patients to erupt into a cacophony of alarms. If Eddie wasn't awake before, he would be now.

The dog concerto settled her soul. Julie loved every woof and whinny that came with a rural practice. Unlike her father's frou-frou

D.C. practice that catered to manufactured teacup puppies, she had it all here—real folks with real pets, a beautiful farm, and a wonderful husband. Sure, her practice kept her busy 24/7. And yes, she did sometimes have to take a hog in lieu of pay. But that's the price for living in "Wild and Wonderful West Virginia."

Julie pulled into the spot closest to the private entrance on the right side of the building. Thanks to Daylight Savings Time ending last weekend, it would only be dark for another hour. The motion-sensor lights chased the darkness from her path up the stairs to the door. She opened her purse and struggled to locate her office keys. How did they always manage to sink to the bottom despite which bag she used? She needed to find a purse that had its own pocket for keys.

Finally. She retrieved the keys and entered the already-lit hallway that ran the length of the building to the supply room, with the waiting room, the office manager's station, checkout corridor, and Julie's office on the left, and the three exam rooms and operating room on the right.

"Eddie? You here?" she called as she secured the door and returned her keys to her hungry purse.

The kenneled dogs renewed their interest in her arrival.

"Doc?" a voice called from the din, along with a couple of woofs.

A leashed beagle puppy working to make traction on the linoleum floor came from Exam Room 3 at the far-right end of the hallway, followed by Eddie, and, of course, Socrates, the black and white office guard cat. Socrates seated himself in a proper king-cat pose at the doorway, annoyed that his favorite staff member was daring to give attention to someone other than himself.

"Mornin', Doc," Eddie said as he met Julie at the counter that separated Angie's domain from her own. Tail beating the air, Rascal sniffed Julie's jeans as if they held the key to a raccoon's whereabouts. "Ain't it a little early for ya?"

"You're not kidding. You're looking at a woman who just successfully delivered her third full breech calf in a row." Julie bowed as Eddie applauded and his charge barked his excitement. They both chuckled.

Julie stooped to acknowledge her patient and check the stitches from his bullet wound. Typical story. His owner had "a little too much to drink" and Rascal got in the way of some target practice—at least, that's what the owner said. It was more likely that he was high on something illegal.

"He's healing up nicely," Julie said. "You would never know he lost so much blood."

"I'll say. He's got more energy than me." Julie stood as Eddie continued, "I feel so sorry for him. He cried and cried all night." Eddie paused, shaking his head. "They oughta arrest that jerk."

"You're preaching to the choir." Julie patted Eddie's shoulder. She had yet to see anyone arrested for pet abuse, even for cases worse than this. Richard would just remind her that things in the country were a whole lot different than in D.C. where her dad had moved their family after he had remarried.

Richard's big concern was the heroin that had given West Virginia the illustrious title of most heroin-related deaths. He was not swayed by Julie's argument that those druggies were doing it to themselves, and the dogs were innocent victims. She had long ago stopped trying to get anything done about it. She just patched them up, sent them home, and hoped for the best.

Julie retrieved a dog snack from the cookie jar on the counter. "Sit," she commanded, to which Rascal just wagged his tail harder. Eddie laughed while Julie handed over the treat.

She leaned over the counter to get the appointment book that Angie had carefully centered in front of her computer screen.

"Uh oh. Wait till Mom finds out you touched her stuff. You're in *so* much trouble," Eddie smirked.

"Do I need to remind you who owns this office?" she asked as she surveyed her back-to-back morning appointments and her one barn call in the afternoon.

"When has *that* ever mattered? You may own it, but Mom rules.

Socrates launched himself up to the counter and sat squarely on the book. He pressed his nose into Julie's cheek for some loving. She scratched under his craning neck, as he purred his appreciation. Rascal jumped up putting his front paws on the wall under the counter, jealous for Doc's attention.

"Okay, that's enough." Eddie settled Rascal as Doc shooed Socrates down. She carefully returned the book to the exact spot where she found it. She turned to be sure Eddie saw the book's perfect placement. "Your mom doesn't have to know a thing, now *does* she?" Julie nodded slowly to invite—or, rather, insist—on Eddie's complicity in the matter.

"Are you kidding? She always knows." Shaking his head, Eddie stared at his mom's chair as if looking back in time. "She's got a sixth sense about this stuff. Trust me—I've got twenty-eight years of dealing with her. The funny thing is she used to do the same thing with Grandpa when he owned the practice. And he's her dad."

"How well I know."

Socrates planted himself on the relocated book, intermittently flipping his tail to remind them of his presence.

"Well, we can always blame Socrates."

"I don't know . . ." Eddie's mouth tipped up with a sly grin. "I still think she'll know."

Julie checked her watch. 6:15. Days like this, Julie was glad Doc Lawrence had had the foresight to install a shower when he had the clinic built. "I'm going to get a shower and take a nap. You gonna be around?"

"Where else would I be?" Eddie said, raising his hands and shoulders. Rascal hopped up on Eddie's leg and whimpered to remind him he was neglecting a promised walk.

They both chuckled.

"Looks like business calls. Wake me up at seven-thirty, will you?"

"I'll try, but you might want to set your phone alarm anyway, just in case I get busy and lose track of time. We have a pretty full house right now." Eddie gave Rascal a tug and they headed out the side door.

Julie retrieved her purse and stepped into the simpler times of her office sanctuary. Placing the purse on the floor beside the sofa, she sat and tugged off her boots. She stood and removed some spare clothes and a towel from the antique wardrobe her stepmother had planned to get rid of when they moved out of her childhood home. Julie had rescued it as it was being loaded on the donation truck.

She stepped into her private bathroom and carefully tucked her pendant under her turtleneck before removing the shirt. Shedding clothes this time of year was a mixed blessing. The soiled clothes were nasty, but who wanted the shock of the chilled autumn air? *Brrr.* She should have run the hot water before she undressed. It took forever to get hot. The shivering took her back to the times earlier that day she had been jolted by the cold. But seeing that calf take its first breath and sharing the Olgrams' joy at Micaela's birth made it all worthwhile.

Finally. Hot water. Julie stepped into the shower and allowed the liquid love to envelop her, chasing away the darkness that had tried to overtake her day.

Shower done. Fresh clothes donned. Darkness gone. Now for a nap.

Julie pulled a pillow and one of her mother's quilts from the wardrobe. Holding it up, she was struck anew with the details of her childhood carefully stitched together in this tapestry. Mom had been a master at every craft she ever undertook. *I miss you, Mom.* Even after twenty-four years.

Perhaps her sister's return had invited this melancholy.

She lay down on the brown leather sofa, wishing her mother could tuck her in. She smiled as her mind escaped to her childhood farm life displayed on the wall across the room. Her mom's paintings captured the essence of her early years. Julie had loved that ranch house and stable full of Arabians who always swept the prizes at shows, each horse with its unique radiant beauty. They lived immortally on the walls of Julie's office. Why had Dad let Catherine talk him into selling their

Virginia farm in favor of life in the suburbs? And what about the four moves since then? That woman was never satisfied. Poor Dad. What had he seen in her?

Oh no! Dad! She had forgotten to call him back again. Had it been a week since he'd called? He probably wanted to invite them for another disastrous Thanksgiving.

She should get up and do it now. But the pillow felt so good . . .

———

6:15 a.m.

UNDER THE CLOAK OF THE EARLY MORNING DARKNESS, Cruz returned to his car. He snuggled the cruiser door closed to avoid detection. His heart pounded in his ears as he scanned for witnesses. He let out his held breath. He had to admit that he loved the thrill, but this … this went too far. It was wrong, and he wanted no part of it. But Uncle Rudy said this was his last chance. He could still hear his words after his last screw-up. *I took you in after your mother died and this is how you repay me?*

How long do you owe a debt?

Headlights off, he slipped the cruiser into drive and moved down the block before stopping to call in. Still checking for six-a.m. life, he touched the boss's name in his Favorites list, then held the phone to his ear. A neighbor's bathroom window illuminated, casting light on the sleepy magnolia outside.

The gravel voice answered, "So?"

"Done. I'm sure she'll get the message."

"Anyone see you?"

"No."

"Good work."

Cruz waited for more, but nothing came. "Boss?"

No answer.

Nothing good about this work. Well, except for Heather. What was he going to do about her? Why had he let his uncle talk him into working here? He had a bad feeling.

———

Tuesday 7:25 a.m.

Richard's welcome ringtone interrupted Julie's restless sleep. What time was it?

Julie pulled her phone from the purse beside the sofa. She squinted to see the time. 7:25. Even in her fog, she smiled at Richard's thoughtfulness. Despite getting up at seven, he postponed calling her in case she was sleeping. He knew her well enough to wait until seven-thirty—her regular alarm time—and that she sometimes forgot to set her alarm at the office—which she had. How had she been so lucky to be married to this man who knew her so thoroughly?

She swept the phone's screen to answer. Clearing her throat, she said, "Good morning."

"Did I wake you?"

Julie envisioned her Prince Charming's face. "*Nooo*, I was just *lying* around the office waiting for my patients to show up."

"Liar," he said with mischief in his voice.

"You know me too well." She sat up, pushing her mother's quilt to the side.

"How'd it go last night?"

"Another full-breech victory. I'll tell you – I didn't think the calf was going to make it. In fact, I didn't think *I* was going to make it."

"Whaddaya mean?"

"I got sick to my stomach this morning. It was really strange. I think it must've been food poisoning or something." Julie paused, remembering her difficulty hiding her discomfort while working on Petunia. "At least I didn't get sick in front of the Olgrams, but it was close. I'd no sooner driven off their property than I had to pull over to throw up by the roadside."

"Are you sure you're okay?"

"Yeah—but you know what's even stranger? When I got back in the truck, I put my head on the steering wheel and fell asleep. Who does that?"

"Sweetie, you haven't been yourself lately. Will you promise to go see Dr. Brown today?"

She froze. See a doctor? She couldn't. Doctors only brought bad news. What if—

"Hun?"

"I can't today."

"I know what *that* means. Do I have to call Angie to get her to clear your calendar?"

"No, no. I'll go. I just can't go today. My schedule is packed." Julie lied, knowing her afternoon was light.

"Tomorrow then?"

He wasn't going to take no for an answer. "Okay, tomorrow."

"I'll call Angie to make sure."

"Thanks for your vote of confidence. But you don't need to." Then she could conveniently forget on purpose.

"You be sure to. I don't want to have to send Jake to pick you up."

Jake. The creepiness of her morning came rushing back.

"Hon, you there?" Richard said.

"Yeah, sorry. I was just remembering that Jake was up when I left at three-thirty this morning. What would he be doing up at that hour?"

"I don't know. Maybe he couldn't sleep. What difference does it make?"

"I guess I'm being silly."

"You? Silly?"

"I guess … but it's not just that. This day has been surreal."

"What do you mean?"

Police lights and Deputy Cruz flashed in Julie's mind. "Do you know Deputy Cruz?"

A pause. "Yeah, why do you ask?"

Uh oh. Answering a question with a question. What was he not saying? "He's the one who woke me up when I fell asleep by the side of the road. Why do *you* ask?"

"What'd he do?"

"He stopped to check on me. So, what do you know about him?"

A long pause. "Let's just say I don't know him well."

Richard stopped talking. A long pause. He was the one who had trained Julie not to be intimidated by the pause. He finally broke the silence. "He's new on the force … Can we just talk about it tonight?"

Richard was being as evasive about Cruz as Julie had been about going to the doctor. This was not her Richard. He used to tell her everything. Lately, he was tight-lipped and tense. Things were changing, and she didn't know why.

"Honey, why don't we ever get invited to social functions with the sheriff's office? We used to be invited to all kinds of things."

Another pause. "I guess we're just too busy."

"Busyness is not new to our lives. At least not new to *my* life. *Your* late nights are another story. So, what's the deal?"

"I don't know. Hang on—Sarah's asking me a question."

In muffled tones, the housekeeper said something, then Richard replied, "No, she got called out last night. It's just me for breakfast … Yes, that sounds good." Another pause. "Sorry, babe. Where were we?"

"Sheriff's office. Events. Too busy."

"Yeah. Will I see you tonight?"

"Why are you asking me? You're the one who hasn't been coming home at night."

"I know. I know. I told you that this case I've been working on is heating up. It can't be helped."

Was it a nervous edge or annoyance that overtook Richard's sweet manner? Work had never affected Richard's life or his loving disposition in their ten years of marriage. Julie didn't know how to respond, so she didn't.

Richard offered nothing more, so Julie said, "I gotta get some breakfast if I'm going to eat before my patients arrive. *Will* you be home tonight?"

"Yes, I promise. I'll see you at seven for sure. You can take that to the bank. In fact, I'll ask Sarah to fix something special."

"It's a date, then," Julie said half-heartedly. Did he mean it this time?

"Great. See you then. Don't work too hard. And don't forget to make that appointment."

"I won't. Love you."

"Me, too."

Julie tapped "end." What an awful word. More foreboding.

Julie stood to fold the quilt, but instead, she opened it and spread it over the sofa. She touched the horseheads, remembering the names of each Arabian beauty as she did. Julie and her mother had spent days riding together before her sister came along just after Julie's tenth birthday. Her mother had made this quilt for Julie's next birthday—perhaps to make up for no longer having time to spend with her "because of the baby."

She wanted to tell her mom all she was feeling this morning. Her mother would have understood. She touched her pendant. "I miss you so much, Mom."

Julie folded the quilt, returned it to its place in the wardrobe, and then carefully closed the doors to her childhood treasures.

Her stomach churned. Hunger pang or queasiness? She waited a minute and thought of breakfast. Breakfast at the Dogwood Diner actually sounded good. She sped up her pace. What a welcome change from how she had felt two hours earlier. Maybe she didn't need to go to the doctor after all.

CHAPTER 3

7:50 a.m.

JULIE ENJOYED THE CONVENIENCE of the one-mile proximity of her office to downtown Hearthstone and the tastes and aromas awaiting her at the Dogwood Diner. And any chance to drive her new ride was a blessing . . . at least until she crested the hill that coasted to downtown. A blaze of brake lights broke her bliss. The elementary school drop-off lines clogged the two-lane highway that became Main Street. Surely, they could come up with a more efficient method of handling the school line.

The last of the cars turned into the school drop-off lane. Julie pressed the accelerator and began to pass in front of the school until the crossing guard held up her stop sign and made her way to the center of the road ahead. There was no one behind Julie. Couldn't she have waited for Julie to pass? But no, ever since Julie had not been able to save Mary Jean's eight-year-old hound dog from cancer, Mary Jean always stopped the well-marked vet-mobile when Julie came along and then took her sweet time about letting her go again. Finally, Mary Jean returned to the curb and lowered her stop sign. Julie raised one hand in a half-wave and resumed her short drive to the Diner.

More than a food establishment, the Diner measured the pulse of the town. The Hearthstone Herald would do well to set up shop there. Julie could count on seeing at least a half-dozen people she loved. Hopefully, Doc Lawrence would be in his usual booth at the back.

In the ten years since he sold his practice to her, she depended on his breakfast counsel to help her with running the clinic and getting along with the clients. He knew them all. No one would appreciate her morning breach story more.

A parking space a few doors down from the Diner invited Julie to pull in. What an ideal spot to show off her new dream machine. After perfectly centering her vehicle, she turned off the engine, grabbed her bag, and slid out of the seat.

She stepped up on the curb beside one of the planters filled with long-dead flowers. Why they didn't plant some kind of small evergreens in those pots, she would never understand. In the spring and summer, the annuals adorned Main Street, but come fall? Just depressing. At least they could have the decency to give those plants a proper burial.

Julie eyed the new treasures in the town's antique shop. Oh! The perfect buffet for her dinette. It would have to wait. The store didn't open until ten. She stopped and sent Angie a text to remind her to call the shop about it when she returned to the office.

The white lace curtains of the Diner framed the window, which displayed the usual full house. The bell above the door announced Julie's entrance.

Sally looked up from refilling coffee cups at a nearby booth. Grinning, she said, "Hey, Doc. Have a seat anywhere," knowing there was not an empty table in the place. Perhaps that's what Julie loved most about coming here—its busyness forced people to sit together, whether you felt like it or not. She was always a better person for sharing a meal or coffee with someone here.

Julie stood by the cash register surveying the twenty or so tables and booths capped with red and white checkered tablecloths.

Doc Lawrence was seated in his usual booth in the left rear corner with his back to the wall. He had taught her when she first came to town to always sit looking toward the door so you could see "who's a-gettin' along with whom." He already had company. They exchanged waves.

Julie did her best not to make eye contact with Paul Cato who was seated in the booth in front of Doc Lawrence's. Thankfully, he was reading the paper and did not notice her entrance. Paul was a defense attorney and Richard's archrival in matters of justice. Julie never had understood how anyone could help criminals get back on the street. Since the time he had tried to hit on her back when she was dating Richard, Julie had done her best to avoid him—not an easy task in a small town. When she was forced to speak to him, he never let her forget that she "could have had the better man." It wasn't funny the first time or any time since. She certainly didn't want to hear it today.

A wall of patrons' backs filled every red stool mounted at the counter on the far side which ran along the front of the kitchen pass-through. Was that Deputy Cruz with assistant sheriff Jerry Hayes? Cruz and Hayes looked pretty chummy sitting together there, heads leaning in. Julie couldn't help but wonder why the county's second-in-command would hang out with a rookie, especially when Sheriff Mack was seated alone two tables away with his back to the duo. You would think that Hayes would be sitting with the sheriff, not the rookie. But, then again, Mack and Hayes were like night and day. Mack had always been gregarious and fun-loving, unlike the somber Hayes. How had Hayes gotten his job anyway?

And Mack … his face could have been a carving on Mt. Rushmore. Staring into space as if unaware of his surroundings. Maybe he could tell her what was going on with Cruz and the sheriff's office since Richard was unyielding.

Without asking permission, Julie removed her jacket and placed it on the back of the chair across from Mack. Her seat allowed her a full view of Cruz and Hayes. Mack's robotic stare turned to Julie as if triggered by a motion sensor. Where was the Mack she had known—the best man at her wedding? His eyes revealed a consuming black hole.

"Good morning, Mack. Long time, no see." Julie said as cheerfully as she could muster. The deputy duo's heads turned in their direction.

The corners of Mack's lips rose in slow motion without improving the droop in his eyes. With no intonation, Mack said, "Good morning."

"How've you been?"

"Hmm," he said, looking at her, but not like he was really seeing her.

"How's Marge?" Julie asked mostly to spark the conversation.

"Marge?" His eyes moistened. His answer came slowly. "Marge is good. She's at her sister's in Illinois."

His monotone left Julie cold. The void consumed the very air.

Sally showed up, pad and pen ready. "Mack? You ready to order?"

Mack mechanically looked up. "No, I think I'll just have coffee this morning." He paused. "I just want you to know that you've always been a bright spot in my life."

"Yeah, you say that now …" She smirked, but Mach did not respond. Sally tipped her head and asked, "Mack, are you okay?"

"Yeah, I'm fine. I just wanted you to know that. Sometimes we forget to tell people things and then … well, I just wanted you to know."

Sally looked at Julie as if she held the clues. Then she asked Julie, "How about you? The usual?"

A southwestern omelet probably wasn't a good choice after her morning. "How about an English muffin today? I've been a little under the weather."

"Juice?"

"Apple."

"Coffee?"

"Not now. I'll take one to go when I leave, though."

"Apple juice with an English muffin coming right up. Coffee to go later." She inspected Mack again. "You sure you don't want something?"

Mack raised one hand as if waving her off and said, "No, I'm good."

"No one ever doubted your goodness," Sally said.

"Hmm," Mack said as his eyes turned down.

Sally looked to Julie as if checking whether she should be concerned. With a slow head shake, Julie shrugged slightly. Sally put her hand on Mack's shoulder as she turned and headed to the kitchen window to turn in Julie's order.

Hayes and Cruz were not talking. Their heads were turned at an angle as if adjusting their radar to pick up conversations. Who were they trying to hear? Mack sat silently, fidgeting with his spoon.

Keeping her voice low, Julie said, "You know, we used to go out together every week. But for the past couple of years—"

The bell rang. Mack looked up toward the door. His eyes became intent as his lips tightened.

Julie turned as Jake walked toward the cash register counter. He took a menu and placed an order. What was he doing here at this hour? He couldn't possibly be done with his chores, could he? She wasn't even sure what he did or when he did them. Richard had hired him without consulting Julie. Julie hadn't even known the old farmhand was leaving until Richard had already hired him. Jake waved at Julie. Julie returned the wave and turned back to face Mack.

They weren't the only ones interested in Jake's appearance. Cruz tipped his head in Jake's direction and said something to Hayes, then they both returned to listening mode.

Mack began tapping his coffee cup.

"Do you know Jake?" Julie asked.

"No." Mack looked up with drooping eyes. "Doesn't he work for you?"

"Yeah … Well, he's new. I haven't really gotten to know him." Julie hesitated a moment. "Do you know anything about him?"

"No, can't say that I do." Mack kept looking toward Jake out of the corner of his eyes and then back at his coffee as if trying to hide his interest.

Julie tried to reel Mack's attention back to their conversation. "How long is Marge out of town?"

Mack began to tap his spoon on the tablecloth. "I don't know." He hesitated. "It's kind of open-ended." Was that code for separating or divorce? What else would explain his behavior and the gaping chasm between them? What kind of friends had she and Richard been not to know something was wrong?

"Well, how about we invite you over for dinner—for a good home-cooked meal while Marge is away?"

Mack glanced at Jake, then said, "Yeah, that would be nice."

"Mack?" Julie waited for him to return her gaze. She whispered, "What's going on?"

Mack shook his head once and lifted his right pointer finger as if issuing a warning. Did he know the duo was listening? Was there something about Jake he wasn't telling her?

He placed his hand on hers. "I gotta go, Julie." Laying down a twenty, he stood and left the table.

Julie turned and said, "What about dinner?"

Without looking back, Mack raised his right hand and gave a half-wave as he made his way to the door.

Ding a ling. He was gone.

Jake finished paying for his order and followed.

Ding a ling. The door closed.

Sally brought Julie's English muffin and apple juice. She picked up the twenty Mack had left and stared at it as if she had never seen one before. "What's up with Mack?"

"I don't know. He's almost morbid," Julie said.

"I'll say." Sally shook her head. "You need anything else?"

"Yep—a start-over for this day."

Sally nodded and said, "You'n me both." She returned to the counter.

As if on cue, Hayes and Cruz got up from their stools. "I'll get this," Hayes said as he looked at Julie and tipped his head toward her, then headed for the cash register. Cruz made his way toward her and stopped beside her table. He towered over her as he shifted his uniform to perfection, his dark eyes intently on hers. This was not the nervous rookie she had met earlier. He glanced toward Hayes, then back at Julie.

Julie didn't like his superior position, but ladies don't rise for men.

"Dr. Wheeler," he said and then just stood staring.

Was he trying to intimidate her? She was not giving up her emotional ground. "Deputy," she said as she steeled herself.

Cruz's eyes stayed fixed on her. "Are you feeling better?" The words were right but mocked her early morning troubles.

"Yes, thank you."

"Good to hear. And how is *Mister* Wheeler?" Why was he asking?

"He's fine."

"Glad to hear it. And how is *Miss* Marley?" Cruz's lips thinned as his facial muscles held back a smile.

"Why are you asking me about my husband's assistant PA? Doesn't *your* department work closely with the Prosecuting Attorney's office?"

"Oh, I just figured, with you being her dog's vet and all."

Dog? Did Nicole have a dog?

While she was still trying to process this information, Paul Cato came to her side, facing off with Cruz. Without looking at Julie, Paul said, "Good morning, Doc. Is this deputy bothering you?"

Had it been that obvious? Julie didn't know what to say. Paul was rescuing her from exposing that she had no idea that Nicole had a dog, but she wasn't looking to be Paul's ally. The lesser of two evils? Without answering Paul's question, Julie pretended to be happy to see Paul and said, "Paul, how are you? Won't you have a seat?" she said pointing to the now-vacant chair.

Paul smiled knowingly. "Yes, I'd love to." He got in Cruz's face and said, "Excuse me," as he pointed to the chair. Cruz let him buy. He pulled out the chair and sat.

Julie looked up. "Is there something else, Deputy?"

Cruz stared at Paul, then looked back at Julie. His smirk returned. "Oh, just one more thing. How's *Heather*?" Cruz shifted in his uniform again in an almost vulgar way.

Her hopes to maintain a poker face now gone, she asked, "How do you know my sister?"

"She didn't tell you?" His grin thinned. "Maybe you should ask *her*."

Could her sister really be attracted to this thing?

Cruz shifted, retrieved his sunglasses from his shirt pocket, and said, "Oh—I forgot. Tell Heather I'll see her tonight." With two hands, he placed his sunglasses on his face. With his index finger, and slid them to their perfect position.

No, no, no. Heather dating this loser? Not again. Is that where she was last night? If there was anything dependable about her sister, it was her poor choice in men. How could she? And it's not like Julie could say anything either. Julie's warning about men drove her sister right into their arms.

Paul looked at Julie, then at Cruz. "Is that a phone I see on your belt?"

"Yeah. What of it?"

"Know how to use it?"

"Ha. Ha. You're a funny man. You thought of taking that act on the road?" A toothy grin crept across Cruz's face sending a chill down her spine. He turned on his heel and met up with Hayes, who was chatting it up with the owner. Hayes waved in her direction, and the duo walked out together.

Julie returned her attention to Paul. She never thought she would be glad to have his company. Paul didn't speak, but waited, his eyes searching her face. His face was kind, his presence patient, like that of a longtime friend. At a minimum, she owed him recognition for running interference.

"Thanks, Paul. That guy creeps me out."

"He creeps everybody out." Paul put his hand on Julie's. She quickly withdrew it.

Paul chuckled. "That was not a pass. It was a gesture of compassion—but I get that you might have misunderstood after the way I've joked with you all these years."

Julie nodded. "What exactly did you overhear?"

"Nothing, really. Your expression screamed that Cruz was doing what he does best … stirring up trouble. He *is* trouble. And for the life of me, I can't figure out how he got on the force."

"That makes two of us."

"Is he really dating your sister?"

"I don't know. It's news to me if he is. But, then again, my sister has no man-sense. I wouldn't be surprised. Just my usual disappointment."

"How's Richard? I haven't seen much of him lately."

That made two of them. But it didn't make sense. Paul was one of the few defense attorneys in town. Paul and Richard were always going toe-to-toe in court. "I thought you guys were regular foes."

"Used to be. The sheriff's office doesn't seem too interested in arresting people these days. It would be nice if that was an indication of crime being down, but it's just the opposite. The jails should be filled with potential clients."

Was she in the Twilight Zone? Nothing was making sense. If prosecutions were down, why was Richard so busy? Julie needed time to think. What should she say or not say?

Thankfully, Sally returned to check on her. "Aren't you gonna eat that breakfast?"

Julie looked at her English muffin and then at her watch. Eight forty-five. Patients in fifteen minutes. "Oh, my. I have back-to-backs this morning. Would you wrap this and get me a coffee to go?"

"Sure thing." Sally picked up the plate as Julie guzzled her apple juice.

"Sorry, Paul. I have to run." At least she hadn't had to lie. Julie stood, as did Paul, who, if nothing else, was always the perfect gentleman. "Thanks again for saving me."

"I always liked playing the part of the knight in shining armor rescuing the damsel in distress."

Julie had a new appreciation for this man. She left him standing there as she made her way to the register to pay and pick up her coffee and muffin. She paid, turned, and waved to him as she left, unsure of where these encounters had left her or what she was going to do about her sister.

8:55 a.m.

MACK STARED AT RICHARD'S CONTACT INFORMATION on his smartphone. He was sure the meeting he had witnessed the night before was a payoff. He prayed they hadn't seen him. There was no other possible explanation. Everything made sense now.

Was his office bugged? Was his phone tapped? He checked the activity outside his glass-walled office to see who might be listening. Various members of the department sat at their stations, some on phones, but no one was close enough to hear. He touched the call button.

"Mack." Richard said, "This is a surprise—"

"Don't talk. Just listen. Remember that place we took cover during a storm when we were hunting a few years ago?"

"Yeah, you mean—"

"Don't say it. Wait twenty minutes so we are not traveling at the same time, then head there—alone. And I mean *alone*! Do *not* tell a soul—not even those you are supposed to be able to trust."

"Mack, you okay?"

Mack touched the end button, closed his eyes, and prayed.

He got up, put on his jacket, and started out his door. Hayes met him in the hallway outside his office. Hayes put his arm around Mack's shoulders. "Good morning, boss," Hayes said, with a broad smile and a chortle. "You're heading off awfully early this morning. Where're you going in such a hurry?"

Mack broke free from his hold to face him. "I was just coming to see you. I think I have a touch of the flu. I've got a commission meeting at nine-thirty. Can you cover for me?"

"Yeah. Those commission meetings make me sick, too. But sure, I'll cover." Hayes studied Mack. Pointing to a deputy seated at a desk, he said, "Why don't I get this fine young man to take you home?"

"No. I'll be fine. I might need my car."

"What about Marge? Can't she come and get you?"

"She's out of town visiting her sister."

Hayes's eyes squinted. In a stern monotone, he said, "How inconvenient for you. You will let me know if you need anything."

"Of course."

Mack needed to move quickly before Hayes had time to react. He headed for the old Hendricks's Mine, careful that he wasn't being followed.

CHAPTER 4

9:00 a.m.

Grabbing her purse, brown bag, and coffee from the truck, Julie made her way to the private entrance. She must have lost her mind going to breakfast on such a busy morning. Instead, she should have checked the condition of her post-op overnight guests from eight to nine—and Angie was not going to let her forget it. She paused at the door to steel herself for the sugar-coated tongue-lashing awaiting her. Julie would have liked nothing better than to slink past Angie's domain to her own at the far-left end of the hall, but that was not allowed until Angie said so. Doc Lawrence had told Julie when she took over the practice to just get used to it. She still wasn't.

Deep breath. And, open.

Julie began the walk of shame past the patient waiting rooms on the right. Several tail-wagging patients in Exam Rooms 1 and 2 let her know they were happy she had arrived. Whatever their ailments, they didn't show them. Julie acknowledged their presence as she proceeded past the patient waiting room entrance on her left to the counter that formed the neutral zone between Angie's and Julie's worlds.

"*Gooood* morning, boss. I'm so *glad* you could join us," Angie said as she stood, held out a pink while-you-were-out message slip, and stared at Doc as she approached. As always, Angie was adorned with a scarf that highlighted her blond perfectly-coiffed bouffant hairstyle, her perfect Mary Kay glow, and her ruby red scrubs tailored to fit her buxom shape. Julie looked beyond Angie's check-in counter to the left to a packed waiting room. Turning and running were not options.

Julie straightened herself as she arrived at "Doc's counter," as Angie put it—not that anyone believed Julie had any say-so over that space. Julie accepted the note containing her reminder to call about the buffet for the dinette. "Oh, thanks," Julie said. "You're the best."

Angie crossed her arms. "I'm so glad to be your personal shopper in addition to handling your practice while you're out running around instead of here taking care of business."

Julie set down her purse and brown bag next to the inbox. Before she could put the stain-making Styrofoam cup down, Angie cocked her hand on her hip and eyed the contraband. It was a no-win situation. Angie would not let Julie pass Go to put the cup in her office or set it down.

"*What*?" Julie said as she chose the evil of setting the cup next to the doggie treat jar to her right.

Bobbing her head and shaking her finger at Julie, Angie said, "How many times do I have to remind you that you can spill coffee or whatever else you want in your office,"—Angie swept her hand like a realtor showing a home— "but this is *my* space. And I have some pride." She returned her hand to her hip and bobbed her head once to punctuate her authority.

"Okay, I'll just go put it in my office," Julie said as she picked the cup up.

"Oh, no you don't, Missy. I know what'll happen. You'll go in there and I won't see you for an hour, and then I'll be here answering all these owners about why you are a-runnin' so late." She swept her right hand again toward the bulging waiting room past the check-in counter. Several waved at her. All smiles. She responded in kind.

Julie set the cup back down and returned her attention to Angie, still glowing like a model for Southern Living. Julie did her best pouty-daughter imitation. "Does delivering a breech calf at four this morning buy me any leniency, warden?"

Wagging her finger, Angie said, "Don't you go a-putting on that spoiled baby-girl face. That might've worked with your daddy, but you know that don't work with me."

"Well then, what do you suppose I should do with my coffee?"

"Go ahead. Set 'er there. But next time . . ." Angie's eyes gave away her love for Julie, as a smile pulled the corners of her mouth to hold up those barely aging cheeks.

Julie would never admit it to Angie—who had raised five boys in her own right—but she was the closest thing to a mom that Julie had had since her own mother died. And her animal-owner clients loved Angie. Probably more than Julie. She reached for her pendant as she thought of her mom and how she wished her mom were there, especially to deal with her sister's man issues.

Angie's smile and tone moderated as she eyed Julie's gesture. "So, baby girl, you a-doin' okay?"

"Do I look that bad?"

"No, it's not yer looks. It's the look in yer eyes. What's going on?"

"I wish I could tell you." Julie didn't know. She still hadn't processed it all. Cruz and Hayes … Mack … Jake … Richard … and what about Nicole's dog?

The private entrance door opened. Heather entered, put her jacket on the tree rack, and punched her timecard in the gray machine on the wall. Julie checked her watch. Five after nine.

"What?" Heather said to the two watching women as she began making her way past them, head tipped down and avoiding eye contact.

"Hold it," Julie said.

Heather begrudgingly stopped and turned to Julie. "What?"

"Who took your candy away this morning?"

"I'm just tired."

"What time *did* you get in?"

"What's it to you? You're not my mother."

Julie reached for her pendant. No, she wasn't. *Now what, Mom?*

Hands on hips, Angie said, "Heather Susan Blanchard, is that any way to speak to your sister and employer—the one who took you in, *again*? If you were my young'un, I'd take you out behind the barn and give you a good whoopin'."

"But I'm not 'yer young'un,' am I?" Heather barked back, almost immediately wincing at her words.

Angie was unflapped. "Don't talk to me that way, young lady. Now you apologize to me and your sister. You understand?"

Heather bowed her head and said, "I'm sorry. I—I—I—" and tearing up she ran off to the back.

"Well, I didn't see that coming," Julie said, looking to sage Angie for anything.

Angie shook her head. "Sometimes it makes you wonder why we ever do anything nice for anyone. Anything a-goin' on at yer house?"

"No. We rarely see her. She was out past my bedtime last night." Julie thought back to Cruz's inference. "Do you know Deputy Cruz?"

"I've heard Eddie talk about him. Those kids all hang out at the Downtown Saloon at night. Eddie doesn't like him, but, then again, he would be a rival for the hearts of the few available women in this town." Angie gave a knowing grin.

Julie chuckled as Buster in Room 1 reminded her that she was needed elsewhere.

"What does our lineup look like this morning?" Julie asked, peering over her counter to the appointment book.

"Like you don't know." Angie took her seat at the helm. "Don't think I couldn't tell that you were a-touchin' my book this morning." She looked up at Julie, waiting.

Busted. She had no answer.

"That's what I thought. Thankfully, your morning is pretty routine, so Eddie can help you get 'em in and get 'em out."

Julie took a sip of her now lukewarm coffee as she pulled the first chart from the inbox. *Eww.* Nausea. It couldn't be the temperature of the coffee. Lukewarm was the status quo in her busy schedule.

"Doc. You okay?" Angie asked. "You're looking a mite green around the gills."

"It's nothing. Probably a bug or food poisoning."

Angie pointed to her cup. "Dogwood Diner?"

"No, that's not it. I got sick to my stomach this morning after I delivered that calf *before* I went to the Diner. And I've been a bit tired. It's likely the flu."

"Hmm. You been missing your monthly friend?" Angie said, smiling from ear to ear?

Julie hated that question. She was as irregular as the church bells. After ten years, she was done with the emotional roller coaster of hoping, then falling apart when she did the at-home tests. She should have bought stock in that pharmaceutical company.

"You know I'm not answering that question."

Angie's perfectly painted red lips drooped, and then rose again. "Well, okay, but the Lord a-told me that it's about to happen."

The Lord? Where had the Lord been for the last ten years . . . or when Mom died, for that matter?

"Angie, we've talked about this. I don't want to go there. I'm sure it's just the flu."

"Are you sure you should be working? I can call my daddy to come in and fill in fer ya."

"No. I'm good. I can get some rest later this afternoon. Now, if it's okay with you, I'm going to put my purse in my office and grab my lab coat."

"Permission granted," Angie said with a smirk and a salute.

Julie dropped her purse and brown bag off on her desk and retrieved a lab coat from the hook on the back of her office door, then proceeded to her day.

Her first patient panted and wagged his body in excitement to see her. Julie entered Exam Room 1 and closed the door. As she washed her hands, she said, "Good morning, Meg."

Meg was sitting on the owner's bench trying to restrain Buster's exuberance. "Good mornin', Doc."

Julie looked over his chart. "I see here that Buster's not feeling well." She picked him up and set him on the exam table, careful to keep the energetic two-year-old from falling off. Meg stood to help keep him settled.

"So, what's going on with him?" Julie asked.

"Well, I noticed he's a little droopier than normal, and his eyes are a-watery. When I felt his head, he seemed to have a fever." Meg reenacted her fever check as she described his symptoms.

"You don't look so droopy to me." Julie pulled his lower eyelids down to check his eyes. "Got a little cold, Buster?"

Buster wagged his tail.

She pulled the otoscope from her lab coat pocket and examined his ears.

A knock came from the hallway door. Angie cracked the door open, beggar-style. "Doc?"

"Yes, Angie?"

"I wouldn't interrupt, but it's your dad on line two."

Dare she take the call? Talking to her dad was the last thing she needed this morning. But she couldn't put him off again. She looked at Meg, trying to measure her annoyance factor with the already late start.

With a sympathetic grin, Meg said, "It's fine, Doc Wheeler. I know how *my* dad is. You jus' go on."

"Thanks, Meg. I'm pretty sure Buster just has a cold, but just in case, Eddie will be right in to get some samples." She slipped through the rear door to the lab area that formed a hallway behind the exam rooms and turned left toward the operating room at the far end of the hall.

Eddie was doing lab tests in his usual spot at the far workbench on the right side, just past the hallway from the kennel behind the building. Socrates monitored his work from the chair beside him. They both turned toward Julie when she interrupted their world. She stopped at the avocado green phone mounted in the hallway between Exam Rooms 1 and 2.

"I've got to get this call. Can you go take some blood samples in Room 1? Looks like Buster has a cold. Oh, and go ahead and take a stool sample. It's about time for his regular exam … and put your lab coat on. Julies smiled, put her hand on her hip, and did her best Angie imitation. "What kind of hick place do you think we're running here?"

Eddie hopped up as Socrates jumped down anticipating Eddie's next move. Eddie collected his tools and laid them out on a tray. He grabbed a lab coat from a wall hook, put it on, but left it unbuttoned. He looked at Julie who shook her head at his rebellion but didn't dare give him the satisfaction of acknowledging it. He picked up the tray and headed toward the exam room, Socrates in tow.

As Julie reached for the olive-colored phone as Heather charged in from the kennel hallway. Julie knew Heather well enough to expect round two. Julie held up her hand to stop her sister's advance. "I don't have time for this. Dad's on the phone, and I've been avoiding him for two weeks."

The color in Heather's face drained. Her eyes searched Julie's. She grabbed Julie's hand on the receiver. Julie shook off Heather's grip. "I can't put him off anymore."

Heather's eyes moved back and forth in full panic mode. Julie couldn't read her. Was she about to explode or burst into tears? It must have been the latter, because Heather asked in almost a whisper, "Then what are you going to tell him?"

"I'm not going to tell him anything. I didn't call him. He's been calling me. But I'm sure it's about Thanksgiving."

Heather stepped toward Julie again and covered the phone with her hand. "I'm not going. You talked me into it last year and look what happened. Richard feels the same way. Heck—you can't stand going there either. You said last year was the last time, *remember*? So, if you cave, it's just you and Richard. Got it?"

Julie brushed a stray blond bang out of her baby sister's blue eyes. Heather's battle-worn face showed she could take no more. "We're not going either. Relax." Julie placed a soothing hand on her sister's shoulder and looked into her eyes. "I've always taken care of you, haven't I?"

Heather's body tensed and shoved Julie away. "What about last Thanksgiving?"

With a calming voice, Julie said, "It won't happen again."

Heather got in Julie's face. "I'm serious. I'm *not* going."

Raising her hands as if surrendering, Julie said, "I got it. Now let me get this call over with." She needed to distract her sister. "Can you go ask Angie if the pharmacy shipment came in? It needs to be stocked."

Heather searched Julie's face as if checking a lie detector printout. "Okay, but . . ." Heather's eyes focused past Julie. Heather reddened from her neck up. Socrates scampered past Julie as she turned to find the source.

Eddie stood frozen outside Room 1 with the tray of samples just taken. Eddie looked between his peer and Julie. *What now?* Not Eddie. Julie looked back at Heather who was motionless. Julie turned back and said, "Eddie, don't you have something to do?"

"Yes, ma'am." He avoided eye contact as he passed and resumed his position at the workbench.

Heather turned back down the kennel hallways and called back, "Remember what I said and stay strong."

Yeah. Stay strong. Easy for her to say.

Eddie had busied himself running Buster's blood sample. He shifted his back toward her. Nothing better have happened between those two. And what about Cruz? Julie couldn't keep up, nor did she want to.

Julie looked at the blinking light on the phone. Was Dad still holding? Pausing for an energy-gathering breath, she picked up the phone, forced a smile, and punched the button.

"Hi, Dad. I'm kinda busy. What is it?"

"What kind of greeting is that?"

"I'm sorry. Long night. A distressed cow needed a little help bringing her calf into this world at four a.m. Add a touch of the flu. I've been up all night, my stomach is queasy and I've been running late all morning."

"Have you been avoiding me? I must have called a dozen times. I've been on hold for ten minutes. I was beginning to think you don't love me."

Love was not the problem. Could it have been a dozen times? Definitely ten minutes. But he was right. She had been avoiding him. "I've just been busy. You know."

"Too busy to talk to your ol' dad?"

What could she say? She didn't know, so she let the question hang in the air.

Eddie shifted in his seat. Thankful for the long phone cord, she retreated to the privacy of Exam Room 1, which Meg had vacated. She took a seat on the stool. Twirling her dark, straight hair and looking up at the dog border wallpaper that held up the ceiling, Julie waited for the movie rerun to start. The same thing happened every year. Dad would call, guilt her into coming, and then—

"Well, kiddo, I can't remember the last time I saw you and your sister. I was hoping you'd come up for Thanksgiving, especially after all your sister's been through. What do you say? It would mean so much to Catherine."

Catherine—Cruella was more like it. Was Dad deluding himself? Cruella always said she was happy when Julie and Heather came, but as soon as they arrived, she would get a sick headache and excuse herself. Dad would cover for her. The whole thing made Julie sick. She reached for Mom's pendant. Mom had made her promise to take care of Dad. But Mom could never have anticipated Dad would marry that witch. Mom would have understood Julie's reluctance to spend time with Cruella.

She let go of the pendant. "Dad, we've talked about this before. I don't have a team of associates to cover like you do. It's impossible."

"What about Angie's dad? I thought he loves covering for you. Did you check with him?"

"I don't know—I hate to impose on him for a holiday, and, besides . . ." Julie was running out of excuses. "We just can't get away. Why don't you come here? You're only a few—"

The sounds of metal clanging and Eddie barking muffled instructions erupted from the lab hallway. Julie hopped up from the stool and rushed to find the source of the noise. Through the operating room door windows at the end of the hall, Julie saw Eddie and Heather moving as if relocating a dog from a gurney.

"Dad, I gotta go. We have an emergency." Julie hung up.

As she started down the hall, Angie came through the door. "Doc! Nicole Marley just dropped off her German shepherd. He's convulsing. Hurry!"

The mystery dog? Here?

———

MACK PULLED INTO THE ABANDONED PARKING LOT of the old Hendricks's Mine and backed into a spot where he could see all, but not so obvious that someone would notice his car if they were driving by. Kids loved these places to do what kids do in the dark.

He did his math again. Richard should have just left the office. It had taken Mack twenty minutes going faster than Richard would have traveled … Well, maybe not. Say fifteen minutes. He should arrive around nine-thirty or so. Enough time for Mack to call his wife before going inside.

He checked his environs again and then tapped his Favorites icon on his phone. Yes, she was.

"Mack?" Marge asked.

"Good morning. Did you sleep well last night?"

"No, actually I didn't. I was restless all night."

"I'm sorry, hon." Mack wished he could take her troubles away, but knew that there was nothing that could be done. They were in too deep.

"No," Marge said, "I'm the one who should be sorry. I got you into all this. I wish I could undo it all." She paused. "Mack, when are you coming?"

"Just as soon as I can. They will be distracted when everything hits. I should be able to get away then. You haven't called anyone, have you?"

"No—but it's so lonely. I can't believe we have to start all over again."

"Don't you worry. A fresh start is just what we both need. You'll see."

"But the kids … our grandkids."

"It's okay, hon. It's just for a little while." He checked his watch. "Well, he should be here in a couple of minutes." He bit his lip to hold back the tears. "I love you so much."

"Me, too."

"I'll see you soon." He touched the end icon and hoped that he had not just lied to her. He got out of the car and entered the mine. He was glad for the kid at the phone store that showed him how to use the flashlight app. Batting spider webs as he entered, Mack ensured he did not disturb any rotting roof support beams.

He found a large rock and took a seat. Avoiding Richard these last couple of years had been easier than exposing his failure. But the time had come.

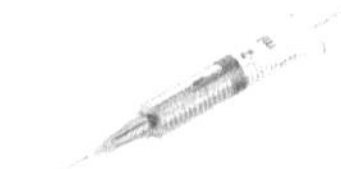

CHAPTER 5

9:20 a.m.

THE GERMAN SHEPHERD'S BODY WAS RIGID, his eyes staring into nothing. White foam-lined his lips. His tongue was hanging as if it didn't know its job. Heather looked helpless while she attempted to comfort the dog. She cradled his head, caressing it like she could rub his troubles away.

Angie stood at the door as Eddie pulled supplies from the cabinets. "Looks like poison to me." He turned and looked Julie in the eyes. Heather was not looking. He slowly shook his head.

Julie hurried to the table opposite Heather. "Let's take a look." She checked the canine's eyes, felt his abdomen, and listened to his heart. "Where's Nicole?"

"She left," Angie said blankly. "She rushed in crying hysterically and babbling. I could barely understand her. She said the dog was a-fine when she got up. She put him in his dog run in the backyard when she went to shower, and he was like this by the time she was a-ready to leave around nine o'clock.

"Me and Heather followed her out to her SUV," Angie said. "The dog was a-lying in the back like this. Heather showed her 'round to the back entrance and we brought him in here. No sooner did we get him out of the truck than Nicole said she had to go and ran out the door. I didn't even get the dog's name or age." She shook her head in disbelief. "In thirty years, nobody's ever left their dog like this." Angie removed a file from a drawer, fastened a page on the right side, and closed the clasp. "Anything else?"

"Yes. Call Richard's office and see if you can get hold of Nicole."

"I'm on it."

"Oh, I think it would be good if your dad can come in to help with the other patients."

"My thinkin', exactly."

Julie continued examining the dog. Who would leave a dog like this? Julie was sure Nicole didn't abandon the dog because she was late to work. Richard would have understood a pet emergency, especially for his favorite breed.

Heather continued to caress and soothe the dog as Julie poked and prodded. "It's okay. You're doing fine."

Heather never had a stomach for seeing animals in pain. From the time she was old enough to go to her dad's office, she had emotionally adopted every animal in his clinic. But her connection with this dog was more . . . As if she'd met a soul mate—a fellow sojourner of life going through needless suffering. Maybe it was because he had been abandoned. The way Heather had been abandoned when their dad married Catherine. With sunken eyes, Heather asked, "Do you think he's going to make it?"

Eddie and Julie's eyes met. As empty as it sounded, Julie said, "We'll do our best."

Julie forced each eye wide open and shined her otoscope into them. "Let's get his stomach pumped."

Before Eddie could move, the dog's convulsions eased, and then stopped. She checked the dog's eyes again. Looking back to Eddie, she said, "Whatever it was appears to have passed his stomach now. His abdomen is relaxed and his pupils are contracting a bit. I don't think there's any reason to pump his stomach now."

Exhausted from the ordeal, the dog didn't attempt to escape the cold metal table, the doctor's prods, or the stranger's tattooed arms in which he found comfort. He raised his head, looked at each one, and then melted back into Heather's arms.

"Good job, Heather," Eddie said as if she was responsible for the dog's good turn.

Heather looked at Eddie and her face reddened.

Blushing again? This was not good . . . Or was it? Unlike Cruz, Eddie was certainly a good young man . . . maybe too good for Heather.

"Eddie, can you grab that file?" Julie asked.

He moved behind Julie to the counter and retrieved the folder Angie had set out. He took a seat on the stool and pulled a pen from his open lab coat pocket. "Ready."

"We have a male German shepherd, possibly purebred." She checked his teeth. "He appears to be five to seven years old. He was convulsing when we first examined him. His stomach was distended and his eyes dilated. He appears to have ingested poison, possibly an insecticide. His owner reported twenty minutes of convulsions before entering the clinic, and he continued to have convulsions for approximately ten additional minutes at which time his convulsions ended. His eyes and his stomach returned to normal. He appears weak, which would be consistent with a post-poisoning state. He does not appear to have any injuries inflicted upon his body. He has a half-inch gash on his tongue, which was likely self-inflicted. It should heal on its own. We need to get him on an IV, but no oral liquids for at least a couple hours."

Julie looked at Heather as she continued to massage the dog. "I think he's going to be fine."

Heather hugged the dog. "See? I told you … you're gonna be fine."

———

MACK SAT LISTENING IN THE DANK SHADOWS of the abandoned mine, rehearsing what he was going to confess. In the distance, an occasional car whooshed by. He checked his watch. Richard should've been there by now. Had they uncovered his plan?

Gravel crunched outside. A car door slammed. Mack rose, pulled his gun, and leaned into the shadows.

The slender outline of a man in a suit came to the mine entrance. "Mack? You in here?"

Richard. "In here."

Mack holstered his gun and retrieved his smartphone to light up Richard's path. Because Mack didn't know how Richard would feel about him after all these months, and all he had done, he didn't cross the divide between them. But Richard did.

"Mack, it's so good to see you, my old friend." Richard came right for him and gave him a man-hug. Then Richard backed off to look him over. "It's really good to see you, but what's with all the cloak and dagger?"

"You're not going to feel happy to see me when you hear what I have to say." Mack hung his head and started his rehearsed speech. "Richard, I'm so sorry."

"Sorry? For what?"

"I've let you down. I wanted to call you a thousand times, but I couldn't. It's bad. It's all bad. But now I have to warn you."

"Warn me?" Richard stepped back. "About what?"

Mack pointed to his previous perch. "Have a seat. I need to tell you what's going on." Richard stepped around Mack and took a seat on the appointed spot.

"It's been a nightmare." Mack rubbed his head. "It started with Marge. She began going to the casinos and gambling. At first, it was occasional, but then she began disappearing for days at a time." Mack paced as Richard sat motionlessly. "I called my buddy in that county, and he told me that a lot of people were getting sucked in. The loan sharks moved in. When Marge finally confessed, she had already maxed out the credit cards. I took out all the equity in our house and emptied our retirement funds to get her out of trouble with those guys. But she went right back. She couldn't help it.

"Next thing I know, I get a phone call and they tell me they have my wife. They tell me where to meet them in an abandoned warehouse.

She was there, tied to a chair. Bruises and cuts on her face. I wanted to kill them." Mack paused to regroup.

"They told me that they would wipe out my wife's debt and give her a gambling stipend if I turn a blind eye at the office. Then they told me to hire Hayes as the assistant sheriff, and he's going to run things—all I have to do is stay out of their way."

Mack stopped pacing to check for Richard's reaction. He said nothing.

"I'm sorry, Richard. I know I've let you down."

Richard's eyes softened. "No, I've let you down. How could I have missed this? I should have known something was wrong."

How could Richard even think about Mack's plight considering how Mack had turned his back on all that he knew was right—and turned his back on the best friend he had ever known? Why hadn't he confided in Richard?

"There's a lot of stuff going on. At the office, I hear loud voices and see movement, but I just can't get a handle on what they're doing. They watch me like a hawk. I've been trying to figure out the players, but last night, I found out that Jake has been getting paid off."

Richard's eyes widened as he looked past Mack. Mack turned toward the silhouetted figure at the entrance. "It's you!"

Jake entered the cave. "I was afraid you saw me last night."

A gunshot rang out as pain ripped through Mack's side and . . .

———

Doc Lawrence entered the operating room, followed by Angie. Concern evaporated from both their faces when they saw the dog calm and comforted.

"Looks like Heather's a natural." Doc Lawrence winked at Julie. "You can tell she comes from a long line of vets."

The old Heather was returning with each encouraging word.

"*You* got here fast," Julie said as she went to give him a welcoming hug. "Saw you at the Diner earlier. I was going to brag on my middle-of-the-night adventures—full breech—all doing well." Julie felt herself puff.

Doc Lawrence put his arm around her shoulder. "Not surprised, considering you've been trained by two of the best vets in the world."

Everyone laughed.

"Thanks for coming in. How'd you get here so quickly?" Julie asked.

"I was just driving home from the Diner. I was only a few blocks away."

Julie looked at Angie. "Well, I'm just about done here. But you know, with the three-a.m. breech and my queasy stomach, I think Angie might have been right—some rest might be a good idea. Would you mind staying?"

"*Might* have been right?" Angie said.

"Okay, okay." Julie looked at Doc Lawrence. "She's never wrong, is she, *Dad*?"

"I warned you." Doc Lawrence said. "So, what's going on here?"

Julie briefed him as he performed the usual inspections and asked the appropriate questions. Then Julie looked at Angie. "This dog appears to be five or so years old. Did you know Nicole had a dog?" If anyone knew, it would be Angie. She grew up here, had cut her teeth on horse bits and dog leashes. She knew every person and animal for five counties.

Angie stood straighter and said, "Well, of course, I did. Nothing gits by me."

"And you never mentioned this *because*?"

"Have you ever known me to gossip? I thought it was strange because she's been here like three years … and she works for Richard … and it *is* a German shepherd." Angie was watching Julie as if trying to read her. Was Angie making some sort of connection because of the dog's breed?

Richard had bought a shepherd eleven years earlier as an excuse to talk to her because she refused to date him. Despite her immediate attraction to him when they met at the courthouse while she was getting her business license, Julie had refused to go out with him, hiding behind a lack of proper introductions, but really just playing the coy southern girl. Julie could still picture him sitting in the waiting room in his Armani suit with that puppy. She made him wait hours out there before allowing him entry to an exam room.

Angie was a party to his scheme that day. But of course, Richard would never have been allowed past the front door if Angie wasn't already sold on their relationship. Angie and that German shepherd witnessed Richard not only ask her out, but he got down on one knee and proposed to Julie right there in Exam Room 3. Angie all but accepted for Julie. And it was all because of that shepherd.

"Maybe she took the dog somewhere else or maybe didn't take him anywhere at all," Angie said.

"Well, he must go somewhere," Doc Lawrence said as he held out the dog collar to Julie. "Where else would he have gotten his rabies tag?"

Julie looked back to Angie. "Did you get a hold of Nicole?

"Not yet. I'm still a-workin' on it."

"We need his background and Nicole's permission to run some tests. He must have gotten into something, but not enough to kill him. I'd like to know what we're dealing with."

Angie nodded.

"If you can't get hold of her, track down the vet who gave him his rabies vaccination with the number on his tag. Then maybe we can get his medical history."

"I'm on it." And if Angie was on it, you could bet it would get done. She left the room.

"There are no apparent bites or trauma anywhere on his body," Julie said as she ran her hand over his body. "Heather, are you sure Nicole didn't say anything else?"

"No, she didn't. She could barely talk. It was almost like . . . well, I don't know what it was like." Heather looked into the dog's dark eyes searching for an answer. "I just know she sure was nervous and in a big hurry."

"Why don't you and Eddie get him settled in? Keep him still. As much as you can. Eddie, start a saline drip to be sure he's hydrated.

Let's get routine blood, fecal, and urine samples. I don't think we can wait for Nicole's permission if we're going to find out what got into him." Julie looked to Doc Lawrence. "Am I missing anything?"

"Nope. You've got it covered."

"Great. How about we go take care of some other patients?"

"Are you sure Dog's going to be okay?" Heather asked.

"Dog? Are you naming him now?" Julie smirked, glad to see *Dog* helping to lift Heather out of her depression.

"Well, we don't want him to feel like an *it*." Heather kissed Dog tenderly on the forehead and rubbed his belly. He was mesmerized by her gentle touch.

"Would it be okay if I stayed with him for a while?" Heather asked.

"Sure, but don't get too attached. You know better. He has a real name and a real owner. He'll be on his feet in no time and back with Nicole—*where he belongs*. Speaking of Nicole . . ."

Doc Lawrence held the door open as Julie passed through. Julie and Doc Lawrence walked through the supply room on the far side of Exam Room 3.

"Wow, I like what you've done with this room. Those shelves sure hold a lot more pet food. Look how many kinds of food there are now. In my day, dog food was dog food. Well, you know. You saw it with your dad's practice. It's amazing, isn't it?"

"Profitable is more like it." Julie led as they went through the door to the front hallway.

Doc Lawrence grinned.

Julie checked her watch as they approached the counter. "I believe we are about four appointments behind. By the time we work on the late ones, we'll have two more late. That's six, or three apiece." Julie sorted through the top six files and said, "How about we do them in this order?" She handed one to Doc Lawrence, set one on the counter, and handed the next four to Angie.

Angie looked at the four and made a sour face. "I don't *think* so."

Julie took the four back and looked at them again and recognized the problem. "Scooter. Pancreatitis symptoms." Julie made a face, knowing that Scooter would likely be making a stinky mess. "I'll take this one now."

She switched the file from the counter with Scooter's file.

"Good plan," agreed Doc Lawrence with a Cheshire smile.

"I thought you'd agree." Julie winked at Doc Lawrence as he headed for Exam Room 2. Julie started for Scooter. "Would you send Eddie in with some extra towels and disinfectant as soon as he can break free from Dog?"

"*Dog*? Is that his name?" Angie asked.

Julie looked at Angie wryly. "No, Heather named him. But seeing's how you're the one who knew he existed, maybe you can shed some light on his name."

"I don't know anything other than I saw Dog in Nicole's yard when I visited my cousin. Like you, I've been surprised that he's not been a-coming here."

"Did you find anything on the tag yet?"

"Not yet. Phones have been a-ringing off the hook this morning."

Backing into Exam Room 1, Julie pushed through the door to the stinky mess.

9:45 a.m.

HAYES SAT AT THE HEAD OF THE TABLE in a creaky black leather chair. The wood-paneled walls of the conference room surrounded the county incompetents. How these commissioners ever got anything done was beyond him. At least their ignorance had made setting up shop here like the proverbial taking candy from a baby. Actually, taking over their burg had been easier – a baby would have at least cried. That was until that idiot Wheeler called in the feds. But, in Hayes' brilliance, he'd figured out a way to fix that little problem, and all was about to be solved.

Everything was on schedule.

The light on the back of his phone flashed. He checked the screen. Cruz. What now? Couldn't he do anything right? He should never have let his uncle talk him into hiring that punk. He'd be doing Rudy a favor if he put him in the line of fire.

Forcing a smile, he said "Excuse me, gentlemen," and slipped out the conference room door.

Irritated, Hayes put the phone to his ear and growled. "I'm in a meeting. What's wrong?"

"Phase one complete—she took the dog to Wheeler's clinic and left right away, just like you said. Message delivered."

"Is that it? You got me out of a meeting to tell me you *did your job?*" Hayes could feel his neck stiffening.

"No, I called to tell you Deep Throat's off the radar."

Deep throat? Did this kid think he was in a movie? "Did I ask you to follow him? Stick to your job."

"I've got a bad feeling about him."

Yeah, well I have a bad feeling about you. Hayes gritted his teeth. "I don't pay you to *feel.* Just take care of your job. *If* you think you can."

"I can. I can. I'm on it."

Hayes ended the call, wishing he could end Cruz instead.

———

WITH THE HELP OF EDDIE'S CLEAN-UP DETAIL, Julie handled the pancreatitis crisis plus the next two patients efficiently and was done in less than thirty minutes. As she walked her last patient's owner to the checkout counter, she said, "You don't need to check out. You can pick up Charlemagne tomorrow in the afternoon. Just give Angie a call to be sure he's ready."

"Thanks, Doc. I'll see you tomorrow." The cat's owner picked up the cat cage and left through the patient exit door.

Angie was busy on the phone making an appointment. No one interrupts Angie. From Angie's black high-back rolling throne, she manned the phone, controlled the pet owners in the waiting room, commanded the computer, and managed each minute of Julie's day with that good old-fashioned appointment book. Doc Lawrence gave a dog's owner instructions as they came out of an exam room. The owner and her pup checked out with Angie.

"All caught up?" Julie asked Doc Lawrence.

"Caught up and took another one. I reckon it's not so bad for an out-to-pasture ol' country doc." He winked, took the next file, and headed into Exam Room 3.

"Thanks, again, Doc," Julie called after him as he disappeared into the room. She checked the files. They were completely caught up and back on schedule. Julie could leave after she got permission from the boss.

Beyond the patient counter of Angie's helm, a handful of pet owners still filled the worn, brown-padded benches, each keeping their own pets in line. The display shelves had been fully stocked with a colorful variety of dog and cat food bags. At least Heather was providing some help around the clinic while she was recovering in life's trauma ward.

Julie wiggled the dog leash hook. Still loose. Eddie should have fixed that weeks before. Julie toggled it loud enough that Angie turned toward the sound while still talking to a client on the phone. Julie pointed at the hook, shrugged her shoulders, and opened her palms up as if to ask, "What's the deal?"

Angie waved Julie off and returned her attention to the phone call. "You don't say. . . Is that right?" Sometimes Angie was the town counselor. That was the problem with having a compassionate assistant—everyone wanted to share their problems with her. Oh well. It was great for business.

Socrates sprung onto the desk by Angie and then up onto Doc's counter, almost spilling her now-cold coffee. Julie steadied the cup. "Socrates! You'll be out on your ear if you make a mess." Socrates ignored her scolding and held up his white-tipped bearded chin, demanding attention. Julie obliged the spoiled cat. "Allow me to pay homage." Amazing how this cat had survived in that house for two weeks until his owner was found dead of a heart attack. Socrates had taken over as king of the office. It was wonderful to hear him purr again.

"Okay, we'll see you at ten tomorrow . . . I will . . . Thank you." Hanging up the phone, Angie looked over her left shoulder at Julie. "You're gonna have a busy day tomorrow. You better catch up on your sleep tonight."

"Did you get hold of Nicole?"

Angie shook her head. "I can't find her anywhere. Richard's office said she hasn't been in or called. They gave me her number. There's no answer. I left a message."

"Can I see the appointment book?" Angie handed up the open book. "Oh, by the way, was Meg okay?"

"Yeah, she's fine," Angie said, then laughed. "She said she was a little short on cash and would have to pay you next month when she gets her support check."

Julie shook her head and grinned. "Some things never change."

"I told her you would call when you get the lab results."

Julie gave Socrates one last chin scratch. He kept his neck stretched, expecting his subject to continue lauding him with attention. When she didn't comply, he meowed his disgust and jumped down to Angie's desktop.

Angie shooed him. "Get off the desk, you brat. You think you own this place?"

Now spurned, Socrates jumped back up to Doc's counter, down into the front hallway, and into the supply room, tail held high. Julie turned back toward Angie giggling. "Eddie's a sucker for his temper tantrums. I'm sure he'll find more compassion for his pitifully sad life in the lab."

Angie rose to replace a patient file in the rainbow-colored wall of animal histories across from Julie. "Yep, I definitely raised a cat lover in that one." She turned toward Julie and pointed to the stale cup of coffee. "You a-done with that?"

Julie's stomach knotted at the thought. She gladly handed over the stained cup. Angie took it as if handling nuclear waste and dropped it in the trash can.

Eddie appeared holding a lab bag and Dog's folder, trailed by Socrates. He handed Angie Dog's lab results. "I haven't found any answers yet. I'm going to run these samples over to the hospital lab to test for some chemicals I don't have the testing supplies for. I'll be back after lunch."

"How's Dog doing now?" Julie asked.

"He's sleeping. Heather's keeping an eye on him, but I told her he'd be fine." Eddie hesitated a minute and then asked, "Doc, is Heather okay? I don't mean to be nosy, but she looks like a skeleton, and her color is awful."

"I wish I knew, Eddie, but Dog sure did lift her spirits, didn't he?"

Eddie nodded. "Yes—*that* he did." He paused another awkward moment, then said, "Well I'd better get to the lab. See you after lunch."

Angie gave Eddie the look that only moms can give. "What, no kiss for your ol' ma?"

Lifting the hinged checkout counter, Eddie made his way into Angie's domain. He kissed her on the cheek. Even at twenty-eight, children are still children.

Julie took the opportunity to rattle the hook for Eddie's benefit.

"Oh, I'm sorry. I'll get to that after lunch." His mom held up the waste basket that was brimming with trash and one dead coffee cup. "Okay, I get it … trash duty too. Is this what I went to vet tech school for?"

"That's why you get paid the big bucks," Julie said.

"Yeah, yeah." Eddie turned and went back around to the hallway, leaving the counter up behind him. "Later." He passed Julie and headed out the private entrance.

Julie returned her attention to Dog's folder, tapping it several times with the top of her pen. Where was Nicole? "Since your dad has everything handled, I think I'll give Richard a call. Maybe he knows something."

———

HAYES ALTERNATELY TAPPED THE BOTTOM CORNERS of his smartphone against his legal pad as the two commissioners droned on about the need for another school zone sign. How did Mack ever tolerate these yokels?

His phone light flashed. He turned the device over. Jake? Hayes stood and said, "Gentlemen, I need to take care of this. I think we're adjourned here anyway. We can take this up next time."

One of the commissioners stood and said, "But—"

Hayes ignored the loser as he walked out of the sheriff's office conference room. He lifted the phone to his head, and said, "Give me a minute." He walked down the hallway to his office, closed the door, and stood looking out the window.

"Why are you calling? Cruz said you were AWOL."

"Listen, we've got a little problem here."

"What's this *we* stuff? Your job was to provide information. You did and you were paid."

"Last night I thought I saw Mack when we were leaving. I followed him this morning. You saw him at the Diner. He went to the office for a while, then left for the old Hendricks's Mine. I followed him there. Guess who showed up?"

"I *don't* play guessing games. Just tell me."

"Richard."

"What?"

"Mack was spilling his guts to Richard about being involved with you when Nicole showed up and shot Mack. Then Richard shot Nicole. I didn't know what was going on, so I shot Richard in self-defense."

Hayes released some unseemly expletives. Things had been going according to plan, and now this.

"They're all dead. I didn't sign up for this. And I'm not going to jail for you. I got Mack's body out, put it in his trunk, and ditched his car in the lake up the road. I hightailed it back to the mine and put Nicole's body in the back of her SUV and covered it with a tarp she had in the back. Before I could get back to Richard, the mine caved in. That place was creaking—more with every shot. I'm sure he's dead, but there's nothing I can do to get to his body. I can't get Richard's keys. They're on him. But I can get a set of keys back at the house. What do you want me to do?"

Hayes unleashed more expletives. "Let me think … were you wearing gloves when you drove that car in the lake?"

"No . . . how stupid of me." Jake paused. "You're the sheriff, can't you cover it up?"

"What do you think?" Hayes said.

Jake's fingerprints on the steering wheel played right into Hayes' hand. If Jake got out of hand, he could eliminate him and frame him as part of a conspiracy. Heck, he was going to get rid of him anyway. It was perfect.

Hayes stared at nothing in the parking lot. That idiot Mack. Mr. Goody Two-shoes. Why couldn't he have just kept his nose out of it? Hayes turned and pounded the side of a file cabinet and vomited more foul language.

Okay. He wanted to get rid of Richard and Nicole anyway, and he had already set the wheels in motion for setting up the killer's motive. He needed Jake to do a couple more errands . . . but after that, done.

"Leave the cars there for now," Hayes said, trying to figure out if he was missing something. "Where are the guns?"

"I've got them."

"And the keys to Nicole's car?"

"Got them."

"Bring me the guns, the necklace, and keys to Nicole's car later. I'll let you know what to do about Richard's car after you get the keys from the house."

"I'm working on getting something to place the killer at the scene. I should have it by midday."

"What about Doc?"

"What about her?"

"What does she know? Nicole dropped her dog off. I need to know what Nicole said to her or if Richard called her to tell her where he was going?"

"Good point." He paused. "I'll find out what she knows. Who would she go to if she knew something?"

"You just took care of them."

"Listen, like you said, I'm not involved in this. This wasn't what I got paid for. This is your mess."

"It's yours now. Your fingerprints are in that car. Get me something."

Hayes hung up. He moved to his desk and punched the intercom button. "Send Williams in."

The door opened. The stocky uniformed deputy entered and stood behind the chair across from him. Of course, she wasn't going to lower herself to the disadvantaged position of sitting. That would put her below him and he knew she hated being in an inferior physical position—good police training. She was tough—something that turned Hayes on. But her barbered hair style was just too much. Even without female allure, there was still something about her no-nonsense, hardball demeanor that revved his engines. He could certainly trust her more than his ex-wives.

"Have a seat." Hayes pointed to the chair she stood behind then sat in his own so she would do likewise.

Hayes gave Williams the details of the telephone conversation. He stood again as he said, "Why didn't *your* people notice anything going on?"

Williams stood and leaned across the desk, her face tense. "Oh, maybe it's because *you* wanted them in other places, like watching transports. Oh, and then there're the little issues like drug overdoses that they have to tend to. All my men are out, and there's still not enough of them. The only one who's not overworked is your pet, Cruz. You two have a thing going?"

Hayes pounded the desk. "Yeah—he's just my type." It wasn't Williams' fault. She knew his plight with Cruz, and he was just as frustrated as she was.

"Okay, let's assess." He sat back down. Williams followed suit. "Number one, is Jake reliable? Send someone out to the mine to check out his assessment. Don't send a uniform, in case someone happens by. That mine is set off the road in a curve so the cars shouldn't draw attention from the highway. They should find two cars and a cave-in. If they can see in the SUV, they should see a tarp, not the body. It's cool enough that we have a day or so before we have to"—Hayes did air quotes—"find the body."

"If Jake is on the up-and-up then he will take care of moving Richard's car. He can dump it in the lake with Mack's."

Hayes tried to remember where a lake was. He looked at Williams. "Lake. Is there a lake within walking distance to the mine that Jake could have dumped a car in?"

Williams thought for a moment. "Yeah. There's one about a mile up the road. You know—where all those girls get pregnant. Keeps our abortion operation in business, doesn't it?"

She smiled, awaiting Hayes's acknowledgment, which he gave. "And then there's that kid who broke his neck trying to dive off a rock a few months back." She shook her head. "Yeah, I'd say that you could ditch a car there."

"How about two?"

"Why not?" She smiled. "We should probably block off the road to it so no one will notice in the middle of the day."

He nodded. "So far, his story sounds plausible."

"Why don't you trust him?"

"Because he was just hired for information—not to do this kind of work. He's just an informant, but he's acting like someone who has experience with one side or the other of the law. Were we just that lucky?" Hayes pinched the bridge of his nose, then let go. "I just don't know. Why didn't he just call me to tell me about Mack seeing him last night?"

"I don't know, maybe he was worried that you'd think it was his fault if something went wrong … or that you wouldn't handle it and that would expose him?" Her face tensed. "I don't know either. You're right to check him out."

"Yeah, but I need him now to watch Doc. Cruz on the outside and him on the inside." Hayes hated needing anyone. "And he's got to get those keys. He's got the guns but not anything that puts Doc at the scene. He's not disposable until everything is set."

Williams nodded, then stood. "I'll send someone out now." She headed for the door, then turned. "Do I need to do anything about Cruz?"

Hayes cursed Cruz's name. "No, I'll stay on him for now. After this, he has to go." He looked out the window then back at Williams. "Did I miss anything?"

Williams shook her head. "No, I think that covers it … and I think we're in pretty good shape for the shape we're in. Isn't that what they say?"

"Yeah. I guess."
Williams opened the door and left, closing the door behind her. Hayes cursed the God he didn't believe in.

CHAPTER 7

10:50 a.m.

JULIE'S OFFICE CHAIR CREAKED as she sat down at the desk just inside her office door. She swiveled to face all the dog, cat, and horse decorations her clients had bestowed on her over her tenure. The Felix-the-Cat wall clock showed it was almost eleven. Richard shouldn't have left for lunch yet. She pushed his speed dial button on her desk phone.

Heather appeared at her door. Julie waved her in. Heather slipped into the chair across from her and crossed her tattooed arms as if hugging herself to keep warm. The girl needed to wear warmer clothes, which would help with covering those ridiculous tattoos. Heather's tired face softened as she gazed above Julie at their mom's painting.

"Good morning, Hearthstone Prosecuting Attorney's office."

"Hi, Donna. May I please speak to Richard?"

"Oh, I'm sorry, Doc. Mr. Wheeler's not in. He left a while ago."

"Do you know when he'll be back?"

"No. He got a call on his cell phone, grabbed his jacket, and ran out the door around nine. Said he had to get to a meeting on the Meadow's case."

Tension manifested itself in Julie's core. She rubbed her left temple. Maybe if she massaged it enough, she could remember what Richard said he was working on. "Is it that case that's been keeping him out so late?"

"Um . . . I couldn't say."

"Oh, that's okay. I'll try him on his cell. Thanks, Donna." Julie started to hang up but then said, "Oh—by the way. Have you heard from Nicole?

"Nicole?"

"Yes, *Nicole Marley*. Who else would I be asking about?"

"Um . . . I'm sorry, Dr. Wheeler." Donna paused. "Um . . . it's just that Angie called and asked the same thing. We haven't heard from Ms. Marley today . . . um . . . maybe she's working with Mr. Wheeler? She does that a lot, ya know. I mean, it's a big case and all."

"Donna, is something wrong?"

"Wrong? What do you mean?"

"What's going on?"

Donna paused. "I don't know, Dr. Wheeler, it's just Mr. Wheeler has been working a lot on this case, you know, outside the office. It's just not normal. Maybe you should ask him."

What did that mean? "Well, okay, Donna. I guess I will. In the meantime, if you hear from Richard—or Nicole—please ask them to call me right away. Okay?"

"Yes, ma'am."

Julie held the receiver away from her head, examining it as if it were foreign. Then she hung it up. "That was strange," she mumbled. Richard had never mentioned working a lot with Nicole ... or outside the office. Not normal? Julie needed to go to Nicole's. She needed answers—now.

"What was strange?" Heather asked.

"Oh, nothing."

"Does she know where Richard is?"

"No. She thinks he's working on a case." Julie wanted to say more but didn't. Julie couldn't confide anything Richard to Heather, who already had a healthy dislike for everything Richard. Of course, Richard had his own opinion. *"Why is it your job to pick up the pieces of her life every time she runs off with some bum,"* he had said. *"How's she ever going to grow up if you treat her like a child? How long is she going to stay this time ... until another Casanova sweeps her off her feet and then dumps her back on our doorstep when he's done using her?"*

What could Julie do? Heather couldn't go to Dad's. Cruella would destroy her. On the other hand, you could say Richard had not been a gracious host. But, then again, Heather was the number one source of Heather's problems and a poor guest.

Heather's gaze returned to the painting. "I miss Mom so much. I know I was only four when she died, but I still remember the way she sat under the oak tree for hours doing that painting. She was so beautiful. Her hair, her mannerisms. Do you think she was really an angel?"

"You know she was."

Heather studied her tattoos. "Mom was so pure ... so full of light ... I miss her."

"Yeah. Me too, kiddo. Me too."

Heather had come to look so much like her mother. Aside from their common penchant for art, Heather was her replica—minus the tattoos and the now-blue-streaked hair. Strange that Heather loved their mother's purity and yet colored her own body.

Julie was all Dad—straight dark hair, brown eyes, tanned skin, and, of course, his love for doctoring animals.

"How's *Dog*?" Julie asked as she got up. She removed her lab coat and hung it on the back of the door.

"He's good. Very tired. He'll probably sleep all day."

"Good," Julie said as she moved to the couch to exchange her sneakers for her favorite pair of ostrich-skin boots. She looked up at Heather and then sat up. "Hey, you want to go with me to lunch? We can stop by Nicole's house to get some answers, and then we can head to the Dogwood Diner. Whaddaya say?"

Heather turned in the chair to face Julie. She scrunched her face. "No, I'm not hungry. I think I'll just stay here and keep an eye on Dog."

"Okay. Suit yourself." They both stood. "Oh, Richard. I forgot to call his cell phone." Heather headed for the door as Julie sat back down at her desk. "Oh, can you do something for me before I leave?"

Heather stopped at the door, turned, and said with a tensed face, "Yes, *boss*?"

Amazing how her sister could be so loving one moment and so selfish the next. Should she have taken her back in again? "Really Heather? Can we not go down this path? It's been going so well."

"I'm sorry. I'm just tired from being out late last night. What do you need?"

Tired? From being out late all night. Whose fault was that? Julie bit her tongue. "Would you please put some gloves in my truck? I used the last pair this morning. And eyeball my other supplies. Oh, and, also, would you get my messy bibs out of there?"

"Sure thing, boss," Heather said, winking and smiling this time. "Door closed?"

"No, you can leave it open. Thanks, sis."

Heather turned and stepped from sight.

Julie lifted the receiver and clicked the speed dial for Richard's cell. No answer. She returned the phone to its cradle. She grabbed her smartphone and texted him "9-1-1," which was code for *leave whatever you're doing and call me right away*. She waited a couple of minutes, staring at the phone. Nothing. Richard always called when she did the code. Where was he?

———

Doc Lawrence surveyed a patient file as he stood across from Angie as she gave him his orders. "She giving you a hard time?" Julie smirked as she approached him at the counter.

He chuckled. "Always."

"Well at least it's not just me," Julie said.

Angie put her hand on her hip and bobbed her head as she said, "And where would you both be without me?"

The Docs exchanged glances. Doc Lawrence put a finger to his check and said, "Ooh, let me think." They all laughed.

Heather emerged from the supply room, a box of gloves in hand, followed by Socrates. She held the box out and said, "See, I'm a good girl." She approached Julie and held out her hand. "Keys, please."

Julie handed them over. "Thanks." Heather left without a coat. Julie shook her head.

Socrates returned from his pursuit to claim the appointment book. Angie scratched under his neck as he purred and held it out for more.

"I can't locate Richard," Julie said. "He didn't even answer my 9-1-1 text. Any calls?"

"I called Richard's office again and Nicole's cell number. Alls I got was voicemails." Angie said.

"What about her house?"

Angie chortled. "Ha. Kids these days don't have house phones."

Doc Lawrence said, "I need to get rid of my house phone. Nobody ever calls it but solicitors and politicians selling stuff, the IRS, and Social Security threatening to throw me in jail, car warranty places warning me my car's gonna fall apart. Oh, and let's not forget your mom … and you. And when my women call, it's always to get me to do something. Yep, I think I'm a-gonna cancel that phone today."

"Daddy! You oughta be ashamed of yourself. Wait 'til I tell Mama," Angie said as she picked up the phone.

"I'm kidding, I'm kidding," he said as he held up a file. "Three more and I'm done here for the day."

"Thanks again for coming in," Julie said as she held out her arms for a cherished hug.

"Eleven down, three to go," he said, walking into Exam Room 3. He paused. "Keep me posted on the dog mystery." He turned and said to the next patient as he closed the door behind him. "Well, Pluto, what's going on with you?"

With Heather outside, this was Julie's chance to talk to Angie alone. "I need answers. Do you know what Donna said to me?" Julie repeated their conversation. "Even she said it's not normal. What does that mean? I'm trying not to think the wrong thing here …"

"Look at you, going and getting all green-eyed." Angie stood and righted her posture military-style. "Where's the Doc Wheeler I know?"

"I'm not green-eyed, but I'm not stupid either. I don't want to be one of those women who say, 'I thought something was wrong, but …' Well, something is wrong, and I'm going to find out what."

"Yes, you are. But not like that, you aren't. You need to take a breath." Angie stood at attention again and did a circular motion with her hand mimicking taking a breath.

Julie stood straight, inhaled deeply, and exhaled. She checked her smartphone again. No text. "Where *is* he, Angie?"

"Does work ring a bell?"

"He's not *at* work, is he?" Julie pursed her lips into a pout.

"Listen, baby girl. I've known Richard for a lot longer than I've known you, and there's not a cheatin' bone in 'im. So, you just a-put that out of your mind."

Julie tapped the corner of her phone on the counter. Socrates jumped up and tried to comfort her. He pushed his face into hers. "Okay, okay. I love you," she said as she rubbed his face. "You're such a pest when Eddie's out."

"You can say that again."

"Okay," Julie said as she considered a reasonable response. "We have a dog whose owner we cannot locate. Right?"

Angie nodded.

"Then I should go to her house. That's logical, right?"

"Absolutely. You might even be able to poke around the yard to see if there's any poison laying around."

"Good thought." Julie pictured sleuthing around Nicole's house. "Isn't her house the one at the corner of Maple and Elm … that adorable two-story brick with the wrap-around porch and the white picket fence?"

"That's the one."

"I've always loved that place . . . and those rocking chairs on the porch just beg you to stop by for some sweet tea." Julie lowered her voice and leaned in. "How do you think she affords that place?"

"Now that's a question," Angie said. "Rich uncle?"

"Hmm." Julie fidgeted with Socrates' collar. "Did you get answers on the dog tag yet?"

"I called and they're backed up. S'posed to get back to me this afternoon."

"Okay. I'm going to Nicole's."

"Hold on just one minute." Angie walked over to a cabinet and pulled out a pregnancy test box and plopped it down on the counter beside Socrates. He immediately nudged it.

Julie's heart stopped. Staring at the box, years of disappointment washed over her. She took a step back. "No. I'm not doing it."

Angie looked toward the waiting room, then lowered her voice and said, "Now you listen here, young lady." Angie was in full momma motion now, head tipping and finger swinging. "I know you say you don't believe in God cause you're all mad at 'im for taking your momma, but that don't mean He don't exist. And I know you don't like it when I talk about 'im, but you're gonna hear this."

There was no point trying to stop her now. Julie had to listen, and a part of her knew what Angie said was right … or at least that Angie cared about her as much as she did for any of her kids—and she was crazy about them.

"I have been on my knees for you and Richard for weeks now, praying. I don't know why. You know very well that when the Lord a-lays something on my heart, there's a reason. Sunday after church I stopped by the drugstore. I felt like I needed to buy this. I know better than to ignore Him when He's a-callin' me to do something. And when you a-come in here this morning and said what you said about being sick, the Lord tol' me it was time. So, young lady"—Angie held out the box for Julie to take— "you take this here box, you walk yourself into that bathroom, and you do this test right now. And don't give me none of your feel-sorry-for-yourself excuses."

Angie was never wrong when she got one of her "messages from God." Since Angie had always been supportive of her pregnancy disappointments, she had never before boldly said that she believed Julie was pregnant. Socrates and Angie waited for her response. Could it be? Julie held out her hand.

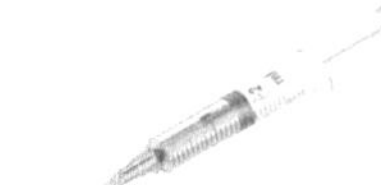

CHAPTER 8

11:10 a.m.

JULIE WALKED THE DARK PATH to her private bathroom, still stunned at the boldness of Angie's proclamation. Even so, the shadow of impending devastation awaited her when only one line would appear on the stick. She set the cursed box on the sink and grasped the counter as if bracing for a bomb to explode.

The specialists had confirmed it wasn't Richard's fault that Julie's family line would end with her and her sister. His little guys were quite happy. Heather's botched abortion had stolen her ability to have children. Heather had brought it on herself, whereas Julie had lived a clean life. Where was the God who rewards right living?

Tears turned into a torrent. She couldn't put herself through this again. But Angie was so sure. She pulled a tissue from the box on the back of the toilet, dried her eyes, and blew her nose. An aging failure looked back at her from the mirror. Maybe she'd just pretend she did the test and tell Angie it was a bust. Richard had stopped asking. Who would be the wiser?

Angie would. She'd want to see the proof.

Julie looked at herself and straightened "Okay, Lord. If you're there, now's the time to show up. If you can pull this off, we'll talk." Julie unzipped her jeans, sat down, and did the test. She raised the stick in her hands as if holding it up to God.

No lines. She dropped her head. Here we go again.

Closing her eyes, she counted to sixty. She peeked ... still nothing.

She shut them again and counted the second sixty, promising herself this was the last time—ever. Holding her breath, she opened one eye.

Now she was seeing things.

It couldn't be. She must have done something wrong. She had read the instructions dozens of times but checked them again. "Two lines, pregnant."

What if it was wrong? Maybe it was a false positive. Maybe she should do it again. She wrestled her jeans up, almost dropping the stick in the toilet. She put the stick on the counter to finish snapping and zipping. She needed a second opinion ... or a witness ... or someone to pinch her. She needed Angie.

She picked up the stick and started to rush out, but realized she had to wash her hands ... and clean the counter where she had placed the stick. As she returned to the sink, a glowing woman looked back. Julie? A mother? Someone to call her Mom. Was she too old? Could she be a mom and run her practice? She had repressed imaging motherhood years ago. Could it be true? She had to tell Richard.

Richard. Where was he?

She washed and dried her hands, picked up the stick, and wiped the counter with disinfectant soap. She looked at the stick again just in case she had been dreaming. Two lines still declared her motherhood. Julie flipped the light switch off to a childless era.

Hiding the stick behind her back, Julie approached the counter as Angie was putting folders away. Angie turned and with one look, raised her hands to heaven and said, "Oh, my Lord! Thank You, Jesus!" Throwing up the hinged counter, she rushed around and enveloped Julie in a swaying hug.

After a long moment, Julie stepped back and held out the stick for Angie to see. "Two lines, Angie. Two lines!"

Angie scrunched her face and she stepped back. "You hold onto that. I know where that's been."

"What if it's wrong? Do you have another one?"

"Baby girl, you don't have to take another one. First of all, the Lord don't lie."

"Hmm." Maybe not. But He did steal. Hadn't He had taken Julie's mother away.

"Besides," Angie said, "you know better than anybody that positives are accurate … *doctor*." Angie reached for the tissue box on Doc's counter and held it out until Julie took a tissue. Angie returned the box to its place.

Still shaking, Julie wrapped up the stick. "I need to tell Richard. I should call him. He's never going to believe it. I don't believe it. I had lost hope." She pulled her cell phone out of her pocket.

Angie reached for Julie's hand. "What do you think you're a-doing?"

"I've got to tell Richard."

"On the phone? What are you thinking?"

Julie stared at Angie a moment as the effervescence rose. "I don't know if I can wait. I feel like I'm going to bust."

"Listen, baby girl. You've been a-waitin' a long time for this moment. Make it special. A moment to enjoy. The good Lord knows you deserve it."

"Richard did promise me a special dinner tonight. Maybe I can wait until then."

"That's a good start, but ramp it up," Angie said as she returned to her spot. "Call Sarah to make his favorite dinner."

Julie ran through his favorite foods and pictured that look of satisfaction that only Richard could exude at the end of a great meal. "Yes—Sarah's famous fried chicken with mashed potatoes, gravy, and turnip greens. And his favorite dessert. Coca-Cola cake." Julie dialed the house as Angie beamed at her.

Julie braced herself for Sarah's chastising. Accommodating changes was not Sarah's forte. While her OCD made for a perfectly kept house with everything in its place, disruption of the schedule was a calamity. But laughter was never far away with Julie's high-school best friend.

"Wheeler residence."

"Sarah, it's me. Can we change the menu for tonight?"

"Change?" Sarah paused.

Here it came. Julie pictured Sarah sitting at the kitchen counter twisting a brown curl that had escaped her bandana with her left hand as she drew a target on the special dinner list and poked it with her pen. Maybe she was drawing Julie's picture on the target. Was she counting to ten? If Julie could only tell her about the baby, then Sarah would be excitedly planning her baby shower—and not the least bit mad about the change in plans. Julie was dying to tell her, but how could she before she told Richard?

"How can I *change* something that I haven't been able to prepare for? Jake has my car, you know, and I'm stuck here trying to figure out how I'm going to get the food for your *special* dinner. So right now, it's just a matter of writing a new list, isn't it?"

"Why does Jake have your car?"

"Said he was going to breakfast in town. Then he was gonna pick up a part for the truck and go by the feed and seed … which was kinda funny. Can't imagine what he's gonna fit in a car." She laughed. "I expected him back before now, but who knows. He's so cute. Always got girls chasing after 'im." She chuckled.

"Does he?" Julie wished she had spent more time getting to know him. She reran the mental tapes of their encounters since Richard had hired him. She had passed all her instructions and work requests through Sarah. Julie had only had cursory conversations with him when he got Jubilee ready for her to ride.

"Oh, my goodness. He's always gettin' calls from babes. At least that's what he says. He has to get out of earshot so he can have private talks."

"Hmm." Something wasn't sitting well with Julie. "I guess I really don't know him."

"He's a treasure. I'm glad you hired him. He's always helpin' out around the house when he's not tending to the animals. And he's real easy on the eyes if you know what I mean."

"Sarah. You're a happily married woman."

"Sure 'nuff, but my eyes still work." She chortled. "So, what's the plan?"

All Julie had to say about the menu was "Richard's favorite meal," and Sarah immediately rattled off his favorites—adding a couple of her own. "Good china and candles?" Sarah asked. She was the queen of special events. She could make a celebration out of a "no cavity" report from the dentist. "What's the occasion?"

"I'll explain later. Oh—and would you get the memory boxes down from the front hall closet and put them in the living room?"

"I'll have to ask Jake to do it when he gets here. My back is out again. Anything else?"

"No, I'm sure I've thrown enough of a monkey wrench in your plans for today. I owe you one."

"Just remember that next time I have to stay home with one of my sick kids." She giggled. "See you later."

Julie hit the end button. Angie was still grinning as if she had just found out she was going to have her first grandchild. "Now for Richard. Text. Don't call. Your voice will give it away."

"You're right," Julie said, trying to stay positive. Still no texts from Richard despite her 9-1-1 text. Maybe he'd missed it. She tapped the icons. Contacts . . . Richard Wheeler . . . Texts. Her thumbs raced over the keyboard display.

"Let me see it before you send it," Angie said.

Julie nodded as she finished her text. *Tried calling earlier. Forgot about your big case. Looking forward to dinner tonight. See you at seven?* Julie showed it to Angie, who approved. She tapped send. The screen confirmed it was sent.

"I'm so excited," Julie said as she looked into Angie's eyes. "I'd given up, but you"—Julie worked to hold back tears—"You never did. How can you always be so positive?"

A Cheshire smile crept across Angie's face. "All things are possible through Jesus Who strengthens me."

"Hmm." If all things are possible then why wasn't it possible for Jesus to save Mom? Was Angie's demeanor just because Angie's glass was always full? But that wasn't it. Angie had had enough pain in her own life. And still, she was always a light in the darkness. The truest example of an angel—the most loving, compassionate, and inspiring woman Julie had ever met. Except for her mom, of course.

Could Julie ever believe God was good? *Oh, no.* Julie had promised God she would if he made this pregnancy happen. But maybe God hadn't done anything. She was already pregnant when she made the deal, so it didn't count. Thankfully, Angie didn't know about her deal. "Angie, whatever this is, thanks for being here for me. Since my mom died . . . well, you know. I'm so glad I can share this with you."

Julie teared up again, this time drawing Angie into a crying party. It was Julie's turn to come around the counter and give Angie a big hug. Angie finally pulled back and straightened herself.

"Now go on. You don't belong back here. And look how you've messed up my makeup."

Julie retreated, lowering the counter. Angie tipped her chin toward the stick. "What are you going to do with that?"

"Should I take a picture of it so I can show Richard?"

Angie's face pinched. "I don't know. It's a little weird, but then again you kids these days are quirky. Maybe. It couldn't hurt."

Julie unwrapped the spent device and snapped a picture. She rewrapped it and held it out to Angie who made a face then held up the trash bin for Julie to drop it in—and just in time. Doc Lawrence emerged from the exam room with Pluto's owner leading the aging golden retriever. "Well, that does it for another year. Angie will check you out."

The owner went to the checkout counter. "Good morning, Doc. I didn't think you were in."

"Yes, we got a little backed up with a poisoned-dog emergency this morning."

"Oh. I hope it's okay. What did the dog get into?"

"That's yet to be determined. But he's going to be just fine."

"Well, we love you both," the client said, patting Doc Lawrence on the arm.

Doc Lawrence handed over the folder. Angie gave the owner a dog treat and got busy running her bill.

Doc Lawrence looked at Julie. "Well, you sure are looking better. In fact, you're glowing. Something good happen?"

Julie and Angie exchanged smirks. Julie wanted to share her good news, but instead said, "It's just girl stuff."

"Uh, oh. That's never good." Doc Lawrence said. Angie winked at him as she finished up with the client. He shook his head, picked up another file, and headed into the next exam room.

Angie collected the payment and handed the receipt to the client. "See you next year."

Julie tipped her head. "Take care." Julie looked around. "Where's Heather?"

"She never came back in. Where did you send her?"

"Just to stock the truck. That should have taken two minutes." Julie walked to her office, grabbed her jacket and purse, and headed for the side door.

As Julie reached the door, Angie said in mama tone, "Just hold on a minute." With a hand on her hip, Angie asked, "What are you a-gonna tell Heather about the baby?"

What was Julie going to tell her? And when? Julie returned to the counter, ordering her thoughts as she walked. "Well, for starters, nothing now."

Angie nodded. "Smart … And what if she's home tonight at dinner?"

"She won't be. She's always out at night."

"But if she is?"

"She's good about vacating for special romantic stuff. I should tell her now to make herself scarce."

"Good. So, when will you tell her?"

"After I tell Richard, I guess."

"How long after you tell Richard."

Julie raised her shoulders and grinned. "On the way to the delivery room?"

Angie's left brow hiked, pulling her pursed lips upward. "I'm serious. How is she going to take it after Rod broke off their engagement because she can't have kids?"

"Shhh! No one's supposed to know about that." Julie lowered her voice. "How would you feel?" Julie looked into Angie's eyes for the answer. Shaking her head slowly, she said, "There's never going to be a good time, is there? If I tell her now, before she's gotten over Rod, I'm afraid it'll put her over the edge."

"And if you don't share your greatest news since you got married and she finds out some other way?"

"It'll put her over the edge."

Angie's sad eyes reflected Julie's pain for her sister. Angie put her hand on Julie's forearm the way her mother used to. "So, what are you going to do?

"I don't know . . ." Julie pulled her arm back and stood straight. "But what I do know is, A, I don't have to say anything until I tell Richard. Everyone understands that. And B, my sister is AWOL, and I need her to get back to work."

Julie turned on her heel and headed out the door.

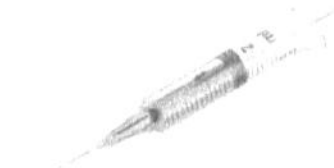

CHAPTER 9

Tuesday 11:35 a.m.

FROM THE TOP LANDING of the side-door stairs, Julie surveyed the staff parking lot. *No, it couldn't be.* Cruz was holding supplies and following Heather around the truck as she restocked the needed items. She laughed at Cruz's every word. Julie had not heard that laugh since they were kids. That sound was welcome, but Cruz? She took a deep breath to steady herself.

Julie paced her five-step descent, turned left, and walked the short ten-foot sidewalk to the parking lot, allowing her boots to do some talking. She crossed into the gravel—each step of her boots punctuated by the crunch. Cruz's sunglasses were perched on top of his head. He turned and smirked as Heather's face brightened at Julie's approach, oblivious to Julie's purposed scowl.

Heather giggled. "Hey, sis. I'd like for you to meet—"

"Deputy Cruz," Julie said, now forcing a smile for her sister's sake. "We've met."

Cruz studied Julie.

Heather scrunched her face and looked at Cruz. "You didn't tell me you knew my sister."

Cruz snorted a laugh, eyeing Julie. "Yeah. I rescued her this morning by the side of the road." He pulled a surgical knife from a tray. "What's this for?"

"What do you *think* it's for?" Julie grabbed it out of his hand and forced herself in between them to put it back in its place, then stepped back.

"*Where* did you see her?" Heather asked.

"Long story," Julie said. "I'll tell you later. I'm more interested in the fact *you* didn't tell me you were dating anyone."

Heather's face reddened. "We're not dating. We met at the Downtown Saloon. We hang out there."

Cruz shrugged.

"I thought you said the Diner." Julie said, "Never mind."

"Diner?" Heather asked.

"Yeah. I was at the Diner for breakfast this morning and he told me you were going to have dinner tonight," Julie said.

Heather looked at Cruz, who raised his hands in question. "I never said dinner. I said I'd be seeing you tonight. I meant at the Saloon."

Was Heather buying this slimeball's story? What a manipulator.

"So," Cruz said, "I hear Ms. Marley's dog is going to be okay. Poison, huh? Isn't that something? I wonder who would do a thing like that to a beautiful German shepherd."

"Yeah, it's crazy, isn't it?" Heather asked as if picking up on Julie's disdain. Cruz shook his head as if he was disgusted.

"Yeah. Who would?" Julie said as she rerun the mental tape of her encounter with the deputy that morning. How could Cruz have known about Dog? Did he have something to do with the poisoning or had Heather run her big fat mouth? She was never good with secrets, especially if she could use them to get something. Cruz had been in a nervous hurry to get somewhere. But at the Diner, he was relaxed—or rather obnoxious. But why would Cruz want to harm a dog? It just didn't make sense that he would have had anything to do with it.

"Why do you suppose Ms. Marley was crying and in such a hurry this morning that she would just drop her dog off like that?" Cruz asked.

That information had to have come from Heather and what was information about Dog or Nicole to him? "I have no idea. Do you?" Julie said.

Julie's lips pursed. Cruz shifted his body and tone. "Did you get hold of her?"

"That would be privileged, now, wouldn't it? And, Heather, it would be good for you to remember that we shouldn't be discussing our clients or their pets with others."

Heather's face blanched. "I'm sorry. I thought he might be able to help out or investigate or something."

Law enforcement investigate? Wouldn't that be a change? But Julie wasn't buying Cruz's act or that Cruz wanted to help in some official capacity. Cruz had to have an interest beyond his ability or inability to arrest the person responsible . . . *if* there was someone responsible. It might just be a case of a dog getting into a household product left carelessly in his way. But Cruz's attitude pointed to malicious intent.

Julie changed subjects hoping Heather might open her eyes to who this little weasel was. "So, Detective Cruz—"

"Don't be so formal." Heather giggled. "Call him Tom,"

"Tom? Tom *Cruz?"* Julie smiled enough for Cruz to feel her mockery. "Mr. Top Gun? Really? Well, I guess if the shoe fits . . . "

Cruz winced—a sight Julie enjoyed. He eyed Julie with contempt and then softened as he turned toward Heather. "Yeah, my dad was watching Top Gun the night I was born. And with our family name, he thought it would be . . . well, what can I say?"

"So, *Tom,*" Julie said, dragging out his name, "Where are you from?"

Julie ignored her sister's glare, relishing the trap she was setting for him. Julie knew Cruz couldn't afford to confront her in front of her sister. Cruz turned to Heather as if she'd asked the question. "Originally the Bronx, but we moved to Chicago when I was a kid."

Heather's face lit up, her voice raised to a schoolgirl octave as she said, "Really? That's *such* a coincidence. I lived in Chicago while I was in college. I graduated from the Art Institute of Chicago six years ago. I loved it there."

"Yeah? Why'd you leave?"

"My ex and I opened a small art studio near the school. My husband began hiring models to pose for the classes, and let's just say that he found them more appealing than me." Heather's effervescence had disappeared. "I wanted to stay in Chicago, but I kept running into him everywhere. Guess Chicago isn't so big when you're trying to avoid someone." Heather looked down and left the rest of the story untold.

Cruz lifted her chin with uncharacteristic tenderness. "He was an idiot. Who would do that to a class act like you?"

Heather blushed. Despite the obvious flattery, she soaked up the compliment like a dehydrated sponge. She was enjoying his attention. A little too much. Not good. Why did Heather always find her self-worth in men's attention? And why the bad ones?

Julie had to find the chink in his armor. "What brought you to West Virginia?"

Heather squeezed her eyelids to let Julie know she was not appreciating her interrogation.

"You mean besides the beautiful women?" he said, winking at Heather again. Her sister pretended not to notice but blushed nonetheless. "Seriously, it was the skiing. I'm looking forward to getting on the slopes this winter."

A large barking dog in the front parking lot announced his visit. Julie looked at Heather. "Would you head on in to help Angie with the patients while I have a word with *Tom*?"

Heather shot Julie the sisterly you're-a-dead-woman look. But Heather couldn't argue. She was supposed to be working. "Excuse me, Tom. Thanks for offering to help with my car. You'll pick me up at the shop around twelve-thirty and then we'll grab lunch?"

Help her out? Lunch with Cruz? She'd just told Julie she couldn't do lunch. Heather was hopeless.

"Sure." He tipped his chin toward her as she passed in front of him. What was up with that swagger she was putting on?

Cruz's gaze followed her down the sidewalk, up the stairs, and through the door. He kept his smarmy smile.

"*So,* you moved here from Chicago for the *skiing*? Wouldn't Colorado have been a better move?"

"Yeah, sure." The fake smile disappeared. "My uncle moved here. Asked me to move with him. You know, help him out. It's a family thing. He knows Hayes. Got me this job." He shifted in his uniform as if it was constraining him.

"Oh? Do I know your uncle?"

Cruz squinted. "Probably not. He works at a farm outside of town."

"Really? What's his name?"

"His name?" Deputy Cruz studied Julie for an uncomfortable moment. "It's Rudy … Rudy Andretti."

"Hmm, I don't believe I know him. Whose farm does he work on?

"The Gleason farm."

"Out on County Road 456?"

He nodded.

"The Gleasons moved away years ago. We almost bought that property."

"That's the one, my uncle's boss bought it."

"Well, I should stop by sometime and meet your uncle."

"You won't find my uncle there. He's in Detroit helping to get things set up."

"Well, I'm headed out that way this afternoon. Maybe I'll stop by."

"You just do that." His look dared Julie to follow through. He straightened into an official police stance. His face softened and his smile returned as his eyes focused on something over Julie's shoulder. Julie looked back to see Heather returning from the building. He adjusted the microphone attached to his shoulder, then greeted Heather with his love-sick smile. If only Heather had witnessed Dr. Jekyll turn into Mr. Hyde and back. But she would never believe Julie, even if she tried to warn her. Heather always accused Julie of being jealous when she tried to rescue her from bad situations.

Julie reached for her pendant, wishing it held the answers for how to deal with her boy-crazy sister.

Heather went to Julie's truck and retrieved the overalls. "Sorry. I forgot." She reddened again and handed the keys to Julie.

Cruz chuckled.

"See you later." Heather giggled and headed back to the clinic.

"Well, I've got a house call to make." Julie stared at Cruz, wanting him to leave. She didn't move.

"Of course," he said, pulling his sunglasses down from their perch and returning to his car. He started the engine but didn't leave right away.

When Heather was out of sight, Cruz rolled down the window. Peering over his shades, he said, "Don't you worry, *sis*. I'll take good care of her."

He punched the gas, throwing enough gravel to drive home his less-than-honorable intentions. Which were . . .? Julie's stomach lurched, but not because of the baby.

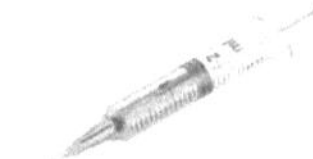

CHAPTER 10

11:45 a.m.

JULIE CLIMBED IN AND TOSSED HER BAG to the passenger seat. She eased out of the parking lot, turning onto Main Street. Nicole's house was halfway between her office and the county courthouse where Nicole worked with Richard. She slowed as she came to the Forest Hills neighborhood and turned right to go up Maple Lane.

The street names aptly described the variety of this virtual forest. Spring and summer brought lush greens. Fall. Bursting colors her mother ascribed to the glory of the Lord. Mom attributed a lot of things to God that was really just nature in all its beauty. Bleakness prevailed now, as the trees had divested themselves of their crowns in late September awaiting the white blankets of snow soon to come.

Julie pulled up to the stop sign at Nicole's corner. No cars in the driveway. She pulled through the intersection and parked along the left side of the house. Under a large oak at the far back corner of the lot was an unoccupied doghouse enclosed in a chain-link fence.

She grabbed her bag, slid out of her truck, and headed for the gate at the front of the house. There were no signs of other dogs. She unlatched the gate and went to the front door. The sound of her boots on the three wooden steps and across the porch announced her arrival. She rang the doorbell and stepped back.

No answer.

A barking dog sounded an alarm from inside the house beyond her truck. She walked to the edge of the porch to look for signs of life on the street. No one. She returned to the door and tried the doorbell again. Still no answer.

Fighting her sense of propriety, she checked again for anyone who might be watching and then walked lightly to the two front windows to the left of the door and peeked in. Living room, all in order. No signs of activity.

Still quieting her boots, Julie crossed the porch past the door to the windows on the right and found the dining room. Same thing.

She returned to the door and rang again. Dare she try the handle? Taking a deep breath, she turned it. Locked. Maybe she should try the back door.

Julie descended the porch steps and turned right to head around back. The barking dog's tone changed from muffled inside to unhappy outside. Mrs. Russell had emerged from the house on the other corner with Jack, one of Julie's beagle patients. Julie had inherited Mrs. Russell as a client from Doc Lawrence. As a semi-retired church secretary, she was also a walking Enquirer Magazine—and you didn't want to be in that newspaper. Julie was glad to live on a farm where no one watched her life unfold.

Mrs. Russell turned onto the sidewalk and crossed the street toward Nicole's front gate. Jack's bark slowed to an insincere *woof-woof.*

"Well hello, Doc Wheeler," Mrs. Russell called out. "Kin I help ya?" Her purple robe started to blow open in the wind, but she grabbed it with her free hand to keep it together. Hard to imagine this well-groomed belle-of-the-south would still be in house clothes at midday.

Julie headed for an unscheduled meeting at the gate. "Yes, as a matter of fact, you can," she said as she reached the rendezvous point. "Hello, Jack." He gazed up at Julie with his graying beard, looking already tired from his day's work.

Still fussing with her robe, Mrs. Russell held out Jack's leash. "Would you mind a-holding this a minute?" Julie took the leash, while

Mrs. Russell finished buttoning her robe. She reached to take the leash back. "Thanks, Doc. I rushed out when Jack a-started barkin'. It was time for his walk anywho. What's a-goin' on?"

"I'm looking for Nicole Marley. Have you seen her today?"

Mrs. Russell studied Julie's face. "If you don't mind me asking, why're you a-lookin' for her?"

"Her dog is very sick, and I need to speak to her about him."

Mrs. Russell's suspicious look now turned to concern. "Oh, you mean Dog?"

Julie almost choked. "*Dog?* Is that really his name?

"Yes. I know it's funny, but that's what she calls 'im. Cain't remember the story now. What a sweet boy. What's a-wrong with 'im?"

Julie smiled. "That's between a doctor and her patient."

Mrs. Russell nodded, the corner of her lip rising ever so slightly, but then her left brow raised and mouth tightened. "Is that the *only* reason you came by? To see Nicole about her dog?"

"Yes. Why do you ask?"

"Ain't none of my business." She paused. Julie could feel the information dam about to break. "Anyways, I ain't seen 'er since she left last night with some men. Don't know who they were, 'cause I never seen 'em before. They had one of those big black vehicles, you know, like the governor er something. Your husband was with 'em. Guess it was some kinda business meeting or something. Like I said, ain't none of my business."

"My husband? Are you sure?"

"Why yes, dearie."

Richard? At Nicole's? Maybe they were picking up something before heading to a work dinner. "What time did they leave?"

"Must've been around seven, 'cause that's when *Wheel of Fortune* starts. I always walk Jack in time to get back soze I don't a-miss it."

"Did you notice anything else? Did she have Dog with her?"

"No. Like I said, it looked like a business something-er-other. Why would you take a dog when yer doin' business?"

"If you see Nicole, would you let her know that I'm looking for her and need to speak to her right away?"

"Sure thing, Doc." Mrs. Russell didn't move but kept staring at Julie. What was she waiting for?

Julie pointed to the backyard. "I'm just going to head around back to check to be sure everything's okay. She seemed kind of upset when she dropped Dog off this morning. Thanks."

"Don't mention it. Let me know if you a-need anything else." Mrs. Russell continued down the sidewalk.

Julie went straight to Dog's pen and doghouse, trying to imagine any way he could have gotten into an insecticide. Everything seemed normal. Gate closed. Nothing out of place.

She walked to the back stairs, scanning for any signs of foul play around the house. Nothing. Because she was intruding on Nicole's more personal space, she punctuated each of the five wooden steps up to the landing with her boot heels. She peeked into the kitchen through the curtains covering the glass panes. Everything in its place. No dishes on the counter. No signs of a struggle. Was she worried for nothing?

There were gouges around the lock. She touched them as if feeling for the reason they existed. Forced entry? Had she seen too many thriller movies? She knocked as hard as she dared. "Nicole, are you in there?"

No answer. She tried the handle. Locked.

She walked down the stairs to head back to the front. A sheriff's car slowly approached along the side street. Not again.

Cruz parked in front of her truck and got out. He strode around the car and approached the fence. He took an official stance, ensuring his uniform was in place.

Julie stayed where she was by the side of the house. "Deputy Cruz, are you following me?" Julie hoped her disdain showed.

"Why would I do that?" That toothy grin crept across his face. He let it hang for a long moment and then said, "Your sister said there might be foul play. I thought I'd stop by to check it out." Julie wasn't buying it.

He walked to the rear gate, reached in, and unlatched it, then headed for the dog run. "What are you doing here? Came to check up on Mr. Wheeler?"

"Now why would Mr. Wheeler be here?"

He stopped to look at her over the top rim of his sunglasses. "Why *wouldn't* he be? He's always here ... with this hot babe ... late into the night." He paused, watching Julie. "Doesn't it bother you that the hottest babe for five counties works alone at night with your husband? Man! I tried to take her out, but she acted like she was already involved . . . If you know what I mean."

Annoyance arose. Was he trying to cause trouble? While Nicole was beautiful and Richard did work with her a lot, Richard was a faithful husband. He was home every night. Although he was getting late. But that was just because of the case he was working on. Right?

"What makes you think he's here *all the time*, as you say?"

He slid his sunglasses back to their perch. "I patrol this neighborhood several times a day ... and night." He bobbed his head. "Always here. Mr. Wheeler should change his mailing address . . . If you know what I mean."

If he said that one more time . . . Julie's stomach knotted. Is that where he'd been all those evenings when he was supposed to be working? Nicole could have been a model. As far as Julie knew, she hadn't had a boyfriend in the three years she'd been in Hearthstone. Richard was spending more and more time "at work." She pictured them together. Was this where he was ... alone with Nicole? Could she believe this punk? Should she?

"I'm sorry. You didn't know, did you?"

"Of course, I knew." She couldn't let him know she didn't. Change the subject. "You're investigating foul play for a dog? I've never known the sheriff's office to concern itself with animal welfare."

"Well, think about it. Your sister will think I'm a hero if I solve this crime."

Julie wanted to spit in his face. "What makes you think there's been a crime?" Now Julie smiled.

Cruz gave the dog run a cursory once-over as he walked the length. "No one home?" he said as he pointed to the house with a very different expression on his face. Was this sincere concern for someone other than himself?

Julie needed answers, so helping his investigation would be wise. "No, I've knocked at both doors. I peeked inside the windows, and everything seems in place. But there were scratches around the back doorknob."

Cruz went up the stairs to look. "Hmm." He didn't share his conclusions. He descended the stairs and looked right at Julie. "Well—I can't forget my lunch date." His toothy grin returned. "See you later, *sis*."

He went to his car as Julie watched after him until he had pulled away. She headed for the front gate. Mrs. Russell was walking back up the street toward her house. Julie let herself out of the yard. She had to act nonchalant so Mrs. Russell wouldn't get wind of her concerns about Richard.

"Was she there?" Mrs. Russel asked.

Julie stooped to scratch Jack behind his ears. "Doesn't appear so. She didn't answer either door." She stood and gazed back to where Deputy Cruz had been parked and then at Mrs. Russell. "Do you know Deputy Cruz?"

"Oh, yes! He's *such* a nice young man. He comes through the neighborhood watching out for us. He checks up on me regular-like. Must come by here three er four times a day. He even stopped to help me a-bring my groceries in last week."

"Really? Have you ever seen any other deputies be that attentive to a neighborhood?"

"Cain't sayz I have. Somebody must've raised him right."

Deputy Cruz's car appeared at the corner and slowly turned in their direction. Who do you call when a deputy is stalking you? Maybe she should call Mack.

Cruz slowed to stop. His window opened to that sinister grin. "Good afternoon, Mrs. Russell. How's Jack today?"

Jack let out a low growl and then barked.

"Jack! Mind yer manners," Mrs. Russell commanded. "He's just fine, young man. Just fine."

"Good to hear, Mrs. Russell. You take care, now." Still grinning, he rolled the window up covering the evil that lurked within.

"Ain't he the *sweetest* thang?" Mrs. Russell cooed.

Jack barked after the car. At least Jack didn't buy what Deputy Cruz was selling. Julie squatted to commiserate with Jack. "I don't know about him, Mrs. Russell. I only just met him." What did her dad always tell her? If you don't have anything nice to say, don't say anything at all.

Julie turned toward the house and pictured her husband leaving with Nicole the night before. Were they really together all the time? Neither of them was at the office this morning. Where were they?

"Is everything okay, Doc?"

Julie looked back at Mrs. Russell. "Did my husband come to Nicole's house often?" Julie asked, hoping for a no.

Mrs. Russell pulled her hands together with the leash over her chest, almost as if about to pray. "Dearie, far be it from me to gossip. But if I were you …" She stopped, checking over her shoulder as if she was afraid someone would hear. She leaned in to share her secret. "Now you understand, this is none of my business and all." Mrs. Russell looked around again. "I've had my concerns about what was going on in that house. Your husband comes and goes like he lives there. He says it's business. I know I'm old-fashioned, but in my day . . . well, in my day . . ." Mrs. Russell reached over and took Julie's hand. "I'm a-sorry to be the one to have to tell you, but I'm glad you found out. It's been killin' me to watch those two carry on the way they do."

Julie withdrew her hand and stepped back as if she could make this news disappear. Richard having an affair? With Nicole? Working so closely? Like he lived there? Was Julie so disconnected from reality?

He said he was working on that big case. Why would they work at Nicole's house? No. It couldn't be true. There had to be a reason.

Julie searched Mrs. Russell's face. Pity. Mrs. Russell was pitying her.

Julie couldn't move or speak. She looked from Mrs. Russell to the house and back. It couldn't be true. Her world began to crumble just as it had when her mother died. Was she so wrapped up in her vet practice that she hadn't noticed? She reached for her pendant.

"Dearie, do you want to come into my house for a cup of coffee or something?" Mrs. Russell asked. "You're looking mighty pale."

Julie wasn't ready to talk to anyone. She needed to process. *Get it together, Julie.* She closed her eyes. Maybe it would all go away.

She opened her eyes to see Mrs. Russell's worried expression. "That's very kind of you to offer, but, if you'll excuse me, I've got to get some lunch before my afternoon appointments." Not that she was hungry now. You learn that your husband is having an affair, and you're going nonchalantly to lunch? How stupid. But it was too late to take it back. Besides, how else could she get away? Anything she said to Mrs. Russell would be spread through town before Julie could get back to her office.

Julie reached into her pocket and handed Mrs. Russell a business card that she only gave to clients who might need to reach her for pet emergencies. "Would you call me if you see either one of them? My cell number is on this card."

Mrs. Russell accepted the card and scanned it to find the number. "I sure will, honey. And you let me know if there's anything I can do fer you."

Julie wanted to say thank you, but how could she thank a person who'd just taken her world away? Without a word, she walked away, around the corner to her truck, and climbed in. She drove two blocks up the hill, out of Mrs. Russell's sight, pulled to the curb beside a hedged lot, and turned off the truck.

The tapes of every minute of every day began playing in her mind as she tried to piece the clues together. Last night she had worked late because of a pet emergency. Richard wasn't home when she got there. He wasn't home when she went to bed.

She grabbed her phone out of her bag and checked the screen. No calls or texts. She called her house.

"Wheeler residence."

"Sarah."

"You're not changing the menu again, are you?"

"Sarah—this is serious. Was Richard home yesterday?"

"Yeah. He came home, showered, and had dinner before he went out." Sarah hesitated. "Is everything okay?"

"How did he act this morning?"

"Tired. 'Bout the same as any morning after he works late. He had his usual breakfast, two eggs over medium with toast and orange juice … What's going on?"

"I don't know. Listen. Think. Did he do *anything* unusual?"

"Now that you mention it, he had on his going-to-court clothes. Something about an important meeting today. He took a gym bag. I asked if he was going to work out later, and he said no, it was nothing like that. Said he needed a change of clothes. Is everything okay?"

Julie seethed with anger at herself. "No! Everything's *not* okay." Regretting her tone, she added, "I'm sorry Sarah … Everything's fine, I'm just worried is all. I'll talk to you later." She pounded the end icon.

If worry was her only problem. A tidal wave of emotions swept over her soul, drowning her former reality. She was pregnant, her husband was having an affair, and she had been too self-absorbed to realize it.

She put her head on the steering wheel and sobbed.

———

Tap. Tap. "Doc?" A male voice said from outside the truck

Oh, no. Someone recognized her. But then again, she was in her vet-mobile. How did it look for the town vet to be sitting in a truck crying her eyes out? She raised her head from the steering wheel and wiped away her tears.

Jake. What was he doing here? She checked her swollen eyes in her rearview mirror. Their farm truck was parked behind hers.

Gathering her composure, she turned the key so she could roll down the window. "Jake, what are you doing here?"

Jake straightened his six-foot, three-inch, muscle-bound frame. "When I brought Sarah's car back, Sarah said she was worried about you. Said you called asking about Mr. Wheeler. She checked with your office, and they said you had come by Miss Marley's house to check on her because her dog had been poisoned." Jake pointed in the direction of Nicole's house. "I drove right over here to check on you. You weren't at her house. I was about to call your cell when I looked up the hill and saw your truck."

It was kind of hard to miss her mobile vet clinic. "Why were you worried?"

"It wasn't me. It was Sarah."

"How did you know where Miss Marley lived?"

Again, the pause. "Well, you see, ma'am, I've been here before."

"Do you know Miss Marley personally?"

"No, ma'am. Mr. Wheeler asked me to do some errands to bring him stuff. Other than that, not really."

Did everyone know where her husband was spending his time? Were Sarah and Jake worried because they knew Richard was having an affair and thought she'd catch them in the act?

"Jake?" Julie waited until he looked at her. "What do you know about Miss Marley?"

"She's Mr. Wheeler's assistant."

Julie opened the truck door and slid out. She hated to pull the employer card, but she had to know. Julie said with more anger than she wanted, "Jake. Look at me." They locked eyes. "Tell me what you know about Richard and Nicole."

Shaking his head, he said, "I'm sure I can't tell you anything." Jake looked into Julie's eyes, "Ma'am, are you okay? You look upset. Is the dog okay?"

"Yes. He'll be fine."

"So, what's got you so upset?"

Frustration overwhelmed her. "I'm pregnant and I can't find my husband to tell him we're going to have a baby, and now I found out he's having an affair!"

Jake's face blanched. Time halted. Had she just said that to Jake—a virtual stranger? What difference did it make? Apparently, everyone knew about the affair but her. Sobs overtook her as she melted onto the pavement. Jake helped her up and held her. "

How could I have been so naïve?"

"That doesn't sound like Mr. Wheeler. He loves you," he said as he stroked her hair.

New waves of emotions came with each tender affirmation. When there were no more tears, Julie collected herself and pulled away from Jake. "I've got to get answers." She couldn't look into his eyes. She felt too foolish.

"Would you like for me to drive you?"

"No," she said as she started back to the truck. "I'm fine. You go on."

"Ma'am, do you have any idea where Mr. Wheeler might have gone?"

Julie got into the truck, then turned back to answer. "No. I haven't spoken to him all day."

Jake came and put his hand as if ready to help her close the door. "And Ms. Marley, what did she say when she dropped off Dog?"

How did he know Dog's name? And why was he asking these questions? Jake's look was . . . intense. Where was the tender face that had just comforted her?

Julie answered slowly, watching for his reaction. "She didn't say anything. I didn't talk to her. Why do you ask?"

"Well, I've only known your family for a short time. I'm just trying to help you piece this together."

She hadn't told him she had something to piece together. Julie's stomach knotted again. Her poor baby—its life was already taking a turn for the worse.

"Are you sure you don't want me to drive you home?"

"Yes. Thanks for coming to check on me. Tell Sarah I'm fine." Julie jerked the door closed, leaving Jake standing. He returned to the truck. He stopped before climbing in and called out, "Call me if you need me."

Julie waved as Jake got in and pulled away. She looked down and placed her hand on her stomach. This was supposed to be the best day of her life. What was it now? She needed answers. Did everyone know about Richard and Nicole but her? She had to find out. And Richard's office was the place to start.

CHAPTER 11

12:30 p.m.

Had everyone gone out and bought a car today and gotten on the main road for the sole purpose of getting in her way?

Finally. A break in the traffic. Neither the beauty of pure blue sky nor the oak-lined, half-mile drive to her office could keep Julie's mind from conjuring images of Richard with Nicole.

Sure, Julie had had the normal concerns about Nicole that any married woman has when her husband works with another woman. But Richard demonstrated his love for Julie continually. He made her feel adored. Julie had seen Nicole with Richard on numerous occasions. She had never sensed Nicole had any romantic interest in Richard.

But now, images of her husband wrapped in the arms of the young and beautiful, emerald-eyed, totally put-together woman, who must work out four hours a day to have such a great body, flooded her mind. How could any man not want to enjoy Nicole's charms? *Stop it, Julie. Richard would never stray.*

She had to focus on why she should not believe anything could be happening between them, like Richard's call that morning, filled with TLC. They were going to have a special dinner tonight—just like their anniversary several weeks prior when he romanced her all the way to heaven. He had planned a romantic Caribbean cruise for the holidays. He was willing to put up with her crazy sister moving back in. Although come to think of it, they had fought it.

But still, Richard was always there for her. He couldn't have feelings for Nicole. He had never once done anything that would make her suspect an affair.

This was all Cruz's doing. It was nothing other than his idle ramblings that called Richard's character into question. Why was Cruz doing this? Was he trying to cause trouble? Did he have an ax to grind with Richard?

But what about Mrs. Russell?

The bronze Cadillac in front of her crept along. "Come on," Julie said aloud as if the elderly driver in front of her could hear. Instead of moving faster, the left turn signal came on and the car stopped. When large breaks in the line of cars came, the old woman did not go. "Come on. Come on. What are you waiting for?"

A big clearing opened in the oncoming traffic. The woman hesitated, missing her opportunity to make the turn. "What do you need, an invitation?" Julie pounded the steering wheel and laid on the horn. The woman raised her hand in acknowledgment. Julie tried to calm herself. She hated drivers behaving the way she was now.

Finally, there was a long break in traffic and the woman turned. Oh no. Angie's mother—one of the town's saints. Maybe Mrs. Lawrence didn't recognize her. Like people wouldn't notice her vet-mobile? How was she ever going to explain?

She finally reached the beginning of the seven blocks of brick buildings that comprised the downtown district. A sheriff's car was parked at the Dogwood Diner. Heather. Cruz. Did her sister know Richard was cheating on her? The courthouse would have to wait.

A parking spot was opening up right next to the sheriff's car. A sign. Julie waited for the driver to pull out, tapping on the steering wheel and muttering under her breath. "Come on. Let's go."

At last, the car backed into the street, and Julie took the space. She grabbed her bag and hurried to the front of the diner. Heather and Cruz were in a booth. As she reached the door, Jake passed by in the farm truck. Was he following her? Their farm was in the opposite direction from town. He didn't appear to notice her or slow when he went by.

The bell above the door rang as she entered. Meatloaf and home-made bread filled the atmosphere. But today her stomach lurched as Cruz stared at her, his lips turning up in that sickening smile. Heather's eyes followed Cruz's focal point to Julie. Heather's gaga grin faded into a scowl.

Sally passed in front of Julie with a tray of drinks as Julie considered her next move. "Back so soon?"

Julie didn't answer. She walked past a number of hellos as she headed toward her sister, mechanically returning their greetings with smiles and good-to-see-you's. She stopped at the edge of the booth and stared at Cruz. She wished her eye darts were poisonous. Heather forced a contrived smile and pleasantry. "Julie, I didn't expect to see you here."

"I don't know why not. I asked you to join me here for lunch long before Deputy Cruz did, and you couldn't make it.

Heather offered no defense.

"Did you ever consider that it might be the company?" He smirked.

Julie tried to ignore him. Why did he make her feel like a worm dangling on a hook? "Heather, can I speak to you for a minute … alone?" Julie tipped her head to the right signaling for Heather to follow.

Her sister looked at Cruz, who scooched out of the booth and said, "No, no. Sit here. I've got to see a man about a dog." He sneered at Julie. "Oh, that's your line, isn't it?"

"Thank you," Heather said in a scolding tone. Cruz left for the restrooms as Julie took his place. She waited until he was out of earshot.

Heather snarled. "What's this all about?"

Julie leaned forward and motioned for her sister to do the same. "Heather, I don't even know where to begin, but I'm afraid you've been holding back. I need to know the truth. What do you know about Richard and Nicole?"

"What?" Heather slammed back in her seat and crossed her arms. "What are you talking about?"

"I don't think this is a hard concept. I'm trying to stay calm here. I know you are not Richard's biggest fan, but I'm asking you a question that is important to me." Julie took a deep breath. This question could not be rescinded. "Is Richard having an affair?"

Sally came to the booth. "Are you going to be staying for lunch, Doc? We've got a meatloaf special."

"No! I'm fine!" Julie said with a bite. Sally's eyes widened. Julie immediately regretted her tone. "Sorry, Sally. I'm fine, really. I've gotta get back to the office."

"Would you like some sweet tea?"

"No, thank you! I'm fine. I'll be outta here in a minute."

Sally stared at her a moment, then bobbed her head and looked at Heather. "Your orders'll be up in a minute." She moved to the next table to clear the dishes.

Heather surveyed the neighboring tables. She leaned toward Julie and spoke in a hushed tone. "You're right. I'm not Richard's biggest fan. I know he's not happy that I moved back in with you two. He's made that pretty clear. But doesn't it make you wonder why he's not happy? In the few weeks that I've been back, I've hardly seen either one of you at the house. You're too busy to even notice what's going on around you."

"You did not answer my question!" She pounded her fist on the red-and-white checkered top. "Is Richard having an affair with Nicole?"

Heather tipped her head to the tables around them. "Everybody's looking."

Sure enough, several people in the nearby booths and at the adjacent tables watched them. Oh great, more explaining to do.

"Is everything okay?" Cruz said as he rejoined them.

Heather smiled up at him the way she did with their father when she wanted her way. "Yeah, everything's fine. Be a doll and give us a couple more minutes."

Cruz straightened in his uniform. "Okay." He headed for the lunch counter and took a seat on the only available red-topped bar stool.

Heather's face was rigid now. "I don't know if he is or not. They're the talk of the town, though. Everyone goes on about how beautiful and young she is, how much time they spend together, you know. Why wouldn't he?"

"What do you mean by that?"

"When was the last time you did anything together? Do you even remember the last meal you shared? Was Richard home when you went to bed? You guys live in separate worlds. Nicole's available, and you're not."

"What are you saying? This is my fault?" Julie pounded the table again.

The entire restaurant grew quiet. Everyone was looking at her. Julie had to get out. "Thanks for nothing, sis!" She yanked her bag and stood. All eyes were on her. Cruz sat on his stool, but this time he was not smiling.

Julie erected herself and walked out. The bell announced Julie's escape from the peering crowd.

———

Cruz stood as he watched Julie run away. He had accomplished his mission. But a flash of grief stabbed him. He gazed over to his crushed confidant. The division he caused had just added to Heather's troubles and her deep grief. Cruz had never had anyone care about him, but Doc did care about Heather. She deserved to be loved. Was this going to put Heather over the edge?

Cruz shook his head as if he could shake off his troubles. He had to stay on task, or he was a dead man. He had to pull his weight. It was his last chance.

He retrieved his cell phone from his pocket and texted. *Mission accomplished. Big scene at Diner. Couldn't have gone any better.*

Instead of praise, the response was: *Idiot. Stop texting.*

Another screw-up. Electronic evidence. How many strikes was that?

He returned to his secondary beleaguered target. Julie's words had crushed Heather's small frame. She was so vulnerable. A screw-up, like him. Both of their mothers had died when they were young and neither remembered much about them. They had no one in their corners, only people who saw them as baggage. He needed to be there for her, but what could he do? Her eyes pleaded for help—help he could not give her.

Sally arrived with food. Just in time.

———

JULIE COULDN'T GET AWAY FAST ENOUGH. She put the truck in reverse and let off the brake. A horn blared, halting her backing procedure. Where had that car come from? The driver flashed around her. He marked his displeasure with a distinctive hand signal. She double-checked as she finished the maneuver and drove halfway to the county courthouse. She pulled to the curb. *Breathe. Think.* Several people walked by. Had they seen her display at the Diner?

She looked ahead to the town centerpiece. Julie had always been proud that Richard was an integral part of the law and order that the building represented. Now what was he? A liar and a cheat. The office was now the place Richard went every day to be with his assistant.

The truth lay ahead of her. She pulled out and went the final block. She turned right on Broadway and pulled around to the rear parking lot of the red-brick, two-story building. The sign, RESERVED FOR PROSECUTING ATTORNEY, marked the vacant parking spot. Why not? Based on everything she had heard, it was unlikely he was going to be using it. He was probably off in some cheesy motel with Nicole.

Julie turned off the engine and checked her watch. Almost one. The staff would likely still be at lunch. *Deep breath.* She should just leave. Richard wasn't there anyway. What good was it going to do to go in?

She started the truck, put it in reverse, and began to back out, but stopped. No. She had to do this now. She needed to see the expressions on peoples' faces when she asked questions. She pulled back in, turned the key off, opened the door, and headed for the back entrance.

Charlie, the regular security guard, must have been at lunch. Another fellow was sitting at Charlie's post, mesmerized by his phone. He barely looked up. She put her bag through the x-ray machine and walked through the security point. The guard looked up and tipped his chin to acknowledge his authority for her to continue.

Hayes was headed down the staircase. "Good afternoon, Doc." Julie shrank when he came around. It wasn't his six-foot-two stature. Almost all the men in her life were tall. He was dressed in his usual white dress shirt, no tie, with a casual jacket. Gruff and graying, but not that old. Irish maybe? Perhaps it was the absence of words. He always left her wondering what he was thinking. He was, in fact, the last person she wanted to see.

"How's it going?" he said, mid exhale.

How *was* it going? The question was simple enough. She wasn't fine—her usual answer. She was furious. "Well, I can't say it's going well. Ask me again later."

Hayes squinted his eyes. "Here to see Richard?"

"Yes. Well kind of. Do you know Richard's assistant, Nicole?"

Hayes smirked and puffed his already-barreled chest. "Ha. Ha. She's the kind of gal it's hard not to notice." He winked. "If you know what I mean."

She didn't know whether to be mad or hurt.

Hayes tipped his chin up. "What do you want with Nicole?"

"Nicole dropped off her German shepherd this morning. He got into something poisonous. She was hysterical when she left, and then she vanished and so did Richard. No one has been able to locate either one of them. I'm hoping to get some answers."

"What did she say when she dropped off the dog?"

Same question as Jake. "Why do you ask?"

Hayes's face began to redden, but then it relaxed. "You said the dog had been poisoned."

"No, I said he got into something poisonous."

"Must be my suspicious detective mind working overtime. Did they disappear together?"

"I didn't say that." But that was exactly what she was implying. She forced her tensed shoulders down. "I don't know."

Hayes studied her. That's what she hated about him. "Well, Doc, I heard they've been working on some big case together. It's some big secret. Has he mentioned it to you?"

Why was he asking her? And why didn't he know about it? Richard prosecuted cases that the sheriff's office brought. They did the legwork to get the evidence. Richard always said his job was—what did he say? Reactive? The deputies made the arrests and they prosecuted.

"Not that I remember." That was the truth, but it was more likely she just hadn't been listening when Richard talked about it because she had been so wrapped up in her world. Maybe Heather was right.

"Well, if I hear from Richard, I'll let you know." He patted her on the shoulder. His words brought no comfort.

"I saw you with Deputy Cruz this morning. He seems to have an interest in my sister. What do you know about him?"

"He's a great kid. Came from Chicago."

"Didn't you come from Chicago?"

Hayes searched Julie's eyes. "Well, Chicago originally. More recently, Detroit."

"What brought you here?"

Hayes hesitated. That shrinking feeling returned as he examined her. "Sick of city life. Ever lived in Detroit?" He made a sickened face. "It's been such a relief to live in clean air and a clean town. And it was a great opportunity." He pointed to the back door. "Well, listen, you let me know if I can do anything else for you." He patted her shoulder once more and walked past.

She headed up the staircase to Richard's second-floor office and turned right down the carpeted hallway. She entered the reception area, and, as she suspected, Donna was not there. She peeked around the corner to check for other staff.

She turned to find Paul Cato in the hallway talking to a pretty young girl she'd not met before—or at least didn't remember.

"Kin I help you?" the young girl asked Julie.

"Paul—what are you doing here?" Julie said, barking her frustration with these human obstacles to her answers.

The young girl lowered her head and went into the clerk's office across the hall.

Paul's brows knit together. "I'm sorry, have I committed a crime?"

"I'm sorry," Julie said. Someone was committing a crime but it wasn't Paul "I was looking for Richard."

"Me too." His face softened.

"What did you want with him?" Julie asked.

"Not that it's any of your business, but nothing in particular. After seeing your behavior in the Diner just now, I was worried about you … and him."

Julie's face heated. "You saw that?" She had been oblivious to who had seen her outburst.

"Of course. Everyone there saw that." Paul reached out to try to touch Julie's arm, but she jerked it away. She was in no mood to be comforted. She just wanted the truth.

"Julie, I've heard the rumors, but I've also known Richard for decades. He's not the type." His head moved forward with pleading eyes. "You know that, don't you?"

Julie wanted to believe it, but after all she had heard today, she just needed to get to the truth. And she had to see Richard. To look in his eyes. To see his reaction. "I wish I did, but neither he nor Nicole is anywhere to be found. Nicole dropped her dog off crying hysterically and disappeared. Doesn't that sound like guilty parties to you? And people are telling me that Richard is spending long hours at her house. Does that sound innocent?"

Several women came out of their offices to see what was going on. Julie had once again gotten herself worked up. The women retreated when Julie glared at them.

"I'm sorry, Paul, but I have to go." Julie entered the clerk's office. Paul came to the door and said, "Call me if I can help."

She turned back. "I'm sorry, Paul. I truly appreciate your offer, but I don't see how you can." She found the young woman and several others working behind old wooden desks.

Julie took a breath. "Good afternoon, I'm looking for my husband, Richard Wheeler. Do you know if he's in?"

"You're Dr. Wheeler?" The young girl's face reddened a bit but quickly recovered. "It's so nice to meet you. I've heard such nice things about you … and you're so pretty." The girl paused as if trying to put together bits of data to form a picture. "My name's Kelly."

"It's nice to meet you too, Kelly. Have you worked here long?"

"No, ma'am. I just a-graduated high school last June and got this job right after."

"Wow. What a great opportunity. I'd love to chat, but I need to speak to my husband. "So . . ." Julie searched her brain for the girls' name.

"Kelly," the cute young thing offered.

"Yes, Kelly," Julie said, trying to remember her name. "Can you tell me if you've seen Mr. Wheeler today?"

Kelly looked toward the other girls who were watching their encounter. She turned back. "Well, you know that I don't work in his office, so I really can't say."

Julie had had enough of this caginess that everyone was engaged in today. Putting on a cross-examination accusatory tone, Julie said, "Do you mean to tell me that you can't say whether you have seen him today? Were you not listening to the question?" She was nearly shouting now. "Let me repeat this so you can understand it. Did you—not Donna, not his staff—did *you* see my husband today?"

Kelly froze, her eyes round, her mouth open. Julie had just attacked an eighteen-year-old baby who might be immersed in a scandalous environment. Tears streamed down Kelly's face. "Excuse me," she said as she stood and ran past Julie down the hall to the restroom.

What had she done? The other girls sat staring at her, frozen.

Julie wanted to disappear. She exited the clerk's office and turned toward the fire escape at the end of the hallway. She stopped inside the safety of the staircase as the door closed behind her and leaned back against the wall. She put her hand over her eyes as if she could make the image of Kelly's face go away, but it made them all the clearer. Tears turned into sobs.

Footsteps from the first floor echoed up the cement stairwell. She had to get away. She wiped her tears and turned toward the corner, looking for a tissue in her bag, and pretending that she had gotten something in her eye. Two girls passed, thankfully no one Julie knew. She escaped down the stairs as soon as the door closed, the hollow footfalls echoing the emptiness in her soul.

She slipped out the fire exit, which led to a sidewalk that ran between the building and a wall that housed the dumpster. She slowed as she reached the opening of the parking lot to ensure she would not be seen by anyone she knew. The coast clear, she headed straight for her truck.

Escaping yet again, she got in quickly and barely looked around before backing up and going around to the exit. She turned left to get out of sight of the building, stopping a street away.

Julie had come into the courthouse with an apparent reputation of being a nice, frumpy wife, and was leaving behind the certain legacy of being a beautiful Wicked Witch of the West. She had no answers, no allies at the courthouse, and no idea what to do next. She grabbed the top of the steering wheel and put her head down. The floodgate of tears opened again.

The image of Kelly's horrified face stayed with Julie like one of those songs you can't get out of your head—until the image of Nicole popped into her mind. Lovely Nicole. She couldn't be more gorgeous. Green eyes dancing when she laughs. Auburn hair falling just off her shoulders and perfectly outlining her Lancôme face. Her body—mail-order perfect. Her impeccably tailored wardrobe wrapped itself around her curves. It's no wonder Richard had fallen for her.

Julie recalled a day the month before when she had come to Richard's office unannounced. Nicole—dressed in a peach-colored Tahari jacquard suit—was leaning over Richard looking at some papers laughing. The surprised look on their faces when she entered had struck her—like two kids getting caught playing doctor. But then, Richard immediately rose, dropped what he was working on, and immediately took her to lunch. Boy, he played Julie well. Making her feel like she was his all-in-all. What an actor.

Image after image of Richard and Nicole together flashed … the phone calls he got when home, after which he'd leave to go *"take care of some business."* Some business indeed. What a fool she had been. Did she not want to see it, or was he just that good at deceiving her?

And all those nights Julie came home to an empty house. Now she knew where he had been. Like Cruz and Mrs. Russell said, he was with Nicole *all this time*. And just like Heather said, Julie was too busy to notice. Her dedication to her practice had come at the expense of her marriage.

Julie pounded the top of the steering wheel. She had to get back to the office.

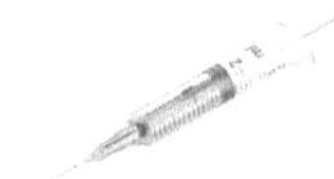

CHAPTER 12

1:15 p.m.

Julie's tears dried as she began to come to terms with the full meaning of Richard's affair. She was a strong, capable woman. She could handle life . . . and parenting without him. Just as quickly as this new confidence came, images of a birthing room devoid of everything Richard burst the dam again. The baby was *their* dream, and now he wouldn't be a part of it.

As she crested the hill, Julie's sacred place came into view. *Oh, no.* The farm truck. Not Jake. What was he doing there? The hair on the back of her neck rose. So much for her safe harbor.

Julie pulled around back. Angie's car was gone. Julie entered through the private entrance and went to Angie's counter. Eddie was standing in Angie's spot across from Jake on the other side of the check-in counter. Socrates was on the counter doing his best to get Eddie's attention.

"Thanks," Jake said, as Eddie handed over a brown paper bag.

"Jake. I'm surprised to see you here. I thought you were going back to the farm." Julie said as she set her purse down.

Jake tipped his head toward the bag as he lifted it off the counter. "Yes ma'am. I was just getting those horse supplements." He winked and smiled with an unexpected charm.

Oh no. Jake had asked her to bring those home a week ago. "Sorry. I forgot."

"No problem, ma'am. I was in town anyways getting some supplies." Isn't that what he'd said he was doing before? Neck hair back up. Still standing, Eddie looked at Jake. "Anything else?"

"No, I'm good." Jake tipped his Red Sox ball cap.

"Well, if we're all good here, I've got to put my training as a vet tech to good use." Eddie smirked. He grabbed the trash can, held it up for Julie to see, flipped up the hinged counter, and headed to the back. Socrates jumped down to follow.

Julie reached for the loose hook on the counter and rattled it.

"It's next on my list of vet-tech duties," Eddie called back as he disappeared into an exam room.

Jake loitered until Eddie was out of earshot, and then said, "Ma'am, if you don't mind me asking, are you feelin' any better?"

Julie couldn't respond. The only person she wanted to confide in was Angie at this moment, and Angie wasn't there. She stared at his face, unable to speak.

"Ma'am?" Jake asked.

"Sorry." She shook her head trying to get her brain engaged. "I'll be fine."

"I saw you were at the Dogwood Diner. Did you get some lunch? If you don't mind me saying, you're looking a bit pale."

So, he *did* see her. "Am I? Well, everyone knows you go to the Dogwood for the gossip." She managed a weak smile, which Jake returned.

"You know how Sarah is—when I dropped off her car, she told me to tell you to make sure you had lunch. She's worried about you."

"Tell her I'm fine."

Jake grabbed the top of the brown paper bag. "Well, ma'am, I'm headed back to the farm. Call me if you need anything." He started for the front door.

Sarah. Oh no. "Jake, hold on."

Jake stopped and turned to face Julie. "Yes, ma'am?"

"Would you tell Sarah to forget the dinner instructions for tonight? Tell her it appears I'll be dining alone. I should be home early. I only have one barn call this afternoon."

Jake nodded. "Anything else?"

"Yes, please don't share with anyone that I'm pregnant."

He nodded. "I would never do that, ma'am."

"Thanks, Jake." Julie watched from the safety of her post until he left, then went into the waiting room to look out through the front picture-box window to ensure that he pulled away. She sat back on the bench and stared at the front desk, wishing Angie were there.

Eddie padded back to Angie's desk, looked at Julie sitting in the waiting room, and then returned the trash can to its place without comment. His face was solemn. Where was the snarky comment about accomplishing his vet-tech duties?

Socrates jumped to the counter to watch his minion.

"Where's your mom?"

"She ran out to the bank. Said she'd be back around one-thirty." He looked at the wall clock. "So, I guess any minute." Eddie looked Julie over as if inspecting her for something. "How are you feeling?"

Why was he asking? Although her makeup was probably non-existent after her crying episodes, which meant her eyes must've been puffy. And she hadn't eaten. She felt queasy—the pregnancy. She really should eat, but how could she?

"Doc? Anything I can do fer ya?" Eddie asked.

Was her catatonic condition that obvious? She shook her head to force the wheels in her head to restart. "Sorry, Eddie." She paused another moment, hoping for brain activity. "Listen, I know you didn't go to school for this . . ." Julie waited for Eddie's acknowledgment, "but could you run over to Burger Shack and get me a burger? I've just been busy and I am feeling a little lightheaded."

"You sure you don't want something healthier?"

That was different. Usually, he was the first one to suggest Burger Shack's legendary burgers. Was he on a health kick? Then again, she was eating for two . . . but he didn't know that. And after her day, she just needed some good comfort food. "No, I think the comfort of a hamburger is in order."

"Then a burger it is." Eddie opened the cash drawer and held up a ten-dollar bill for Julie to see. "You sure you don't need anything else?"

"No, thanks."

"I'll be back in twenty." He passed by the open waiting room door.

The private entrance door opened and closed. A muffled exchange began outside. Angie's voice grew louder as the door opened again.

Angie appeared at the waiting room door, stopped to look at Julie, then came to Julie's side and wrapped her in her arms. Julie was glad no patients were in the office this afternoon. She wanted Angie to herself.

Stroking the back of Julie's hair, Angie said, "Baby girl, I heard you made quite a fuss in town today."

Julie's tears turned to torrents as her body gasped for hope.

———

HAYES PASSED BY MACK'S OFFICE on the way to his own. No more Mack to worry about. He had free reign—at least until he was replaced. But not having Mack as the friendly face of the sheriff's department was going to mean Hayes would be assigned to cover these insufferable committee meetings. At least Mack had done something helpful.

Then there was the replacement problem—get their guy in or "win over" a new sheriff after the elections. Worse, Mack's absence would put Hayes more fully in the public light. And light was his enemy.

Hayes took his seat behind the oversized wooden desk. Among the envelopes in his stack of mail was a hand-addressed greeting card. Who would send Hayes a personalized card? He opened it. A Thanksgiving card from his insurance agent, signed by staff he didn't care to know. How personal. He stood it next to several family photos, including the framed picture of him with his former wife, daughter, and two sons. The juxtaposition mocked him. His family would be spending Thanksgiving together—on his dime—without him. He had never even seen his four grandchildren. He snatched the photo and shoved it in a drawer.

His mother's eyes stared at him from another photo taken of the two of them when he was eight—the year his dad went to jail. She died of cancer the next year. It was the only thing he had left from his mom. They didn't let you keep your personal stuff when you got shipped from one foster home to another. How could his kids reject him after he had given them what he never had?

He picked up the Thanksgiving card. What did he have to be thankful for anyway? He threw it in the trash, picked up his smartphone, and dialed Jake.

"Yeah?"

"Did you talk to her?"

"Yeah, I spoke to her. She knew nothing."

"Good. Did you take care of getting Richard's keys?"

"Not yet. Sarah was around. I'll take care of it this afternoon."

"What about that item?"

"I got it."

"Good."

"She's pregnant."

"Who's pregnant?"

"Doc."

"Hmm." Doc pregnant? With Richard gone, what did that mean? He couldn't think about it. He had a job to do that demanded results— or else. "Changes nothing. Just take care of your mess. And bring that item to our meeting place. I'll explain everything then."

Hayes tapped end.

Pregnant. No dad. But hadn't he done fine without a father?

———

How did Angie always know what Julie needed? Angie stroked Julie's hair and said, "Come on, baby girl. Let's get you outta here before somebody sees that mascara." Angie guided her to the couch in the sanctity of her office. Julie folded in half, sobbing and rocking as Angie rubbed her back. Angie didn't say a word until Julie stopped rocking.

"Tell me what's going on, baby girl." Every time Julie started to lift herself to talk, she would just fall apart again. Angie retrieved a handful of tissues from Julie's desk and put them in Julie's hand. "There, there, baby girl. Just let it out."

Socrates came into the room and rubbed against Julie's legs. He hopped up beside her and nuzzled her side. Julie couldn't help but laugh. Inasmuch as cats were self-centered, they sure came to your rescue when you needed a friend. She sat back and rubbed his head. With resignation, Julie said, "I've lost him."

"Richard?"

"Yes," Julie said as numbness settled into her soul.

"Have you talked to him?"

Socrates crawled in Julie's lap and began purring. Julie caressed him from head to tail. "No, I haven't talked to him. Not that I haven't tried." She looked at Angie. "Everybody in town knows he and Nicole are having an affair. I've lost him to Nicole."

"What you've lost is your mind. That man adores you."

"But Mrs. Russell said Richard was over there *all the time*."

"Mrs. Russell? That old gossip? That woman has an imagination that doesn't end." Angie brushed Julie's bangs out of her eyes. "One time she told me that one of my boys was making out with the preacher's daughter. I reckon he was eleven or twelve at the time. I went home ready to whoop on that boy. Instead, I found out that Johnnie's youth group had been doing community service, and they were a-painting a house on her street. She saw Johnnie a-comin' out of the backyard with the preacher's daughter and assumed they had been up to no good. That woman is trouble. You should know better than to listen to her."

Julie blew her nose again. "What about Deputy Cruz?"

"What about him?"

"He said they were together *all the time* … and he would know because Mrs. Russell says Deputy Cruz comes by there several times a day."

"Mrs. Russell? Again?" Angie took hold of Julie's chin, turned Julie's head toward her, and looked her in the eyes. "And Deputy Cruz? That hot shot? You met him. Do you believe anything he says?" Angie smiled at Julie as if she was looking at a silly five-year-old who believed she could fly if she jumped off a roof with an umbrella.

"What about Heather?" Julie said.

"*There's* the pinnacle of truthfulness and light. Don't get me wrong—I love your sister. But she's only interested in everything Heather. Did she *say* she saw Richard being unfaithful?"

Julie thought for a moment, and then weakly said, "No."

"How long has Heather been back in town?"

"A few weeks."

"And where has she spent her evenings?"

Feeling more foolish by the moment, Julie said, "Drinking. At the Downtown Saloon."

"And who hangs out with her?"

"Deputy Cruz."

"Yeah, well Eddie hangs out there too, and he does *not* have a high opinion of Deputy Cruz—*or* your sister's drinking, for that matter."

"What about the clerk at the courthouse? Everyone's been acting so evasive?"

"How would you react if someone asked you to report on their spouse?"

Now Julie felt downright stupid. "I guess you're right. I'm so confused." Julie leaned sideways onto Angie's shoulder. "What am I supposed to think?"

"Now that's the million-dollar question. I know you don't cotton much to the Bible, but it says that we cannot rely on our own thinking. It's flawed."

Julie pulled away. "No sermons, please."

Angie's face dropped.

"I know you mean well, but now's not the time," Julie said.

Angie dropped it and instead asked Julie to recount every detail of her pursuit of the truth. Julie complied as Angie redirected Julie back to the facts every time she tried to go down a rabbit trail. When Julie was all done, Angie said, "Here's what strikes me as odd. That Deputy Cruz is there *all the time*, as you like to stress. And that Richard and Nicole left her house with some men. Don't you think that's weird? Why is Cruz spying on your husband and Nicole? Answer that question and I believe you will have your answer as to why Richard is working outside the office."

Julie's phone rang. *Heather.* Julie held it up for Angie to see. Angie shrugged. Julie looked at her sister's picture on the phone. She needed to talk it through, but not at that moment. She let the call go to voicemail, even though she'd probably pay for that later.

"You're the one I'm worried about right now. Your sister is . . . well, your sister. And the package that comes with that." Angie searched Julie's eyes. "Where are you now with what you believe about Richard?"

Julie thought for a moment. She still had good reasons to doubt him, but they were either founded in gossip or questionable sources. She had equal reasons to trust him—he had never once done anything but love her. In a lawyerly manner that Richard would have been proud of, she determined there was not enough evidence for a guilty verdict. "Is it awful to say I don't know?"

"No, baby girl, it's honest. It means you're not holding onto stinking thinking." Angie grinned and winked. She was right as usual.

Julie checked the time. "Oh my!" Julie stood. "I've got to get to Sam Beckers'. It's already a quarter to two. I'm late."

Angie rose and shook her head. "Surely, you're not going out there after all you've been through."

"What else am I going to do? Sit around and worry? The drive out there will do me good. Give me a chance to breathe and process this crazy day."

"I don't guess it'll do me any good to argue. Besides, I'll bet Mary Jo will have some of your favorite pie waiting." Angie started for the door and then turned and said, "Speaking of pies, did you get something to eat today? Gotta think of that baby now."

"Eddie's bringing me something."

"I'll call the Beckers and see how late you can come. With eatin', you're gonna be more than a few minutes late."

Julie sat at her desk, ready to try Richard again. Seeing a dog collar, she asked, "Do you know how Dog is doing?"

"I just got back. Let me find out. By the way, did you find out his real name?"

"It's Dog."

"What? Who told you?"

"Mrs. Russell. And you know Mrs. Russell knows everything."

They both laughed.

———

HAYES STOOD UP FROM HIS DESK CHAIR and checked his pockets to be sure he had everything. Keys, wallet, cell phone. Something was missing. He looked around his desk. Nothing. The only thing missing was his peace about the plans, and how he had not been able to control the timing on this week. Everything had been on schedule until Mack screwed everything up.

He had just enough time to make the two o'clock meeting at the Gleason farm. They had to reorganize to be sure they'd have no problems with the delivery of the labs this week. Relocating them to this sleepy town would make the operations so much more efficient. And there was a big bonus in it for him if it all went well. It had looked like easy money. Now he wasn't so sure.

It had been a piece of cake to turn Mack to their ways . . . until he lost his mind. The former coal miners would do just about anything to put food in their bellies. This was the perfect place. Now he just had to cover up the tracks that Mack, Richard, and Nicole had left. Just a couple more days.

Hayes headed to his Grand Marquis. He reached for his keys just as his phone rang. He pulled the phone from his belt clip and cursed as he read the screen. The boss. This call couldn't be public, so he unlocked the car and got in. He raised the phone to his head. "Hayes here."

"What the heck is going on there? I thought you had everything under control. That's what you said, wasn't it?"

"You heard about Mack."

"Why would you think that? I just sit up here with my thumbs tucked where the sun don't shine and hope that everything's going to be okay. Like I can trust you. Idiot! I have eyes everywhere. And it's not just Mack, is it? Richard? Nicole? Really? You're useless!"

"Nothing has happened that wasn't supposed to. It's just the timing. There's nothing to worry about—"

"Yeah, well just in case, I'm sending Smitty down to be sure."

Hayes pinched the bridge of his nose. That's all he needed—the boss's henchman watching over his shoulder. "You don't need to do that. It's all handled. It'll just draw attention to us if you send him. People down here don't like out-of-towners. There have been enough transitions here in the last couple of years."

"He'll be there tomorrow. In the meantime, don't mess up anything else." The voice paused. "You're such a disappointment." The phone went dead.

Hayes hit the steering wheel and cursed Mack for being weak, Richard for being a good guy, Nicole for showing up at the wrong time, and Julie for being a loose end. That would soon be taken care of, but would it be soon enough? He had to keep Julie away from the truth.

Everyone had better be at the meeting so they could nail this down.

CHAPTER 13

1:45 p.m.
"Hello, you've reached Richard Wheeler. I'm not available right now to take your call …" Julie held the receiver away from her head. The lovers' image popped into her mind again. *Stop it, Julie.* Angie was right—there had to be a rational explanation. She would laugh about all this at dinner that night when Richard explained his day.

Oh, no. She had told Jake to tell Sarah to cancel. What if Richard showed and there was no special dinner on the night she would be sharing about the baby. She picked up the phone to call Sarah just as Eddie showed up at her door carrying a brown paper bag with a grease spot forming. Julie set the phone receiver back in its cradle.

"Come on in, Eddie." Julie motioned to the chairs across from her desk. Eddie handed the bag and a cup over as he took a seat.

"I got you a chocolate shake, too. Figured you'd be pretty hungry this late in the day." He had the sweetest smile. Angie had done a good job with this one. In fact, she had done a good job with all her boys. Was Julie's a boy? She held up the cup as if toasting his good nature. "Thanks, Eddie."

Angie came to the door carrying Dog's collar. She looked at the food bag as Julie emptied the contents. "Healthy eating?"

Julie smirked. "At least I *am* eating, *Mom*."

"Really? Hamburger, French fries, and what? A shake? We have to talk about your diet for the next—" Angie looked at Eddie. "Could you go check on Dog? Doc wants a status report."

"Sending the kids out of the room so the adults can? I'm sure I don't want to know." Eddie didn't look either of them in the eyes as he exited the room.

"Sorry. I hope I didn't let the cat out of the bag."

"I doubt it."

Angie set the dog collar on Julie's desk "I got the scoop on the tags. It's a vet's office in Charleston."

"Did you call them?"

"Of course. The girl with the records is taking a late lunch. I'll let you know when she returns my call." Angie looked at Julie's lunch again. "I'll leave you to your sinful ways." She turned and headed out the door.

"Thanks, Angie," Julie called after her as Julie returned to her meal. Sarah. She had already forgotten. Was this absentmindedness pregnancy related?

She picked up the phone and dialed her house.

"Wheeler residence."

"Hi, Sarah."

"I'm glad you called—Jake just got back and said to cancel dinner? He said he couldn't tell me what was going on, that I should talk to you. So, spill it, sister."

"I know this sounds strange, but I don't know." Julie's body tensed again and she almost began to cry again. She shook her head and tried to squelch these outbursts.

"Julie?"

"I'm sorry. I'm trying not to cry here. Today has been a roller coaster. I've been tired, sick, and I haven't been able to get a hold of Richard today—even when I texted our special 9-1-1 code. I don't know what's going on with him. I was thinking the worst thoughts." Julie dug deep to keep from falling apart again.

"What kind of thoughts?"

"I can't talk about it now. I'm still processing. You know I'll tell you everything later, but I just can't now. Let's just say one of two things is going to happen. Either Richard will show up as planned and we will have one of the best evenings ever or he won't, in which case I will surely die."

"Julie? You're not making sense."

"I know. Nothing makes sense. But let's hope that Richard shows up for the best night ever and you have prepared the best dinner ever. Okay?"

"Okay." Sarah hesitated. "So, what you are saying is that you want me to fix Richard's favorite meal for seven o'clock."

"That's what I'm saying."

"And you will tell me everything later?"

"Yes. I'll be home early and spill it."

"Well, that's a good thing, because if you canceled after I just made a special trip to the grocery store, there would be heck to pay."

Julie knew better than to be offended that Sarah was calling this good because her best friend knew her better than anyone and knew how to get her to smile.

"First Richard tells me to make a special dinner, so I make a list for your favorite meal. But can't go to the store 'cause Jake has my car. Then *you* call and want me to change the menu, so I throw that list away and make a new one. Now Jake says *you* canceled it. Then *you* call and say it's back on. I feel like I'm back in high school." Sarah paused, but as usual, broke into laughter, which, of course, Julie joined.

Sarah's tone became sincere. "Don't you worry—I'm gonna make the best dinner ever. If Richard doesn't make it, I reckon I'll have dinner with you, so it don't go to waste."

"Thank you, Sarah. I don't think anyone else gets me like you do."

"You know it. See you this afternoon."

Julie hung up the phone, unwrapped the burger, and took a bite. She was so hungry it didn't matter that it was now cold.

Angie came to the door. "First, I called Sam Becker, and he said to take your time. He just needs to run to the feed and seed before five today.

"Great," Julie said with a mouthful of hamburger.

"Now, for the dirt on Dog. I told you the tag was issued by a vet's office in Charleston?"

Julie's mouth was full, so she made a circular motion with her finger for Angie to continue.

"The girl called back and said Dog was healthy and had no medical issues and only came in for routine stuff. They confirmed his name and, like you guessed, he's five years old. They've been treating him for three years. I explained that he was dropped off and his symptoms and they said nothing in his history would cause that."

Angie scrunched her face and leaned in like she had a secret to tell. "Here's the really weird thing. The dog's owner's name isn't Nicole Marley. It's Jayne Jones."

"What?"

"That's right. I asked her to describe the owner and the girl described Nicole to a T. I asked if she was sure, and she said she couldn't forget Jayne because she was beautiful, had piercing green eyes, a perfect figure, and carried herself with grace and poise."

"Hmm . . ." Julie ate the last bite of her hamburger and then sipped her milkshake. She picked up Dog's collar and turned the tag in her fingers. She looked up at Angie. "Would we know if someone came in and gave us a fake name?"

Angie shook her head. "No, we don't check IDs. Never have. Course we know most everybody."

"At least you do." Julie paused, still looking at the dog tag. "You would think that the prosecuting attorney's office would have run a background check on her. So, if she's really Nicole Marley, then is it possible that she has a twin sister who really owns Dog and takes him to the vet up there?"

"I don't know. Isn't it usually criminals who change their names? Or someone hiding from their past? I reckon you're right about the background check."

Julie said, "Or maybe she had an affair up there with a public official and had to hide her name? Or maybe she's known Richard for all this time and she used that name when they got together?"

"Stop it, baby girl. I told you—"

Julie put up her hands in surrender. "I'm kidding, I'm kidding." She looked at the dog tag and then at Angie. "So where is Nicole—or whoever she is? Why did she leave here crying hysterically?"

Angie turned to look in the direction of an animal trying to make traction on the linoleum. "Speaking of Dog, look who we have here."

Dog came around the corner—tail wagging—followed by Eddie. He went straight to Julie and put his front paw in her lap. Julie was always amazed how dogs knew when someone had saved them. Of course, she really had not. Whatever he had gotten into hadn't been enough to kill him.

Julie leaned over to accept his kisses. "Good boy!" Julie sat back and looked into his eyes while rubbing his head. "Where's your mama?"

"Still haven't found her?" Eddie asked.

Julie took the leash from Eddie's hand. "Eddie, have a seat for a minute. We're trying to pool our information about Nicole." Eddie went around her desk and sat. Angie remained at the door. Julie continued to stroke Dog's head. "Eddie, you're twenty-eight, right?"

"Yeah."

"In fact, . . ." Julie paused, then looked at Angie. "Come to think of it, is everyone in this town twenty-eight? Cruz, Nicole, Heather— aren't you all twenty-eight?"

Eddie nodded. "Yeah, I think so."

Julie grinned at Angie. "Must have been a good year for babies."

"There were many good years for having babies at my house."

They both chuckled, then Julie got serious again. "Don't most of the kids your age hang out at the Downtown Saloon?"

"Yeah. Especially on the weekends when the bands play. But I've never seen Nicole there."

Julie looked at Angie, who shook her head. Julie asked, "What do you know about Nicole?"

"Not much, really." Eddie squirmed a bit.

"Why do I get the impression that you are uncomfortable discussing this?"

Eddie looked at his mom and then back at Julie. "Well, it's just that, you know, a lot of people in this town talk. And most of it's trash talk. So, I hate to repeat it."

Julie checked Angie's reaction. "You see what I mean?" She looked at Eddie and said, "Sorry, Eddie, I'm not picking on you, but"—she looked back at Angie— "see how he became evasive? That's about how everybody acts when I ask about her."

"Son, what do you know personally?" Angie asked.

"Personally?" He drummed his fingers on the arm of the chair for a long moment. "Nothing. I never see her in any social setting. I've never talked with her, and I don't really know anything personal about her. It's like I said—all trash talk."

"See? Notice the words he used. 'Trash talk.' It's all just idle gossip. That's why you need to ask Richard."

"So how do you explain that this dog sees a vet in Charleston instead of coming to me?" Julie asked. "Don't you think that shows a guilty conscience?"

"No, it shows me Nicole is loyal to her vet. Who knows—she might have relatives there."

"Yeah? And why then does *Ms. Jones* use an alias?"

Eddie's face twisted. "Ms. Who?" Julie explained what his mom had discovered. Eddie shook his head. "That's too strange."

Julie leaned forward. "And how do you explain the rumors and that her neighbor says that Richard's there *all the time*?"

Angie shook her head. "I don't know, and that's exactly where you are. You don't know. And until you do, you are not going to jump to any conclusions. Right?"

"Right."

Dog nudged Julie's hand with his nose. "How does your mom just drop you off here? I wish you could tell me what's going on." Julie searched his eyes. "Are you hungry?"

Dog wagged his tail.

"Eddie," Julie said as she caressed Dog's head, "Let's feed him some soft food now and give him some water. Let me know how he does with the food. Maybe I'll take him with me—at least until we get some answers."

Eddie took Dog's leash and led him out of the room. Angie followed.

Julie sat for a moment, fatigue suddenly enveloping her. Her eyelids felt like they had weights pulling them down. She couldn't drive like this. She buzzed Angie.

"Yes, ma'am?"

"Since Sam's in no hurry, I think I'm going to catch a thirty-minute nap. I can't keep my eyes open. Can you wake me up in thirty?"

"Sure, and you'd better get used to it. First-trimester sleepies. We'll have to start scheduling your afternoon naps. I never could stay awake with *my* boys."

How nice it was going to be to have an experienced mom around.

Julie pulled out her mama's quilt, went to the sofa, removed her boots, and cuddled up. *Oh, Mama. I wish you were here.*

Your mother is safe with Me. Trust in My ways.

She settled in with a smile. If she could only believe it was God and not her imagination trying to make her feel better.

She reached for her pendant. It was gone.

Julie sat straight up, checking her layers of clothing. She jumped up and felt around the quilt and the sofa. Where could her necklace be?

Julie sat back down. She had it when she showered that morning in the office. She had been careful with it when she dressed. How could she lose her most cherished gift? What if she didn't find it? Her hands began to shake.

"Angie?" Julie called out as she rose, went to her bathroom, and searched around the counter and floor.

Angie appeared, face scrunched. "What is it? You okay?"

Julie began to hyperventilate. "I can't find my pendant." Her mind raced as she went back to the sofa and removed the cushions.

"I don't remember you having it when I came back from lunch."

Julie returned the cushions to their place. Julie put the back of her wrist to her forehead as she looked around the room, and then at Angie.

"Take a deep breath." Angie modeled taking a deep breath, motioning for Julie to follow. They exhaled together, and they did it a second time.

"Baby girl, you know these things always have a way of turning up. We just have to figure out where you've been and when you had it last."

"I know I had it this morning . . . when I showered . . . here."

"Where did you go after that?"

Julie looked at the floor as if she was watching a video of her day. "I went to the Diner … then back here … then to Nicole's … then to the Diner … then to the courthouse and back here." Julie searched Angie's eyes. "What if I don't find it?" Tears began to flow.

Angie grabbed Julie's hands. "I'll get Eddie to look for it around here. In the meantime, I'll call around to get people looking right away."

"No, I have to go. I know where I went." Julie attempted to leave, but Angie latched onto her arm.

"Listen—you need to listen to me." Angie was quiet until Julie looked her eye to eye. "You caused some scenes at the Diner and the courthouse today. We can call security at the courthouse to check your path, and we can call the Diner to look inside and out to the street for it. Other than that, it's just a matter of going to Nicole's house, right?"

Julie looked from eye to eye and considered the suggestion.

Angie continued. "I'll get Eddie to check your truck right now, okay?"

"Okay . . . you're right."

"And I'm going to insist that Eddie go with you to Nicole's. You get yourself put together. Do you still want to take Dog?"

"Yeah. I think that would be good."

Angie left. Julie folded the quilt and put it away. Could this day get any worse?

Julie glanced at her watch as she pulled on her boots. She stood and retrieved her cell phone from her pocket. A text message from the Olgrams thanking her for her early morning rescue. Julie went to her bathroom to freshen up. Angie was right about her mascara. She finished fixing her face and stood back. She didn't look the same without the pendant. Why hadn't Angie mentioned it? Angie knew she always wore it.

Julie snatched her purse and jacket. The sound of Dog trying to gain traction came closer as he reached the door, followed by Eddie, who was holding him back. Eddie let go of his leash and Dog ran to her. Julie bent down to acknowledge him. "That's a good boy. How'd he do with the food and water?"

"Great. You would never know that he'd been on death's doorstep this morning. I didn't give him a full serving—just in case."

"Did you check the truck for my necklace?"

"Yeah—with a flashlight. I checked the path. The gravel. Nothing."

Socrates came to the door to investigate. Tail up, he walked in and sat on the arm of the sofa. "Look who's getting jealous," Julie said. Dog sniffed Socrates but did not bother him.

"You ready for a little road trip?" Julie asked the handsome dog. "I'm gonna take you with us so we can find your mama. Maybe you can help me find my pendant." Dog's tail beat the air as Julie rubbed behind his ears. "Can you get his collar and put a regular leash on him?"

"Sure." Eddie picked up his office leash and guided him back to the hallway. Socrates jumped down to follow. "Oh, would you also get a safety harness from stock to put on him in my truck?"

"Sure. The way you drive, he'll need it." Eddie said, checking Julie's reaction. The audience was in no mood for jokes.

"Did you walk him?"

Eddie called back, "Of course. I'm a well-trained vet tech, you know."

Julie headed to her counter where Angie was waiting.

"Dog looks really good," Angie said.

"He sure does. Especially considering his day." Julie said.

"I'm going to call the Diner," Angie said. "Where did you park and where did you walk?"

Julie described her parking spot, the path she took, and the booth she sat in. Angie wrote every word.

"And the courthouse?"

Julie was sure to include her alternate departure route via the fire escape. Not that people didn't use it regularly, but it wasn't her normal path. The rest was easy—the back entrance, Richard's hall and office, the clerk's office, and the fire escape. It really would have been silly for Julie to go—especially after the scene she caused. Would she ever be able to go there again? It was where she and Richard had met when she first came to town.

Julie retrieved several treats from the jar and then tugged at the hook on the counter. "Wow. Eddie got the hook fixed."

"Surprised?" Eddie asked as he came back with Dog and his paraphernalia.

"Nope. Just glad you condescended to do it." Julie checked Angie to ensure a smirk, which she got. "Eddie, when will the hospital's lab results be ready?"

"Ha! I'll be surprised if we get them back within a week. The regular guy is out, and the girl that's filling in acted like she just graduated high school last week." Eddie shook his head. "We may never know."

Julie held out her hand for Dog's leash.

"Are you sure you want to take him? He's pretty strong." Eddie said.

"Are you questioning my strength?"

Eddie's face blanched. "Uh, no." He paused. "It's just … um … you've had a long day."

Julie snagged the leash from him, then looked at Angie. "I know it's weird, but I can't shake this feeling. It's like he needs to be with me until we find Nicole."

"Do you have dog food?" Eddie asked.

"No, would you grab some and bring it out to the truck while I buckle him up?"

"Sure."

"I'll drop Eddie off when we're done. I'll see you tomorrow, Angie. Let me know if you hear from any missing persons."

Angie frowned. "You be safe. Go straight home after you get done at Sam's place."

"I will, *Mama*." Julie smirked and pushed the side door open with her back.

Dog must have been well-trained. He stayed by her side without pulling his way to the truck. Funny how even the most well-trained dogs will try to pull on the linoleum in the office, but once outside, they heel.

"Good job, Dog. You heel so well." When Julie opened the rear door behind her seat, he jumped up to the floor and into the seat. She opened the packaging for the dog harness and read the instructions. "It's been a while since I had a dog. They sure have improved these things. Looks like you'll be good and safe with this."

Eddie brought out a bag of dog food. "Where would you like this?"

"Just put it on the floorboard on the other side. Thanks."

Eddie opened the door opposite her and set the food down while Dog watched with great interest. "You want me to drive?"

"My new vet-mobile? Are you kidding?" She smiled, despite her concern for the pendant. No sense taking her troubles out on anyone else. She'd done enough of that for one day. Julie stepped up on the running board and dressed Dog in his new harness.

"Do you need any help with that?"

"No, I think I've got it."

"Okay, then. He climbed into the passenger seat.

Dog sat patiently as Julie pulled his paws through the straps and finally finished hooking him up. She scratched behind his ears and looked him in the eyes. "Good boy."

He sat up, eager to go on this adventure, tongue hanging out as if anticipating a treat. Having a dog by her side again felt good, especially with the crazy day she'd had.

She stepped down from the running board. Dog was content as she closed the door. She paused for a moment. Dog looked good in her truck. Maybe the time had come for her to get another one. It had been five years since Lucky got shot by those hunters.

"Ready for a ride?"

Eddie got into a crash position. "Okay."

She checked Dog in the rearview mirror. She could have sworn Dog smiled.

———

As Julie and Eddie approached Maple, Dog's front feet began to march in place on the seat. His tail beat a rhythm. A school bus turned into Nicole's—*or Jayne's*—neighborhood in front of them and stopped just before her corner. A half dozen elementary-age kids got off, the smallest holding hands with the tallest. Julie touched her stomach. Would this be her only child?

The kids formed two groups that headed off in opposite directions. The school bus retracted its stop signs and the lights stopped flashing. It turned right down Elm. Julie stopped at the sign, looked ahead, and froze, thinking about Richard and Nicole being there *all the time*. Mrs. Russell was nowhere to be seen.

"Which one is her house?"

Dog barked, breaking the tension and making them both chuckle.

"That one's home, isn't it boy?" Julie pointed and then proceeded through the intersection to take the spot a couple of spaces away to avoid crushing the necklace in case it had fallen on the street.

They got out of the truck. Julie retrieved Dog who wanted to go in through the back gate. Julie needed to retrace her steps, so she led Dog to the front. As they searched the ground, Eddie followed to ensure she hadn't missed the necklace. Jack barked from his perch in a side window of the Russell house. Dog returned the greeting.

Please don't come out. Please don't come out. Please don't come out. Perhaps if she thought it enough times, it would come true. By now, Mrs. Russell would have tapped into her gossip vine and heard about Julie's public outbursts.

When they got to the front door, Julie knocked in case whatever-her-name *was* there. Dog sniffed frantically and whined. She more boldly looked inside again. Nothing had changed.

They went around back. Julie handed Eddie the leash. "Keep him here just in case that poison is still around." Julie entered the dog run and checked inside the dog house. There was no evidence of any foul play. Dog whined while she looked around.

She returned to take his leash. They walked up the backstairs. Dog whined again. As Julie looked in the window, Dog began to bark and pull toward the street. Cruz drove by slowly but didn't stop. What, no tormenting? Was it because she had a witness? Or maybe he was afraid of Dog.

Sure that no one was there and her pendant was not to be found, they returned to the vet mobile. As Julie climbed in, she remembered driving up the hill to where Jake had found her. They retraced those steps to no avail, then headed back to the clinic.

As they drove away from the house, Dog lay down and gave that sad-eye look, like he'd lost his best friend. He mirrored how Julie felt.

Julie dropped Eddie off at the clinic, ready to get her mind off the day. She thought about going in to get the status of the others' search efforts, but knew that if the pendant had been retrieved, Angie would have called. Julie began the process of reconciling herself to the fact that her mother's pendant may be gone forever—just as she was start-ing her own motherhood journey. A tear formed, but she pushed it back. She was done crying. Time to put her big boy pants on and face whatever her new reality was.

CHAPTER 14

2:40 p.m.

Julie watched as Eddie walked up the side steps to the clinic. Both Julie's mom and Angie preached the benefits of counting blessings. With a baby on the way, it was time she learned how to do that. Necklace or no necklace, her mother was still with her. Dog was buckled in and ready to go anywhere. She was on her way to see people she loved. And a pie was likely waiting. She had friends who cared for her deeply. Her baby was growing inside her. The sky was clear blue. The sun warmed her soul.

She pushed the buttons on the door panel to let the beautiful fall day spread life into her truck. She breathed in the smell of the fallen leaves mingled with the scent of wood-burning fireplaces. *Carpe diem.*

"Do you like music?" she said as she checked Dog in the rearview mirror.

His look acknowledged that he would enjoy anything that she did with him.

Julie popped in her favorite CD. "You'll love this one. It's from when Richard and I got married." She pulled right out of the driveway onto the main road, serenading Dog as they headed out of town.

Richard had surprised her by secretly getting the church to play this song at the end of their wedding ceremony. The words invited her to the greatest adventure of her life with Richard—off to the fairy tale. Romance was his specialty. All the women in the county had dreamt of catching this handsome man with the mystique of a secret agent and the charm of Prince Valiant.

The song changed to the one Richard had used to romance her into the bedroom just three weeks before. Through all their years of mechanically monitoring fertility, Richard had always ensured Julie felt loved, desired, and cherished in every aspect of their love life. Tears slipped down Julie's cheeks. On that night, she never would have believed that Richard could love another woman. Could a man love a woman so completely if he was having an affair with another? Angie was right—Richard could not have been fooling around. His love for Julie was so complete.

As the song ended, Julie wiped her tears. She checked Dog in the rearview mirror. "You still doing okay back there?" Dog licked his lips and looked ahead longingly. He was happy to be alive. What a handsome dog. Why hadn't Nicole called to find out about him?

She approached the left turn on County Road 456, one of Julie's favorite byways during the summer when the trees were full of leaves. An oncoming semi tractor-trailer with Illinois tags slowed and turned right in front of her. It had no advertising to indicate its business. Why would a semi from Illinois be headed down this road? There were no warehouses or factories—and there were faster ways than this road to get everywhere.

The truck blocked her view and her thoughts as she followed it for the four of the five miles to her destination. She stayed back so she could still enjoy her view of the now barren trees. The sun mingled with the bare limbs. It already felt like winter—minus the snow, of course.

Several farms sprawled across the landscape before she got to the Becker's. The old Gleason farm, where Cruz said his uncle lived, was coming up on her left. The beautiful white antebellum southern home with towering white columns was nestled in maple and oak trees and mounted on a bed of boxwoods standing guard around the porch. The homestead was only visible when the trees gave up their foliage.

She and Richard would have bought it if it had been available when they got married.

The truck signaled a left turn and slowed. It stopped for an oncoming car to pass. The truck made the turn between the two brick pillars that used to hold cement planters filled with flowers in the spring and summer. Was it a moving truck? It struggled down the pitted gravel and dirt driveway that led past the left side of the house to a barn hidden behind.

Julie slowed to a stop to see if the truck was perhaps lost and needed directions. She turned off the music. A man came out of the house and intercepted the truck. He hopped in and the semi continued past several cars and trucks parked by the house. *What?* Julie squinted to be sure—two sheriff's cars. Did Cruz live here with his uncle? Wasn't his uncle supposed to be out of town?

Julie checked her mirrors. With no cars behind her, she backed up off the road until she could get a better look between the trees to the parking area. Two old pickup trucks, an official-looking black passenger car like the ones around the courthouse, and the sheriff's cars. Dog began a throaty growl that grew into full-body barking.

"What is it, boy?" His barking intensified as did his pulling against the harness. Without it, he would have escaped the truck.

Julie pushed the buttons to close the windows. "It's okay, Dog." She reached back trying to calm him. A half dozen men poured out the house's front door looking in her direction. One pointed at her as several of the men headed for their vehicles. Julie's heart beat in her neck. Dog's snarling, barking, and pulling was beyond anything Julie had ever witnessed. Dog's hatred was obvious. But why? And who?

Worried for both her safety—and her new leather seats—she pulled back onto the road and shot straight to the Beckers' place. Whoever was there would know it was her. Her vet-mobile was unmistakable. A sheriff's car pulled onto the road behind her. Julie sped up, trying to increase the distance. It went out of view as she crested a hill. Dog's barking slowed. Maybe it was just her imagination. Or maybe it was Cruz wanting to inflict more pain on her.

The sheriff's car topped the hill just as the Beckers' farm came into view. Dog renewed his desperate warnings. She turned left down the drive toward Sam's house and barn—never so happy to get somewhere. She stopped in front of the house and raced around the truck to get a look at who was following her. The sheriff's car slowed to a stop. Between the tint and the distance, Julie could not make out the driver.

Dog did not relent until the cruiser drove on and went out of sight. Julie opened the rear door to check him. "What's going on? Is there something I need to know?" Julie released the harness from the seatbelt clips so Dog could lie down. He whimpered as Julie rubbed his head and scratched his ears. Sadness shrouded him.

Julie returned to the driver's seat and turned the key so she could roll down the windows a bit for Dog to enjoy the cool autumn air. "I'll be back in a few minutes, boy."

———

WITH WILLIAMS BY HIS SIDE, Hayes looked at the others around the folding table in the middle of the otherwise empty farmhouse dining room. This was not your Norman Rockwell painting from the Saturday Evening Post. These hardened men could handle routine or brute operations when called for. But in every other way—just plain dumb. "Any questions?"

"No, boss," they said in unison. Of course not. They were either too scared or too stupid to ask.

"Are you sure? Smitty's coming tomorrow. Need I say more?"

They grumbled no's then stood. Williams looked at Hayes and opened one hand upwards and mouthed, "Smitty? Really?"

Hayes held up one finger to let her know not to say any more. He called out to the last of them leaving the room. "Okay, then. No screw-ups.

Everyone left through different doors. Hayes got up to be sure they were alone. Williams remained seated. Hayes went to the window and looked up the drive to where Julie had been spying on them.

"Smitty? This can't be good," Williams said.

"You're telling me." Hayes continued staring at nothing as he processed the moving parts of his day. "What do you think Doc saw?"

"She saw two cruisers. That's bad enough." A moment later she said, "I guess a lot of things could explain that, especially since Cruz lives here."

"And what about that dog? Did you know she had a dog?"

"None that I know of. Looked like it could have been a shepherd. You don't think—"

Hayes's phone rang. He pulled it from his belt clip, looked at Williams, and said, "Boy wonder."

He answered. "So?"

"She went to the Beckers' farm. She looked right at me when I passed. I think she had Nicole's dog with her. Not sure, but it sure looked like a shepherd."

"Why would that dog still be alive?" Hayes asked.

"Like I know. You gave me that stuff."

Hayes cursed. "Did you give it *all* to him?"

"Of course, I did. You think I'm stupid?"

Hayes was tempted to answer. Had that wimp chickened out?

"Oh—one other thing," Cruz said. "This morning Doc told me she was coming out this way this afternoon. Said she might drop by the farm to meet my uncle. I told her he was out of town, so I doubted that she would actually come."

Hayes unleashed a string of curse bombs. "Did you *think* that information might be important when we were having a meeting here this afternoon?"

"I thought she was blowing smoke. Trying to intimidate me when I was goading her—like you told me to do. I guess she was telling the truth."

More curse bombs. "Maybe it's time for you to quit guessing and thinking. Anything *else* you forgot to tell me?" Hayes's blood pressure was rising.

"Seems like good news that she still came out here. Means she's going about her regular business. Means she doesn't know anything about the mine."

"Yeah, maybe." Hayes looked at Williams, who was still sitting at the table watching his every move. "Stay in the area. Let me know when she leaves. Do you think you can do that?"

"No problem."

"I wish I could believe that." Hayes hung up and crammed his phone back in its holder.

"What's wrong?"

"Cruz—that's what's wrong." Hayes profaned the Lord's name. "She told him she was coming out this way this afternoon. Do you think he could have mentioned that before we called a meeting *here—now*?" Using a mocking tone now, Hayes said, "I thought she was blowing smoke."

Williams shook her head. "What's done …" She crossed her legs man-style and left the rest unsaid. "What about the dog?"

"He thinks it's Nicole's."

Williams was silent for a moment. "Does it make a difference? It was just to send a message, and the message was delivered, and the target can no longer threaten us."

"Yeah. Maybe poisoning that dog sent Nicole over the edge. Maybe that's why she shot before thinking."

"What else could she have done?"

"Yeah, you're right. But I don't like it. That dog is going to be a problem. I just know it." That dog had always hated him. Every time he went to Nicole's house, she had to put him in the dog run. "I hate dogs. They're nothing but trouble." How many times had he been attacked by dogs when he was just taking care of business?

"What is it with you and dogs? I thought the idea of poisoning the dog was over the top to begin with. Maybe it had more to do with you retaliating against her for dumping you."

"She didn't dump me. I was done with her."

"Yeah?"

There was no defense.

"Doc went to the Beckers' place." There was something about the name. "Aren't they the ones that came snooping over here a few weeks back . . . bringing a pie or something?"

"Yep."

"Do you think they're a problem?"

"Not if we're nice back at them. Just get someone to take something over to them. That should smooth things over. Make sure to tell the guys that if they come over again, they need to ask them in and act self-conscious about not having furniture. You big-city guys have to learn how to blend."

"Oh—like *you* blend."

William's face fell. Hayes often forgot that Williams was a woman under all that tough-guy stuff. Hayes had not meant to hurt her. "Sorry, it's just that—"

"Never mind. I know my lifestyle is not welcome here. But it's time for them to get used to it."

"You don't have to explain. I shouldn't have said anything." Neither spoke for a minute. "What do *you* think she knows?"

"I'd say nothing. If she knew about Mack and Richard, she wouldn't be going to the Beckers'—although I heard she made a pretty wild display of jealousy at the Diner and the courthouse. Heard a clerk quit, she was so upset." Williams uncrossed her legs and stood, joining Hayes at the window. "If she knew Richard was dead, she'd be at home or her office doing something or being consoled. She wouldn't be out here working on the animals and going about business."

"That's what Cruz said. Not that I put stock in his opinion. But yours …" He smiled at her to let her know how valuable she was to him. And she was. "Well, I guess we'd better get out of here in case Doc comes a-knocking."

"What does that mean?"

"Cruz said she threatened to come here to meet Rudy."

Williams scrunched her face with her mouth open. "What?"

"Wanted to meet his uncle. Wouldn't that be great?" Mocking Cruz with a girlish voice, he said, "*I told her he'd be out of town.*" He returned his voice to normal. "Like that matters. I'm surprised he didn't invite her to the meeting."

"Didn't he?"

"Might as well have," Hayes said as he opened the door for Williams. Of course, she would never allow a man to open a door for her, so she motioned for Hayes to go ahead, and then followed.

They went to their respective vehicles. Williams said, "You sure you don't want me to have someone else watch Doc?"

"No. Maybe it'll keep him out of trouble. *If* that's possible."

Hayes got in his black Grand Marquis and closed the door. He needed a drink, but a piece of pie would have to do for right now.

CHAPTER 15

3:00 p.m.

Julie closed the truck door as Dog whimpered his protest. Time to take care of business. But was she safe? The cruiser would not have moved past if she wasn't—right? If it was Deputy Cruz, he was probably just wanting to taunt her some more. So why this feeling of dread? No cars had passed since the cruiser went on. Dog was quiet. It must be safe. Julie forced a smile and turned back toward the house.

Mary Jo Becker waved from the front bay window, then opened her screen door and stepped onto her wrap-around front porch. True to form, she was sporting one of her fall-leaf-applique sweatshirts and stretch blue jeans. The plump middle-aged woman created one for every season and holiday. "Come on in, Doc. I've been a-waitin' for ya. I've got a fresh apple pie all ready with some homemade vanilla ice cream."

"That's the real reason I came." Julie checked the road one more time.

"Everything okay, Doc?"

That question was becoming her theme today. Julie turned back to Mary Jo, who stood holding the screen door open. "Sorry, I was distracted." That was an understatement, but how could Julie describe her state of mind? She willed her feet to move and started for the porch. As Julie reached the door, Mary Jo opened her arms and gave Julie a bear hug. She released her and then looked beyond Julie. "Who's that handsome guy?" She said, tipping her head toward the truck.

"That's a story for another day. Let's just say he's a house guest until I can find his owner."

Mary Jo waved an arm in his direction, "Don't keep him in there. Bring 'im on in. Go fetch that handsome thing.

"You sure?"

"Of course. You remember that ol' shepherd we used to have. I think we still have some of his dog toys a-layin' around."

Julie returned to the truck, opened Dog's door, and removed his harness. "Come on, boy. This is your lucky day." Dog checked each step down before taking it and headed for the door Mary Jo was holding open. He stopped and sat at the welcome mat as if awaiting permission to enter.

"Well, look at that—a dog with manners. Come on in, fella." Mary Jo patted her thigh twice authorizing his entrance. Dog and Julie moved past her and went straight back to the kitchen where Mary Jo always had Julie's treat waiting. It was one of the perks of being the local vet—everyone treated her like country royalty.

The smell of fresh pastries and coffee enticed her senses. Julie followed her hostess to the kitchen. Mary Jo must have just hit the button to make a fresh pot of java before she got there. Good. Julie hated stale coffee. *Oh*—was she supposed to have coffee in her condition? Well, she couldn't tell anyone yet. At least until she told Richard. One cup couldn't hurt.

Angie got a bowl out of the cabinets and filled it with water.

"Where's Sam?" Julie asked.

Mary Jo turned holding the dog's water and tipped her chin back. "Oh, he's out on the back forty. Angie called to tell me you was on yer way. She also said you didn't have no appointments after us. I told Sam to scoot so we could have some girl time before you have to take care of business." Mary Jo's face beamed. "That ol' mare can a-wait."

They both chuckled.

"What's the pup's name?"

"Dog."

"No, come on. What's his real name?" Mary Jo walked toward the dog and looked him over.

"Really. Dog."

Dog sat with his ears perked, anticipating his water.

Mary Jo smirked. "Well, Dog, here's some water fer ya." She set it on the floor. Dog lapped it up.

Julie took a seat on a barstool at the kitchen counter. Dog came to sit by her chair. He looked up at her with pleading eyes. "It's okay, boy. You can lie down." Julie pointed to the green and tan braided rug under the kitchen table where he immediately found a good spot.

Mary Jo stood on the other side of the counter watching his movements. "Boy, he minds good, don't he?"

"Well, it's either that or he's tired. He's had a hard day. Poor thing got into something or someone poisoned him."

Mary Jo looked at Dog and spoke in "coochy-coo" baby talk. "Who would do a thing like that to such a handsome boy?" Dog looked up, wagged his tail, and then put his head back down.

"He looks pretty good now," Mary Jo said.

"Yeah, the strange thing is his owner dropped him off on the brink of death, left before giving us any information, and hasn't called to follow up. I've never seen anything like it." Julie shook her head. She dared not say more, but the thoughts came rushing in. Was she in Richard's arms now? Augh. Just when she thought she had conquered her unfounded jealousy.

Julie changed the subject. "Wow, Mary Jo. When did you redo the kitchen? I love this butcher block counter. And the oak cabinets? What a difference! It invites company to set a spell."

"You know, Sam and I have lived here for thirty years. We never updated nothing. We don't travel. All we do is work and go to church. I have a ladies' Bible study here every Thursday morning. The girls a-love to hang out in the kitchen. Well, I told ol' Sam, you know, we oughta have a nice kitchen for the girls to enjoy." Mary Jo smiled as though she was seeing the look on Sam's face. "He said, 'darlin', all you a-have to do is ask.' The next thing I know, he's got one of those guys out here that does those drawin's … what are they called?"

"An architect?"

"Yep, that's it. He asks me all kinds of questions, and then before you know it these men showed up, and boom, here it is." Mary Jo motioned a full circle around the room. She pointed to a glass-front cabinet. "That's my favorite part. A cabinet just for my coffee cups. The girls have always gived me coffee cups fer my birthdays and such. Now I get to show them off." She shook her head. "I am truly blessed."

"That's amazing." Julie stood and opened the cabinet. She picked the cups up one at a time to inspect their inscriptions while Mary Jo started to work on the pie. Many had Bible verses: *Be still and know that I am God. Psalm 46:10 . . . As for me and my house, we will serve the* LORD. *Joshua 24:15.* Some cups were funny: *We'll always be friends. You know all my secrets.* Julie chuckled and held that one out toward Mary Jo.

"I love this one."

Mary Jo looked up from cutting the pie. "Yeah. It's such a good 'un, I got the same cup from four of my friends." Mary Jo giggled "And get this. On the *same* birthday. I guess I know lots of secrets." Shaking her head, she snickered again. "The best part of my friends is that we're sisters in the Lord." Mary Jo smiled, looking beyond the cupboard through the history of her friendships.

A tinge of jealousy tweaked Julie. She didn't have those kinds of friendships. Sure, Angie loved her, but she was an employee and more like a mom. Sarah was a great friend—perhaps her only friend—and she had a whole other life with her family. Julie didn't have time to do life with other friends. She didn't even have time for Richard. Her only friends fit into her routine by employment.

Julie examined Mary Jo. Her face was beaming as she spoke of her friends. Here was this plain country woman with a simple haircut, clothes, house, and life, but she was filled with friends, joy, and peace. Julie's life was full, but instead of peace, it was filled with busyness and casual acquaintances. There was something special here—something she wanted—something missing from her life.

Julie had never understood the Bible study part. How many times can you read a book? In a book club, you read the book once and then go on to the next. These people needed to get a life . . . but then, they were the ones who seemed to have a full life.

Mary Jo opened the freezer to retrieve some ice cream. Julie returned to her barstool and spun around, drinking in the room's country charm. Wooden plaques bespoke of the Beckers' faith life.

> *Only one life, 'twill soon be past,*
> *Only what's done for Christ will last.*
> *—C.T. Studd[1]*

An arrow pierced Julie's heart. What would last in Julie's life?

"Here you go, honey." Julie turned back as Mary Jo served up a whopping piece of lattice-covered hot apple pie with ice cream melting off to the side. She loved that Mary Jo always sprinkled a hint of cinnamon on top. The sprinkling of cinnamon made it perfect. Julie's mouth watered.

Mary Jo asked, "Did you pick out a mug?"

"Ooh! My pick? How fun." Julie returned to the cabinet and picked out the cup with the "secrets" inscription. She handed it over.

A wry smile crept across Mary Jo's face. "You know, it's been my experience that when a woman picks this one, it's 'cause she's got a secret." Mary Jo watched Julie for a moment. "I had a feeling you a-needed to talk about something when you came in. Care to share?"

Julie didn't like to "share" her personal life with anyone. She looked from Mary Jo to the cup. If Mary Jo had that many friends give her the same cup, she was probably a secured vault of untold tales. *This* was a safe place, and Mary Jo was a safe person. Maybe Mary Jo could help

---

[1] C.T. Studd, "Only One Life, Twill Soon be Past," Public Domain

give her the perspective she needed—and boy did she need it. "How much time do you have?"

"All the time in the world, baby girl." That's what Angie always called her, and it made her feel safe. "Let me just get our coffee and my piece of pie." Mary Jo penguined to the cupboard, chose her mug, and then returned to the coffeemaker to pour two cups. She deposited them on the counter, then retrieved some cream and sugar.

Julie reached across to turn Mary Jo's cup so she could read the whole inscription. *Then you will know the truth, and the truth will set you free. John 8:32.* What truth would set Julie free? The truth about Richard would be a good starter.

Mary Jo grabbed her piece of pie and took a seat across from Julie.

Julie checked Mary Jo's plate. "No ice cream?"

"Nope. I'm on a half diet. I only eat half what I normally would." She made an hourglass gesture with her hands. "I've got to keep my girlish figure."

They both giggled.

Julie took a bite of her pie. Heaven. How did she do it? It wasn't that this was Julie's favorite dessert—it was just that Mary Jo's was the best. "Oh my, you have outdone yourself." Julie closed her eyes to absorb the flavors of love.

"My grandmother used to say that there ain't nothing a-better than apple pie and coffee to bond a friendship." Mary Jo reached across the counter to take Julie's hand. She gave her a warm squeeze and then withdrew it so she could give her own piece her full attention. "So, what's on your mind?"

Julie took a deep breath. "I don't even know where to start. So much has happened—and all of it today."

"Why don't you start at the beginning?" she said as she took another bite.

Julie started with her getting sick, worrying that she was going to die like her mother, getting sick alongside the road, and meeting Deputy Cruz. They both chuckled over his name. She described how he got increasingly creepy with each encounter, and that her sister seemed to be dating him. She recounted breakfast at the Diner, Mack's morbid breakfast conversation, Cruz's weirdness, and how Paul rescued her. Then Dog came in poisoned, Nicole mysteriously disappeared, and what the dog tag had revealed.

Mary Jo shook her head in disbelief. "Well, ain't that the strangest thing?"

"Oh, it gets worse." Julie paused, remembering the pregnancy test. "Well, not all of it was worse." Julie stopped again, still deciding whether it was okay to tell Mary Jo before Richard. She tapped the secrets cup and looked into Mary Jo's warm brown eyes. "I know you promised confidence, but this next part, even Richard doesn't know yet."

Mary Jo crossed her heart. "Your secret's safe with me. But I bet it has something to do with you being in a family way."

Julie's pie-stuffed fork stopped midair. "What? How did you know?"

"I don't know. I've always sensed when women get in the family way. Something changes in the way they move and their countenance. So, I'm right?"

"Yeah. I guess I could have saved the price of the pregnancy test by just coming over here."

Mary Jo giggled and patted Julie's hand. "You've waited a long time for this. I'm so excited for you. And Richard doesn't know yet?"

"No. He's not answering his phone and neither is Nicole. Neither of them is anywhere to be found. Then when I went to Nicole's to check on her, Cruz showed up and talked about Richard and Nicole working at her house *'all the time.'* He was so creepy." The sheriff's car out front came to mind.

"You know, I think he was at the old Gleason farm next door when I came here. Did someone buy that farm?"

"It's funny you ask. We've noticed a lot of comings and goings there, but we haven't heard nothing about the Gleason kids selling the property. And we haven't seen no farmin' going on and no animals.

Just people." Mary Jo inspected Julie's empty plate and cup. "Would you like some more?"

"You know—I don't think I'm supposed to be drinking coffee in my condition."

"Oh, that's okay." Mary Jo laughed to herself. "It's decaf. Sam ain't spozed to drink regular no more, but he fusses about it. I just let him think it's regular soze he won't complain. He don't know the difference." She slapped her leg. "The things we do to love our husbands."

"So?" Mary Jo pointed to Julie's cup.

"Sure, I'd love some more coffee then, but I'm still hoping Richard shows up for a special dinner we had planned for tonight."

"So, no more pie?"

"No, but know that it was the best." Julie checked Dog, who was happily dozing while Mary Jo refilled the cups. Mary Jo slid back into her seat.

"So, that's all you know about the people next door?" Julie asked.

"Yep. They keep to themselves. I took one of my apple pies over a couple of weeks ago. A man answered the door and thanked me. He apologized for not inviting me in. Said he didn't have furniture yet. Said he'd invite us over sometime when it arrived. We haven't heard from them since."

"Have you seen any sheriff's cars there?"

"Yep. I think a deputy must live there 'cause I see it there in the late evening and early morning." Mary Jo bit her lip. "Cain't say who it is, though. Never seen him."

"So, you don't have any idea what's going on over there?"

Mary Jo shook her head slowly and searched Julie's eyes.

"Deputy Cruz told me his uncle worked there. The weirdest part is I saw a semi pull down their drive and head past the house toward the barn."

"Maybe delivering farm equipment?" Mary Jo scrunched her nose.

"Have you ever seen farm equipment delivered in a semi?"

A look of suspicion etched Mary Jo's face. "Nope, always on a flat-bed or open kind of trailer. You got me. Maybe it's time for me and Sam to pay another visit."

Panic surged through Julie. She didn't want this dear couple to come to harm. "I don't think that's a good idea. I can't say why exactly, but I've just got this feeling." She looked at Dog who was resting peacefully. She felt safer knowing he was nearby. She turned back to Mary Jo, who was leaning in. "Let me tell you more about Deputy Cruz."

Julie told of her investigation of Nicole's house, what she learned from Mrs. Russell, and how the deputy acted away from and in front of Mrs. Russell. "You know, when Deputy Cruz drove up, Mrs. Russell's dog started barking. I don't mean like the normal stuff when a stranger comes, but he was really upset … and he's so old, he doesn't get upset about much. And if Deputy Cruz was such a regular visitor, you wouldn't think he'd be bothered at all. Dog went crazy in the truck when we went by the Gleason place. He practically tore loose out of his harness trying to get out. He quieted until the deputy's car followed us. He didn't calm down again until it disappeared from sight in front of your place."

Dog started growling. His head popped up and his ears perked. He came to Julie's side and whimpered.

"What is it, boy?" Julie ran a hand over his coat.

Something heavy fell or got kicked on the front porch. Dog let out a low, throaty growl and crossed the kitchen to the hallway door.

Julie started to get up, but Mary Jo held out her hand. "You be still. Let me check it out."

Mary Jo headed out the kitchen, down the front hallway. Julie was frozen. A door creaked, then the muffled sound of the door seating against the weather stripping. Dog stood and barked his alarm. Julie went to her right through the dining room door near where Dog had been resting. She moved away from the front hallway toward the mahogany china cabinet around the matching table. Dog's barking intensified. Julie saw no one through the front window. Where was Mary Jo?

Julie crossed the room to the front hallway. She rounded the corner. The front door was closed. She looked back at Dog as he continued his warnings. Julie patted her thigh. "Come, Dog." He obeyed and came to her side.

She acknowledged his obedience with a pat on the head as she kept her eyes on the door. Julie reached for the door, just as it opened, causing Julie to jump. Mary Jo came in laughing, while Sam stayed behind her on the porch. Julie let out the breath she had been holding. She knew them well enough to know they were not pranking her, but their laughter felt like a betrayal.

"Doc. Are you okay? You look terrified. I should have come right back in." She opened her arms to hug Julie, which Julie reluctantly accepted. "Sam just came up to fetch you. He was a-droppin' off some tools to use on the side porch. I've been asking him to fix a loose board for months." Mary Jo released Julie.

Sam waited on the porch with his cowboy hat, red plaid shirt, jeans, and boots. He always looked the farmer part.

"Hey, Sam."

Sam gave a beer-belly laugh. "Sorry I sceered ya. Are you a-ready to come down to see that mare? I think she's ready to drop."

"I told him he was jus' trying to horn in on our girl time, but he said he's got to make it to the feed and seed before they close." Mary Jo said. "How about you go on down and check that mare and then come on back here so we can finish our talk."

Julie's legs were still jelly, but she did come for business. "Okay, let's get her done." Julie called Dog.

"No, you leave him here with me. Like you said, he's had a hard day. I'm sure he can use the rest."

Julie nodded then left to catch up with Sam.

"You want to ride in my new Gator down to the barn?" Sam beamed from his green machine. It put her old Gator to shame. "Wow. Is that a farm utility vehicle or an all-terrain toy?" Julie teased.

Sam laughed.

Julie walked over to inspect all the bells and whistles. Sam patted the passenger seat. "Come on, gal. How about a ride?"

"That's a hard offer to refuse, but I might need some doctoring tools. I'll follow you down … or you can ride with me."

Sam hopped up. "I'll catch a ride with you. Not every day a pretty lady offers me a ride in a souped-up truck."

———

HAYES SMILED FROM THE BACK-CORNER BOOTH as he watched Sally flit around to the half-dozen tables around the Diner. This between-crowds time of day was particularly sweet. One of his few pleasures. Sally was virtually all his. And he could take care of business here and these yokels would never know. He routinely used the two-block walk from the sheriff's office to clear his head and get away from the incompetence that defined everyone in this town. Sally was one of the few people who broke the mold. She knew her job and did it well. She kept her nose to herself. She knew what he wanted but didn't hover. Best of all, she always made him fresh coffee.

"The coffee's almost done a-brewin', Jerry." Sally grinned as she outfitted the table with the necessary utensils. "The usual?"

"Of course."

"Today you have a choice—peach or apple."

"You pick."

Sally returned to the counter, cut him a slice of peach pie, and delivered it and a steaming cup of coffee. "Anything else?"

"No, thank you."

"Okay, I'm a-headin' home. I'll see ya tomorrow."

Hayes hated paying at the register. The owner asked too many questions. He held up a twenty-dollar bill. "Here, would you take care of this? Keep the change—in case they don't treat you right."

"Wow, thanks, Jerry. You always know how to make my day." She winked and walked away.

Something about her walk reminded him of Nicole. He pictured what Nicole's body must look like in the back of the SUV. What a shame. That was one passionate woman—until she caught him with that cute little rookie. Spurned women. He shook his head. But Nicole had been useful. Everything has its season. Her purpose had come and gone. Jake just saved him the trouble. Now that Julie had walked into the motive, he just needed the gun and necklace. Then he'd finally be able to get Smitty off his back.

He tapped the phone to check messages. As if by telepathy, it lit up. Jake.

"Well?"

"I got the keys to Richard's car. Going to move it shortly. Did you decide where you want it?"

"What about the same lake you took Mack's car? I had the department close off the road. Just move the cones and go in. Take them with you when you're done."

"I've got the other stuff. Listen—I don't think it's good for us to meet. I've been moving too much today, and it was noticed. It's pushing it for me to go out one more time. Plus, I think I need to be here tonight to watch Doc. I'll put the items in the regular place. You can pick them up there."

Hayes thought for a moment. Was he trying to make a run? He needed Jake to stick around one more day. But seeing him wasn't going to ensure that. And he was right about too much movement. "Okay. Oh, and by the way, Doc drove by the farm today. Supposedly vet business. I think she had Nicole's dog with her. It was barking its head off. I don't know what Doc saw. She could have seen me, my car, two sheriff's cars—I need to know. Find out."

"I'll do my best, but you know I don't usually have contact with her in the evenings. Maybe if she takes her horse out for a ride. Otherwise, I'll think of an excuse to come up to the house. I'll talk to you later."

Silence.

Did Jake just hang up on him? Not much more time for him either. He was going to have all new people working for him before long— except for Sally, that was.

CHAPTER 16

3:30 p.m.

JULIE STEPPED ONTO THE RUNNING BOARD and up into her vet mobile. Sam climbed in the other side.

"Wow, I gotta git me one of these. Sam touched buttons and opened the sun roof and windows like a third-world child stepping into an American toy store. "Is there anything this truck doesn't have?"

"A coffee maker."

"Ha. This puts my new Gator to shame."

Julie drove to the barn only a few thousand feet behind the house.

"Did you guys leave me any apple pie?"

Julie stopped at the opening of the barn. "Well, maybe a little piece." Julie smiled wryly at Sam as they opened their doors to get out.

Sam pointed to the back of the barn. "She's in the last stall."

Julie followed along after Sam. He opened the stall and guided Julie in to check out the mare. "Well, she started waxing a couple of days ago," Sam said. "See her nipples?"

The mare's nostrils flared at the intrusion. She nodded and shuddered.

"Yep, looks like she's ready," Doc said. "I can see you've wrapped her tail and put clean straw down. Did she eat today?"

"Nope, she's been very affectionate, but doesn't seem interested in eating."

Julie got out her stethoscope and listened to the mare's belly. The mare fidgeted at first and then relaxed as Sam stroked her face to soothe her.

Julie pulled the earpieces out and wrapped the stethoscope around her neck. She walked around the back end of the mare. "Her muscles have softened." She moved back to face her patient, who nudged Julie's hand as she stroked her. "You're looking good, girl. Looks like you're gonna be a momma tonight."

"That's what I figured." Sam puffed.

"Seems like she's good to go. I'll be home if you need anything, but I think she's gonna do just fine. You probably know this, but keep the lighting low when you come out. These girls are kinda private when they birth." Julie rubbed the mare's head once more.

Julie loved the elegance that horses had through the whole mothering process. They rarely had birthing problems, and they were quick to take on their roles as mothers—always so dignified.

Sam held the stall door open for Julie to exit. They walked together out to Julie's truck. Sam opened her door and said, "I've got my truck back here. Tell Mary Jo I'll be home in an hour or so."

"Will do," Julie said as Sam closed her door and headed for his truck.

Julie looked across the field toward the Gleason farm, then opened the passenger window and called to Sam. "Hey. Do you know if the Gleason farm sold?"

He stopped just as he reached his truck and turned toward her. Sam's face puckered. He walked to her passenger window. "No, but there's been some people at the place for a while now. Why'd you ask?"

"I saw a tractor-trailer turn into their drive on my way out, which I thought was strange. Then I saw two sheriff's cars there and some other vehicles. Do you know if someone is renting it?"

"Cain't says I do. Mary Jo tried to visit, but they sent her a-packing. She was a-mighty upset. I wanted to go tell them off for shunning my sweetheart after she worked hard to make them her pie. She told me to stay put, that they said they didn't have furniture, but I didn't like it. Is something wrong?"

"I don't know, but I wish I did. Mary Jo said the sheriff's car is there pretty routinely. I can't believe anything would be wrong if a deputy is staying there. Something about it doesn't feel right, though."

"You want me to go over there and check them out?"

"No. I'm probably just being silly. But if you hear about someone renting or buying that place, would you let me know?"

"Sure thing." Sam turned back for his truck. Julie stared across the field looking for answers. None came.

———

JULIE ROLLED UP TO THE FRONT of the Beckers' house, ready to collect Dog. The intimacy with Mary Jo had been broken by the scare. She was exhausted from the day and wanted to head home. She checked her watch. Close to four o'clock. Her special dinner was just three hours away—*if* Richard showed up.

Julie removed her stethoscope from around her neck and placed it on the seat beside her. She gathered her resolve, knowing that Mary Jo would put up a fight if she didn't stay. Julie slid out of the seat and headed in. She knocked and listened for Mary Jo.

"Come on in."

Julie pulled the screen door open. Mary Jo was sitting on the sofa in the living room. Dog sat beside her on the floor as Mary Jo patted Dog's head in her lap. Mary Jo looked up and stood. "He sure is a good watch dog."

Dog's tail wagged at the praise. He trotted over and sat at Julie's feet as if waiting for more.

"You *are* a good boy." Julie rubbed his head and then looked up at Mary Jo. "You know, I've had a tough day. I think I'm just going to grab my purse and head on home."

"Don't be silly." Mary Jo walked over to Julie and gave her a quick hug—her second specialty aside from her pies. "Besides, you can't leave me in the middle of your story." Mary Jo pointed to the kitchen. "Come on. We've got some work to finish." Mary Jo didn't wait for Julie's protest. What could she say? She followed.

"Go lie down." Julie motioned for Dog to return to his spot as she took her seat. Mary Jo freshened coffee as Dog returned to his spot.

"Lie down."

Once down, he kept his eyes on her, raising each eyebrow independently as he listened for trouble. He raised his head. "It's okay, boy." Julie had been so concerned about her safety, she had forgotten what Dog had been through.

Mary Jo smiled as she put the cups down and took her seat.

Julie pondered Mary Jo's cup again. She still didn't know the truth, but she had to admit that sharing her day had lifted its burden. Maybe staying was a good idea. "Where were we?"

Mary Jo leaned forward with anticipation. "You were telling me about the Gossip-in-Chief, Mrs. Russell. And then you got sidetracked with Deputy Creep … I mean Cruz." She giggled, proud of her play on names.

"I guess the bottom line is that when I left Nicole's, I was sure that Richard had been cheating with her *all the time*."

"I have to say that it doesn't sound good if what they were saying was true, but, so far, has anyone actually seen Richard being intimate in any way with Nicole?"

Julie thought for a moment. "No—just that they were spending a lot of time together."

"But no intimate behavior?"

"No. But why were they spending so much time at her house—or any time at her house for that matter?" Julie's body tensed as she envisioned them together.

"It's a good question. But that's just it. It's a question."

Mary Jo paused as if trying to retrieve some bit of information buried deep in her memory bank. "You know, I had a counselor once who taught me that life is full of puzzles. When we don't have all the pieces, we try to fill in the gaps. We get into trouble when we assume the worst—which is most often wrong. What's silly is that all we had to do was ask in the first place, and then we wouldn't have been worrying about the missing information. And you haven't asked."

Julie shook her head slowly as she considered the implications.

Mary Jo tapped her cup with her fingertips. "Has Richard acted differently toward you lately?"

"No, he's been the same guy I thought I married. He's been completely devoted to me when we're together. It's just that we're both so busy." Julie reran the tapes of all the times one of them had worked late and missed dinners.

Mary Jo patiently waited as Julie processed her thoughts. "Everybody's busy, baby girl. It's not a sin … unless it keeps you from what you're supposed to be taking care of—relationships. We're supposed to keep our eyes focused on God and on the ones He gave us to love. That's why God is called Love."

Couldn't she leave God out of this? But the truth was Julie had not been focusing on Richard. She pulled her cell phone out to look for a message.

Mary Jo frowned.

"Sorry, just checking for messages."

"It's okay. I know how busy you are."

Julie set her phone on the counter. "It's not just the gossip and the creep. Everybody has been acting like they're hiding something." Julie described everyone's reactions and how she lost control.

Mary Jo shook her head. "Has anyone said anything *not* rooted in gossip?"

Julie paused. "No. Angie, Heather, and even Eddie said it was all what they heard."

"So, is it just possible that all this trouble may be caused by one woman who has a history of running her mouth about things she doesn't know?" Mary Jo had that motherly smile that let you know that maybe you should have been paying better attention to life. It wasn't judgmental, but, rather, welcomed Julie to a place she needed to go.

Mary Jo searched Julie's eyes. "I don't know what's going on with your husband. I've heard some of the town gossip, but over my sixty years in this Podunk town, I know one thing for sure—you can't know anything for sure from gossip. It's usually wrong and causes a whole lot of misery." She looked at Dog and said, "It's just as sinister as the poison that almost killed this beautiful animal. You know . . ." A pained look crossed her face ". . .maybe it's more insidious—gossip can poison a whole town's water supply and ruin lives for years."

Mary Jo turned her cup to read the scripture as if it was somehow different. She shook her head. "Oh my, not now."

Who was she talking to?

Taking Julie's hands, she said, "Lord, help me." Mary Jo paused again and then looked into Julie's eyes. "Now I know why God sent you here today."

Mary Jo got up from her stool, retrieved an old photo from a cupboard drawer, and returned to the counter. She looked at the photo for a long moment, then pushed it across the counter in slow motion for Julie to see. Mary Jo fetched a glass of water for both of them, leaving Julie to examine the picture.

A family of five … maybe one of those church pictures … probably Sam and Mary Jo thirty years ago, but there were three kids in the photo. Julie only knew of two.

"Is this you and Sam?"

"Yes, it is." She set the two glasses of water on the counter.

"Are these your kids?"

"Yes, they are," Mary Jo said, face puffing around the eyes. She took her seat.

"When was this?"

Mary Jo took the photo for a minute and looked at it longingly. "Twenty-four years ago."

A pain stabbed Julie's heart—the same year her mother had died. Julie reached for her mother's missing pendant. Another stab.

Mary Jo held the photo for Julie to follow as she pointed. "The oldest one—on my left—is Sam, Jr. He was twelve there. The one on my right is Joey. He was ten. You've met them."

Julie nodded. "Yes, just as handsome there as now." Julie forced a smile, trying to elicit one from Mary Jo, who instead bit her lip.

"You never got to meet Hannah, my baby girl. She was four there. It was the last picture I have of her." Mary Jo choked up. This time Julie reached for Mary Jo's hand. Julie decided not to share that Heather had been four when her mother died.

"I've never shared with another person—not even Sam." Mary Jo examined Julie's face as if deciding whether to continue. "I guess it's time." She tapped her coffee cup with her nails. "Time to set us both free." Tears streamed down Mary Jo's face.

Mary Jo got up to retrieve a tissue box. She stared out the back window for a long moment. She returned to her stool and took a deep breath. "I don't know if I can do this." She studied Julie's face. Julie couldn't remember anyone ever entrusting her with a secret that ran so deep. The enormity of this moment weighed on her heart.

"Are you sure you want to do this?" Julie asked, half hoping she wouldn't have to carry the secret burden.

Mary Jo studied the picture again. "Yes, it's time. I've held onto this way too long. Do you mind if I pray first?"

Despite her disbelief, this was right. "No, please do."

Mary Jo reached for Julie's hands and then bowed her head. "Lord, give me the words to share. Let my words be Yours, and may Your will be done." Mary Jo released Julie's hands.

"Whew. Here we go." Mary Joe drew in a long breath. "Twenty-four years ago, I worked in town at the Diner. I was just tryin' to pick up some tips to help with our finances. The crops were bad that year, and we knew it was going to be tight. While I was a-workin' there, the Mrs. Russell of those days asked me how I felt about Sam foolin' around with one particular waitress at the saloon. She said her husband had seen Sam leaving there with the woman.

"In those days, Sam liked to head up to the Saloon after a long day on the farm—said to shoot pool—leaving me at home to take care of the house and the three kids. I had to do all the cookin', the cleanin', help the kids with their homework, and get 'em ready for bed. I was angry all the time.

"Sam never did anything to make me believe that he was a-foolin' around, but that lady's words kept running around my head. I was obsessed. One night when he left, I got good and mad. I told the boys to watch Hannah while I ran into town for some milk. I headed straight for the saloon. I snuck in the back soze Sam wouldn't see me.

"There he was, shooting pool—just like he told me he was a-doin'. The waitress came over and tried to flirt with him, but he sent her packing. That gossip's words were just a pack of lies. I was so embarrassed that I had ever doubted him."

Mary Jo bit her lip again and looked at the photo. "We were just two stupid kids. Sam was a good man, but he didn't know how to handle the responsibility of being a dad and husband. His dad died when he was young, so nobody taught him. I was a self-centered girl trying to make do, but I was really a brat. I'd been spoiled growing up and didn't know how to handle real life. I was so stupid."

Mary Jo broke down crying again. She grabbed several tissues and blew her nose. She walked to the doorway of the dining room and looked out the front window. "When I got home, there were two sheriff's cars in the drive and the paramedics in front." She stopped again as if she were watching it.

"I rushed in. The boys came a-runnin' from the dining room and said, 'We're sorry, mama. We didn't mean it.' They buried their heads in my arms as the paramedics brought a stretcher down the stairs. A blanket outlined my little Hannah's lifeless body."

Mary Jo stopped to watch her memory unfold. She walked back and took her seat. "The boys had given her a bath, but they'd gotten distracted when they heard the dog a-barkin' at something out back. They went outside to check it out. When they got back, Hannah was a-floatin' in the tub. They called 9-1-1, but they didn't know how to do CPR or nothing. Best we know, she must have tried to get out, fell, and hit her head. But the truth is she died because I believed the pack of evil lies." Mary Jo broke down, heaving sobs.

What could Julie say? She couldn't believe what she was hearing. Mary Jo and Sam were pillars of the community. They were the most level-headed folks she knew. Was this even possible?

"I never told anyone where I'd been. I let everyone believe that I was getting milk. If anyone had paid attention, they would have realized that I didn't come back with anything except the certainty that Sam had not been a-cheatin'. I should have just asked him about it, instead of doing something so stupid that it cost the life of my only daughter—and living with this guilt."

Mary Joe returned to face Julie. "The boys had to go to counseling for years to get over their part in this … and it wasn't their fault. They still carry the weight today. And Sam—he took the blame on himself because he figured if he'd been a proper husband, he would have been there to get the milk. And me, I've been living this lie all these years and not shared it with anyone. It's time." Mary Jo pointed to the scripture on her cup. "God called you here today for both of us."

Julie was speechless. Did God bring Julie here for Mary Jo to expose her truth? "Are you going to tell Sam?"

"Absolutely. God sent you to tell your story to me so yours didn't end up like mine. You don't have a young'un yet, but one is coming, and your choices now will forever impact your life, Richard's life, and that young'un's life. God wanted me to tell you that, but He also wanted to remind me that it was time to expose the lie and get rid of my guilt. Only Satan wins when lies and guilt abound.

"You know, Doc, from what you've said, I believe that your husband loves you. He's never given you a reason to doubt him. He may have a simple explanation for what's happening and you need to give him the benefit of the doubt." Mary Jo reached for Julie's hand. "Whatever is going on with your husband, God has given you a wake-up call for your marriage. For me and Sam, the wake-up call was tragic. I don't know what it means for you and Richard."

A wake-up call? Was that what this was?

"You said yourself that you've been absorbed with your work. I was absorbed with my work and my kids. I was treating Sam like a meal ticket instead of my prince. Thankfully he wasn't fooling around, but if he had been, it would have been because I let him believe he was a failure. I'm not condoning adultery as an excuse for bad relationships, but what I am saying is that God calls us to love our husbands, regardless of how they behave. The same way that Jesus loves us—while we are yet sinners."

"I don't think I treat Richard like a failure."

"I'm not saying you do, I'm saying that's what I did. Sometimes we say it with our words. Sometimes our actions. Sometimes by doing nothin' at all. Some husbands feel like they don't matter to their wives. Other women will make them feel like they do matter. We open the door to trouble when we don't let them know they are our princes."

"Are you saying that if Richard is cheating, it's my fault?"

"No, no, no. Men are responsible for their behavior. One of their responsibilities is not getting ensnared by the adulteress. That's why there's so much about it in the Bible. There are always women out there trying to lure them into sin. Our husbands' jobs are to avoid them even when their wives make them feel unloved—like I did."

Julie thought a long moment through all her encounters with Richard. Did she make him feel bad about himself? "I don't think I do that. He's always attentive to me and makes me feel loved."

"I'm so glad to hear that. But that's how he treats you. How do you treat him?"

Julie took residence in Richard's shoes. She could not think of a single instance when she had made Richard feel special. Most of her thoughts about them as a couple were directed at her inability to get pregnant, which was not his fault. The only time she focused on Richard was when the calendar said it was time. Richard was the only one doing the romancing. She did nothing to show her love for him. Oh, no. What had she become?

A knot formed in Julie's stomach. Tears came to her eyes. "What have I done?"

"Don't beat yourself up, baby girl. Nobody teaches us these things. But when God is ready, He shows us what love truly looks like so we can get it right. It sounds to me like you've been blessed with a guy who still loves you. I'm praying that the rumors are wrong, just like they were for me." Mary Jo paused. "For me, the lesson was costly—I lost my little girl."

"Why didn't you ever tell him?"

"I always intended to, but it never seemed to be the right time. At first, I was afraid he'd leave me for sure. Every milk carton reminded me of my need to confess, but I always talked myself out of it. After a while, the containers lost their significance, and though the guilt remained, it became easier and easier to put the truth away. Things were going well for all this time, so it didn't seem to matter. And here it's been twenty-four years. Now's the time."

"What do you think he'll say?"

"I don't know. It's a puzzle, and the answer will come only when I tell him … just like your answer will only come when you ask Richard."

Julie checked her phone. "I wish he would call." She noticed the time—4:20 p.m. "Oh my, I need to get going."

Julie swiveled in her chair. Dog's head popped up with perked ears. "Are you ready to go?"

Dog got up and came to Julie's side, tail wagging. Julie moved around the counter to hug Mary Jo. "I'm so sorry for your loss. I cannot imagine."

They hugged for the longest moment. Mary Jo touched the back of Julie's head. "Dear Lord Jesus, take this woman and her child and watch over them as they go forward this day. Bless their marriage.

Protect her husband from whatever danger is surrounding him. And for myself, Lord, prepare my husband to hear the truth so we can be set free. In Your name we pray. Amen."

Mary Jo released her hand from Julie's head and squeezed her once more before releasing. Amid all the happenings of the day, Julie had never felt safer than she had being wrapped in that prayer.

Julie looked into Mary Jo's eyes. "May it be so." She walked to the front door. "How can I ever thank you?"

Mary Jo's humble smile turned serious. "I'm the one who should be thanking you. Now you go on. I'll be a-prayin' for you."

Julie hated to admit she liked the sound of that.

CHAPTER 17

4:15 p.m.

THE VIEW FROM THE BECKERS' PORCH would never be the same. Images of red and blue lights, firetrucks and sheriff's vehicles, a gurney taking away a lifeless baby girl … and two boys tucked in their mama's arms trying to make sense of it all. And the guilt … How had Mary Jo made it past that day?

Julie opened the back door for Dog to take his seat. He jumped up and readied himself for his harness as if they had done this dance for years. She buckled him in and then climbed in herself. At the end of the driveway, she met Sam coming back from town. They rolled down their windows in unison.

"Finally done with your girl talk?"

"Yep." Julie forced a smile, knowing the conversation that awaited Sam. Would Mary Jo put it off again? "Let me know if that mare has any troubles. I'll be home all night. I'll stop by to check on the new foal before I head to the office in the morning. Probably around seven or so."

"I'll put the coffee on. I'm sure I'll need it after a long night." He winked.

Julie chuckled to herself knowing that coffee wouldn't do him a lick of good. "I'm looking forward to it. I'll bring the donuts."

"That's a deal." Sam tipped his cowboy hat and drove on.

She would normally turn right to go back the way she came, but she didn't have enough emotional energy to pass by the Gleason farm again.

She didn't want to think about who was there and why. But, then again, she had never been one to let fear direct her course. She gathered her resolve and turned right.

She checked Dog in her mirror. He was looking to the future and happy to be alive. A dog's worldview would be nice right about now.

The sun hung low in the trees, casting long shadows on the road. She slowed as she reached the Gleason farm. Only an old truck remained.

Dog growled from deep in his throat.

"What is it, boy?"

He whined a bit and moved his feet in a dance. Then he barked. Julie hurried past.

As she got to the main road, she reached for her phone. Oh, no. She had forgotten it on Mary Jo's counter. She made a U-turn and headed back. Of all days. She drove quickly past the Gleason farm as Dog's barking reached another crescendo.

Julie pulled up to the Beckers' home next to Sam's truck. It had only been a few minutes since she left. Julie hoped Mary Jo had put off the conversation at least this long. "I'll be right back, boy." Dog yielded a slight woof.

Julie approached the door and stood quietly for a moment. She heard low voices inside. She knocked sheepishly. Mary Jo came to the door, eyes puffy.

"I'm so sorry to bother you—I left my phone." Julie pointed in the direction of the kitchen. Sam came up beside Mary Jo and put his arm around her.

"Well, I wouldn't have called and invited you over at this moment." She peered over her shoulder at Sam. "But this is hands down one of the best moments of my life."

Sam nodded at Mary Jo and squeezed her.

"Sam knew. All these years, he knew." Mary Jo gazed at Sam with love-light in her eyes. "He even saw me in the saloon that night and knew I hadn't been out getting milk. He did check the refrigerator though after all the emergency folks had left and I was knocked out with tranquilizers." She smiled at him. "He didn't confess he knew to protect me." Tears flowed down Mary Jo's cheeks.

"It was all my fault that she had to leave the house," Sam said. "If I'da been where I belonged, we would still have our Hannah. I was such a stupid kid. I thank God that He gave me this wonderful wife who has stayed by my side through all of our years. She is such a precious gift." He hugged Mary Jo again.

"Now that the truth's out, it's one less thing Satan can use to trap us. Thank You, Jesus." Sam raised his left hand off Mary Jo's shoulder in praise, then squeezed Mary Jo and headed back to his recliner in the living room.

Julie had never witnessed such pure love. She tried to imagine what Richard would have said in the same situation.

Mary Jo pointed to the kitchen. "Let's get that phone."

"I am so sorry that I had to come back. I'm so forgetful lately." Julie grabbed her phone and checked for messages. None from her husband, but one from her dad. Augh. Dad—

"That forgetfulness?" Mary Jo leaned back against the counter by the sink. "Count on it getting worse. In fact, here's a little secret that women never share. Right after they deliver the baby, they deliver one-half of your brain. I read about it. Fact is, your IQ drops a whole bunch after you have a baby. But it's all worth it."

They chuckled.

"Oh great. Now I know what to look forward to." She headed for the door. "Well, I've got a dinner to get to—and hope I'm eating with Richard and not Sarah."

"Speaking of dinner, I think I'm gonna have to do something special for my hero husband. I can't believe he knew all these years. How much grief I could have saved myself—and him. That's why God warns us that we can be slaves to the wrong master. I was a slave to my secret sin all these years. What a waste."

What on earth was Mary Jo talking about? Slave to sin?

"Let me walk you out."

Sam was sitting smiling in his rocker. "Goodbye, Sam"

"Goodbye, Doc. Tell Richard we said hi."

If only she could.

———

TURNING RIGHT TOWARD THE GLEASON FARM would stress Dog again—and neither of them needed that right now. What difference would another ten minutes make in getting home at this point? Julie turned left.

It was too late to take Jubilee for a ride . . . Oh. Horseback riding. Another thing on the list of things she wouldn't be doing for eight or so months. But still, she needed a Jubilee fix. She pushed the call button on her steering wheel and asked her system to call home.

"Wheeler residence," Sarah said.

"Hey. It's me. Is Jake back?"

"No. He just called. Said he'd be here in twenty minutes."

Julie checked her mirror for any sign of him still stalking her. "Where is he?"

"He didn't say. But, then again, I didn't ask." Sarah paused. "Dinner's still on, isn't it? 'Cause if you're a-changin' your mind again—.

"*Yes*, dinner's still on. Are you saying I can't change my mind again? I am a woman, you know."

They both laughed.

"I should be there in twenty. I guess the same time as Jake." She checked her mirror. Still no one. "Have you heard from Richard?

"No, should I have?"

"No." Julie's heart dropped. She needed answers and was clinging to the hope that Mary Jo had given her.

"You know, you're acting really weird. We need to talk."

"Later. Is everything ready?"

"Of course. I'm setting the table. I'll get the chicken a-cookin' around six-thirty so it's nice 'n fresh for dinner."

"Terrific. See you in a few." Julie pushed the red phone icon on the steering wheel and turned right at the next road and headed back down to the highway. She pushed the green phone button. "Call Dad."

After three rings, her dad answered. "Hello?"

"Hi, Dad. You called?" Julie turned right to head toward her house.

"Is everything okay? You don't sound right."

How did he do that? He always knew when she was having a rough time. "Yeah, Dad, I'm fine."

"I called the office and they said you were out making barn calls. Sometimes I envy your rural doctor's life. My clients get crazier by the day. You should have seen the dog carriage this lady had today. It had a stereo system in it to play music to soothe her dog's nerves. Her dog's *psychologist* recommended it."

"*Nooo.*" That was one thing Julie didn't miss—ridiculous extravagance.

"Are you sure you're okay? You sound tired."

"I *am* tired, Dad. I was up all night last night, and I had the craziest day."

"Trouble with the patients?"

Dog started growling. Julie looked in the rearview mirror—a sheriff's vehicle. Dog barked.

"It's okay, boy."

"Who's that barking?" Dad asked. "Did you get another dog?"

Dog continued to bark. Julie picked up her phone and took it off Bluetooth. "No, it's not my dog. That's part of the reason my day's been crazy. Let me call you back when I get him calmed down. Love you."

Julie clicked the red phone icon to hang up and pulled to the side of the road.

The deputy's car pulled in behind her. Cruz got out and came to her window—without his previous swagger. He looked serious. She rolled down the window.

"Doc?" He stood looking like he wanted to say something.

Julie was determined not to get caught up in his banter. But he wasn't offering any. Dog was going crazy. He looked at Dog. "Glad to see he's doing okay." He smiled. It almost looked genuine. Dog was not fooled.

"Well, Deputy. It seems like Dog doesn't share your sentiments. Why would *that* be?"

His smile disappeared. He didn't answer the question. He looked into Julie's eyes. The evil was not there. He looked at Dog and back at Doc, still saying nothing.

"As you can see, Deputy," Julie yelled over Dog's protests, "I need to get Dog home so he can calm down. It's strange—so far you are the only person he can't stand. He's had a hard enough day. If you'll excuse me, I'm headed home. And please don't follow me."

"Did you think I was following you? I just stopped when I saw you pull over—public safety stop."

"Well, I'm concerned for the safety of my patient, so if you don't mind." Julie pulled away, leaving Cruz by the side of the road. Dog only relaxed when Cruz went out of sight. If Dog hadn't been restrained, he would have attacked Cruz. Part of Julie liked that idea.

The phone rang. She touched the green phone icon. "Hi, Dad."

"Is everything okay?"

"No, everything is *not* okay." Julie regretted the words almost before they came out. Before Cruella, Julie had loved sharing the details of her life with her dad. But Cruella always managed to worm her way into their conversations and life. Later, she would make Julie regret sharing her private information because Cruella would use it to hurt Julie's feelings. Julie had vowed never to share anything else with Dad to protect herself from Cruella's attacks. How much should she tell him this time?

"What's going on?" Her father asked.

Despite her best efforts to hold back, something unleashed her tongue and spilled the details of her day in one long unending sentence. She did, however, manage to leave out the being pregnant part.

"I'm coming down there."

Oh, no. That's all she needed. "No, please don't." Visions of Cruella's know-it-all face flashed before her. "I'm sure everything will be okay. I'm just tired."

"Listen, I'm concerned for your safety, and I'm coming down there. Catherine is visiting her sister up in Maine. I'll get my associates to cover for me. Nobody's going to hurt my little girl, and it sounds like you need a little reinforcement right now. I'll give that deputy a thing or two."

No Catherine? Dad all to myself? A protector sounded good. And someone to deal with her sister. Still . . .

"I'm not taking no for an answer. I'm going home to put some things together, and then I'll leave. I should be there by eleven. It'll be good for us to be together, just the two of us. Or should I say three? Me with my two girls."

Truer words had not been spoken. It would be good for her *and* good for Heather.

"Okay, Dad. I'll ask Sarah to get your room ready."

"Is the key still under the frog—in case you're asleep when I get there?"

"I doubt that will happen, but yes, it's still there."

"I love you, baby girl."

Now it was getting ridiculous. Why was everyone calling her baby girl? "Me too, Daddy," Julie answered. Had she just called him "Daddy"?

The phone call cleared the Bluetooth system, and her playlist came back on. She located the father/daughter song that she had played for her dad at her wedding. She did love her dad . . . when Cruella wasn't around. What a joy it would be to have the old dad back. And what a great time to tell him she was going to be a mommy. She couldn't wait to see the look on his face. She sang along to the song, remembering how her dad cried when they played it at her wedding. Tears flowed as she remembered that day. Yes, she was glad Daddy was coming.

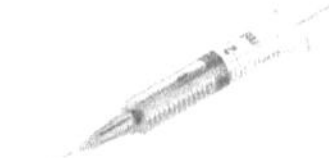

CHAPTER 18

5:00 p.m.

JULIE'S HOME HAD NEVER LOOKED AS BEAUTIFUL as when she crested the hill, giving her a full view of her stone, a two-story haven. She would finally be able to shut the door on this day's roller coaster—and be able to talk to Richard. She pushed the garage-door-opener button and pulled in. She shook her head. She was still not ready to hide her dream machine. She backed out and parked in full sight of the road.

She raised her head to look at Dog in the rearview mirror. "We're home." He cocked his head as if not understanding. Of course. It wasn't *his* home. A part of her wished it was. She was enjoying his company more than she wanted to admit.

Julie got out, opened the back door, and unhitched Dog from his harness. Having already proven his obedience, she didn't bother with the leash. She patted her upper thigh. "Come on, boy."

Dog cautiously found his way down from his high perch and hopped to the ground. His tail wagged and his feet pranced as he looked between Julie and the house, ready for this new adventure. She retrieved her purse and the dog food. They walked to the columned porch and climbed the steps to the front door. Dog was taking it all in. Julie reached for the screen door handle but hesitated at the sound of the farm truck on the gravel drive. Jake was headed toward the barn.

Julie patted Dog's head. "What do you suppose Jake has been up to?"

Dog wagged his tail. What a contrast to Dog's vehement reaction to Cruz. Dogs always know. Did Dog like Jake? Should Julie?

Julie opened both doors. Dog entered looking in all directions, then back at Julie as if asking for permission to explore. "Make yourself at home." Even so, he stayed with her as she set the dog food bag on the third step of the staircase and walked to the living room entryway.

The memory boxes were stacked on the oriental rug next to her vintage paisley flared-arm sofa in the living room. Across from them, the crackling fire warmed Julie's heart. Everything was in place, including candles throughout the room. Sarah knew her too well.

"Well it's about time," Sarah said, wearing her ever-present smile and her favorite print apron. Julie especially loved those dimples.

Sarah made her way around the partially set mahogany dining room table in the adjacent room. Dog headed straight for Sarah, tail wagging his body. "And who do you have here?" she asked as she squatted to meet Dog—not an easy task for her body shape.

"Dog, I would like you to meet Sarah. Sarah, meet Dog." The beat of his tail increased as he licked her face.

Sarah scrunched her nose as she relished his love. "This beautiful animal is no stray, is he?" She forced herself up and put her hands on her round hips as Dog returned to Julie.

"Do I look like someone who would bring home a stray?"

Sarah cocked her eyebrow and held her hands out toward Dog as proof.

"Okay, I get it. But you have to admit—I haven't brought a stray home in years."

"That's true, but what about this one?" She asked as she moved a wayward strand of hair back behind the scarf that matched her apron.

"He belongs to Nicole."

Sarah's mouth dropped open and her eyes widened. "*Nicole*? As in Richard's hot assistant?"

Et Tu, Sarah?

Julie willed herself not to be mad at her friend. Sarah had no idea how the idea of Nicole's beauty was affecting her, and how hard Julie was working not to go there.

"Come on, sister. There's a story here, and you're going to tell me."

Julie pointed to a chair adjacent to the head of the dining room table. Julie took the seat at the head. Sarah sat awaiting Julie's tale of woe. Dog sat between them. Sarah stroked his head while Julie weighed how much to say. She checked her watch. 5:10. "How much time do you have?"

Sarah checked her own watch. "Tell you what—you come to the kitchen so I can keep on schedule."

Julie welcomed the delay. It gave her more time to compose herself. They moved through the swinging door into the warm aroma of Coca-Cola cake baking. Julie held the door open for Dog, who circled the island, then took a seat on the breakfast nook area rug. Julie got Dog a bowl of water. He lapped it up.

Sarah checked the potatoes, then the cake, as Julie took a stool at the counter. Sarah joined her. "Five more minutes." Sarah sat up straight. "So, tell me. Starting with why you bristled when I asked about Nicole."

"Was it that obvious?"

Sarah nodded.

Julie described her emotional journey from blissful ignorance to public humiliation and ugly accusations.

"And you believed those people? *Richard?* Are you kidding me?" Sarah's puzzled face made the embarrassment all the deeper. "I've known my share of cheaters, and Richard's not one of them."

"Are you just trying to make me feel better?" Julie took a breath, measuring her next words. "I shouldn't be telling you before Richard, but I've known you longer and you need to know anyway. You just have to promise me not to tell him."

Sarah's face lit up and she launched off her stool. "You're *pregnant!*" She grabbed Julie off her stool and they hugged.

Sarah held Julie back to look her over. Was she wearing an "I'm pregnant" sign?

"Thank you, Jesus!" Sarah looked up to the ceiling, raised her hand, and did a happy dance. Beaming, she squeezed Julie again. Sarah took Julie by the shoulders and held her back once more. "An answer to prayer!"

"You can't tell Richard . . . I didn't even tell you."

"You didn't have to." Sarah giggled. "You're glowing." Sarah went for her smartphone on the counter and pushed a few buttons. A happy song began to blare, and Sarah danced around the room. Dog, who had lain down on the rug in the breakfast nook, held one eyelid up and then raised his head. Julie laughed.

When the song ended, Sarah sat down. She was panting and her face had pinked, "Whew—I'm getting too fat and old for that. And what about you? Wow, you've had quite a day." She squeezed her face. "And still no word from Nicole?"

"No ... *and* no word from Richard."

Sarah's smile turned upside down—a bad sign from Miss Effervescence. She reached for Julie's hand. "I'm sure there's a reason." She forced a smile. "And I'm sure we will be laughing about this in a couple of hours. Speaking of time . . ." She checked her watch and then opened the oven door to retrieve the cake and set it on a cooling rack.

Julie gathered her strength to smile. "Yes, I'm sure there is." She retrieved her phone and pointed to the counter on the other side of the cake. "Stand there and show off your cake." Julie snapped a photo as her friend did her cooking temptress face holding the cake at an angle for the perfect picture. "If that doesn't get him here, nothing will." Julie found the icon for messages and hit the send button.

Sarah set the cake down and came around the counter to her friend. "Let's pray."

Sarah had *found the Lord* after Julie left for college. Sarah put her hand on Julie's shoulder and prayed for peace and guidance. Julie's body tensed at first, but then warmth overcame her—a feeling that all was going to be well. Sarah prayed for God to guide Richard, and for God to give Richard and their child safety. She also prayed for some word from Richard.

When Sarah finished, she hugged her friend, then backed off and said, "How about a cup of green tea?"

Julie grimaced. She was a coffee girl.

"No coffee for you, mama," Sarah said.

"What about decaf?"

"Okay, but *tea* would be better," Sarah said in a sing-song voice, batting her eyes, still trying to coax tea.

"Decaf. You know me—I can't be *that* good."

Sarah started the coffee pot.

"I just saw Jake pull in." Julie pointed toward the barn. "What's he been doing all day?"

"I couldn't say." Sarah turned to face Julie. "Why the sudden interest in Jake?"

"I don't know. He's been popping up everywhere. I never saw him outside of the property before. But today it's been like four times. He was even at the diner."

Sarah shrugged her shoulders. "He *has* been kind of distracted today."

"What do you mean?"

"Well . . ." Sarah straightened her collar and pressed her apron ruffle down. "I don't know. He's been on his phone a lot. But maybe I just noticed it because he's been up to the house a bunch today, getting down the boxes and borrowing my car." Sarah crossed the room to look out the back picture window by the nook toward the barn. "I'm sure it's nothing. I just love having him around. And the way he fills out those britches." A broad smile crossed her face as she looked back. "Mmmhmm." Dog looked up and moaned. They both laughed.

"Okay, married woman. Come down from Cloud Nine."

"Yeah . . ." Sarah fanned her face, then retrieved a plate of uncooked chicken from the refrigerator.

Julie walked to the window and looked back at the barn. "I think I'm going to run up and grab a sweater, then go brush down Jubilee,"

Julie said. "I guess I'm not going to be able to ride him for a while. He's going to be mad." Dog lifted his head. "Will you feed Dog?"

"Sure. And just where did you leave his food?"

"You mean you don't believe I put it where it belongs?"

"That would be a first. Let me guess. The dumping ground—third step on the staircase."

"Isn't that where it belongs?"

They both chuckled.

"Just give him a cup of dry food with a little water mixed in. And, please, no table-food." Julie gave Sarah a look that let her know she meant it. Sarah had a habit of wanting to share her good cooking with every stray. "He doesn't need a case of pancreatitis after being poisoned."

"If you say so." Sarah smiled. "Dog, I guess you're on dietary probation. Come on."

Dog followed Sarah to the front hallway as Julie headed up the backstairs to find some warmer clothes. Pausing mid-flight, Julie called to Sarah. "Is Heather coming home for dinner?"

Sarah called back, "No, she's going over to the saloon to shoot some pool is what she said."

Good. Julie would have the house all to herself when she talked to Richard. Julie climbed the rest of the stairs and walked into her bedroom. She paused as she looked at the bed and remembered the night their child was conceived. Richard had put candles everywhere—a sea of warm light and love.

She walked into her closet. She was face to face with herself. She touched her stomach and turned from side to side, checking her slim figure. She would be getting bigger day by day. She had secretly envied her uninhibited friends that posted Facebook pictures with signs marking the growth of their bellies. Vain friends didn't want anyone to see their pooching tummies. Julie always thought pregnant women were beautiful, but she was sure she didn't want to share her burgeoning stomach with the world. But it would be fun to catalog her development. She took her phone out of her pocket to get the before picture . . .

well, at least before there was a visible sign. The viewer magnified the fact that she needed a change of clothes.

She found her favorite red sweater and mindlessly reached for her missing pendant. How odd that she would lose it just as she began her own journey of motherhood. She would not be able to pass it along to her daughter—if it was a girl. Would Richard want to find out the baby's sex before it was born?

Julie donned a turtle neck blouse and sweater over. She touched her belly again and looked in the full-length mirror. *Soon, Momma, soon. I'll have a little one. Wish you could be with me.*

Julie turned sideways as she imaged her tummy in a few months. She pulled her phone from her jeans pocket and snapped a photo. *Month #1.* She couldn't post that to Facebook anyway. Nobody was supposed to know until Richard learned. And then maybe no one should know until she got past her first trimester . . . just in case.

Stop it, Julie. She had a team of prayer warriors working. Not that she believed God would help her.

She turned her back on the unpleasant thought and headed downstairs.

———

JULIE HAD INSISTED ON RED PAINT when they had their barn built—just like the one at her childhood home. She had ordered a full apartment built above the stable to house their farmhand. And now, Jake lived there. A shiver went through her.

Dusk now muted the barn's color, especially when the lights inside stole the attention away from the structure's glory. Dog stayed by Julie's side as they approached the shadows cast by the interior glow. The backlighting didn't improve the look of their old pathetic Gator. Maybe Richard could get her one like Sam's for Christmas.

The main door was open. Jake was on the phone. Julie paused to listen to Jake's strained voice.

"No, that wouldn't be good ... He'll get it later ... I'll handle it."

Dog's ears perked and he ran into the barn barking. Julie turned the corner to find Jake squatting, getting his share of love. It was as if Dog found his long-lost friend. He stood when he saw Julie. "Is this Dog?"

"Yes. How did you know?"

Dog continued to dance around him. "I met him at Nicole's once." He patted Dog's head.

"He really likes you." Dog continued as if trying to engage Jake in a game.

"Yeah, they call me the dog whisperer." Jake gave Julie an inviting smile. She could see why Sarah melted at the thought of him. He had that rugged country-boy ease in a tall dark package with just enough brawn to let you know he could handle himself, but not too much to intimidate.

"I'm sorry. Did we interrupt a phone conversation? I thought I over-heard you speaking to someone."

Jake's face froze for a moment as if searching his memory for the conversation, then relaxed and laughed. "Oh, no. You weren't sup-posed to hear that." He paused, checking Julie's face. "I'm not sup-posed to tell you what that was—per your husband's instructions. It's a surprise."

Julie didn't know what to think. She had never known Richard to spend much time speaking to Jake. Much less make secret plans with him. The farm was Julie's gig. She didn't have good reason to believe him . . . or doubt him, for that matter.

"A surprise, huh? Tell me about it."

"Then it wouldn't be a surprise."

"Hmm," Julie said as she watched for more clues. They didn't come. "It's funny. I didn't know you and Richard were so chummy."

"Oh, we're not. He just asked me to take care of something for him. But I'm not telling you another thing. You're just trying to get it out of me, and it's not going to work." He grinned.

"Was that Richard on the phone?"

"No, ma'am. I haven't heard from him all day."

Julie's stomach dropped. A feeling of dread. If Richard was planning something with Jake and he hadn't heard from him, what did that mean? She couldn't think about it.

"I just came down to tell Jubilee about the baby—since I won't be able to ride for a while." She walked to Jubilee's stall and opened the door. "Good evening. How are you doing?"

Jubilee bobbed his head a couple of times as Julie began to rub his face. She slipped a bit into his mouth and the bridle over his head and fastened it under his jaw. Julie loved the white paint down his chestnut-colored nose. She led him out into the open area of the barn and hooked his harness to a beam.

Dog didn't know what to think of the horse. He and Jubilee sniffed each other. Jubilee nodded his approval and said hello in the way only horses can.

"Could you get me his brushes and mane comb?"

"Yes, ma'am. I already groomed him, so you won't need to curry him. I think he was hoping you'd take him out today." Jake retrieved and handed the implements to her. His smile disarmed her. Sarah was right about him. Julie tucked the comb into her back pocket and slid her hand into the brush strap. Jake took a seat on a bale of hay across from Julie. Dog went to him seeking his attention, which he fully gave.

"Well, Jubilee, it looks like we're not going to be able to go riding for a while." She began her labor of love, stroking his neck in downward motions. Riding Jubilee was the closest she could get to experiencing her mother's presence. There was nothing like the feeling of riding side by side down through country pastures and pine-matted forests. It was what they did on tough days. It's what she wanted to do now.

Jake looked up from stroking Dog. "Are you going to want me to ride him for the duration, ma'am?"

Julie paused to look at Jake, trying to gauge whether she could trust him with her treasure. She was going to lose a precious year in the life of her horse. Jake was gentle enough. "I suppose that would work. You know I don't trust him with just anyone." Julie caught herself smiling.

"Yes, ma'am, I know. Mr. Wheeler told me all about your mom and how you named him after her favorite song. I get that. I lost my dad when I was young too. It was hard growing up with no dad. He was a good man."

Could this guy have been any more endearing? Jubilee bobbed his head up and down and puffed out a breath, not happy that Julie had been distracted from him. Julie lifted his chestnut mane to brush under it. She separated the tangled mane hairs with her fingers as she went.

"So, I heard that you delivered a full breach this morning. Back in my days on the farm before Dad died, those calves didn't make it."

"Back in your days? You couldn't be that old."

"Still, ma'am. The calves didn't survive. But, then again, I guess we didn't have vets like you."

There was that smile again. "I don't know about that, but I am glad for the Olgrams. They are a lovely couple. They've had a rough go acclimating to farm life." Julie smiled as she remembered the photos taken that morning. Hard to believe her day had started so long ago."

"I'm surprised you're still awake. My sister couldn't make it past noon without a nap her first trimester. Didn't you go out to the Beckers' this afternoon?"

She hadn't told him that . . . Or had she? What had they discussed when he was at the office? Maybe she had. The hair raised on her neck again. She proceeded with caution.

"Do you know the Beckers?"

"Yeah. In fact, I saw Sam at the feed and seed today."

That explained it. Her body relaxed. Jubilee shifted and huffed— reminding her that she had stopped brushing again. She got the comb out of her pocket and began combing Jubilee's tail.

Jake held Dog's chin up and asked, "Did you go with Doc to the Beckers'?" Dog's tail wagged. "Did he like going on a barn call with you?"

Why these questions about going to the Beckers' . . . and Dog? But, then again, he seemed to be in tune with Dog. Maybe it was an innocent question.

He must have read her, because he asked, "I mean, it's not often you bring a patient on a barn call—or home, for that matter."

"I guess not. I think he enjoyed it."

"He seems like he'd make a great veterinary companion. We had a vet when I was young who had a sidekick dog. Old Doc Hanson wouldn't go anywhere without that dog. I think people liked the dog better than Doc Hanson." Dog lifted his head for some petting, and Jake obliged.

She guessed his questions made sense, so she let down her guard and told Jake about his reaction to going by the Gleason farm.

"That's strange. Dog doesn't usually react so strongly. He's so gentle. But, then again, we don't know what he's been through—with the poisoning and all. I will say that you look happy with him. Mr. Wheeler told me about your shepherd. And how he bought that dog to win you over." He grinned as he looked at Julie. When she returned the smile, he said, "I bet it's been kind of nice having him around today."

"Yes, it has."

Julie was liking Jake more by the minute—and hating that she did. Her day had started with seeing him outside the barn at three in the morning, and now here she was enjoying his good graces. It wasn't right.

Julie finished combing Jubilee's tail and handed the implements back to Jake. "It's been nice getting to know you better. I need to get dressed for dinner. I get to tell Richard about the baby now."

A sadness flashed across Jake's face, but the smile returned. "The pleasure was mine."

Julie didn't like that look, albeit temporary. What did he know?

"Come on, Dog." We have a dinner to attend.

———

6:15 p.m.

Julie and Dog descended the back stairs to the kitchen. Sarah had changed into a black, formal maid's uniform complete with a white apron, collar, and hat.

"Look at you!" Julie said.

Sarah put her hands in the air and did a model's runway turn. "Nothing but the best for milady," Sarah said in her best British accent. They both chuckled.

"Oh, I forgot to tell you, Dad's coming tonight. He's supposed to be here late. Is the guest room ready?

"Always—but you realize you're going to be one guest room short in about eight months." Sarah giggled, making Julie smile. Making people smile was Sarah's greatest gift. She could always find the silver lining in anything.

Sarah's face scrunched as if she were afraid to ask. "Speaking of guest rooms. How's Heather doing?"

"I wish I knew. I would have said better until I saw her with Deputy Cruz."

Sarah nodded.

"Is she being a pest when I'm not at home?" Julie asked.

"No. It's almost as if she's avoiding me. Is she mad at me for something?"

"Surely not. Who could be mad at you?" Julie grinned.

"Well, I can remember a few times …"

They both chuckled.

Richard was another story. He was not going to be happy having Heather there when the baby came—that is if he *was* there. Her heart sank.

"So, what's up with your dad coming?"

"I don't know. Catherine is out of town, and I'm sure he's coming to pester me about Thanksgiving." Sarah loved Julie's dad almost as much as she did, but Sarah hated the effect that Cruella had on Julie. She hesitated to say anything negative about Cruella because Sarah was sure to launch into her boundaries' speech. Sarah affirmed the things Julie knew she should or should not do, but then Julie just let her dad drag her into these unhealthy encounters, only to have her feelings hurt again. It was all for her dad, right?

Oh well. At least she was going to have her dad to herself for a little while.

They both looked at the wall clock—6:25—and then at each other. Sarah's eyes betrayed her concern for Julie's breaking heart. Even the smell of the fried chicken could not distract them from the elephant in the room: Richard was not there.

Dog raised his head and whined.

"Well, I guess we're ready for dinner," Julie said. The expensive china with fancy silver covers awaited the Southern royalty fare. Sarah looked the part. Still no word from Richard.

"Well, not quite. I'd better get back to it." Sarah returned to her food prep. It was looking more and more likely that it would just be the two of them.

Julie propped herself up with the counter. She didn't think she could stand another moment. This entire day had been a paradox—problems and encouragement. Hurt by her enemies. Buoyed by her friends.

Julie wanted her husband. Why hadn't he called or at least texted? She patted her pants pocket. "Oh, no!"

Dog's head popped up.

"What? Did I forget something?"

"No. I left my phone upstairs. Maybe Richard called." Julie raced up the stairs to her bedroom closet with Dog in tow.

She found the phone on the closet shelf. The only messages were from the office. She found her favorites in Contacts and touched his name. It went straight to voicemail.

Julie went to the armchair and crumpled into a ball of tears. Dog sat next to her. He put a paw on her lap to console her. She sat up, patted his head, and then fell back into her tucked position.

Sarah came to the door. "What can I do?"

"Nothing," she said between sobs.

"It's still not seven," Sarah said in a quiet tone, even though she surely knew better. If Richard was coming for a special night, he would have already come home, showered, and dressed the part.

Sarah retrieved a box of tissues from the nightstand and placed it within Julie's reach, then gently touched her shoulder. She disappeared, leaving Julie with her undelivered news.

Just when Julie had convinced herself to trust Richard again.

CHAPTER 19

6:59 p.m.

JULIE STARED AT THE ALARM CLOCK. 6:59. One minute and counting. Cycles of fear and anger gave way to numbness. She surveyed the empty bed. What was life without Richard? Would she be raising their child without him? The seven chimes of the downstairs grandfather clock confirmed that Richard was gone. Mary Jo was wrong. The gossips were right. Tears began to trickle down her cheeks. She was unable to move . . . to think . . . to breath.

Sarah appeared at the bedroom door. "Oh, hon." She knelt beside Julie next to Dog. Sarah leaned in to hug Julie.

Julie robotically accepted the hug. Sarah leaned back and put her hands on Julie's cheeks, turning Julie's head to face her own. Julie's focus stayed on the empty bed.

"Listen," Sarah said, holding Julie's face until Julie looked back at Sarah. "Something's wrong. This isn't Richard. Remember, I just saw him this morning. I know—like I know that I am—that he was looking forward to tonight. This isn't Richard, and it's not another woman. There's something wrong. I know it in my spirit. And you know it, too."

Julie heard the empty words. The reality of the moment was oppressive. Her eyes returned to the bed. "He's not here—Richard's gone."

"No, I'm telling you. Something's wrong . . . look at me."

Julie's eyes returned to her friend's.

"Are you hearing me?"

Sarah's question reached into Julie's numbness. That was the question her wise friend had asked so many times when Julie was being obstinate. It was time to snap out of it. Julie shook her head to release the grip of the catatonic state. She now saw her friend in Sarah's eyes— her true friend who would never say something just to make Julie feel better. These were not platitudes. They were from an unknown source deep within.

Sarah stood, reached for her friend's hand, and pulled Julie up. "Now, I want you to go fix yourself up and come down for dinner. I know I'm not Richard, but you're going to eat this chicken you ordered, canceled, then ordered again. And we are going to talk this through. Do you understand me?"

"I'm not hungry."

"Well, now that you're pregnant, it's not about you, is it?" Sarah had that coercive smile that wasn't going to let Julie frown anymore.

Julie forced her lips up. "No."

"Okay, girlfriend. Say it. It's not about me."

Julie pursed her lips, then said, "It's not about me."

"That's better." Sarah released Julie's hands, turned Julie's shoulders toward the bathroom, and gave her a swat on the behind. "You have five minutes, then I expect you downstairs."

"Yes, ma'am," Julie said as she headed for the bathroom.

Julie checked her puffy face. So much for the greatest moment of her life. She pushed the wayward brown bangs from her face and gathered her resolve. At least Sarah's home-cooked fried chicken wouldn't go to waste … and she was eating for two.

She returned to the bedroom. Her new companion was still by the chair. How could Nicole have just left him? "What's going on, Dog? Is your mommy having an affair with my husband?"

Dog cocked his head and whined.

Julie wanted to grab her keys and go looking for them, but where would she look?

Dog wagged his tail—a picture of rebirth after being on death's doorstep earlier that day. She looked at the bed once more, glad Sarah was keeping her from getting lost in those dark imaginings of Nicole and Richard sharing what Julie had thought only she shared with Richard.

A cowbell rang from downstairs. Julie half chuckled at the memory of her mother ringing that same bell to call her and Sarah to dinner. Someday, Julie would be able to call her own child and his or her friends with that same cowbell.

"Come on, boy. Let's go have some chicken." She patted her thigh for Dog to follow.

They descended the stairs to the front hallway. Julie checked the living room in the vain hope that Richard would be there dressed, waiting to escort her to their celebration. Instead, the memory boxes mocked her plans.

She pulled back from the pain and forced herself to the kitchen. Sarah had changed into her "street clothes" as she called them. She was standing at the kitchen counter wearing a smirk—cowbell in hand. "I see it still works."

Julie nodded, unable to smile. "It's really sweet of you to stay here with me, but what about Joe and the kids? I can fend for myself." Not that she wanted to.

"I already called him. He said to take all the time we want. He's watching a game." She chuckled. "Imagine—I don't have to watch the game or get the kids ready for bed. And I get to spend time with you planning for that baby." Sarah did her happy clown face, head tipped right, eyes wide open, and pulled her lips up at the corners with her index fingers. With her curly, light-auburn hair, she was like Raggedy Ann. How could Julie not smile when she was blessed with a friend like this?

"Are you sure? Won't the kids annoy him if he's watching a game and has to put them down?"

"Nope." Sarah bobbed her head. "He wouldn't notice if the house burned down. But somehow, they manage to survive. I'll probably get home to find them all passed out on the sofa." She giggled. "The truth is, the boys love hanging out with daddy and gettin' away with things . . . plus, I get a night off. And boy do I need that. You'll be finding out what I mean soon enough." Sarah reached for Julie's stomach.

Julie instinctively pulled back.

Sarah laughed. "You'd better get used to that. Especially once you start to show. Even strangers want to touch the bump. It's like your body becomes public property."

"Really?" Julie did do that with pregnant women. But she always thought it was because of her vet training. With her own body, she was very personal and had a closed personal space. People touching her belly? *Eww.*

"Speaking of belly, we'd better feed that baby. Take your seat, milady." Julie took her seat as Sarah put on oven mitts and removed two plates from the oven. She closed the oven door with her knee, removed the foil, and set the plates on the table. The aroma of the freshly cooked fried chicken made Julie's mouth water. How long had it been since she had eaten?

"Be careful. These plates are hot." Sarah retrieved the pitcher of sweet tea from the refrigerator and grabbed a glass for herself, then joined Julie at the table. "Guess I'll have to make decaf tea for a while." She winked.

"Wow, this looks great. Richard doesn't know what he's missing." How true that was on so many levels. She forced herself to pick up a fork.

"Not so fast, missy. I know your momma taught you better." Sarah reached across and took Julie's hands to say the blessing. Julie didn't protest.

"Dear Lord, we thank You for the miracle of this child. May he or she grow to be mighty for You and a blessing for these parents. May You bless Julie as she carries this child and raises him or her. And now, please bless this food. Amen."

"Amen," Julie said as she had at every meal her mother had prayed over. While she didn't want to talk to God, she longed to sit around her family's table for just one more prayer with her mom.

Julie dug in, surprised at her appetite after her crazy day. Every juicy morsel of chicken tickled her taste buds. The conversation flowed from life with babies to decorating nurseries and new-fangled baby equipment. Julie had heard much before, but it had been with an unbelieving heart that it would ever happen for her. And now that she was finally going to be a member of the motherhood club, everything came to life.

Sarah retrieved the Coca-Cola cake still in the pan along with two forks—a great girlfriend tradition. They dug in and giggled like only six-year-old girls can.

With half the cake devoured, Julie held up her fork in surrender. Sarah cleared the table. Julie's thoughts returned to Richard. Sarah had been a wonderful distraction, but she had her own life. It was time for her to go home.

"Thanks for staying with me."

"This was fun, wasn't it? *And* I didn't have to watch the game." Sarah laughed and then turned to Julie. "Are you going to be okay?"

"Yeah. I think I'm going to get a cup of herbal tea and curl up with a book. I'm just so tired."

"I think that's a wonderful idea. I'll get it."

Sarah put a cup of water with a teabag in the microwave and delivered it to Julie when it was done. "Can I get you anything else?"

"No, you go on home." Julie stood and gave Sarah a big hug. "Take care of your man."

Sarah retrieved her bag and jacket from the laundry room. Julie walked her to the back door. They hugged again. Sarah descended the back porch steps and got in her car. Julie watched as Sarah drove away. Julie had never appreciated her friend more than this day.

Julie returned to the table to retrieve her cup. Dog looked up at her and tilted his head as his ears perked.

"Are you ready for bed?"

He whimpered.

How could Julie have forgotten? He needed to go out. Julie headed for the front hallway closet to get her jacket. Dog barked from the kitchen. She returned to find Dog wagging his tail at the back door looking at Jake's face through the window. What was Jake doing at the back door at this hour? Had he been watching for when Sarah left?

Dog's tail beat the air in anticipation. Julie cracked the door open as Dog stood ready to greet his friend. "What's up?" she asked.

"I saw Sarah leave and thought you might appreciate it if I took Dog for a walk so you didn't have to come out in this cold air."

"Have you been watching me? Seems like every time I turn around, you're there."

Jake's face searched Julie's and reddened, but there was no shock in it. "I guess I have been, ma'am. I was raised to watch after the fairer sex, and since I found out you were pregnant, I guess my protection mode kicked in. I hope it's alright. It's just how I was raised."

Part of Julie was embarrassed, but there was that niggling feeling that wouldn't leave. What she did know was that she was exhausted and Dog needed to go out. What could it hurt?

"I'm sorry, Jake. I guess it's true what they say about pregnant ladies getting a little crazy." Julie did her best to look happy.

"I understand. It's okay."

"I left his leash in the truck, but I don't think he needs it."

"No ma'am, I don't think he does." Jake patted his upper thigh. "Come on, boy."

Dog trotted out, happy to have a new companion. Emptiness opened its mouth as she shut the door behind them. She was alone. No husband. A dog that wasn't hers. A farmhand she didn't trust.

Julie returned to the oak dinette table that had been passed down from her great-grandmother. She watched through the bay window as Dog sniffed his way around the moonlit lawn behind the house. Jake stayed in sight, watching Dog. Julie sat with her cup of tea and rubbed her belly. She reached for her mother's pendant. How could she have lost it?

Oh, Mom. Why aren't you here to help me? What should I do?

The ring of the house phone jolted Julie. She got up, picked up the phone from the counter, and returned to her seat. The caller ID only indicated a local number she didn't recognize. Who would be calling her at this hour? She clicked the phone on. "Hello?"

"Oh, thank God I got you." A woman's panicked voice spoke. There was a familiarity, but Julie couldn't place it.

The woman continued. "I can't get hold of Mack anywhere. I'm afraid something has happened to him. I'm out of town. I've called everywhere, and no one's seen him since this morning. Is Richard there?"

"Marge?"

"I'm sorry—yes, it's Marge. I guess we haven't talked in a while."

Julie thought back to Mack's state of mind that morning. "It's okay, Marge. Richard's not here. I don't know where he is."

"Oh no. Not him too."

"Him too? What's going on?"

"What do you know about what's been going on with Mack and the sheriff's office?"

"Nothing. Is there trouble?"

"That's an understatement. It goes way beyond trouble. I don't have time to explain, but this morning, Mack was going to meet with Richard out at the old Hendrick's mine. He was going to confess his involvement with the corruption going on in the sheriff's office. I haven't heard from him since."

Julie's mind raced, trying to put the pieces together. Meet with Richard? Corruption? That morning?

"I saw Mack this morning at the diner. What time was their meeting supposed to be?"

"Around nine-thirty."

"Richard didn't mention a meeting with Mack when I spoke to him a couple of hours before. He acted like he was going off to a normal day. Sarah said the same about him when he left here this morning."

"I don't know. I don't think Mack called him until he got to the office."

"That's weird. When I saw Mack at the diner, he was distracted or depressed or something." Julie pictured his robotic gestures. "Just what was his involvement?"

Marge briefly explained her gambling problem and how, because of it, Mack had been blackmailed to turn a blind eye to the corruption in exchange for her safety. "I'm the reason he got into this mess, and now I'm afraid he's in trouble or dead. They're horrible people. I'm sure they've done something to him." Marge broke down crying.

What did this mean for Richard? *No.* Richard couldn't be dead. "Marge?" Julie said to calm Marge down so she could find out more.

"Yes?" she said between sobs.

"I am totally in the dark about all this. When you say corruption, what does that mean?"

"Hayes controls everything. He answers to somebody in Detroit, but Mack didn't know who—he didn't want to. Hayes brought in his people to cover up all their activity. Drugs mostly, but they have their hands in everything. Hasn't Richard mentioned any of this?"

Julie tried to remember. "No—nothing."

"He never mentioned the lack of arrests and prosecutions?"

She remembered that he said a few things a couple of years back— about the time Nicole showed up. Nicole. She dropped off Dog around nine-thirty—poisoned. Was that part of it? What had Paul Cato said that morning about rarely seeing Richard … and crime? Prosecutions down? Crime up? Was this what Richard had been working on? And what about the changing face of the department? And how they no longer had relationships with anyone at the sheriff's office?

"It's all beginning to make sense," Julie said. "That's why we haven't been getting together for a few years, isn't it?"

"I'm afraid so."

"I'm so sorry. What kind of friends have we been?"

"Oh, it's not you. Richard kept asking Mack about getting together, but we've been pushing you guys off. We had to."

"Does Richard know what was going on?"

"Mack was pretty sure Richard knew something and thought he was working with the FBI. He saw things but kept his mouth shut hoping Richard would uncover everything—especially when Nicole came in. Mack found out she was FBI. So did Hayes."

Mary Jo was right. They weren't having an affair. Julie was thinking the worst of Richard, and he was being a hero. Why didn't he tell her?

Julie looked out the window. Where was Jake? She got up and moved to the right side of the table to locate him. He was over by the edge of the drive calling for Dog, who came running back into sight. Jake looked toward Julie, then started toward the house. What was his role in all this? Did Hayes set him up to work here? To spy on them?

"Julie?"

"Yeah, I'm here. What do you know about our farmhand, Jake?"

"Mack said he saw Jake was talking to Hayes last night. It looked like a payoff. It's what prompted Mack to confess now. He was afraid for Richard. He wanted to warn him."

"Call me back in two minutes. He's bringing Nicole's dog back in, and I don't want to alarm him."

"Nicole's dog?"

"Yeah—I'll tell you later."

"Okay. Be careful."

She hung up just as Jake knocked. She walked to the door and let Dog in. He was panting and headed right for the water bowl. "Everything good?"

"Yes, ma'am. Anything else I can do for you?"

"No, I think I'm good," Julie said, almost shutting the door in his face.

Julie watched him go back to the barn, then sat back down at the table so she could watch the barn. The upstairs lights came on in his apartment.

The phone rang.

"Marge?"

"Yeah. Everything okay?"

What a question. Did Julie even know? "Well—he's gone back to his apartment in our barn. I don't know what to do. Should I call the FBI?"

"That didn't help Richard, did it? I hate to ask you this, but could you go out to the mine and see what's there?"

"I don't know . . ." But what else could she do? "Who have you called?"

"The sheriff's office. Not that they would tell me anything, but I tried. I called our house, his cell phone, and the hospital. I even tried Richard's cell phone. Unfortunately, we've been cut off from all our friends. I don't have anyone else I can trust."

"Who can *I* trust?"

"No one that I know of. All our deputy friends are gone."

"What do you know about Deputy Cruz?"

"Not much. Hayes brought him in because of some relative. He doesn't like him, but he's kind of stuck with him. You know? Why do you ask?"

"My sister's been hanging out with him."

"Bad news."

How like Heather to pick the wrong one.

Marge interrupted Julie's mental rerun of her encounters with Cruz. "Can you do it? Can you go out to the mine?"

"Yeah, I'll do it. Where is the Hendrick's mine?"

Marge gave her directions, which Julie typed into her smartphone's memo app.

"You'll be on this number in case I get lost?"

"Yes. And please be careful."

"I will." Like Julie knew how to do that.

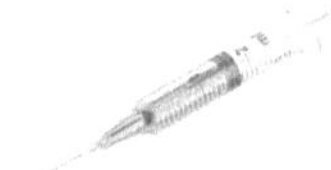

CHAPTER 20

9:30 p.m.

JULIE CHECKED THE WALL CLOCK—nine-thirty. Her dad would be arriving by eleven. Dog lifted his head and cocked it as if to ask what she was doing. What *was* she doing?

Dog tilted his head the other way. What about Dog? Should she take him? His barking might alert the wrong people of her presence if someone was there. It was too risky.

Her dad could take care of him. Should she call him? No—there would be questions. He'd try to talk her out of it. She needed to go. A note would have to do.

Julie padded down the hallway to the study. Dog followed. Should she tell her dad everything? She began with all she had learned from Marge, including an admonition not to trust Jake—or even Heather, since she was with Cruz. She stared at the paper. What about the baby—just in case? No, it wouldn't be good news if he had to learn it from a note.

And so, Dad, if something happens, please know how much I love you. I always have. And, please, take care of Heather. Let her know how much I love her as well.

All my love,
Julie

She finished the letter, wrote "Dad" on an envelope with a big heart on it, and sealed it. Hopefully Heather wouldn't snoop if she got there first.

Dog was at her feet. He looked up. How had it come to this in just a few short hours?

Julie returned to the hallway and carefully placed the precious information on the table, then returned to the kitchen to check for signs of life at the barn. Dog followed her every step.

Jake's lights were still on. She needed to leave without him noticing. Should she wait until his lights went out? No, he was less likely to notice her truck leaving if his lights were still on. She would turn off the automatic setting and leave without headlights.

What about the brake lights? Maybe she should cover them. A little cardboard and some blue painter's tape would do the trick.

Dog followed as Julie found her tools in the garage, then returned to get her jacket. "I'm sorry, Dog. You need to stay here. Dad will be here in a little while to take care of you—in case . . ."

Julie knelt and let him lick her face. She was still amazed by how quickly dogs gave their love to strangers. So trusting. Often misplaced, but not here.

Julie stood and went out the front door, turning to lock it. As she fumbled for her keys, she realized that she had not locked the other doors. She set down her purse, the tape, and the cardboard on a porch table near the door and went back to secure the house.

Dog began to bark furiously at the front door. He alternately growled, then barked with his lips curled. Only Cruz had elicited that response. But it was Heather's slurred loud voice that came through the door. Julie listened. Cruz was with her.

Julie opened the wood door a crack. Dog was almost rabid. Julie slid through, leaving Dog to his warnings. His growl deepened.

Heather was clinging to Cruz's waist—an unwelcome sight until Heather swayed. Was she that drunk—at this hour? "So, there you are, M-a-a-a-a—m-a-a-a." Heather spat as she spoke.

Julie buttoned her jacket. "What's going on?" She looked at the sober deputy, now dressed in street clothes. Instead of a smirk or any other brashness, his eyes were sad. Concerned.

Dog continued his protest.

"She's upset about—"

Heather pulled away from the deputy and pointed her finger in Julie's face. "Don't act so innocent, Miss Preggo." She came at her sister, stabbing Julie's sternum. "You didn't even tell your ol' sis you're gonna be a mom-m-m-y-y-y-y I had to hear it from trash-boy at the Saloon." Heather swayed but caught herself as she stared through her droopy eyes into Julie's.

Julie looked to Cruz. "Trash boy?"

The unwanted ally said, "Eddie was at the bar. He congratulated Heather for becoming an aunt. When he realized she didn't know, he explained how he found your pregnancy test thing in the trash."

Heather fell back against Cruz.

"I'm sorry you had to find out this way," Julie said.

"No, you're not," Heather said as she lunged at Julie again.

Julie tried to help steady Heather, but Heather pushed her arm away.

"What's your problem?" Julie asked.

"*You* are my only problem." She stabbed at Julie again. "You ask me to come and stay here, and then you treat me like dirt. You accuse me of not telling you about *Richard and Nicole*, but then you don't tell me about your baby. I thought we were best friends—or am I too much of a screw-up?"

Heather leaned back into helpless Cruz's arms. "Don't worry. I'll be out of your hair in the morning … maybe tonight." She turned to look at her support. "What about you? Would you like to take in a screw-up?"

"Me?" Cruz's eyes widened as he tried to take her back in his arms. "Get real. You're a great girl, but your sister cares about you. Why don't you listen to her?"

Dog's barking subsided a bit.

"Listen, Heather, I didn't tell you because I wanted Richard to be the first to know."

Heather broke free of Cruz's embrace again and got in Julie's face. "Well, big sister, the who-o-o-ole town knows now." Heather staggered back.

Jake came around the house at the right end of the porch, taking in the scene as he approached. "Everything okay, Doc?"

"No," Julie said, working through which man she trusted more . . . or less. But she needed help getting her sister to her room, and right now all she had were two men she didn't trust—both pretending to care. Julie looked between them.

Cruz said, "Hey man, would you mind giving me a hand getting Heather inside?"

"Sure." Jake started up the stairs to the porch. "Ma'am, where would you like me to take her?" His muscle-bound, six-foot-three frame lifted her waif of a sister. Julie opened the doors for her, Jake, and Heather to pass through while keeping Dog at bay.

"Please take her to her room at the top of the stairs to the right and the first door on the left. It's the blue room."

Cruz stayed on the porch, watching the now quiet, but alert, Dog through the screen door. He noticed Julie's cache on the table and bent over to pick them up. He stared at the cardboard and blue tape as if trying to figure out what they were for. He lifted his head. "Going somewhere?"

The heat rose in her face. "Oh, yeah." She hesitated. "I'm doing a little painting. Would you hand me those?" Would he figure it out? What if Jake saw it?

Cruz passed it through the screen door as Jake returned down the stairs. Julie quickly placed them around the corner in the study, hoping Jake hadn't noticed. When she turned, Jake was looking in the direction of the pile.

"Well, if that's all, ma'am, I'll be heading back." Jake opened the screen door carefully, as Dog was still at attention. He stood on the porch with Cruz as if he were her protector and this was his territory.

Jake—always the gentleman. Without Marge's admonition, she would have trusted him implicitly by this point. Nothing was menacing about him.

And Cruz. What was up with his change of attitude? Had Hayes instructed him to get on her good side? Dog had sure calmed down. Nothing made sense.

Cruz looked between Jake and Julie. "You know, I care about your sister." He beheld Julie's eyes. "I'm sorry—sorry for everything."

Sorry for everything? What did that mean? Did he care about her sister? He worked for Hayes. He had to be bad news. Julie didn't respond.

Cruz tucked his chin and walked down the stairs. Jake tipped his hat and did the same. Jake waited at the foot of the porch and watched as Cruz drove away, then left.

Julie shut the door on the scene, then went upstairs with Dog to check on her sister. The guest bathroom door was closed and a light was on inside. The sounds of violent heaves broke Julie's heart. "Heather? You okay in there?"

Heather moaned. "Go away!"

Torn between her need to be gone before her dad arrived and tried to talk her out of going, and her sister's sickness, Julie decided she had to go now—for Richard's sake.

"Heather, I have to go out for a while."

"I don't care—go!"

"I need you to take care of Dog until Dad gets here. He's coming around eleven. I should be back by then."

"Why should I care? You don't care about me."

"Listen—Richard disappeared. I'm worried for his life. I'm going to look for him. Please!"

"Go away!" Her sister vomited again.

Did Heather really not care about Richard's disappearance? Julie's heart hurt. Was everything in Heather's life about Heather? Even after Richard had allowed Julie to take her in again? But she loved her sister. And her mom had left her in charge. She knelt and told Dog, "Take care of Heather. Okay?"

Dog's eyes pleaded.

Julie patted his head and stood. "Stay here, Dog. Watch out for her." She headed down the staircase, grabbed her stuff from the study, then headed out the door, locking it as she left.

With tail lights covered, she climbed into the truck, turned the headlights off, started the engine, then headed down the drive . . . hopefully unnoticed.

———

JULIE WAS ALONE AGAIN. If Richard was gone, no one could walk this road with her into parenthood. No phone calls to friends or family were going to change that reality. Was she going to find bodies? She had never been in a mine, not even a tour. Even if the mine was open, would it be safe?

She reached for her missing pendant. *I'm sorry I lost it, Mom. I've messed up everything.* If Julie had been paying attention, then maybe Richard would still be there. Julie bit her lip. No more tears. She turned onto the main highway. When she was out of the barn's sight, she pulled over and removed the taillight covers to avoid an excuse for some tainted deputy to arrest her.

Marge's directions were very specific. Not that the roads were complicated. Just a couple of turns to get to the right highway. But the old mine had no signs, which meant that Marge had to be right on with the landmarks on the windy road through the old mining area. Julie hoped Marge's memory was as good as her descriptions.

Headlights appeared in her rearview mirror. Would the driver be able to see her with her tail lights covered? The mobile clinic? How could they miss her monster vehicle? But what if it was Cruz ... or Jake? She pulled over as she envisioned Cruz making his third traffic stop behind her within twenty-four hours. The car passed.

Julie checked her directions again. She was close now. Marge had given descriptions of road signs and the bends in the creek that ran along the road. The parking lot would be just after the next S-curve.

The parking lot was barely noticeable. Bushes sprouted up in the middle of parking spaces. Branches blocked inlets. Richard's car was not there—only a maroon SUV near the mine entrance. Julie pulled in beside the SUV and got out. If Mack was still driving one of those land barges, like a Grand Marquis, then he wasn't here. Whose car could this be?

Thank goodness for flashlight apps. Only the front seat area was visible through the tinted windows. There was a coffee cup in the center console, some papers on the passenger seat, but otherwise clean.

The driver's door was locked, as were the other three. The hatch would not open. Could the owner be in the mine? She shined the light in the cargo area. Maybe a blanket, but nothing else discernible through the tinting.

The mine entrance was dark. She wished there was a sign. What if this was the wrong place? Or what if the owner of the SUV was dangerous? Julie hesitated at the dark entrance. She reminded herself to breathe.

She had come this far. If there was an answer here, she needed it. But what if something happened to her? No one would know—except Marge—and she would never know if Julie made it there. She returned to her truck, climbed in, then touched Marge's contact icon.

"Julie?"

"Yeah. Sorry. I got delayed. But that's another story. I'm here. There's a maroon SUV. What does Mack drive now?"

"A black Grand Marquis."

"I was right. I'm sorry, his car is not here. There's no one around—at least not in the SUV."

"What's in the mine?"

"I don't know yet. I was afraid the owner of the SUV might be in there. There're no markings to be sure I'm in the right place."

"There *are* no markings there. If you walked around the parking lot, you might find some no trespassing signs, but no company signs. They went out of business—a common trick of the mining industry to ensure miners never collect on their lawsuits."

"Okay, I guess I'm at the right place. I wanted to let you know what I found before I went in. I'll put you on speaker because I have to use the flashlight on my phone, but don't talk in case someone is in the mine. Okay?"

"Yeah—good thinking."

After walking about fifty feet into the mine, Julie found rocks piled so high that no one would be able to pass any farther. "Marge?"

No answer.

The screen showed the phone call had been dropped. Of course. No signal could reach through this mountain. She was glad she found nothing.

"Dr. Wheeler?" a male voice called out.

Julie turned toward a blinding light. "Who is it?"

"It's Deputy Cruz. Would you please come out?"

What else could she do? She made her way out toward the light to find Cruz, three sheriff's vehicles, and three other deputies standing at the open back end of the SUV. One pointed and the other two shook their heads. Another deputy came to Cruz's side.

In a monotone voice, Cruz said, "Dr. Wheeler, you are under arrest for the murder of Nicole Marley. Please hand this deputy your purse and cell phone."

Murder Nicole? Julie was stunned. Who would believe that? *Oh, no.* The Diner … the courthouse … Who wouldn't believe it? She had been set up. She glared at Cruz. His words at the house came back to her—*I'm sorry. Sorry for everything.* He knew then what was coming. He's the one that incited her to her jealous rage. He framed her—and she walked right into it. But what about Richard? And Mack? Were they under that pile of rubble in the mine? Did Cruz know?

"Ma'am?" the other deputy said as he held out a clear plastic bag for her valuables.

As Julie mechanically dropped her purse then phone into the bag, the phone rang. The other deputy removed it, looked at the screen, and showed it to Deputy Cruz. He nodded, but neither of them spoke. It had to be Marge. If only she hadn't saved Marge's name with her phone number to her contacts …

This was bad—so very bad. What if Marge came snooping because Julie didn't answer? And now Hayes would know that Julie had been talking to Marge, which meant Hayes would know that Julie knew about the corruption. How stupid could she be? Richard had always been after her to put a passcode on her phone. Now they would just be able to slide the screen and see when she and Marge talked and for how long. Julie was officially a loose end.

Is that what Richard had been? Julie glanced back to the mine entrance. Was he in there?

A gloved deputy walked over and showed Cruz the gun. Then he held up Julie's necklace. "Look what we found in Ms. Marley's hand." He turned to Julie. "Is this yours, ma'am."

Julie just looked at it and didn't say a word—not that she could have. She felt like she was having an out-of-body experience. Watching the scene unfold from the outside. Richard's words began to seep into her consciousness. *Defendants are so stupid to talk. There is zero benefit from explaining anything. You might as well hand them a shovel to dig their own hole.* He said it always made prosecuting them easier. How easy had she just made it for them to put her away? A corpse. Means. Motive. Opportunity. They had it all.

The gloved deputy put the evidence in two separate bags and walked away. Another deputy came with handcuffs and asked Julie to turn. Two men in plainclothes showed up, one with a camera and the other with a notepad, taking notes and asking questions.

Julie looked at Cruz and said, "Really?"

Cruz's eyes were sunken. Helpless. This was not the puffed-up deputy who was at Nicole's house twelve hours before. Where was the gloating?

The man with a camera snapped her photo.

The deputy with the cuffs snugged them on and then led her to a cruiser. The photographer continued to take pictures of the crime scene. The deputy opened the door and helped her in. The door closed, emphasizing the finality.

11:00 p.m.

HAYES LEANED ON HIS DESK, his legs bounding in anticipation of Cruz's call. The office was buzzing—all hands on deck. Word was spreading of Nicole's death and Julie's arrest. All eyes were on him. And with Smitty coming …

At least Julie was cooperating with her part: being an easy target.

Hayes' phone vibrated. He checked the screen. Cruz.

"Yeah?"

"We've got her."

"What did she say?"

"Nothing. She was at the mine entrance when we arrived. We're fingerprinting Nicole's car. She likely touched all the door handles— not that we need any more evidence, or that you couldn't make it."

Hayes enjoyed his power. "How did she react to the gun and necklace?"

"She didn't—she wouldn't even admit the necklace was hers."

"Hmm." Hayes tried to imagine the scene. He wished he could be there, but his presence could raise questions he didn't want to answer.

"Any press there?"

"No. We kept it off the radio like you said."

"Anything else?"

"Yeah, just one thing. When we took her phone, it rang, and guess who was calling her?"

Another guessing game. He gritted his teeth. "Unlike you, I don't guess."

"Marge McConnell."

"What? Are you sure?"

"Yep. Looks like they talked earlier tonight too. Twice."

"Make sure *you* drive her back here yourself. And be sure to find out what she knows. If she knows too much, we'll need to call in Jonesy. Don't let Doc talk to anybody—*no one*, got it? Can you do that right? I'll make sure that Magistrate Harris takes a day off tomorrow so Doc can't make bail. *No* visitors. Got it?"

"Yeah, I got it." He hesitated. "You can't call Jonesy. She's pregnant."

"What difference does that make?"

"Nothing ... I guess."

Great. He should have sent Williams. Cruz was a liability. A friend's kid or not, Cruz was history.

"What are you going to do about Marge?"

Like he was going to confide anything else to this kid. "I don't know. Just get her back here now—and don't screw this up!"

Hayes hung up and pinched his nose. He had to get ready for any questions in case the press got wind of it. He had to keep it out of the paper so the FBI wouldn't find out.

He got up and looked in the full-length mirror on the back of his door. He pictured himself answering questions about poor Julie, who found out her husband was having an affair and went into a jealous tirade. People would be shocked at the news. But then the press would interview the nosey neighbor who saw her snooping around the house and those that saw her blow up in the Diner. He chuckled to himself. "Dumb broad."

Where was Jake? Why hadn't he called when Julie was on the move? He returned to his desk and called.

"Jake here."

"Did you hear?"

"Hear what?"

"That's what I was afraid of. How did Doc leave the house without you knowing it?

"You didn't hire me to watch her twenty-four hours a day, remember? I'm sure I accomplished what you sent me to do."

"Well, you'll be glad to know we arrested her for Nicole's murder. It was great. She went out to the mine, and with the gun and necklace *you* provided, she's mine."

"So, you called to thank me?"

"Not hardly. We have a problem."

"We?"

"Yes. Because of you, any trouble I have is yours. Doc was in contact with Mack's wife. What do you know about that?"

"Nothing."

"Did you see her acting suspiciously?"

"No. All I saw was a woman who was struggling with a missing husband and a drunken sister who's dating Cruz."

It took Hayes a moment to decipher what Jake meant. "Nothing else?"

"No. Nothing. I just was at the house an hour ago. Cruz brought Heather home drunk and I carried her upstairs so she could puke out her guts in the john. No way Doc was planning on going anywhere."

"Well, she did—and it must have been right after you saw her."

"Okay, then. What do you want from me?"

Hayes stood and looked out the window. "I need your ears at the house with her sister and the housekeeper. You said the housekeeper trusts you. Use it."

"So, same as always."

"No—it's more. You are listening for anything that can help us find Mack's wife. She's a big loose end. And so is Julie *if* she knows about what we're up to … well, we have to take care of that. So, you need to be sure there're no more loose ends at the house. Got it?"

"Got it."

Hayes hung up.

Time for the show. He smiled. Not long now.

———

Deputy Cruz slid into the driver's seat in front of Julie. He raised his hand from the steering wheel to acknowledge the blue-gloved coroner as they backed away from the SUV . . . and Nicole's body.

They pulled onto the main road. Julie turned back. The mine entrance grew smaller and disappeared. Was Richard buried there? Was that as close as she would ever come to seeing him again?

She turned back. Cruz's eyes filled the mirror but turned away. Julie glowered at him, daring him to return the gaze. She steeled herself, determined not to talk. Despite her exhaustion, the adrenaline pumped her to a heightened state of awareness. She could make no mistakes now. She listened for Richard's voice to prompt her.

The smell was intense. How many drunks had he picked up? Her queasiness returned but produced nothing. She almost wished it would.

Cruz's eyes met hers in the mirror. He averted them to the road.

The minutes passed as they traveled through the shadows cast by the barren, moonlit trees. Less than twenty-four hours ago, she was delivering a calf. Now? Framed for murder.

Images flashed. A gun. Her necklace. Nicole's body. The pile of rubble in the mine. Richard. Prison. Would she be able to raise their child?

Cruz met her again in the mirror, but this time did not look away. "I'm sorry about all this."

Remember what Richard said. She girded herself and remained silent.

"There shouldn't be any press there. Hayes is trying to keep this quiet. When we get there, don't say anything—to *anyone*."

Like you? Was he trying to help her or was this good cop/bad cop now? His eyes were soft—no glare, no hatred. She *wanted* to trust him. But she knew better.

She was alone.

Julie looked away. What had Richard told her about what was going to happen? Did she get one phone call like they showed in the movies? Richard said it was bad to answer questions, but what about asking.

"Deputy?"

"I wish you'd call me Tom. I do care for your sister. I guess it's too late for forgiveness."

Forgive him? What *was* his part in this? He was so young. So vulnerable. If Julie had not been facing a life sentence, she would have felt sorry for him. But he *was* the one who had goaded her into her jealous rage—the motive that she did not have before Cruz. How could she have been so easily manipulated? How could she have believed the worst about Richard? Shame engulfed her. Richard had been trying to save the town, and she had believed the worst about him.

Tears trickled. With no purse and her hands cuffed behind her, all she could do was rub her face on her shoulder or knees. She opted for her knees. She bent over and willed herself not to let this punk see her cry.

Cruz said, "Yeah, it's me."

Julie sat up. Cruz was on his phone.

"Five minutes … yeah … got it."

He hung up.

"Deputy?"

"Yes?"

"What will happen to me when we get there?"

"I'll walk you into the building. People will be able to see you, but it's late, so I doubt anyone will be around. I'll take you into an interrogation room. Someone—probably Hayes—will read you your rights. Then he'll ask you questions to try to get you to make a statement. Tell him you want to speak to an attorney before you answer any questions. I'm sure your husband would tell you not to say anything. Hayes is supposed to end the questioning when you say that."

"Will I get a phone call?"

"Yes. Do you know who you are going to call?"

Julie wasn't going to tell him. But who would she call? Maybe her dad. He should be at her house by now. She needed his counsel, but he wouldn't know who to call or have their phone numbers. Sarah was her best friend, but Angie was the one who knew everyone and had been in town longer than anyone else. Angie could call her dad for her. But what was Angie's cell number? It was stored on her smartphone. The only numbers she knew were her own and the clinic's. And the only one that would be answered would be her home phone. Between Heather and her dad, someone should answer. Heather would have numbers, but her dad . . . Think.

They were at the edge of town. She only had another minute to decide. The house phone has numbers stored in memory dial. That would work. He just needed to get hold of Angie. Then together they could call everyone needed. And right now, she needed an attorney. Paul Cato? As much as she hated the idea, he was probably the only one she could trust. He was certainly baffled enough this morning with the lack of prosecutions, and he had a vested interest in getting rid of the corruption.

"When will I get to make it?"

"I would ask right away, but don't be surprised if it's not until later. Keep asking." Cruz made the right turn off Main to the side parking lot of the two-story brick building across from the courthouse that doubled as the Sheriff's office and the county jail.

Cruz was right. No one was around. Cruz got out and opened the back door. "I need to act tough. It will keep him from figuring out that I'm trying to help you. Don't be put off."

Was he for real? He looked sincere. Cruz helped her out as she emerged from the cruiser. He guided her up the stairs to the side entrance, entered a code on the keypad, and entered the corner of the L where two hallways converged at the door. Two elevators were to her left. The sign indicated booking to the right and Sheriff straight ahead. She had visited once before as Mack's guest right after she got married, but had come in through the front entrance. This must be the perp's entrance. This couldn't be happening to her.

Cruz directed her straight down the hallway that opened into a large room with a short wall on the left that hemmed the deputies' bullpen. Mack's and Hayes' glass-front offices formed the right side of the hallway. Hayes emerged from his office wearing a half-smirk. "Dr. Wheeler." He didn't even try to hide his sinister nature. Looking at Cruz, he said, "Take her to the box. I've gotta make a call." Julie knew from Richard's stories that making a call was code for letting her simmer for a while to wear her down.

"Let's go!" Cruz said as he guided Julie left at the end of the sea of old desks, past a glass-doored conference room, to a windowed metal door. A handful of deputies stood gawking at her as if she were breaking news. Cruz opened the door to a yellow room. The color would make anyone break, just to get out. Four mismatched, tube-framed, metal chairs, stained cushions, one fluorescent light in the middle of the ceiling, and the smell of . . . What? Urine?

"Sorry," Cruz said in a whisper, looking toward the mirrored wall as if someone might be watching and listening. "Let's get these handcuffs off you." He turned her away and removed them. "Have a seat. I have to go."

She rubbed her wrists as Cruz left. She inspected the chairs and sat in the one with the least stains. Someone peered in through the door's window but ducked away when they saw her. She crossed her arms on the table and put her head down—numb exhaustion set in.

CHAPTER 22

11:45 p.m.

Cruz retrieved the evidence bags from the cruiser and returned to his desk in the bullpen. Hayes was in his office with Deputy Williams. Fellow deputies came by and patted him on the back as he logged the evidence bags.

"Way to go."

"Nice job."

There was nothing nice about it.

A month before, Hayes' dirty business had not fazed him. But this stuff? He had even convinced himself that poisoning Dog was okay—but killing a pregnant woman? It had gone too far.

He stared at Julie's necklace. Was he going to be returning it to Heather along with Julie's other personal effects after . . .? Heather would be devastated. Especially if she took off like she had threatened to do last night. When would Heather find out? Grief with a side of guilt.

Heather.

Cruz pictured her eyes lighting up at his jokes … her tender touch as she consoled him over his past. Why had he let himself get involved with her? He was only supposed to get information from her. He hadn't meant for it to happen. They had so much in common and yet Heather was unique. Cruz wanted to take care of her. And now here he was, checking in her sister's trumped-up evidence while Julie waited for her "accidental" death.

How could he stop it?

Wait. Hayes said he was going to keep Julie from talking to anyone. Her phone call …

Hayes was still talking to Williams. Cruz left the bags on top of his desk, hoping they'd disappear while he was gone. He rushed to the interrogation room. Julie's head popped up from the table. "Come on—hurry!"

"What?"

"Your phone call. Don't ask questions, come on. Hayes will be coming. He'll never let you call. Now's your only chance."

Julie's face crinkled, but she followed.

No time to cuff her. He checked out the window to ensure Hayes was still in his office, then took her to the adjacent glass-doored conference room and pointed to the phone. "Dial nine first."

She dialed. "Hello, Dad?"

He stepped out as she called and watched Hayes' office. He turned back and made a circular motion with his finger for her to speak in a hurry. He turned back.

Williams came out of Hayes's office, looked his way, then turned back to Hayes and said something.

Cruz signaled a timeout T to Julie, then moved away from the door.

Hayes came to the window-front of his office and looked Cruz's way. Cruz leaned against a wall, trying to look cool—like he was doing his job letting the accused have her phone call.

The red-faced Hayes's hurried out the door Williams was holding for him and headed straight for Cruz. "What do you think you're doing?"

"She asked for her phone call," Cruz said.

"Get her out of there—*now!*" He stalked off to his office where Cruz knew he was going to have to answer for his pretended guffaw.

Cruz opened the conference room door. "You have to hang up."

Julie's eyes pleaded, but she didn't argue. "Dad, I have to go. I love you."

Julie erected herself, came to the door, and looked into Cruz's eyes. "Thank you. I know what this means for you."

Did she? Cruz was a dead man walking. He opened the door for her to return to the interrogation room. She looked back at him for a long moment with sad eyes.

Now to face Hayes.

———

Wednesday, 12:00 Midnight.

JULIE CROSSED HER ARMS ON THE TABLE, put her head down, and sighed as she reran the conversation with her dad. She had left out so many details. Would he be able to retrieve the phone numbers he needed? He had never been good with electronics. Or would he be able to find Angie's house by her directions if he couldn't? Would Paul help her after Julie had treated him like a mortal enemy all these years? And Heather—where could she be? Her dad had said she wasn't there when he arrived. Heather had been so drunk. Julie pictured her car in a river off a mountain curve. Julie had brought all this on herself.

The door opened. Julie sat up. Hayes stood in the door like a bull ready to charge. His eyes narrowed to slits against his red face. His neck and shoulders tense—no longer the cool assistant sheriff who had gloated earlier.

He tossed a legal pad on the table and sat without a word. He yanked a pen from his shirt pocket, held it airborne for a moment while he examined her, and then scribbled the date at the top of the paper. He tapped the pad once with his pen, then set it down and sat back. He crossed his arms and said, "I guess you got your *phone call.*"

Julie took a breath to measure her response and maintain neutral body language. "Yes, I did. Good to see that things are being done by the book," she said purposing to neither gloat nor threaten. Either would only exacerbate his anger against Cruz, who was now, what— her ally? She was not ready to give up her hatred for Cruz that easily. But he had helped her get her phone call.

"Yeah, right. By the book—that's me," he said, mouth tight. He didn't speak. He didn't move. He glared. Was this some sort of silent treatment? Was he waiting for her to talk? She knew from Richard the first to speak loses.

He slapped his leg and stood, went to the door, and called out. "You coming today? We've got to get her statement. Let's go!"

He returned to his seat and wrote her name and the time.

"I'm not making a statement. I want my lawyer."

Hayes's face steeled. He didn't respond.

Julie repressed a squirm, unsure of what she should do. "I need some water. I have rights. I'm pregnant."

"Yeah. I heard. Seems like everybody's heard."

What did that mean?

He pounded the desk and cursed, then got up and called to someone outside. "You. Bring a bottle of water! And tell that idiot to get in here." He sat back down, said nothing, and began to pen geometric shapes.

A deputy brought in a bottle and handed it to Julie. She took it trying to avoid eye contact. She didn't want anyone to see her like this. The deputy left. She opened the bottle and took a long drink of room-temperature water. Without warning, a wave of nausea hit her, and what was left of her fried chicken dinner hurled across the table, covering Hayes's pad and hands.

Hayes jumped straight up, uttered an expletive, and shook the putrid mess off his hands. He picked up the vomit-laden pad and tossed it in the metal wastebasket, gagging as he did. He turned and looked at her— eyes wide—then rushed from the room, leaving Julie to face the stench and contents of her stomach.

A part of her relished his look of repulsion, but the smell overtook her. Shaking, she pushed back from the table, turned sideways, and put her head in her lap.

The door opened. Julie looked up as a young deputy opened the door and surveyed the mess. He covered his nose and mouth. "Oh, man, that's disgusting!" He shut the door as quickly as he had opened it.

She put her head back down. Time passed. Was she in timeout? Julie's mouth tasted awful. Did she dare take another sip? What else could she do?

She sat up, held the bottle to her lips, and allowed a small amount into her mouth, then swallowed. No reaction. It cooled all the way to her stomach. She took another sip. Still no reaction. She dared not drink more for a few minutes. She moved to the far end of the table.

After what must have been thirty minutes, a kind-looking gray-haired woman wearing tired clothes came in with a cleaning caddy and, seeing the mess, said, "Oh my. You musta had some kind of night, chile." She looked Julie over. "But then again, you don't look the type."

Julie tucked her chin. From behind her bangs, she forced a weak smile. "I'm pregnant." The words brought about a gush of tears as she lowered her head to her knees. Her hair covered her face. "I'm so sorry about the mess."

"It's okay. Mmmhmm. Don't you a-worry, little momma. I've seen worse—and usually for no good reason." Julie raised her body and peeked out at the slightly-hunched woman with well-worn hands. She was shaking her head at the mess. She began humming a familiar tune that Julie couldn't place. It had been one of her mother's favorites. Probably Christian, knowing her mom. The woman picked up the trash can and pulled some paper towels from her cleaning caddy. She swept the mess into the trash then disinfected the table with a pine-scented cleaner. What was that tune?

She stopped and turned her face toward Julie. "Your first?"

"Yes. I've heard that crackers help with this nausea. Do you have any?"

"I don't know, but I'll ask." She replaced the trash bag. She put her hand on her cleaning caddy and looked across the table at Julie with a loving smile. "Does they know you're in the family way?"

"Yes."

The woman's face almost glowed. She held up her left hand, looked up, and said, "Yes, sir," as if answering someone. She left her cleaning caddy on the table, ambled to Julie's side, and touched Julie's shoulder.

Julie was inclined to pull away, but she didn't move. There was something about this woman.

"Don't be afraid, little momma." She squeezed Julie's shoulder and warmth radiated from the woman's touch. "Lord, I pray that You watch over this chile. I know You have great plans for her. Umm-hmm. Oh, Lord, protect her from the evil that lurks in this place and give her wisdom for the days to come. Umm-hmm. Protect Your baby that is growing in her womb. In the mighty name of Jesus, we pray. Amen and amen!" The woman squeezed Julie's shoulder again and released her.

Evil? Julie looked up into the woman's kind eyes. "Is there something I need to know?"

The woman's wrinkled face and deep-set eyes said it all. Julie knew the woman couldn't speak without jeopardizing her job—something you didn't do in an economy where the coal-mining industry is drying up. Julie wanted to comfort her.

The woman retrieved her caddy. "I'll remind 'em you're pregnant. They have to take special care of you, ya know." The woman winked at her and left. The image of Della Reese and doves from that 90s TV series came to mind. Had she just been touched by an angel? No. Couldn't be. She didn't believe in those things. Julie put her head back down.

Before she could doze off, a woman deputy with barbered hair came in and slung a legal pad onto the table. Had she taken a lesson from Hayes? She sat, crossed her legs like a man, then stared at Julie for a long moment. She leaned forward, took a pen from her shirt pocket, and played with the clicker. "I'm Deputy Williams. They tell me you're pregnant." Williams shook her head.

"Yes."

Williams didn't react. With no intonation or interest, Williams said, "How far along are you?"

"I don't know. I just did the at-home test this morning. I'm ten days overdue."

She made a note on the pad then looked up and asked, "You gonna keep it?"

"What kind of question is that? Of course, I want to keep it! I've waited ten years for this child!"

The deputy held up her hands. "Don't freak out. Most of the girls that end up here don't need more mouths to feed. Puts a crimp in their lifestyle, if you know what I mean." The deputy paused. "We'll get you checked out in a couple of days."

"*Next couple of days*? Won't my attorney get me out tonight?"

"You're kidding, right?" The deputy smirked and stood. "I don't *think* so." She bobbed her head. "You of all people should know better. Your husband's the P.A.?" She laughed. "You must have confused us with TV. If you're lucky, Magistrate Harris will be here tomorrow, but I wouldn't count on it. I'm sure he's going to be sick tomorrow. I'd count on being here … let's just say for a while. Then there's the little matter of whether you'll even make bail. Which, in your case"—The deputy shrugged her shoulders. She moved toward the door, adjusting her belt as she went. "Did you eat today?"

"I just threw up my dinner."

"How about I order you a nice bowl of soup and saltines?" She cracked a crooked smile. "You allergic to anything?"

Julie shook her head.

The deputy left through the metal door. The emptiness of the room engulfed her. Reality began to creep in. What if she was put in prison for something she didn't do? Surely Richard wouldn't let that happen.

Richard. He would have known what to do. If only . . .

Stop it, Julie. You know he's alive.

———

HAYES RETURNED TO HIS OFFICE AFTER CLEANING UP, stewing the whole time. Stupid pregnancy. Stupid legal rights. Well, we won't have to worry about legal rights after tomorrow. That's one kid saved from a life with no parents.

Williams passed in front of his plate-glass wall and rapped on the door. Hayes motioned her in. She pushed the door open but didn't enter.

Hayes rose. "Did she say anything?"

"Nope."

"Not surprised," he said as he started for the door. "Where's Cruz?"

"He's in the evidence room." Williams held out two packages of saltines for Hayes to take.

"What's this for?" Hayes asked.

"Self-defense." She laughed.

"Very funny."

"You'll love this—I told her we ordered soup and crackers for her—like we have a 24-hour diner ready to cater her meals." She chortled.

"Did you take care of that other matter?"

"Yeah, I called her. The boss has her on some errand. I'll send a squad car to pick her up when she's done."

"I need her now."

Williams got in his face. "*You* want to call the boss?" Hayes's mouth tightened. She backed off. "I don't want anyone else for this one. It'll be both our heads if anything goes wrong."

"It'll be your head if she doesn't get there soon enough."

"Patience, boss. It's all under control."

"Yeah, we all know that patience is my strong suit." He sneered as he moved past her on his way back to the interrogation room.

"Yeah, we'll put that in your epitaph," she said after him.

He stopped and looked back at her. "*Epitaph?* Something I need to know?"

"Not if you make it through this week." Williams headed back toward her office.

"Oh, and, Williams . . ." She turned, as Hayes scanned the room to ensure Cruz and other deputies weren't listening or watching. He lowered his voice. "Cruz." He motioned across his neck to cut him off from intel … or slit his throat. Both were on the program.

Williams nodded her understanding. That's what Hayes loved about her. She could read his thoughts. No blabbering on like the others.

He turned back and looked for that wimpy rookie to take notes. "Let's go," he said. The deputy jumped up and grabbed his laptop. Like it mattered. *By the book* . . . at least for the things that didn't interfere with the objectives and would make everything appear copasetic. Once Julie was gone, Marge would be the only loose end.

Hayes looked through the small window in the door. Julie had her head down on the table. Even with her tousled hair, she was a babe. What a waste.

He opened the door for the deputy to pass by and pointed to the seat at the head of the table. "Sit over there." Julie looked up through her bangs as Hayes sat across from her. He tossed the crackers across the table.

Julie pulled her hair back and glared at him. He loved his power.

She opened the first package of crackers, then took a sip from the water bottle. Hayes watched for a gag. Nothing. Safe.

The deputy nodded and said, "I'm ready."

"When am I going to make bail?" Julie asked.

Hayes didn't want to smirk in front of the deputy. He remained stoic. "That depends on whether the magistrate is in tomorrow. He's supposed to be, but he's been known to get sick sometimes. You never know." He grinned until he was sure Julie had gotten the message. Her glare let him know that she had.

He looked at the deputy and pointed to the laptop. "Let's get on the record." The rookie looked at him and nodded, but didn't type. "That means put down the date and time and who is in the room."

The deputy nodded and began typing.

"Julia Wheeler, you're under arrest for the murder of Nicole Marley." He recited her Miranda rights.

Julie sat straight up and listened as if she had never heard them before.

"Do you understand these rights as I have explained them?"

"Yes, that's why I want my attorney here."

"Did you or did you not murder Nicole Marley?"

She didn't flinch. "I want my attorney."

Well trained. Better for him. He didn't want her spilling her guts in front of the deputy, but he did want to see if she'd tell him what she had learned from Marge. "Why were you at the mine tonight?"

"I want my attorney."

"Who's your attorney?"

"Paul Cato."

"Great." Cato was the last person he wanted snooping into their business. He had an ax to grind with Hayes. Had Julie gotten hold of him? *That stupid Cruz.*

Hayes forced a smile. He didn't need Julie to comment on the record if he made a face or did anything to make her uncomfortable. Transcripts only recorded words—not actions. Richard had probably shared that attorney trick with her. He could always have the transcript "fixed" later, but that left room for screw-ups and more people who could spill their guts later. There were enough of those running around.

"Have you spoken to Mr. Cato?"

"I want my attorney."

"Yeah, yeah. I heard you the first three times. So, is it your statement that you are not going to give a statement related to the murder of Nicole Marley?"

"That's right. Not without my attorney present."

"Okay, that's a wrap." He knocked on the table, looked at the deputy, and said, "Get that typed up and on my desk first thing tomorrow, okay?

"Yes, sir." The deputy closed the laptop, stood, and made his way out of the room.

"That's it?" Julie asked?

Hayes stood as soon as the door closed behind the deputy. Hayes planted his knuckles on the table, leaned across, and, emphasizing each word, said "You *said* you weren't going to talk without Paul here, didn't you?"

"Yeah, but you just stopped." Her face blanched and her mouth was open.

He expected her to be surprised he hadn't pushed her for answers. The truth was, he didn't need anything from her—except her permanent silence. Only a few hours to go.

Hayes opened the door and called a deputy. "Get Williams to book her." He turned back. "It's late. I'm tired." He yawned for emphasis. "I'm going home to my nice, warm bed with clean blankets and lice-free pillows."

Julie's eyes narrowed.

"Sweet dreams."

CHAPTER 23

Wednesday 12:45 a.m.

WHAT NOW? Julie followed Hayes to the door after it closed and peered through the window. No Cruz. A couple of deputies milled around. One looked her way. She ducked back and leaned against the wall. Didn't Hayes need for her to make a statement? Why wasn't he pushing? That was not that he was supposed to. Utter fatigue compounded her confusion. Julie began to pace.

Williams entered swinging handcuffs. "Let's go." She motioned for Julie to turn.

Julie complied. "Is this necessary?"

"You think you're *special* just because you're married to the Prosecuting Attorney?"

Williams cinched the handcuffs, then held the door open. "Let's go."

Must be her favorite expression.

"Head over toward the elevators." Williams pointed across the room to where she had entered the building. The deputies watched in silence as she made her way down the hallways toward the elevators. Hayes was standing on the other side of his glass-front office wall as she passed. He just stared. No emotion.

Mack's office was empty and the lights were out. What was Marge doing? Had Dad and Angie figured out how to get hold of her?

As they reached the elevator area, Williams said, "Turn left. We're going to booking. First door on the right." Julie complied.

They entered a large vacant room lined with benches on the three barren walls. A scale, a short counter, and a measuring chart were on the other. She pictured herself being photographed. Was her mugshot going online?

In the center were two gray-green metal desks with rolling chairs behind them and folding chairs to the side. Williams removed Julie's handcuffs and pointed to a folding chair. Williams sat in the rolling chair and pulled a form from the bin on top of the desk. She searched the drawers and cursed the sloppiness of her fellow deputies. She left the room, then returned with a handful of pens that she shoved all but one in the top drawer.

Julie was parched. "Can I get some water?"

"Does this look like a restaurant?"

"I need some water . . . now!" Julie said.

Williams cursed and left the room. She returned with a coffee cup that looked like it hadn't been cleaned in a month. Julie was so thirsty that she drank it despite the million organisms that likely filled the cup.

"Full legal name?"

Julie answered that and a host of personal identity questions.

"Who is your emergency contact?"

Julie answered rotely. "Richard Wheeler."

Williams looked up like she knew something, then wrote his name.

"Wait, he's out of town," Julie said as she watched for Williams' response.

Williams looked up and glared at Julie. She did know something.

Julie gave her dad's information and her house phone number.

Williams opened a file drawer, pushed some hanging folders around, then pulled out a paper. "I need for you to read this and sign at the bottom."

Julie started reading the paper describing her pregnancy rights. Three options were listed with a box to check beside each:

I CHOOSE TO KEEP MY CHILD.

I CHOOSE TO CARRY THE CHILD TO TERM BUT PUT IT UP FOR ADOPTION.

I CHOOSE AN ABORTION, WHICH WILL BE PROVIDED FOR ME.

Could that be true? The same government that was charging her with murder was providing abortions? She couldn't read any more. She checked the first box, signed the document, and pushed it back toward Williams, who matter-of-factly clipped it to the top of the other form.

Williams rose. "Get up," she said as she pointed to the counter where they did Julie's fingerprints. Williams weighed her then took her mugshots next to the height chart as she held up a board with her number on it. It was official. Julie was a criminal.

Williams replaced Julie's handcuffs. "Let's go." Williams held the door for Julie to exit. "Head for the elevators." Julie turned right to the elevators. Williams pushed the up button. The doors opened, they entered, Williams pushed 2 on the elevator panel and took her place behind Julie. The doors opened to the nurse's station, flanked by doors marked WOMEN'S BLOCK to the right and the MEN'S BLOCK to the left.

"Go stand in front of the nurse's station." Julie complied as Williams approached the door to the women's block. She pushed a button on the wall. A bell rang on the other side of the door. They waited for a couple of minutes.

Bzzz.

The tone of the buzzer sent an electric jolt through Julie. A female corrections officer opened the door, and, seeing Williams, said, "What are *you* doing here at this hour?"

"Short-handed."

The officer eyed Williams. "What gives? There're at least a half dozen flunkies down there that could have brought her up. Is she the queen or something?"

"Well, she thinks she is." Williams handed her some paperwork, then returned to the elevator, pushed the button, and left.

The officer cursed, then motioned for Julie to enter the fluorescent-lit hallway with a dozen doors on either side and a large metal door at the end of the hallway flanked by a well-lit glass cage on the left. "First door on the right."

The officer opened the door to the changing room that was about the size of one of her clinic's exam rooms. Cubbyhole cabinets filled the wall to the left with plastic bags filled with clothing and bundles of supplies and orange uniforms. A counter with drawers ran across the far wall. A metal bench centered the room. The officer shut the door behind them and took Julie's handcuffs off. She grabbed a bundle from a cubbyhole and handed it to Julie. "Here's your bedding, your uniform, and a bag to put your street clothes in. There are markers on the counter to write your name on the bag. She stepped back against the door.

Julie set the bundle on the counter and removed the strap. She separated the orange uniform, the undies, the linens, the toiletry bag, and a large, clear plastic bag with a pull-string. She wrote her name on the bag. "Take off your clothes and put them in the bag."

"All of them?"

The officer just looked at her.

Julie sat on the bench and removed her socks and shoes. Thank goodness she didn't have her favorite boots on.

"Come on, we don't have all day."

Julie stood and removed her blouse and jeans, keeping her back to the deputy. "Including underwear?"

"All of it."

Julie had never been so humiliated. At least at the gynecologist, they let you undress in private. Was this woman a lesbian? Was she enjoying the show? She carefully folded each item of clothing as she went. She put her bra and undies in the middle of the clothes so they wouldn't show through the clear plastic. She pulled the handle ties closed and started to put on the prison clothes.

"Not so fast. Come around the bench."

Julie covered herself as much as she could with two arms and came around to face the officer.

"Open your mouth."

"Really? I've been here for hours. You think I could be hiding something in my mouth?"

"Just do it."

Julie complied as the officer checked under her tongue and around her mouth. Julie couldn't imagine what for.

"Put your head down and flip your hair over."

Julie did as instructed. The officer checked behind her ears and around her neck."

"Okay, flip your head back, then squat and cough."

Julie was disgusted. The officer looked bored. At least she wasn't smirking. Julie complied.

"Okay. Stand and turn away from me and spread your cheeks."

"What?" Julie hoped she had heard her wrong.

"You heard me. You think I enjoy this?" The officer had a look of annoyance.

Julie turned and did what was asked of her. Was this done for legitimate reasons or just to show who was in control?

"Okay, now you can get dressed." Julie never thought she would be so glad to get on a pair of white cotton grandma undies and a sports bra. She was thankful to have some modicum of modesty restored. She held up the orange jumpsuit that must have been two sizes too large. She sat on the bench and put on the matching orange shoes. What a time for color coordination. She was glad there was no mirror.

"Put your bag in a bin and grab your bedding and toiletry bag." Julie gathered her things. The officer opened the door and waved Julie to come out. "Go stand at the yellow line at the end of the hall."

Julie walked toward the metal door and found her spot at the yellow line that crossed the hall about five feet from the metal door beside the elevated guard station. The uniformed guard behind a plate glass window looked down at them as the officer joined her at the line. Behind him, the clock announced it was just after one-thirty. Was this still the same day she had delivered the breech calf?

The guard looked them over, then pushed a button.

Bzzz.

The sound zapped her to her very bones. Would she ever get out of here? The electronically operated door swung toward her. And with it, the smell that only stale women's room trash cans can emit. Julie covered her mouth. How did the workers come here day in and day out? She expected to see flies buzzing around piles of trash.

"Step through and to the right."

The lights came on as they entered, and the other inmates screamed obscenities and demanded lights out. It was a door to the Twilight Zone. The out-of-body feeling came over her again. Inside to the left, the same guard station was visible behind another plate glass window, which she imagined was the men's cellblock, but with the station's elevation, she could not see into the other area. In front of her was a large empty cell lined with benches. To the right were seven or eight cells with two bunk beds hanging on the right side and toilets at the back. The walls were gray, like the color of her soul.

Bang.

Julie jumped as the door closed, punctuating her dilemma. The officer directed her to the last cell. Street-dressed women came to the front of their cells jeering at her and making crude remarks as she passed. Julie kept her head down. Why had they changed her and not the others? Did they expect her not to make bail?

Julie stopped behind the yellow line at the end of the row. Julie was thankful that there was no one else in the cell. Each bunk had a rolled-up mattress—if you could call it that. The officer pushed the door open.

Bang!

Julie just stood at the opened door fearing being sealed in like a coffin.

"Let's go!" Had she been trained by Williams?

Julie stepped forward as the metal door clanged shut behind her. It was all so final.

As the officer's footsteps faded, the inmates cajoled.

Bzzz.

The sound resonated between the metal bars and right through her soul. Would she ever get used to it? Would she have to?

"Now what?" Julie said aloud to no one. Julie inspected the filth of the yellow-crusted toilet at the back of the cell. At least they could put a lid on it. And that sink. How would her teeth ever feel clean? Was there a shower somewhere?

"Top or bottom?" she asked herself out loud. She paused. "I think top, thanks." She was officially losing her mind, but she didn't want to be below anyone else who might come.

She set her things on the metal wiring that formed the base of the lower bunk. She decided against placing her toiletries on the sink. She unfurled the stained mattress on the top bunk. At least they gave her a fresh pillow. She made the bed and placed her toiletries close to the wall by her pillow.

Finally done, she climbed up to lay down. The lights dimmed to a twilight setting. She closed her eyes. She was exhausted and hungry. Would she eat here or be taken to a cafeteria for meals? Was this the scope of her existence? What if she never got out? Thank God that West Virginia didn't have the death penalty. What about her baby? Did anyone care? Why was she believing the worst? She was innocent. Surely, she would be set free. Right?

CHAPTER 24

7:35 a.m.

Bang!

Julie jumped. A gruff voice said, "Sleeping beauty! Get up!"

Julie opened her eyes. Drab gray walls covered in vile graffiti surrounded her. It wasn't a dream. Early light peeked through the windows at the top of the room above the cells. Julie sat up and rubbed her neck. The lack of sleep was taking its toll. Her mouth tasted like cotton.

"Let's go!" the stout woman on the other side of the bars barked.

Julie slid off the top bunk and landed harder than she intended. Next time she would have to be more careful. Next time?

She shook her head and ran her fingers through her hair. "I need to pee. Is there a restroom where we are going?"

"What planet did you come from? Go, and hurry it up. You think I have all day, Miss America?"

Julie wriggled out of the jumpsuit and went to the bathroom. Of course, the toilet paper was likely in her toiletry kit that was on the top bunk. She bobbed to try to drip dry. She pulled her jumpsuit back up and came out of the cell and headed for the yellow lines at the door. She felt like an accomplished trained dog. How sad.

The guard behind the glass looked down and pushed a button.

Bzzz.

The sound still ripped through her soul, before echoing through the cell block. She shook it off. The door opened to the tan hallway. At least it wasn't gray.

"Third room on the right."

Julie turned into a yellow room that was barely large enough to fit the wooden picnic table in the middle where Paul Cato was seated. He stood and she rushed into his arms and held on. A flood of tears followed. Twenty-four hours ago, she would have been repulsed at the sight of him. But now, her very life was in his hands.

The officer shut the door behind them.

"Thank God you're alright." He pulled her back to look her over. "I never dreamed I'd see you like this. Orange is definitely not your color."

"I can't tell you how glad I am to see you." Julie wiped her face on her sleeves.

Paul pulled a couple of tissues from a box on the table and handed them to her. "Are you kidding? I would do anything for you. As much as Richard and I were adversaries in the courtroom, I had the utmost respect for him."

"Had?" Julie's knees gave way as she dropped to the bench seat.

Paul's face pinched as he sat across from her. "I'm sorry to have to tell you this, but it appears Richard may have been killed at the mine yesterday morning. They haven't found his body yet, so there's still hope. But here's the big caveat . . . it's all based on what Deputy Cruz heard from Hayes."

"Cruz? Are you kidding me? What does he know?"

"All he knows is what Hayes told him. I know it's third party, so I'm relaying what he said, which is that Jake shot Richard at the mine, and then there was a cave-in before Jake could determine if he was dead."

"Jake?" Julie reran the mental tapes of Jake's activities that day. "Why would Jake shoot Richard?"

"According to Hayes, Jake said it was self-defense."

"Wait. Did this whole story come from Jake? Why would he have been at the mine? I spoke to Marge and she told me Richard and Mack were meeting there."

"Jake was working for Hayes undercover to spy on Richard. But listen, we don't have time for all this right now."

Julie couldn't let him redirect her. She needed to know what was going on. "So, all of this is based on what Cruz said? Cruz hates me. This is more of Hayes's plan. They're playing me."

Paul's demeanor did not change. "I believe him. At least I believe that he's telling us the truth about what he knows. I'm not saying Richard is dead, I'm saying that I believe that is what Hayes said to him. Hayes told Cruz not to let you talk to anyone. Cruz is the one who got me in here before Hayes got to the new shift."

"But *I'm* here because of *him*."

"Yeah, I know. He admitted that. He can't fix that, but he's the reason I'm here. He pretended he was acting under Hayes's orders. He's already given a statement to the FBI and he's going to testify. He's putting it all on the line. I'm telling you, Julie. I believe him."

"FBI? If the FBI is involved, why aren't they getting me out?"

"They are working on a court order as we speak. We should have it any minute."

Julie began to weep. "Why? Why would Cruz try to help me now? *Why*?"

Paul handed her several more tissues. "He loves Heather. He called your house looking for her after you called your dad. Your dad answered. Cruz had a hard time getting your dad to talk to him. When Cruz found out that Heather had left and that your dad couldn't reach her—"

"She's missing?"

"Well. She's not answering her phone. Everyone is worried."

"She was so drunk when I saw her."

"That's what Cruz said. Said it was his fault. Said he had to help. Your dad was trying to get hold of me so Cruz drove to my house at three in the morning. He broke down at my house. Babbled like a baby about how it was his fault and how much he loves Heather. Of course, I wasn't going to talk to him, so I called your dad. He explained as much as he knew. Then Cruz told me what he knew. I called the FBI. He gave them his statement. He's the real thing."

Julie studied Paul's face. "That's all well and good, but that doesn't mean Richard is dead."

"You're right, and we won't know now, but here's what I do know. Hayes is not planning on letting you leave this jail alive."

Julie's stomach knotted. "What does that mean?"

"Hayes was framing you for Nicole's murder. But he doesn't plan on letting you get to trial because you know too much. He has everything in place to eliminate you. The magistrate is on the take so he's not going to show up. No hearing, no bail. While you're sitting in jail, Hayes has a hitman . . . Well more like a hitwoman who he's planning to use to take you out."

"What?" Julie tried to process the idea. Someone killed in a jail cell? Richard had never mentioned anything like this. There were no news reports. But would the news care or would they even find out that Hayes is in charge? "I don't believe this."

"Cruz said Hayes did this once before. People were suspicious last time, but no one dared question him. They knew better."

"Why didn't he just kill me at home or somewhere else?"

"Hayes didn't count on Mack's confession and death at the mine. He was supposed to stay in place as sheriff. At first, the mine incident seemed to play into his hand—Nicole and Richard were dead, and they could frame you for their deaths. But then when Marge called you, and you found out too much. Hayes realized you would expose him. The only thing he could do was knock you off before you talked to anyone. That's why you weren't supposed to get your one phone call. Hayes was going to take care of you before you talked."

"What am I going to do?"

"You have to stay alive any way you can until we get the court order. This is big, Julie. With what is going on here this morning with you, the FBI will be able to nail the coffin on Hayes's activities."

"Oh, so I'm the sacrificial lamb?" Julie got up and began to pace. "I don't have anyone in my cell. They put me in the last cell, out of anyone's view."

"That's not good."

Julie continued to pace as she reviewed the last twenty-four hours. "This explains why Hayes didn't push for a statement from me last night." She stopped pacing and looked at Paul. "He's planning to kill me." Julie reached for her belly. "I'm pregnant, Paul. Hayes knows that and he still wants me dead?"

Paul looked helpless. "I know." He waited a moment, then said, "Come and sit down." Julie sat across from him, still with her hand on her stomach. She had to get out for her baby's sake—for Richard's baby's sake. "We should have the court order any minute, but they may take you back before we get it."

Determination bloomed as she considered the baby. She had to get out.

"What do I have to do?" Julie asked.

"Cruz said Hayes usually uses a woman named Jones, aka Joneszilla. Cruz said you would understand the Joneszilla reference when she shows up in your cell. She's an Amazon woman. All muscles. The only ones that likely know about her are Hayes and Williams."

Julie nodded. "Williams booked me last night."

"They will process her like normal. They'll set a pre-arranged time—enough time for her to go through the normal booking process so there aren't any more loose ends than they already have. When the time comes, they'll call the guard watching the cellblock to get him away from his post." Paul looked like he wanted to cry. He continued, "We should have you out by then, but if we don't, this is what you need to do—"

The door opened. The detention officer waved Julie out. "Time's up."

Paul stood and said, "We're not done here. My client has rights."

"Not *now* she doesn't. You aren't even supposed to be here." said the glaring woman.

He looked back at Julie and nodded. Julie stood. Paul hugged Julie while he whispered, "Watch the guard. You're pregnant. Use that. Don't let them put you in there alone with her."

Julie held onto the last hug she may ever have.

"Let's go!"

Paul released her. "A lot of people are praying for you, including me."

She knew it was true, but how was that going to help her?

———

HAYES SLAMMED THE PHONE DOWN. Williams sat across his desk from him—not with her usual man-crossed legs, but feet planted on the ground. How could Williams have screwed this up? She should have known. He pounded his fist on the table and let out a string of expletives. Williams flinched but remained stoic.

He stood and began pacing. If she was a man . . . He cursed again. But he had to restrain his fury. Right now, Williams was the only true ally he had left. She had been with him through this entire hick-town ordeal and never let him down before. He forced himself to sit back down and examine her again. "How could you have let this happen?"

Williams lurched forward in her seat, like a cat ready to pounce. "How did *I* let this happen?" *Really? My* job was just to get Jones here." Williams stood and began pointing at him with each statement. "You never said anything about giving no-visitor orders. That's your job. They would look at me cross-eyed if I told them that. They were already asking why I was bringing her up there last night. How would that have looked? You're the only one who can do that. Don't give *me* your crap." Williams remained standing for a minute and then sat back down. "You're a total jerk, you know that?"

Nobody talked to Hayes like that and got away with it. But she was right. "You know a lesser man would be dead by now." Williams put her hands up in surrender and nodded. "I hate to admit it . . ." He just couldn't bring himself to say she was right. He should never have left last night. He should have given the orders himself. Was there any way to stop this runaway train? If Jonesy didn't work, it was all over. Anytime now the FBI would find out about Nicole. They would be working to get a court order. Even if the Feds didn't get him, Smitty said it was his last chance.

"So . . ." Hayes paused, still not knowing what to say. He wanted to ask her if it was time to run. But where would they go that Smitty couldn't find them? Could his run be over? He had to think. Helping him think was what Williams did best. "Where is Cruz?" he asked as calmly as he could muster.

"Nobody knows."

"How could you not know?" He said before thinking.

Williams stood as if ready to come across the desk. "How could *you* not know? You . . . you . . . you . . ." She spewed several expletives, ultimately landing on "idiot."

He held up his hand to defend himself. "Sorry. Sorry."

She gave him a look before speaking slowly. "No one has seen him since he got Cato in here. He just disappeared."

"In his car?"

"No. It's still here."

Hayes unloaded every expletive in his vocabulary. Hayes rose and started pacing again.

"They have him."

"Maybe . . . or maybe he took off to save his own skin." She steeled her look.

Hayes stopped pacing. "If he wanted to do that, why did he come back here and help the doc?"

"Are you that naïve? He fell for Heather." Williams smirked. "He wouldn't be the first man that let his sex drive blind his mission."

Williams knew too much about him. Smug wench. Hayes returned to pacing. "You have a tail on Cato?"

"Of course."

"I need to know if he does anything other than return to his office."

Williams shook her head. "He'll go to the Diner. That's his modus operandi."

"Yeah, but today I would think he'd head back to the office. This would be a big case for him. The two of them have never been friends, but Cato would love to take me on. I've been bad for his business."

"You can say that again."

"Where's Marge?"

"At her sister's. Men on the way. They should be there any minute."

"Good. No Feds?"

"Nope."

"Is she talking to anyone?"

"Not since they started surveillance."

"Good."

Hayes pinched the bridge of his nose. At least some things were going right. He let go and looked at Williams.

"What other loose ends do we have—other than Cruz and Doc?"

"Jake."

"Where is he?"

"He's at the farm, listening. Julie's father got there last night. Heather's gone. She got mad at her sister and took off. She doesn't know anything unless she talked to Cruz. But Jake talked to Sarah. She said that nobody's been able to get hold of Doc. She's out of play. At least for now."

"He's still doing his job then?"

"Yep. Good information. Then again, I don't think we have a choice but to trust him for now."

"We can deal with him later. Has anyone been to their house?"

"Nobody other than the dad and Sarah."

"Good. What does Sarah know?"

"Nothing. She left last night before Marge called. Jake's positive because he said that Doc changed when she got a phone call after Sarah left. He questioned Sarah this morning and she didn't know anything."

"Good."

"What about the dad? He talked to Doc. What do you think he knows?"

"Jake said the dad's acting like a concerned father who only knows his daughter was arrested. Doesn't matter anyway. It's all hearsay. By the time anyone gets warrants, the lab at the Gleason farm will be gone. You did call the boss to close it down, didn't you?"

"Yeah." She glowered. "I did your dirty work for you."

"How bad was it?"

"Let's just say he wasn't happy that you didn't have the guts to call yourself. You can imagine the rest."

Hayes knew the trouble he faced, but if he could pull out of this, he might live to tell the tale. "So—if we take Doc and Marge out, and, later, Jake, we're home free?"

"It's not impossible."

For the first time since he got word about Cato's visit, Hayes felt hopeful. He pulled a bottle of scotch out of his drawer, along with two bar glasses. He poured tall shots. This was either his last drink or the door to many more to come. He handed a glass to Williams and took the other. They held them up as Hayes said, "Here's to working with you. It's been a run. May it not be our last."

8:15 a.m.

Bzzz.

Julie jumped as the door swung open. Her fellow inmates cackled and mocked her, but her heart pounded louder than all the noise they could muster. Julie held her breath as she reached her cell. Still empty.

She entered her solitude. She stood at the right side next to the bars planning her moves in case the monster arrived. She could see the guard in position behind his glass barrier. How would he be able to tell if she were attacked? Surely, he would sound an alarm or something. He would be able to see her if she stood here.

She climbed up onto the top bunk and lay down. Even the ceiling had graffiti. Where had they gotten the markers?

Bzzz.

Julie climbed down and took her position. Was this it?

A young girl in orange with a food tray scuffed her shoes as she came through the opened door and slowly made her way to Julie's cell. The others called out for the girl to wait on them. Keeping her head down, the early-twenties inmate pushed the tray through a slot in the bars for Julie to take. Her name was stamped on her uniform. Vicki.

She tipped her chin up and asked, "What's yaw name?"

"Doc Wheeler."

"A doctor, you say? What kinda doctor are you?"

"I'm a veterinarian." Julie accepted the divider tray containing . . . Well, except for the apple, she wasn't sure what.

Turning her head sideways, the inmate asked, "Whatchu in for?"

"Murder." Was she really saying that?

"Ha." The inmate pushed the air away from her with her right hand. "Naw. For real?"

Julie nodded.

"You don't look like no murderer." She said slowly with no intonation. She shook her head and left, scuffing her shoes and mumbling to herself. "Now I done seen everything."

The others cajoled her as she walked back to the door. Julie called after her. "What do I do with the tray when I'm done?"

"Just set it on the bed till I comes back to get it."

Bzzz.

Julie sat on the lower bunk and stared at the tray. Jerky-like dried mystery meat and soupy scrambled eggs. The dividers kept them from running into the overcooked biscuit and an under-ripened apple. The coffee smelled good, but she wasn't supposed to have it. The juice would taste good. She bit off a piece of the meat and tried to chew it but gave up. She picked up her spork, sliced the biscuit with the handle, then rounded up some eggs, put them on the biscuit, and downed it with a juice chaser. She put the apple away for later—if there was a later.

She stood and leaned against the wall closest to the other cells listening to the chatter, but was unable to make out the words or how far away. Could she be killed here without anyone saying anything? Even with the guard's intervention?

Bzzz.

Julie took her position as an Amazonian woman dressed in street clothes stopped in the doorway and looked in her direction. This was it. The woman proceeded toward her glaring the whole way as the others called out, "Hey, Jonesy. What you doing here, man?" She was followed by a small officer who couldn't stop Jonezilla if she wanted to. The officer smirked as they came to a stop in front of the cell.

"Wheeler. Got a present for you." Time slowed as the officer rolled the cell door open. Jones was every bit of six feet. More muscles than the strongest man she knew. Her dark hair intensified the dark look in her eyes. Julie jumped when the cell door banged to its open position. Jones stepped in and stood face-to-face with Julie as if daring her to move. Julie stood her ground, hoping the inmate didn't notice her shaking knees. Julie wasn't sure if it was fear or Jones's wretched smell that caused her to tremble. The officer shoved the door back.

Bang.

The officer grinned. "You two love birds have fun." She turned and walked away. Julie remained at the front of the cell where she could see the guard.

Bzzz.

The officer exited the block. The guard was still at his post. Safe for now.

"Nice of you to make my bed for me." She knocked Julie's tray to the floor as she climbed onto the top bunk. Jones leaned against the wall. Julie was glad she took her smell with her. Where were Jones' linens? Julie picked up the tray and scooped whatever it was that spilled back onto the tray.

Bzzz.

Julie's caterer returned among the cacophony of taunts. Her face blanched when she saw Julie's cellmate. "Jonesy, when d'ya get here?"

"Just now. What of it?" Jonesy glared at the girl.

"You want some breakfast?" The inmate fidgeted with her jumpsuit.

"Yeah, but make sure it's real food. Not that stuff you brought her. I'm hungry."

The young inmate pointed to Julie's tray. Julie handed it through. Vicki turned and left.

Bzzz.

The guard was still there. How long would Julie have to stand here?

Bzzz.

The door opened. Vicki returned with a tray of fresh and appetizing food. Pointing to the tray, Jonesy said, "You! Get busy. Hand me my food."

Julie complied, thankful Jonesy didn't come near. If she was busy, maybe she'd miss whatever clue she was waiting for. Jonesy checked her watch before accepting it. A watch? How'd she get that in there?

Julie returned to her spot just as Julie left. Just before the door closed, two jail tenders entered. One pointed to the guard behind the glass, and the other cell doors opened. "Let's go, girls. You've all made bail."

"That's what I'm talkin' 'bout," one of the other inmates said as the others whooped and hollered. The others joined her as they all filed out of the holding area, leaving Julie alone with Jonesy, who continued eating her meal without a word. Julie tried to remember her self-defense class from high school. She wasn't good at it then. She'd probably just make Jonesy more violent if she tried it now.

"Hey, you." Julie looked up from her standing post. "Take this."

Julie accepted her tray trying not to look her in the eyes. She set it on the lower bunk. The waiting was interminable.

Bzzz. Julie jumped.

Vicki returned. She pointed to the tray as she averted her eyes to avoid eye contact. Julie handed the tray through without a word. Vicki took it slowly, looked up at Julie, then dropped her head and left.

Bzzz. The sound punctuated the air.

Jones jumped off the top bunk. "Move," Jones said with a taught face as she pointed to the back of the cell. Julie stepped back as Jones took Julie's place and looked toward the guard. This must be it . . . Julie's appointed time.

"Help!" Julie screamed as loud as she could. Julie moved back to the front as she waved her arms frantically through the bars. The guard looked her way. "Help! Help! My baby! I'm having cramps, please help me. I don't want to lose my baby!"

The guard hit a button on a panel and an alarm sounded. Two officers rushed through the door toward Julie. Jonesy was glaring at her. The officers looked in as Julie doubled over. "My baby! Help me!"

They opened the door and pulled Julie out of the cell, then closed death behind her. Julie turned her head to see Jonesy returning to the top bunk. Her angry expression had disappeared. Did she get paid by the hour?

The deputies took Julie to the now-closed door while the guard behind the glass picked up the phone. The clock behind him read eight forty-five. The guard shook his head, waved a hand toward Julie, then put the phone down. Still shaking his head, the guard looked at Julie, then he pushed the button.

Bzzz. The sound of safety . . . for now.

The phone call. It must have been Jonesy's signal.

The officers escorted Julie to an unstaffed nurse's station. They opened the door, flicked on the lights, and pointed to a rugged old doctor's exam table surrounded by worn gray cabinets. Rubber gloves, cotton balls, a sink. The basics. "Wait there while we get the nurse." The door closed behind her.

Julie stepped up on the foot of the table and sat on it. No hygiene paper. The officer posted outside the door blocked the small window. She closed her eyes. She was alive for the moment.

A woman about Julie's age stepped into the room wearing khaki pants, a light blue polo shirt with an official county logo, and a stethoscope. "My name is Sandy. I'm a nurse." The officer closed the door behind her as Sandy checked her clipboard. "Wheeler." She gave Julie the once-over. Julie folded over to keep up the act. "You sure don't look like your picture on the news and you sure don't look like no killer," she said as she shook her head.

"I'm not a killer. I'm a veterinarian for God's sake. I save lives. I could never hurt anyone. I'm being framed."

"Umm-hmm. First time I've heard that."

"No, really." How could anyone believe Julie could kill someone?

"Well, as I said, you don't look like no killer. News says you flew into a jealous tirade when you found out your husband was a-steppin' out on you and you gunned her down."

"It's not true . . . The only thing I did was save Nicole's poisoned dog. You have to believe me."

"Well, actually I don't." The nurse shook her head anew. She took her pulse. "My job is to patch you up and send you back so the jury can decide if you killed that girl." Sandy noted her pulse on the clipboard. "So, what's the problem?"

"I'm pregnant and I'm having awful cramps. I'm afraid I'll lose my baby."

"Umm-hmm." The nurse unwrapped the stethoscope from her neck and grabbed a blood pressure cuff and wrapped it around Julie's arm. "You say you're pregnant? You're not just saying that to get out of your cell, are you?"

"No, no. I just did the test before . . ." Julie made a circle in the air with her hands. "Before all this craziness." Julie tried to read the nurse's eyes. Was there a heart inside that stoic body? "I just got the greatest news in the world . . . that I was finally pregnant after waiting ten years. And then my world fell apart. I had given up on this baby. Ten years I waited. Ten years!"

"Umm-hmm." The nurse looked Julie over again. "So, I guess you forgot about your *greatest news.*"

"I didn't kill her!"

"What kind of cramps? Like menstrual cramps?"

Julie wasn't good at lying. "No, no. Worse than that. But I've never been pregnant before. I just don't think I should be having cramps when I'm pregnant. I'm afraid."

She took off the blood pressure cuff and made a note. "Are you cramping now?"

"Why else would I be here?"

"To get out of your cell, of course." Sandy paused. "Any bleeding?"

"I don't know."

"You need to check for me." She opened the door. "Take her to the ladies' room, then bring her back."

The officer escorted her to a restroom in the hallway. "Hurry up," he said as he pointed to the door. Julie knew she wasn't going to find anything, but she was thankful to be able to use the bathroom in private. It may be the last time. She moved as slowly as she dared.

The officer knocked on the door. "Let's go!"

"Okay, okay." She washed her hands in slow motion and dried them with a paper towel.

"Come on!"

She opened the door and was escorted back to the nurse's room.

"So?" Sandy asked.

"No bleeding."

"Well, then I guess there's nothing to do. You just need to lay down when you go back," Sandy said as she scrawled a few notes.

She couldn't go back. Maybe Julie could help the nurse see what was going on. "Listen. How long have you worked here?"

"Ten years."

"Haven't you noticed changes since Jerry Hayes came to town? Bad things are happening here. Hayes is trying to frame me to get me out of the way. My husband's the chief prosecuting attorney. He was trying to expose him. You've got to help me."

The nurse paused a moment as if considering her words. "Wow, you've got an active imagination, don't you? They say your husband is missing too. Did you kill him as well?"

"No!" Julie almost yelled. "I don't know where he is. Listen! They're going to kill me in my cell. They just put a woman named Jones in my cell. She's Hayes' henchman . . . or henchwoman. I don't know. You've got to help me!"

"Got a little paranoia going on with that cramping?" Sandy stared at Julie. "I can see what's going on. You're using your pregnancy as an excuse to plead your case. That's not what I'm here for. There's nothing wrong with you. Let them know if you find bleeding."

She opened the door. "Take her back."

"No!" Julie said. "Jones is going to kill me."

"Get a life." She shook her head. "I'm sorry. You already took one—or two—didn't you?"

"My death is on your head," Julie said as the officer escorted her back to the women's block.

"I'm not going to lose sleep," the nurse called after her.

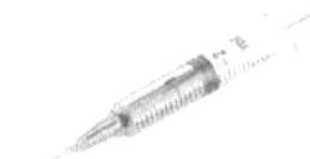

CHAPTER 26

9:30 a.m.

JULIE'S HEART BEAT WITH EACH STEP she took toward her cell. Maybe Jones wouldn't try again since she missed her chance. But Jones had been too content when she crawled back up to her perch as Julie had left.

The guard behind the glass looked up as she approached. Julie stopped at the yellow line awaiting the death knell. The guard pushed a button. The door swung toward her. She couldn't move.

"Let's go!"

Julie turned to her escort, then back to her green mile. She gritted her teeth and walked past the empty cells. Jonezilla was standing … waiting. Julie dropped her eyes to avoid contact. No need to make it personal. That might make it easier for Jonesy to hurt her—or might make it more brutal. But, then again, she had probably already crossed that line when she faked her illness.

Heart pounding, Julie stepped to the yellow line and waited for the officer to play his part in this staged death sentence. She smelled Jonesy's proximity. Sensed her scowl. Julie focused on Jonesy's feet.

"Step back!" the guard said. Jonesy didn't move. Was she waiting for Julie to look at her? "I said step back!"

Jonesy's shoes moved to Julie's self-prescribed safety zone on the right. Where was she supposed to go now? No one would see her at the back. Her bunk? Jones could suffocate her with a pillow.

"Come on, I ain't got all night!"

Did her captor know what was awaiting Julie? "Listen, now that the other cells are empty, can I move over there?"

"Does this look like the Hilton? Move!"

Julie passed through the door to the back of the cell. She could only hope to fight Jonesy off. The officer slammed the cell door closed and moved toward the glass-enclosed guard who buzzed him out. She was all alone with her murderer. Her fate was sealed.

Jonesy didn't move. "Think you're smart, don't you? I know what you did."

Julie didn't answer and didn't make eye contact.

"Well, it ain't gonna work *this* time. They should be calling the guard out any minute now."

Julie didn't move. There was nowhere to go. Would Jonesy beat her? Did she sneak in some weapon like she did her watch? Was this how her life was going to end?

Julie might be able to dodge her a few times, but if that guard wasn't in place to push the alarm, there was no hope.

Julie's legs grew weak. She shifted so they wouldn't go to sleep. Jonesy continued leaning against the wall watching toward the guard. Julie listened intently for sound. Nothing. She was on her own.

Jonesy stood erect then turned toward Julie. "Time's up."

———

HAYES SAT IN THE DOGWOOD DINER'S BACK CORNER booth with his back to the wall. He checked his smartphone. He should have heard by now. Things were either going to go very right or very wrong. The Diner was a good place to be either way. If they went right, someone at the office might catch him gloating at the news. If they went wrong, he would at least have a chance to escape.

Sally left another table and came toward his. "Done with your breakfast?

Hayes smiled. "Yep. Delicious as always." His phone lit up. Williams. "Excuse me."

"I'll be back to check on you." She took his dishes and headed toward the kitchen.

Hayes put the phone to his head. "Give me good news."

"There was a hitch, but it's been resolved," Williams said.

"What kind of hitch?"

"Somehow, Doc figured out our plan. She started screaming that she was having a miscarriage right when the guard picked up my call. He hit the alarm and the next thing I knew the siren was going off. The officers on duty took her to the nurse's station. Don't worry. Sandy was on duty. Doc started pleading, telling her that Jonesy was going to kill her. Sandy called her paranoid and sent her back. We just made the second call a few minutes ago. Sent the guard on a long mission to be sure Jonesy had enough time. I'm sure Doc's toast by now."

"You mean you don't know?"

"No. It's not like you can walk up there and ask if she's dead yet. I should hear any minute. I knew you would be stewing, so I called to update you."

Hayes cursed. "Call me back when you know it's done." Hayes hung up. Could it be true? Had he finally eluded justice? It just didn't feel right.

———

JULIE'S BODY STIFFENED as Jonesy came toward her. She grabbed Julie by the collar and shoved her between the toilet and the side wall. There was nowhere to go and no one to call. She couldn't just give up.

"Help! Help!" Julie cried out as her voice echoed in the empty cement walls.

Jonesy laughed. "No one's coming to rescue you *this* time." Jonesy pushed Julie against the wall and got in her face. Her stench alone could have suffocated Julie. "You thought you could outsmart me." She pushed Julie again. "But here you are again."

Julie looked into Jonesy's eyes. Pure evil. She tried to push her off, but Jonesy was too strong. Jonesy wrapped her massive hand around Julie's throat as she anchored Julie's flailing arms with her other arm. A gloating look came over her face as she slowly applied more pressure. "I'm getting paid well for you." She laughed. "You must be something special."

Julie tried to open her mouth wider to get air, but she couldn't breathe. She felt her eyes bulging. She struggled against Jonesy, but Julie was no match. She squeezed her eyes closed and prayed. *Dear Lord, if you get me out of this, I will be forever yours.*

Bzzz. The door. Someone was coming.

Jonesy released her clutch. Julie opened her eyes. Jonesy backed off and swore under her breath. She climbed onto the top bunk.

Julie bent over as she tried to recover her breath. She rubbed her neck and stumbled to the front of the cell. An officer and a deputy approached. What now?

"Wheeler. Let's go." The deep, bold voice came from a compact female officer. She unlocked the door that rumbled open to her temporary reprieve. Julie's legs felt like jelly, but she managed to get out of the cell.

Bang. The cell door closed off the danger behind as they moved to the yellow line and awaited the guard to open the door. She didn't dare look back at Jonesy or tell the officer what they had just interrupted. She just wanted to get out of there. "Where are we going?" Julie asked.

"Bail hearing."

Could it be? Had Paul pulled it off?

Bzzz. The door swung open. One step closer to freedom? Would she be released? Richard always said people with local businesses usually got out, but, then again, he probably wasn't talking about murder trials. She walked the corridor to the next yellow line in front of the door to the elevator.

A deputy retrieved a leather belt with chains from a nearby cabinet. Her escort stood back supervising as the deputy put the belt around Julie's waist and placed the cuffs on her ankles and wrists. Unlike her previous encounters with deputies and officers, this deputy handled her with TLC.

When the deputy was done, the officer pushed the door open and let them pass by. The deputy pushed the elevator button as the officer said, "We're all good."

"See you soon." The officer turned back through the door to the women's wing.

Despite the ankle chains, Julie maneuvered herself into the elevator. She looked away from her orange-clad image on the shiny wall. When would she get her clothes back? Maybe she wouldn't. Maybe they were taking her to finish her outside the jail. That didn't make sense though. They would have just let Jonesy finish her off unless the nurse reported what Julie told her.

The doors opened to the first floor. With each successive door, the air became fresher, but was it the air of freedom? Another deputy joined them as they exited the building and made their way across the street to the courthouse. They entered through a special door, and then an elevator to the second floor. They proceeded toward a door with a sign. JUDGE RANDOLPH. AUTHORIZED PERSONNEL ONLY.

Judge Randolph? Could it be?

———

HAYES HELD UP HIS EMPTY CUP TO signal Sally who was pouring coffee refills a few tables away. She tipped her chin and headed his way.

"Good news?"

She must have overheard him when he picked up the call. He'd better not gloat here either. She'd eventually connect the dots. Maybe starting a little rumor would serve him well.

"No. I'm worried about Mack. We haven't heard from him. It's not like him."

"He was just in here yesterday. You remember. You were here too," Sally said.

"Yeah. He came to work after breakfast and then left. Very strange. Said he wasn't feeling well."

"He was acting strange, too. Didn't seem like he was sick." Sally shook her head. "More like he was depressed or was going to die."

Seed planted. This gossip was going to make anything he came up with for Mack's disappearance all the more believable.

The bell above the door rang. Hayes looked past Sally.

Smitty stood inside the door scanning the Diner. He headed toward them. "Excuse us, Sally," Hayes said as he pointed to Smitty.

Sally's face scrunched. "Who's that?"

"An old friend."

"Well, my pot's empty anyway." Sally returned to the counter.

Hayes forced a smile and stood to shake his hand. "Smitty. Good to see you."

"Not likely." Smitty ignored Hayes' extended hand and sat. Hayes followed suit. Smitty turned toward Sally, snapped his fingers, and pointed to Hayes's cup. Sally's mouth dropped open.

Hayes smiled and made a circular movement with his hand, hoping to stave off her indignation. He was used to Smitty's ill manners, but Sally didn't deserve it. She topped off the pot and headed back.

She placed an empty cup on the table, poured Smitty a cup, and refilled Hayes'. "Anything else?" she asked without a smile.

"No, we're good," Hayes said, hoping Sally would know Smitty's bad manners weren't at his behest.

Sally gave Smitty a once-over. She frowned. "Good. I'd hate to have to spit in your food too."

"Funny," Smitty said. He waved a hand in her direction. "Now get out of here."

Sally turned on her heel and left.

"Some service," Smitty said.

Hayes knew better than to speak up for her. Hopefully, the tip would smooth things over. "You made good time," Hayes said, trying to size up Smitty's mood.

"Cut the small talk. The boss is concerned. Have you cleaned all these messes you made yet?"

"Just waiting for the all-clear now. What's the word with Marge?"

Smitty's eyes narrowed. "Don't change the subject."

Neither freezing temperatures outside nor the coolness of the Diner could stave off the sweat that formed on Hayes's brow. "Seriously, it should be done. I'm just waiting for confirmation."

"How about I wait with you?" He picked up a knife and began tapping the table. "You know this is your last chance. The boss gave me one more chance to help you clean up. I've covered for you for years. This is it."

Would they order Smitty to take out his only brother? Okay, half-brother. But still. Could Smitty do it?

Hayes's phone vibrated. A text from Williams.

Trouble. Get to the courthouse now.

Smitty's phone vibrated and he read the screen. He looked at Hayes. "Sorry." Smitty stood.

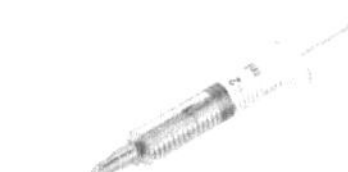

CHAPTER 27

10:00 a.m.

JULIE STOOD OUTSIDE THE COURTROOM as the only deputy who had shown her kindness unlocked and pulled away Julie's shackles. How had Julie missed the angel wings on this short redheaded deputy's lapel? The redhead handed the manacles to the other deputy who turned and left. "Thank you, Deputy . . ." Julie read her name badge.

"Trocaire." Her escort answered. "It means mercy. I'm praying for God's mercy for you."

Julie needed all the prayers she could get. "Thank you." She shook her head as she rubbed her sore wrists. "I can't believe I need it. I'm being framed."

"I believe you." Trocaire entered a code on a keypad and opened the door. "You can go in." It was good to know someone did.

Despite being married to the prosecuting attorney, Julie had never gone into a courtroom to see how everything worked. How could she have so completely ignored her husband's life? She had heard his stories, but now she was the one on trial. He would have been the one prosecuting her.

Julie froze after crossing the threshold next to the dark wood-encased jury box. The massive judge's platform was to her right. Judge Randolph was not there, but the bailiff was in place by the door to the judge's chambers.

The court reporter waved at Julie, but her eyes were sad. Julie recognized her from the office, knew she had treated her sweet rescue dog, but couldn't place the girl's name.

Another woman sat in the booth attached to the right of the judge's seat in front of where the Bailiff was standing. It had to be the judge's judicial assistant.

Paul was standing behind the nearest table to her left, talking to the people Julie held so dearly—her dad, Sarah, Angie, Doc Lawrence, and Eddie. The picture should have included Richard and Heather.

"Julie!" the small throng called to her as she entered. They were constrained from rushing toward her by the wooden rail that separated the court from the spectators. Tears overflowed from the fullness of her heart knowing she would not be alone—at least not for now. Julie rushed into her dad's arms over the rail that kept them apart. She cried.

Trocaire gently intervened. "Step back, please, and take your seats," she said as she held up her arm to separate them. The others touched Julie's hands before taking their seats. Trocaire stepped back and stood nearby against the wall.

Julie turned to Paul. "Thank you for all you have done. Jones almost got me." She pointed to her neck.

Paul turned Julie to face forward with her back to her friends. He pulled her hair back and examined her neck. He whispered, "I can't believe it. There's even a handprint." He put her hair back in place. "Don't say anything yet." Paul looked her in the eyes. "You understand?"

"She was choking me when the officers came." Julie felt her neck. "I don't even think my feet were touching the ground. One more minute and . . ." Julie couldn't even say it.

Paul put his hands on her shoulders, looked into her eyes, and said slowly. "It looks like your friends' prayers paid off."

"I was praying too." Julie couldn't believe she had just admitted that. What had she promised God?

"We might be able to use this to our advantage, can we go forward?" Julie nodded. "Okay. Try not to let anyone see for now." Julie pulled her hair to cover her neck. His eyes looked past her to the back. Julie turned.

A slight man in a mismatched blue suit entered through the rear door carrying a briefcase. The man eyed her entourage as he made his way to the other table and set his briefcase on top. The enemy. The man who would be trying to put her away. What if he succeeded?

He turned back to Paul and, with a warm smile, held out his hand. "Paul Cato?"

"That's me." Paul shook hands. Julie didn't like that Paul was being friendly with the man who was trying to put her away.

"Joshua Wright." He stepped back. "I'm afraid you have me at a disadvantage. I got a call about an hour ago and was asked to come over. I'm from Coalrock County. I was asked to cover for the missing prosecuting attorney.

Paul grinned. "Well, I always like the advantage."

"I was told this was an open and shut case. But that's what they always say, isn't it?" Wright shook his head. He looked at Julie. "May I assume this is Dr. Wheeler?"

"Yes, this my client," Paul said, turning to Julie.

Julie tucked her head as Wright reached for Julie's hand. Shake with her adversary? But then again, he was just doing what her husband did—trying to find and preserve the truth. At least that's what prosecutors were supposed to do. Right? But now she was on the side of the innocent defendant. Did Richard ever put away innocent people? Her hand responded and shook his without her consent. She pulled it back behind her defender.

Wright motioned for Paul to step closer and said in a low voice, "What's going on that a judge is presiding over a bail hearing? Where's the magistrate?"

Paul leaned in to whisper making it impossible for Julie to hear the answer. After a moment, Paul stepped back as Wright nodded and said, "I guess we'll find out then. Thanks."

Wright turned back to his table, opened his briefcase, and removed a single file folder and a yellow legal pad. He set his briefcase on the floor and took his seat. He began to make notes on the pad.

"Have a seat," Paul said as he pointed to her chair. This was it. Paul had already laid out his folders. The top page of his legal pad only contained the date. A pen was ready to fill it, but Julie was uneasy about the blank pages. Was Paul ready for this?

While the courtroom was well-lit, the lack of windows, the dark wood paneling, the worn furniture, and the industrial gray and maroon carpeting oppressed her soul. Courtrooms were supposed to expose the light of truth. Would the light of the truth shine forth here? Julie leaned toward Paul and whispered. "What are we waiting for?"

"The judge. They have their own timetables."

Julie looked around to see who else was there to witness her moment of shame. Two men dressed in dark suits, white shirts, and ties entered through the back doors, scanned the courtroom, and sat flanking the doors they had just entered. Julie nudged Paul. He turned.

A moment later, Hayes opened the door and held it for Mrs. Russell and for Williams who was carrying a box—likely holding the "evidence" they had trumped up against her. Hayes directed Mrs. Russell to a chair on their side. Mrs. Russell averted her eyes.

Julie elbowed Paul, who turned toward the action. Hayes glared at Julie as he headed for Wright. The three of them huddled and talked in voices too low to hear. Wright nodded as Hayes spoke and pointed to the contents of the box and then toward Mrs. Russell. Williams kept an eye on Julie. Julie pulled her neck in like a turtle protecting itself from another attack.

Paul turned Julie back forward. "I can't believe Mrs. Russell is here. That's bad, isn't it?" Julie said.

"Stop worrying," Paul said softly and patted her hand.

The bailiff disappeared through the judge's door then returned and said, "All cell phones off, the judge is about to enter." The judge's door opened again as the bailiff's voice boomed, "All rise!"

Everyone stood. Silence fell over the courtroom. The judge entered and took his position. Would he remember Julie from the part the judge played the day Julie met Richard in this courthouse? "You may be seated."

The soft whoosh of the spectators taking their seats affirmed the courtroom compliance. Silence followed as the judge scanned his courtroom and settled his papers. The court reporter's fingers hovered over her steno machine awaiting the words she would record.

The judge looked at Julie with a sad smile. "Well, Dr. Wheeler, I didn't think I'd ever see you in county orange."

Julie shrank. "Me, neither, Your Honor."

"We are here in the case of the State of West Virginia versus Julia Wheeler. Would everyone please state their names for the record, starting with the prosecution?"

The attorneys announced their names and representations.

"Dr. Wheeler, the court is faced with an unusual situation. In most instances, you would appear in front of a magistrate and have a different path to my courtroom. However, the magistrate seems to have taken leave for some yet-to-be-determined reason." The judge glanced at Hayes. "Your attorney contacted me this morning to conduct this emergency special hearing. He presented some evidence *in camera*, which is a fancy way of saying outside the public eye." He paused for a moment. "Based upon his assertions and the evidence presented, I was convinced of the emergency nature of this situation and agreed to preside over this rather unorthodox hearing. We will hear probable cause from the prosecution and refuting evidence from the defense." He looked at Mr. Wright. "I'm anticipating an objection from you, Mr. Wright."

"Yes, sir. I was just respecting Your Honor's explanation." He stood and said, "Your Honor. The state objects to this special hearing on the basis that we have not been afforded the time to review the evidence and interview the arresting officer. I do not work in this jurisdiction and have only been called in an hour ago. I have been unable to locate the arresting officer, Deputy Cruz. I have only just spoken to Assistant Sheriff Hayes and reviewed the evidence, and have not even had time to speak to the witness for the prosecution. I fear the state will be handicapped. The state, therefore, requests a continuance."

"Gentlemen, in my chambers."

The two attorneys nodded and joined the judge, who left through his chamber's door.

Richard had told Julie many going-into-chambers stories. She hoped Paul was as good as Richard was. Julie turned in her seat away from Hayes to her entourage. She could feel his stare. Angie reached for Julie, but the deputy motioned her back.

"What do you think they're doing in there?" Eddie asked.

"Paul's a-tearing that fella to shreds, that's what's happening," Angie said.

Her dad's face showed what must have been a long night rallying her troops. "I'm sure Paul's got it all handled. That judge seems like a reasonable man."

"He's more than that," Julie said.

"Do you know him?" her dad asked.

Julie puffed a "ha." She gazed at the door she had come through as if it were a door in time. She kept her voice low so Hayes wouldn't hear. "That's the funny thing. I never really did know him." She looked at Angie. "Do you remember when I met Richard?"

"Yeah. Wasn't it the day you went to get your business license here at the courthouse?" A knowing grin crept across her face. "Didn't you refuse to talk to Richard?"

Julie nodded. "Richard was in the business office when I came in. He came to try to woo me. I explained that we had not been properly introduced, so he told me to wait right there, that he'd be right back.

"Well, you know me. I finished my business and started for the back door. Richard came running down the staircase with Judge Randolph. He had gotten him out of a hearing." Julie grinned at the memory. "He asked Judge Randolph to introduce us and vouch for him.

"That's Richard," Angie said. "A case of love at first sight if there ever was one."

Yeah. Love at first sight. That's what Richard had always said. Julie had felt the same but never admitted it to Richard. Now she'd never be able to.

CHAPTER 28

10:15 a.m.

Julie's dad pointed forward. "They're back."

Julie's heart pounded. She turned as the bailiff emerged from chambers and said, "All rise." The judge entered. He motioned, and said, "Stay seated." Mr. Wright was expressionless and looked at no one on his way to his seat. Paul patted Julie's hand when he took his seat. He whispered, "All good."

Was everything good? She still saw no light.

"I have heard the prosecution's objection and we have met in chambers. The defense has proffered statements which it will now have the burden of proving with evidence. For the moment, I am overruling the objection. However, if the defense does not prove its position, I will sustain a second objection from the prosecution on this matter. Overruled for the moment."

The judge looked at Julie and spoke softly. "Dr. Wheeler, the purpose of this hearing is to decide whether or not you should be bound over for trial. If the court finds that you should, then we will discuss bail." He smiled at Julie, then looked hard at the prosecutor, raised his voice to a boom, and said, "And, Mr. Wright, if at any time you feel that you wish to drop charges, feel free to speak up."

"Duly noted," Wright said, his Adam's apple displaying his gulp.

The judge turned back to Julie. "Dr. Wheeler, please rise."

Paul and Julie stood.

"Dr. Wheeler. You have been accused of the crime of the murder of Nicole Marley. An affidavit has been filed by the sheriff's office describing the evidence to support their case and the facts and circumstances as they see them. Have you had a chance to review these charges?"

Paul answered. "Yes, we have, your honor."

The judge watched Julie as he said, "You have the right to retain counsel …"

Julie's out-of-body feeling returned. She tried to focus on the words, but her mind would not clear.

"… You have the right … You are not required …"

Julie forced herself to focus.

"You have the right to a preliminary examination, which we are doing today. If the court deems there is sufficient evidence to hold you over, then the court can set bail. If there is not sufficient probable cause, then the charges will be dismissed. A dismissal does not preclude the state from instituting a subsequent charge for the same offense. Do you understand these rights as I have explained them?"

Julie said, "I do," even though she had not heard them. It's not like she could ask him to repeat them or she could stop this by saying no.

"Mr. Wright?" the judge said. "Your opening?"

The prosecutor looked back at Hayes who put his hand to his face and squeezed the bridge of his nose. Wright stood with his pad and a bag, then moved to the oak podium centered in front of the tables. He took a deep breath. "Your honor, the state's case is based upon certain evidence which would put Dr. Wheeler at the scene of the crime, both because she was there when the arresting officer arrived and because the deceased was holding the defendant's necklace in her hand." He held up the bag containing Julie's necklace.

How could something so precious be used in such an evil way?

"Her motive was jealousy. The deceased, Ms. Marley, worked with the defendant's husband late into the night at the deceased's house. Several witnesses have testified that when Dr. Wheeler learned of the deceased's apparent affair with the defendant's husband—who I might mention is still missing. She began what witnesses describe as a jealous tirade. We will call Mrs. Russell as a witness who saw the defendant at Ms. Marley's house under suspicious circumstances earlier in the day. Dr. Wheeler had the motive, the murder weapon, and the opportunity. This is the evidence that the state currently has, which we believe is irrefutable."

He was right. The evidence was irrefutable. She would convict if she was the judge. But what about the setup? Could Paul show that? Julie knew better than to react, but every ounce of her wanted to stand and scream, *"Liar. It's all a lie!"*

Wright turned toward Julie, then back to the judge. "Further, your honor, the prosecution is concerned that a double homicide may have occurred. Dr. Wheeler should be held over for trial without bail." He turned toward Julie again, shook his head, and then returned to his seat. Hayes nodded his assent.

"Mr. Cato?"

Paul rose but did not go to the podium. "Your honor, my client is innocent of these charges. We will prove that she was framed by a corrupt sheriff's office." Paul turned and looked at Hayes and Williams, who glared at him. "My client would be put in mortal danger if she is returned to this county's jail. My client was at her office at the time of the murder yesterday morning. She was treating the decedent's German shepherd, a dog that had been poisoned earlier in the morning. She's not a killer, she's a saint." Paul sat.

"Mr. Wright, are you ready to proceed?"

"Yes, your honor." Wright picked up his legal pad and went to the podium. "The prosecution calls Assistant Sheriff Gerald Hayes."

Hayes stood, straightened his tie, and went to the witness stand. He sat back in the stand with an air of confidence until he saw the two men in suits at the rear of the courtroom. He looked at Williams and motioned to her with his eyes. Williams turned toward them and then turned back forward. She hunched down in her chair.

The judge swore him in and Hayes stated his name and position for the record, all the while staring at the back of the courtroom. Wright said, "Tell us the circumstances that made you seek an arrest warrant."

Hayes leaned forward and fidgeted with his tie. "I received a report from Mrs. Russell and Deputy Cruz that Dr. Wheeler had been seen trying to enter Ms. Marley's home in the morning. That afternoon, I received reports that Dr. Wheeler was causing disturbances at the Dogwood Diner. In fact, I believe that even Mr. Cato witnessed her outburst." Hayes smirked at Paul. That couldn't help Julie's case, but Paul didn't flinch.

"Later I received reports from courthouse employees that Dr. Wheeler was ranting about people knowing of her husband's affair but not telling her. Later that night, Dr. Wheeler was found by Ms. Marley's vehicle at the old Hendricks' mine. Inside the vehicle, we found Ms. Marley's body. She was holding Dr. Wheeler's necklace in her hand. We also found the murder weapon—a gun."

Wright retrieved pictures from the box. "May I approach the witness?"

"Go ahead," the judge said.

Wright moved back and forth from the evidence box to Hayes and asked him to identify and explain the evidence, including pictures of the crime scene, Nicole's body, the necklace, and the gun.

"Assistant Sheriff Hayes, is there any doubt that the defendant killed Ms. Marley?"

"No sir, it's clear. Dr. Wheeler discovered her husband's affair and killed Ms. Marley."

"I have nothing further." Wright sat down.

Paul, without a notepad, stood, buttoned his jacket, and went to the podium. "Good morning, Mr. Hayes. Can you tell the court who was the arresting officer?"

"Deputy Tom Cruz."

"Did Deputy Cruz arrest her on your orders?"

"Yes."

"Have you ever disciplined or had any reason to discipline Deputy Cruz?"

"No. Although . . ." Hayes looked at Williams. "Never mind. No, he's new and he's made mistakes, but nothing serious."

"Do you believe that he handled the evidence properly and maintained the chain of custody?"

"Yes."

"Where is Deputy Cruz now?"

"I don't know. I didn't have a chance to call him in as I just got called to this hearing within the hour."

"Can you tell me where Sheriff McConnell is?"

"Objection." Mr. Wright stood." The location of Sheriff McConnell is irrelevant to this case."

Looking at the judge, Paul said, "Your honor, we will tie this in if you will give us just a few questions."

"Overruled. The witness may proceed."

Hayes looked to the back and then back at Paul. "No, we have been unable to locate him since yesterday morning when I saw him at the office. He left early complaining that he felt sick."

"Has anyone reported his whereabouts?"

"No."

"Do you know the Wheeler's farmhand, Jake Johnson?"

"Yes. In a small town, you know just about everyone." He nodded and smiled at the judge.

"Was Mr. Johnson in your employ?"

Wright rose. "Your honor. I renew my objection."

"Your honor, I am laying the foundation. Just a few more questions. I promise," Paul said.

"Mr. Cato. I'm about to agree with the prosecutor, but I will give you just a little more leeway. Overruled. You may answer the question."

"No, Mr. Johnson is neither a deputy nor a civil servant."

"Didn't Mr. Johnson report Ms. Marley's death to you?"

"How could he?"

"That's a question; I get to ask the questions."

Hayes glared at Paul.

"Did Mr. Johnson report Ms. Marley's death to you?"

"No."

"Did you get any phone calls from Mr. Johnson yesterday?"

"No."

"Did Mr. Johnson not call you yesterday and report the circumstances under which Sheriff McConnell, Richard Wheeler, and Nicole Marley were shot yesterday?"

Hayes glared. He looked at the back of the room, then back at Williams, who shook her head slowly.

"Well, maybe I got a phone call from someone, but they wouldn't say who they were. We sent out a cruiser, but there wasn't anything to the story."

"Where is Richard Wheeler?"

The prosecutor jumped up, thumping the table as he did. "Objection—Mr. Cato is attempting to distract the court from the evidence. These questions are unrelated to this hearing."

"Your honor. All these facts are related to the veracity of this witness's testimony. If you will allow it, I will tie it all up in another minute."

"Overruled. The witness is directed to answer the question. I'd like to know where Mr. Wheeler is."

"We don't know."

"Did you hire Mr. Johnson to report to you on the activities of Mr. Wheeler?"

Hayes glared at Paul and shifted in his chair. "No."

Paul turned and motioned to the two men at the back of the courtroom. The man on the left rose and opened the door. In walked Deputy Cruz, escorted by Jake wearing a dark suit that matched the two other men, with Dog on a leash. Dog began a low growl as they got close to Williams. They took a seat two rows back from Julie's entourage.

What were Jake and Cruz doing together—and with Dog?

The judge pointed to Dog. "Can you tell me why a dog has just entered my courtroom?"

Jake stood. "Sir, this dog is an FBI agent. He's been involved in this case."

FBI? What did the FBI have to do with her?

"Don't tell me he's going to testify," the judge said, shaking his head.

"He has before," Jake said. He grinned and sat back down.

"And who are you?" the judge asked.

Jake stood and said, "I'm Max Enders, a special agent with the FBI." He returned to his seat.

Julie's mind raced to put the pieces together. Nothing made sense.

The judge pointed to Paul. "Please continue."

Paul turned back to Hayes who was pinching the bridge of his nose. He dropped his hand and sat up. "Do you recognize the two men who just entered the courtroom?"

Hayes's face tightened. He sat back in his seat and glared.

"Answer the question!" Judge Randolph leaned toward Hayes.

Hayes turned to the judge. "I am invoking my fifth amendment rights."

"You waived those rights when you took the stand," the judge said. "You do not have the right to pick and choose what questions you answer. Answer the question!"

Hayes's face reddened as he stared at Jake.

"I'll rephrase," Paul said. "Isn't it true that Mr. Enders, known to you as Jake Johnson, reported to you that he had shot Nicole Marley at the mine yesterday?"

Hayes scowled at Jake but did not answer.

"Answer the question!" the judge said, his face reddening.

Hayes turned to the judge and glared.

"Since you are not answering the questions," the judge said, "You are in contempt of court. I am going to defer my contempt ruling until I hear from Deputy Cruz, who I am *sure* the prosecutor is going to call since he was the arresting officer."

Wright stood, wide-eyed. "Yes sir. That was my plan."

The judge looked back at Hayes. "Please step down and return to where you were sitting until I decide what to do with you." He swatted his hand as if waving him off.

Paul sat and patted Julie on the hand. Julie was still trying to figure out Jake's—or Max's part in all this. She whispered, "I don't understand. Max, an FBI agent?" Julie reviewed the events of the last day—Jake outside the barn in the early hours, at the Diner, all over town, at the house . . . it just didn't make sense.

Paul whispered, "You haven't heard the best part."

Wright took the podium without his notes. "The state calls Deputy Cruz."

Cruz stood, looked down at Max, took a deep breath, stepped around him and Dog, then walked to the witness stand. The judge swore him in.

Wright looked back at Hayes, then at Cruz. "Were you the arresting officer for Dr. Wheeler?"

"Yes."

Wright returned to his table for his legal pad. "Is it your belief that Dr. Wheeler killed Nicole Marley?"

"No. I'm sure she didn't."

Wright's mouth dropped open. He looked at his pad, then at the judge.

The judge said, "Just so we have a clear record here, I would like to have some answers. Are you saying that Dr. Wheeler was falsely arrested?"

"Yes, sir. That is what I am saying."

"And how did you come to that conclusion?"

"Mr. Jake Johnson confessed to me that he shot Nicole Marley yesterday morning at approximately 9:35 a.m. But even without his confession, I have personal knowledge that Dr. Wheeler could not have killed Nicole Marley. I saw her at her veterinary office at the time of death, which was mid-morning yesterday. She was resuscitating Ms. Marley's dog from the poison that I was ordered by Assistant Sheriff Hayes to leave in the dog's kennel that morning."

Looking at Julie, he said, "I didn't give him the whole thing. I couldn't." His eyes pleaded.

Julie nodded. There was some glimmer of good in him.

Cruz continued. "Hayes wanted to send a message to Ms. Marley by poisoning her dog. Ms. Marley was also an undercover FBI agent. But she turned bad when she got caught up in a romantic relationship with Hayes. She was giving him intel on the FBI's movements. They must have gotten suspicious when their ops became ineffective. That's when Agent Enders came. When Ms. Marely caught Hayes with another woman, Hayes got worried that she was going to do something stupid. So, he told me to poison the dog to send a message."

The judge looked at Hayes, then back at Cruz. "So, who do you believe shot Nicole Marley?"

"Agent Enders. In the line of duty."

"What about the physical evidence that the state brought against Dr. Wheeler?"

"Agent Enders turned those items over to Hayes at Hayes' request. Agent Enders had the gun from the crime scene and got the necklace from Dr. Wheeler earlier in the day."

How had he done that? Julie reached for her aching neck.

"Agent Enders, can you confirm this?"

Max rose and nodded. "Yes sir."

"What about Richard Wheeler and Sheriff McConnell?"

Max pointed to the men at the back. One opened the door, and in walked Richard, perfectly fine and healthy.

"Richard, you're alive!" Julie started toward him but Paul held her back.

Angie gasped, and blurted out, "Thank you, Jesus!"

The judge knocked his gavel. "Order in the court." Everyone settled as Richard came to the end of the row next to Jake and remained standing. Richard's eyes remained locked on Julie. Julie ached to hold him. To love him.

"Your honor," Jake said, "you can see that Mr. Wheeler is alive and well. Sheriff McConnell is healing from a gunshot inflicted by Nicole Marley at the mine. The sheriff was confessing to a crime when Ms. Marley showed up and shot him. I was sure Mr. Wheeler would have been next as part of her cover-up. I shot her to protect Mr. Wheeler."

"Mr. Wheeler, is this true?"

Richard stood straighter and said, "Yes, your honor. He saved my life."

"Mr. Richard Wheeler and Agent Enders, hold up your right hands." They complied. "Do you swear or affirm that the testimony that you have just offered is the truth, the whole truth, so help you, God?"

Both men agreed and the judge had them state their names and positions for the record and then had them sit. Judge Randolph said, "Mr. Wright, would you like to withdraw the charges against Dr. Wheeler."

Wright stood straight. "Yes, sir, the state withdraws our charges."

"Agent Enders, in deference to your department, I have withheld my adjudication of Assistant Sheriff Hayes. Will you be taking him into custody?"

"We will, your honor."

The two men opened the door at the back and four more men in suits entered and went to Hayes. One touched his shoulder, but he pulled away, and then rose defiantly. The same agent read Hayes his charges and cuffed him. As they did, Hayes turned back to Max and said, "This is not over." The agent with the cuffs grabbed Hayes's arm and two of the agents led him out.

The agent then looked at Deputy Williams and said, "Ma'am, please step out." She glared at them then rose. The agent read her charges, cuffed her, and led her out.

Did this mean she was Julie free to go?

"Dr. Wheeler."

Julie turned to face the judge as Paul said, "Your honor. May we bring to the court's attention that Dr. Wheeler was assaulted in her cell this morning before being brought here." Paul turned and gently pulled

Julie's hair back for the judge to see. Everyone gasped. Richard rushed to Julie and looked at her neck. "Jonesy?"

"Order!" The judge knocked his gavel. "Is this true?" the judge asked.

Julie nodded, tears forming in her eyes as she relived the feeling of Jonesy's hands on her neck.

Richard did not retreat, but stayed by Julie's side, holding her under his right arm. Her fear dissolved.

"Who did this to you?"

"I only know her as Jones or Jonesy. If you hadn't called for me when you did, I wouldn't be here now." Julie nuzzled into Richard's arms, feeling safe for the first time since she left his side a day earlier.

The judge's eyes softened, then his face tightened as he looked at the bailiff, then at Max. "Dr. Wheeler, part of the reason I agreed to this hearing is that there was a belief you were in mortal danger. I was not convinced that was possible until now. No one would believe how deeply our justice system could have been poisoned by these criminals. I don't know what to say. It's not enough to say that the state of West Virginia apologizes for the pain that you have suffered at the hands of those who were hired to protect you. Please know that your pain will go a long way in helping to rid our community of the cancer that has taken over."

He looked back at Max. "Is this Jonesy woman in custody?"

"Yes, sir," Max said.

"Dr. Wheeler, I hope you will get that checked out. Mr. Wheeler, I am charging you with the responsibility of taking care of this woman."

Richard squeezed Julie. "I will, your honor."

"All charges are dismissed. You are free to go. Court is adjourned." The judge pounded his gavel.

The bailiff's voice boomed. "All rise!"

Everyone erupted in cheers as the judge left through his chambers' door. Her friends came to her side, hugging and loving on her. Mrs. Russell hung her head and slipped out the back. Richard held onto Julie and said, "We need to take you to the ER to get that neck checked out . . . after all, you're carrying our baby." He patted her stomach.

Tears slipped down Julie's cheeks. "I wanted to be the one to tell you."

"I know, Babe. It doesn't matter. All that matters is that you and our baby are safe." Come on. Your fan club can come by the house later."

Angie stepped forward and said, "You're not leaving this room before I get a big ol' hug." She wrapped her arms around Julie then pulled away and put her hands on her hips. "I told you your man was a good egg. And I told you God was watching out for you. When are you going to learn to listen to me?" Everyone laughed. "And besides, I think you two don't need a bunch of folks around when you get home. Julie's dad can stay with my dad, right?" Angie said as she looked at Doc Lawrence.

Doc Lawrence said, "You betcha. I want to hear all about life as a big city vet." He grinned. "And speaking of vets, I'd say the two of us had better get to the office and do some vetting to cover for our lovebirds."

Angie said, "I'd say we all have places to be so you two can get moving."

Sarah said, "I'll head to the house and get everything ready for when you get home. And then I'll scoot out."

Julie asked, "No word from Heather?"

Sarah's dimples disappeared. "No. Sorry. I'm sure she'll show up soon. She always does."

Angie said, "Okay folks, to your stations." Julie's entourage disbursed. Jake and Cruz had disappeared. She needed to be right with both Jake and Cruz . . . and thank both of them. Cruz's confession would put him away for a long time.

Richard touched her shoulder, and she turned to him. He scooped her up in his arms and twirled her around. He set her down and looked deeply into her eyes. "I'm so sorry about all this. I should have told you about my undercover work, but they said I had to keep it quiet. Said you would be safer if you didn't know. None of this should have happened."

The power of his presence overwhelmed her. He was so much more than she had ever known. "I can't believe you're here. You're alive, Richard! I thought you were dead!" She put her head on his shoulder, never wanting to leave. Richard held her for a long moment, then said, "Come on, Mama. Let's get you out of here."

They walked out. Wright was saying goodbye to Paul. Richard approached Paul and said, "I cannot thank you enough." He held out his hand and they shook.

"Being a part of cleaning up this town is thanks enough. Now you need to get that little lady to the doctor . . . well, maybe after you get her out of that orange."

"I don't know, I kinda like it," Richard said. Julie punched his side. "Come on." He wrapped Julie in the safety of his arms again. He guided her from the courthouse and the nightmare.

11:45 a.m.

MAX WAS LEANING BACK AGAINST THE WALL outside the courtroom as Julie and Richard approached the top of the staircase. The suit masked the cowboy Julie had come to expect—and distrust. A broad smile emerged as he pushed off the wall and walked to meet them. There was nothing different about his smile. It had always looked sincere. But now Julie was sure good intentions were behind it.

"I'll bet you're ready for this day to be over," Max said. She and Richard paused to speak with him. Several employees emerged from their offices, looked in their direction, and held hands in front of their mouths as they talked to each other. Julie tucked herself into Richard's arms, ashamed.

"Jake—or whatever your name is," Julie smiled from behind her bangs. "I'm so sorry—"

"Max. The name is Max Enders." He held out his hand, and they shook. "And, no, you're not allowed to be sorry. We let *you* down. We should not have let it get that far in the jailhouse. Unfortunately, the red tape at headquarters got messed up and we had bad intel on your status there. But it's not an excuse. I hope you know that your pain will go a long way to give teeth to the charges against Hayes and his crew."

"What about Cruz?" Julie asked.

"He's in custody. We turned him over to the U.S. Marshals for transport to a safe place. I'm sure he'll get some leniency, but, even so, he'll be in jail for a while. He saved your life, you know. We would have thought you'd be safe in jail if he hadn't told us about Jonesy."

Richard held out his hand, which Max reciprocated.

"Well, I don't want to be rude," Richard said as he winked and tipped his head in Julie's direction, "but I need to get this little lady to the hospital."

"I agree, but . . ." Max directed Richard's attention to the clucking tongues. "Ladies?" The women scattered back to their offices. "I've been assigned to tag along."

Julie looked at Richard.

Tag along?" Richard asked.

"Yep, unless you want a different agent. We believe you're safe, but . . ." Max checked around them again "… our agents noticed a person of interest in town with Hayes. He goes by Smitty. They're not ready to arrest him. The case against him is still too circumstantial. But he's a very dangerous man. We thought he would leave town when Hayes was arrested and head back to Detroit so they could lick their wounds and regroup. But he gave our agents the slip, and we don't know where he is."

"You believe Julie's in danger?" Richard asked.

Julie held onto him more tightly.

"Dr. Wheeler is an unlikely target. Except for her testimony against Jones, she's no threat. Jones should be expendable to them. Anything else Dr. Wheeler knows is hearsay, and not admissible.

"You, on the other hand, witnessed a lot, but nothing direct against Hayes. The only thing you witnessed was Nicole getting shot by me, and her shooting Mack. With Nicole gone, you have no other direct knowledge. Getting rid of Nicole was the best thing for them. They were planning to get rid of her all along—and you for that matter— and to frame Dr. Wheeler." Max looked at Julie. "That's why Cruz was getting you all worked up. He was supposed to set you up for a jealousy motive."

Julie felt her face flush.

Max turned back to Richard. "Your knowledge is hearsay and circumstantial. Like I said, it's unlikely that he would do anything now, but we have to be sure."

Julie's knees weakened. "I don't understand. This isn't over?" She looked at Richard and then into Max's eyes.

Max frowned. "No, I'm afraid not. The organization that Richard helped us infiltrate isn't going to take kindly to what's just happened here. There are a lot of ways this could play out. And there is one more concern. Mr. Smith is Hayes's half-brother. He has a history of protecting his little brother. We just want to be sure you are both safe." Max looked at Richard. "You knew this was part of the deal."

Richard nodded and looked into Julie's eyes—his own sad. Julie had seen that helpless look only a handful of times before. Her hero was helpless. Every word Max uttered rang true and carried with it a weight that Julie wished Richard had not taken on. But Richard's call to duty ran deep. She did not doubt that he knew what he was getting into when he agreed to help the FBI rid Hearthstone of this evil.

But what did this mean for their lives?

Julie took a deep breath and stood tall. "Okay. We're in this together. I'm by your side." She looked into Richard's eyes, then turned to Max and pointed to the door. "Max. Lead on."

"One more thing," Max said as he moved on the top step and turned to face them. One corner of his lips rose. "I hope you like publicity. Your paparazzi awaits."

"What?" Her newfound resolve disappeared. "What do you mean paparazzi?"

"Your story is quite the news. Let's just say it's not only the Hearthstone Herald out there."

Julie was exhausted, bruised, and just wanted to hide. She looked down at her orange attire. And what did her hair look like? "No one can see me like this." Julie swept her hand down over her jailhouse getup.

Max squeezed his face. "I know. We have a couple of agents who will go with us. I'll take your right side and Richard your left. Just tuck your head and keep walking when we get out there." Max turned without waiting for Julie to respond.

"Come on, honey," Richard said. "We'll get through this together. You may even set the fashion trend. You'll be the most popular vet in town."

"Very funny. I'm—"

"—The only vet in town." Richard chuckled.

She elbowed him as he nudged her to follow Max down the stairs.

"I think you should consider orange uniforms at the office. And what about this—change the name of the clinic to Jailhouse Veterinary?"

Julie elbowed him again.

"Think of it. Your slogan could be, 'It would be criminal to go anywhere else.'"

"Not funny," Julie said in a sing-song voice. At least Richard had not lost his sense of humor even after the worst day of their lives. How long would they live under this cloud? Was their child going to be born into this mess?

———

Two agents were waiting at the exit. They opened the door and led them into the mass of reporters covering the scene. Even the television stations from Charleston had managed to get their news vans there. How had they made it in such a short time?

Julie looked down and huddled behind the two agents in front as the lights flashed and the mob hurled questions at her. Most were not discernable, but one question reached into her huddle.

"Dr. Wheeler, how did it feel to know you took the drug cartel head-on?"

Drug cartel? Is that what they were dealing with? In Hearthstone? The cartel was after Richard? Was it after her?

Julie kept her head down until they reached the sheriff's building and entered the hallway that led to the offices. She turned to Max. "The *cartel?*" She looked at Richard. "The *cartel?* You agreed to take on the *cartel?* What does this mean, Richard? What does it mean?"

His helpless look reappeared. "First, it's not the cartel. That's just a news reporter trying to hype his story. Secondly, what else could I do? I didn't know it was a drug organization when it started. It was just little things … things that were off. Changes in the sheriff's office. Prosecutions down. I had to call in the FBI. What else could I do? Turn my back on it? Let them set up shop here?"

"Yes. That's exactly what you should have done!" Julie pounded Richard's chest with her fists.

He pulled her to himself and squeezed her as she melted into sobs. She had thought her crying was over. Richard just held her as she did. He was right. What else could he do? But would they ever be free? Ever be safe? Would they be looking over their shoulders for the rest of their lives? This sacrifice was too great.

An agent came through the door and pardoned himself as he passed them in the corridor. Julie put her head down so he wouldn't see her meltdown state. She turned to Max once he'd passed.

"How bad is this?"

Max looked her directly in the eyes. "I want to tell you this will all go away, but it won't. At least not until the trial. I promise to explain everything, but I think the best thing we can do now is to get your stuff and get you checked out at the hospital, then get you home. We have agents watching your house. Like I said before, it's highly unlikely that there's any imminent danger, but we want to be safe. We can talk about your next steps at the house."

"Okay." Julie looked to Richard who nodded. "I think I'm ready."

They walked down the corridor in the direction of the elevator. The sheriff's office was a full-scale war room. Dark-suited men carried boxes of papers out the door. Williams was in the conference room being interrogated. Had it only been a few hours ago that she was intimidating Julie?

They went to the elevator and to the second floor where Deputy Trocaire was waiting. She took one look at the men and said, "I'm sorry. You can't go with her. This is the women's area."

"I'm Agent Enders with the FBI." He flashed his badge to the deputy who nodded her approval. "Dr. Wheeler is in protective custody. Please clear the area of any women if that's the problem. I will be escorting her throughout her time here."

"Good. And, no, we don't have any women in the area at the moment." Trocaire turned and looked at Julie with soulful eyes. "I'm glad you're getting out of here. This is an awful place. I hope what you went through will be worth it to get this place cleaned up." A sad smile crossed her face. She nodded toward Max and Richard. "It looks like you're in good hands here."

Julie had thought so until the word *cartel* was tossed out there. She forced a smile. "Let's hope so."

The deputy led Julie and Max to the changing room, leaving Richard behind. The separation from Richard spooked her. She had been in constant physical proximity since they hugged in the courtroom. Max checked to be sure no one was lurking in the room, then nodded for Julie and the deputy to enter while he stepped back. The deputy handed Julie her clothes. She pointed to the counter. "Just leave your designer orange over there." The deputy closed the door behind her.

Julie hurried out of the orange, never so happy to put on a pair of jeans. Restoration slowly came as she slipped on her turtleneck blouse. *Ouch!* Her neck. At least the turtleneck would cover the bruising.

Knock. Knock.

Julie cracked the door open, despite being fully dressed. The deputy was holding several clear envelopes.

"Mom's necklace!" Julie accepted her treasures, closed the door, and set the bags on the counter. She restored the necklace to its rightful spot and patted the pendant. *Oh, Mom. What am I going to do?* Tears seeped from her eyes.

Richard entered and she melted into his arms, weeping. "The deputy said I'd better come to get you or we'd never get you to stop crying." Was it just the hormones? He held her until she collected herself.

He put his hands on her shoulders and held her back, looking into her eyes. "Come on, Babe. Let's get out of here."

She turned back to the contents of the bag. Her cellphone was almost dead. It didn't matter. The only person she wanted to talk to was standing by her side. She held up the bag with her wedding ring. Richard removed it and slipped it on her finger.

"Still want me?"

"More than ever," she said.

A smile grew across his face.

Max stepped in. "You guys ready to go?"

Richard guided Julie out of the room and back to the elevator. She almost stopped at the yellow line but forced herself to move past it. Trocaire pushed the button for them. "May God protect you and your baby."

God. Why would God have saved her from death only to be the cartel's target?

Julie said her obligatory thanks for the prayer and entered the elevator.

As they exited to the first floor, Julie caught a glimpse of Hayes in his office, being interrogated by two agents. He glared at her as she walked by. Her stomach knotted.

"This way," Max said, as they headed for the front door. Julie pulled back at the sight of several men wearing deputy jackets, ball caps, and sunglasses. Touching her elbow, Max said, "It's okay. They're our agents dressed to be decoys for you. You'll see."

They continued to the doors where agents handed them the same garb. Julie, Richard, and Max put their ensembles on as four waiting agents went out to a waiting dark SUV, got in, and left.

"We're going to give them a five-minute head start. It might distract people from you."

Julie snuggled into Richard's arms, then looked at Max. "Why is Hayes still here?"

"They have to transport him safely. We're waiting for more marshals to arrive. After all that went wrong here under his direction, the drug ring will likely want to eliminate him. Unfortunately, eliminating him would eliminate any possible threat to you or Richard—and me, for that matter."

Julie had not considered Max's position. He was an eyewitness to it all.

"So, you're saying that my prayer should be that the drug ring gets to Hayes so we can be free?" Julie asked.

Max frowned. Julie regretted saying it as soon as the words departed her lips. "If they get him, all the work we did here for two years will have been in vain. We need him alive."

Julie knew she should care about the work, but right now she just wanted her life back.

Another SUV drove up. Max said, "Ready?"

Julie pulled the bill of her cap down and said, "As ready as I'll ever be."

Max pointed to the vehicle and said, "Richard, you come to the other side of the vehicle with me. Dr. Wheeler, you enter where the agent is standing by the vehicle on this side."

Richard and Julie nodded. They hurried to the SUV. Max got in the front passenger seat as Julie and Richard followed their orders. Dog was in a kennel in the back end. He began whining and wagging his tail as the doors closed behind them.

"Dog!" Julie said as she and Richard turned to pet him through the wire fence. "How's he doing?" she asked.

"He's great," Max said.

They traveled the back streets of the town. Julie looked back at Dog, then at Richard. "Have you met Dog?"

Richard's face pinched.

"Oh, of course you have."

"He was the only good thing about the job . . . and the only good thing about Nicole. He's a great dog. Reminds me of—"

"—Shep," they said simultaneously.

"He's yours if you want him," Max said. "The agency will release him from service. He's been through enough and is ready to be retired."

Julie looked at Richard, doing her best "please daddy" face. "What do you think?"

"Is there anything to think about? Of course, we'll take him."

Julie hugged Richard, then looked at Dog and said, "Did you hear that? You're going to stay with us."

Dog wagged his tail harder as the driver made his way through the town toward the hospital. Richard turned and looked out the back window.

"Don't worry, Richard," Max said. "We've got things under control."

"That's what you said about Julie in the jailhouse," Richard answered with uncharacteristic sharpness.

3:00 p.m.

JULIE SNUGGLED IN RICHARD'S ARMS in the back seat of the SUV after being checked out at the hospital. Finally, going home. Since her mother's death, Julie had avoided hospitals. But today was different. The news had been good. The baby was fine and so was her neck. She'd have some soreness, but she would also have Richard. And Dog.

She had managed a few cat naps while awaiting tests at the hospital. Richard nodded off several times on the ride home. What a wild thirty-six hours they had all had. With her dad and Doc Lawrence covering for her, she could rest for a few days, especially after Angie had shown up at the hospital and confiscated Julie's cell phone. Always the mom.

Dog's tail banged against the side of his crate. Julie opened her eyes and sat up to take in the scene. A dark SUV was parked outside their house.

"Where's my truck?"

"How do you think the dads are going to be able to cover for you? Richard said. "They promised to take good care of your baby—so I can take care of mine."

Was her practice safe in their hands? Did it matter? With a baby on the way, she was going to need their help. She had to let go. It was worth it. And when was the last time she'd had Richard all to herself?

They stopped in front of the house. The driver got out and opened Julie's door. Max released Dog from his kennel. He came to Julie first. She knelt and took in the unmistakable love that only a dog could heap on its owner.

Max said, "Yep, looks like he's home."

Richard joined Julie as they loved on Dog together. Then they both stood and surveyed their home. "Are you ready?" Richard asked.

"Ready for what?" Julie said.

"I just put that ring on your finger. Now, I need to carry you across the threshold."

"Oh, Richard! Forever the romantic. How could I have ever—"

Richard put his index finger to her lips. "Never. We will never speak of this again. I know that you love me, and you know that I love you. From this day forward, until death do us part."

Julie kissed his finger, and then his face. "Okay. But if it's okay with you, I've had enough *death* talk for a while."

Richard guided her to the front door. An agent inside opened it before they could. Richard picked up Julie and carried her past the agent to the sofa, which still had the memory boxes next to it. How perfect. They could relish their love and look forward to their new lives as parents. And create new dreams.

Richard knelt beside her. "I'm going to spoil you rotten, my love." Julie closed her eyes as he kissed her deeply.

Julie opened her eyes as Richard straightened himself. Her man was a glorious vision. Dog sat by the coffee table taking it all in. The scent of pastry cooking made her stomach growl.

"Okay, lovebirds," a familiar voice interrupted.

Julie sat up and turned to see Sarah coming through the dining room with a tray holding two glasses, an ice bag, and a towel. Richard took a seat by Julie. Sarah smirked and said, "You know, these guys almost shot me when I came in."

One of the two agents in the front hallway called out, "We did not."

Sarah winked as she set the drinks on coasters and then handed the ice bag and towel to Julie and pointed to her neck while scrunching her face.

Julie applied the ice pack to her bruises.

"I know I told you I was going to leave before you got home so you two could be alone, but . . ." Max walked into the living room. Sarah pointed to him. "Case in point—you're going to have company anyway. I thought the least I could do was serve you—and these guys—some food before heading out." Sarah turned back to the kitchen and said as she walked away, "I don't think they're here to protect you anyway. They've already been eating you out of house and home."

The same agent from the hallway called out in a sing-song voice, "We have not."

"Is that smell what I think it is?" Julie called out over her shoulder toward the kitchen.

Sarah came back through the kitchen door. "Your favorite … cherry pie and homemade vanilla ice cream."

"You are *truly* my best friend."

"I know," Sarah said as she turned and went back through the swinging door to the kitchen.

Max took a seat in the armchair across from the sofa and looked at them. "As you can see . . ."

Sarah returned with a drink for Max. He stood as she entered. Always the gentleman.

"Thank you, Sarah."

"Anything for *you*." She turned and winked again at Julie and started back to the kitchen. Was her winker on overdrive today? Julie hadn't seen Sarah this giddy since high school. "Oh, and by the way, those boys ate all the leftover fried chicken and coca-cola cake, so I'm making another batch."

"We did not."

Richard's grin stretched across his face. "Coca-Cola cake?"

"But of course," Sarah answered in a French accent as she pushed her way through the door once again.

Max cleared his throat and said, "Okay now—"

Sarah returned with a dish of fruit. "Gotta take care of the little one now." She handed the dish to Julie with a fork and a napkin. "Either of you gentlemen need anything?"

Richard's eyes grew big as he eyed the cut-up melon, strawberries, blueberries, and banana. He pointed to Julie's dish and said, "I'll take one of those."

"Me too," Max said.

Sarah nodded and headed back to her domain. "When would you like dinner?" she called back.

Julie checked her watch. 3:20. "What about your kids? Don't you need to get home to them?"

Sarah shook her head. "Nope. Carol's getting them. I've got all night."

"Well then, if it's okay with you, I'd like to get a nap and then eat. But I'm hungry, so I'd like to eat early. Does five o'clock work for you?" she asked Richard.

"Perfect."

"Five it is." Sarah curtseyed playfully and left again.

They all chuckled.

Max called after her. "Anything else before I be—"

Sarah returned with their fruit, delivering a plate to each one, then curtseyed to the group and returned to the kitchen. Dog cocked his head as everyone dug into their fruit.

Max watched the kitchen door. "Worried she's not done?" Richard asked.

Max nodded. "You noticed." Max stood. "Might as well let Dog take care of his business before we get started so he doesn't interrupt." He patted his upper thigh. "Let's go, boy."

Dog followed Max out of the room to the front hallway, then Max returned alone a moment later and took a seat. Julie leaned into Richard's arms. He stroked her hair.

"Okay, now that everyone is settled, let's talk about the plan." Max turned toward the hallway. "Gentlemen?" He said in a raised voice. The two agents from the hallway came in. "These are agents Mitchell and Romero. They will be stationed outside."

Julie nodded to the agents, even as she struggled to keep her eyelids from closing. Hopefully, Richard was taking it all in. Her plan was to stay at Richard's side every moment.

Max continued. "I'll be in my place in the barn for now. As soon as we find Mr. Smith, then the agents can stand down."

"And then we can have our house back? All to ourselves?" Julie asked.

"That's the plan. If there're no other questions . . ." Max stood. "I'm headed back to my barn for some overdue sleep. I'll see you tomorrow."

"Hold up," Richard said. He tenderly leaned Julie away from him toward the pillow on her right and stood to shake Max's hand. "Thanks for all you've done."

"No, thank *you*, Richard. You are truly a hero. Not too many men would have stepped up like you did. I'm a better person for having known you."

Max withdrew his hand and headed toward the kitchen through the dining room. Richard returned to sit by Julie's side and pulled her back into his arms. She moved the ice bag and covered it with the towel.

"That's cold," he said.

Julie knew she should head up to bed …

"Julie?"

Julie felt a nudge. She opened her eyes. Sarah was standing over them where they had fallen asleep on the couch.

Julie grumbled. "What's wrong?"

"Nothing's wrong," Sarah whispered. "You said you wanted a nap. Why don't you and Richard's head upstairs so you can get a proper nap, and you won't get that neck thing you get." Sarah's face squinted. "Especially with that." Sarah pointed to the bruise on Julie's neck.

Julie sat up and handed the ice pack to Sarah. What time was it? The clock on the mantle read quarter to four. Dog was sitting upright waiting for a cue.

Julie nudged Richard. "Come on, sleeping beauty. Let's go upstairs."

"Hmm?" Richard opened one eye and looked around. "Whew, we must have dozed off. What time is it?"

"Three forty-five," Sarah said.

"Could you wake us for dinner?" Richard asked.

"You betcha. Now go on."

Julie stood and pulled Richard up. Dog stood, ready for adventure. Still holding Richard's hand, Julie said, "Let's go."

"Now that's an offer I can't refuse."

They headed upstairs and fell on the bed without taking down the covers. Dog took his place by the armchair.

The sights and smells of the jailhouse began to play with her senses. "I think I'm going to take a shower."

"Ummhmm." Richard began to snore.

Julie was so tired . . .

———

5:12 p.m.

Dog growled. Julie had been sound asleep. She reached for Richard. He wasn't there. She sat up and surveyed the room. The door was cracked open. It was dark—the sun must have set. The fried chicken aroma reminded her she needed to eat. The red numbers on the bedside stand declared it was 5:12. It wasn't like Sarah to let her sleep past a wake-up time. But, then again, Julie didn't have to be anywhere, so did it matter?

Dog snarled again. Julie's stomach knotted.

"What is it, Dog?"

He faced the cracked bedroom door, lip curled.

Julie called out, "Richard?"

No answer.

Julie stood and crossed to the bedroom door. She listened. It was quiet. She pulled the door open and went to the top of the stairs overlooking the downstairs entryway. No lights had been turned on in the living room. Only a dim light cast in the front hallway from the kitchen. The front door was cracked open.

Grrr.

"Richard?"

No answer.

"Sarah?"

No answer.

She looked in Heather's bedroom. No one.

Was this a dream? Julie reran every scary movie in her mind. Bad guys and demons. She was on her own. She would have the element of surprise if she went down the back staircase to the kitchen. She trod lightly on each step, wishing she knew where all the creaks were like she did when she was a kid trying to sneak out at night. Dog matched her step for step.

Creak. Creak.

Julie peeked under the bottom of the second-floor wall into the kitchen. Steam rose from pots on the stovetop. The cake and pie were on racks cooling on the island. The fried chicken was ready to be served. Had aliens abducted her loved ones? Or maybe it was the rapture and she had been left behind.

She came down the rest of the stairs into the kitchen. She checked out the back window. No one.

With Dog by her side, she entered the dining room, ensuring the swinging door did not swing. The front door creaked. Julie moved back to the corner behind the buffet so she couldn't be seen. The door shut. Julie dropped to a squat by Dog. The music from the shower scene in the Hitchcock movie *Psycho* playing in her mind froze her. Had Smitty come to finish them off?

"Okay, I'll go upstairs and awaken my bride," Richard said from the front hallway. Footsteps went down the hallway to the kitchen, and a softer set made its way up the carpeted staircase.

Julie looked at Dog and whispered, "I won't tell them how silly you were if you don't tell on me." She stood—knees still weak. Dog cocked his head and wagged his tail. "Don't look at me. You're the one growling."

Julie went into the living room and called to Richard. "I'm down here." She continued to the base of the staircase and paused to collect her thoughts. She knew she needed a shower, but that scene from *Psycho* was still haunting her. Sarah came into the hallway as Richard appeared at the head of the staircase.

"There you are. Everything okay?"

"Yes, I'm fine." She looked at Dog to ensure his complicity in their cover-up.

"I'll start your shower for you."

"I'll put the chicken in the oven to keep it warm," Sarah said. "Take your time." She winked.

Winking again?

Sarah called Dog. "Come on, boy. I have your dinner ready." Dog followed. His tail acknowledging his love for her.

The fear of the movie was overtaken by the fear of the germs she'd been in contact with at the jail. "How about you take a shower with me?" Julie said as she headed up the staircase where Richard waited.

"Another offer I can't refuse? They just keep coming." He put his arm around her as she made it to the top step and escorted her to the bedroom.

"What were you doing outside?"

He chuckled. "You know Sarah. She wanted to feed the agents. I just tagged along to chat."

Richard walked Julie to the bathroom and looked in the mirror. "*Oooh*. I could use a shave." He removed his shirt.

Whew! That view never stopped taking her breath away. Julie came up behind him and wrapped her arms around him. He turned in her arms to kiss her deeply.

Whew indeed.

She pulled back. "Later."

"I like the sound of that," Richard said as he began to lather up. Julie slipped out of her day's troubles in the bedroom, placing her clothes on the bed. Putting them in the hamper could wait. She needed to see Richard. He eyed her in the mirror and stopped his lathering. "How am I supposed to concentrate on my shaving? I'm holding a dangerous weapon here."

Julie laughed.

Richard turned when she passed from his mirror view, eyes following her to the shower.

She stopped at the entrance to turn for a side view. "Pretty soon my profile won't look like this." She paused long enough for Richard to consider the image and then quickly retreated behind the shower wall before his passion could not be constrained.

The warmth of the water enveloped her and dislodged the grime of the day, sending it far, far away, down the drain.

Richard began humming "As Time Goes By," a hint of the night they would have later. Julie found herself swaying to the tune and singing a lyric or two. In the midst of this romantic prelude, questions about Richard's operations began to invade her thoughts. When had he noticed the oddities going on around him? What was it like working with the FBI … with Nicole? How did Max play into all this?

"Hon?" Julie said.

"Yeah?"

Julie peeked around the shower wall as Richard swiped troughs through his shaving cream. "Do you think it would be okay if we invited Max to dinner? I have a thousand questions about what's been going on. I know it's supposed to be a romantic dinner, but—"

"Don't worry," Richard said, stopping to look at her. "That's fine. Although I'm not sure he's going to appreciate the wake-up call." He returned to his task, sweeping another stroke through the cream. "But I do have a few questions myself. I'll text and see if he wants to come up."

"Thanks, hon." Julie retreated behind the wall.

Richard continued the *Casablanca* courtship. He ran the water and said, "All done here. I'll see you downstairs."

She finished scrubbing away prison life, then stood in the cocoon of warm water. She rubbed her belly, considering her child and the belly button she would soon lose.

She wanted to stay until the warm water gave out, but she hated the shock. She emerged from the shower a contented new woman and mother.

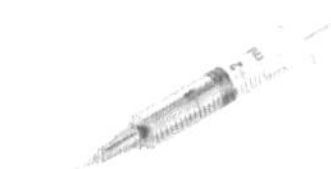

CHAPTER 31

6:10 p.m.

THE BLUES AND PURPLES on her neck were deepening with intensity—as was the soreness. Julie feared it would affect her postponed romantic evening later. For both of them. Men were visual, after all, and she sure couldn't wear a turtleneck to bed.

Her closet was her ally. She chose Richard's favorite—a midnight-blue cashmere sweater that was sure to keep him close by. She slipped on some black jeans cut to fit her every curve. At least for another month, maybe two. Satisfied with her reflection, she pulled her pendant out from under her sweater.

How had Max gotten this away from her? Then she remembered him rescuing her by the roadside when she had been to Nicole's. That was right before she discovered it missing. She'd have to remember to ask him how he did it.

Even though she had not seen Nicole's dead body, the picture of her necklace in Nicole's hand made her shiver. She wanted the image to go away, but it didn't. Would she ever be able to look at the pendant as a loving remembrance of her mother again?

Julie tucked it back into her blouse. She wanted no reminders of her day. But she wouldn't want to be reminded later, either. She pulled it back out and unhooked it from her neck. She carefully placed it in her jewelry box on the shelf. "I do love you, Mama, but I have to try to forget this day." She lowered the lid to her treasure box and went down the stairs.

Laughter from the kitchen welcomed the evening. She peeked out the window to the right of the door to see the two agents minding the house. She turned and followed the sounds of joy to the kitchen.

Dog was curled up on the dinette rug. Richard and Max were seated at the island telling college frat stories. Had they gone to the same college? They talked as if they had attended together, but Richard was Max's senior by more than a decade.

Sarah was leaning against the counter opposite them listening. She took one look at Julie, shook her head, and said, "Boys." She forced herself upright and began to pull the pan of chicken from the oven.

"You ready, hon?"

"You'll never know how ready I am. It all smells so wonderful. In fact, can we skip dinner and get right to the cherry pie?"

"Eh, eh, eh. We'll have none of that. Gotta take care of the baby," Sarah said.

Julie looked at her friend, who had always been by her side. Maybe it was the events of the day, but Julie saw her for the whole care package that made Sarah, Sarah. The need for a hug moved Julie to open arms and hug her friend. "You'll never know how much your friendship means to me." Tears again.

Sarah returned Julie's hug, but then pulled away. "It's the hormones. You'll get over that crying thing pretty soon . . . and then you'll see me for who I really am."

Richard said, "Hey, what about me?"

Julie laughed and went to his side. "You too. But Sarah will always be first in my heart."

"You're just saying that because I made you a cherry pie," Sarah said.

"Probably," Julie said. "We'll know more after I've devoured it." Everyone chuckled.

Richard stood. "Shall we?" He pointed to the swinging door. Sarah opened it for them all to pass, including Dog. Max took over door duty. How had Julie misjudged him?

Sarah pointed to the living room. "Dog, you've had your dinner. Go lie down." He hung his head, moped to the living room, and curled up on the Oriental rug. At least Nicole had trained him not to beg.

Sarah had already set the table for three. Shame washed over Julie. "Sarah, you should join us." She never would have in the past, but today, it just seemed like she should be there.

Sarah shook her head. "No. I've got rugrats at home who think Dad is too swell. Two nights in a row is asking for disaster. If it's okay with you, I'm going to get your food plated and get out of here. I'll clean up in the morning. Besides, I think you guys are going to talk super-sensitive secret-agent stuff, and I left my decoder ring at home." She held up her right hand for all to see.

Julie nodded. Sarah was right about their conversation, but she felt bad that her best friend didn't feel like she belonged. That was the trouble with hiring your friends to work for you. But it was also the best part. You got to hang out a lot more.

"I guess you're right. But tomorrow, I want to spend some time together."

"That would be great. We'll do lunch?"

Julie looked to Richard, who was taking his position at the head of the table. "That's fine with me. I need to check in at the office for a couple of hours. But you have to promise not to go by the clinic."

"That's a deal. I really need a break. I didn't realize how much," Julie said, nodding.

Sarah returned to the kitchen. Richard stood at his chair and pointed to his right for Max to sit.

Max shook his head. "Do you mind if I sit on the other side? LEO's are trained to sit with our backs to the wall."

Richard nodded. "I get that." He looked at Julie. "Do you mind being deposed to the other side?"

After the attack earlier that day, Julie didn't know if she wanted her back to the front windows, but with the agents right outside, what did she have to be worried about? She smiled. "No. It's fine."

They all sat. Sarah returned with plates of favorite foods and some not-so-favorites. "What's this?" Julie said, pointing to some greens.

"It's called spinach."

"I know that, but what's it doing on my plate? Tonight was supposed to be food I love. What about you, Max?" Julie said as she tipped her plate toward Max.

"Don't look at me," Max said, holding up his hands.

Julie looked back at Sarah.

"Do you know how much iron you need for your baby?" Sarah asked.

"Yes, and I do believe they make a pill for that."

"Natural is better," Sarah said in a sing-song voice.

Julie looked around the table for some backup, but both men were nodding in agreement. "Okay, spinach it is."

"I cut the pie and cake and plated them. They're all ready to go. I heated water so you could have some decaf tea. Is there anything else?"

"Sarah," Richard said, "You have outdone yourself. Everything looks perfect. Thanks for staying to take care of us. Especially my bride."

"She may be your bride, but she's my best friend. You boys had better take care of her."

"We will," they said in unison.

Sarah left through the swinging door, then returned. "Music— you need music." She held up the smart speaker device that had a cute name that Julie could never remember. "How about Elton John?"

"Sounds good," everyone agreed.

Sarah called the device by name. "Play Elton John.

Julie was still spooked by a device that could carry on a conversation, although Julie often found that smart devices were not so smart. Part of her hoped it would get smarter, and part of her worried about the devices taking over the world. Definitely too many sci-fi movies.

"That's perfect," Richard said.

"Okay, then. I'm outta here." Sarah looked around the table. "You sure there's nothing else?"

"What else could there be?" Richard asked. "This is a feast."

Everyone said goodbyes again and Sarah returned to the kitchen. The clanking of pots and pans—a hallmark of her OCD—ensued. Gotta have everything in its place. She was never done.

Oohs and ahs accompanied the ritual filling of their plates. The sights and sounds of sitting around a dining room table brought back images of family time growing up. Julie's mom had always insisted that everyone eat together—and she always ensured a blessing was said in the most meaningful ways. Sometimes they went around the table and said something they were thankful for. Mom always thanked God for their blessings. Should she ask that they pray? That would be simple enough. But what would Richard and Mack think? Maybe later.

They all dug in, grateful for Sarah instead.

———

JULIE DEVOURED EVERY CRISPY MORSEL of her drumstick and thigh. Of course, the white meat was healthier, but the flavor of the dark— who could argue?

Richard and Max were back on their fraternity stories.

Julie had a million questions, but Richard was enjoying reliving his college days. It was good to see both of them laughing after such an intense couple of days. Julie still couldn't believe that Max was a good guy, but here he was, across from her in her dining room.

"I hate to break up this frat love-fest," Julie said as she finished her thigh, "but can you guys tell me what's been going on around here?"

Max and Richard exchanged serious glances. The joviality ended as abruptly as a head-on collision.

Max finished his bite of chicken, wiped his hands. "I'm not at liberty to tell you everything, but after what you've been through—"

"Let me tell her what started it all," Richard said, putting down his fork.

Julie held up a finger, then pointed to the swinging door. Richard nodded. Things had gotten too quiet in the kitchen, and Sarah had not announced her departure. She was good for at least three goodbyes before she got out the door.

"Sarah?" Julie called.

Sarah cracked the door, looking like the proverbial kid with a hand in the cookie jar. "Yes?" She wrinkled her face. "Did you need something else?"

Max yielded a knowing grin but didn't turn for Sarah to see.

Julie smiled. "Yes. Would it be too much to ask you to take Dog out for a walk?"

Dog's head popped up. "Come on, boy," Sarah said as she pushed the door wider for the tail-wagger to pass. He had likely already figured out that he only had to cross the kitchen threshold and treats would abound. Sarah let the swinging door shut behind them. They waited for the kitchen door to shut.

"Sorry," Julie said to Max. "Always the curious one."

"Curious?" Richard said. "She's a downright snoop. She knows more about this house and our lives than I do. The good thing is that she's not a gossip."

Max chuckled as Richard started to explain what he had noticed going on in town. Julie had heard much of this before. She interrupted him. "Hon, how about I tell you what I know and you can fill in the blanks."

"Good idea," Richard said.

"Okay." Julie looked toward the swinging door again. No Sarah yet, but it would only be a couple of minutes. "You know what? Why don't I go powder my nose before I start? I don't want to be interrupted if you know what I mean."

"Sounds good," Richard said as he chuckled. The men returned to their college days.

Julie went through the living room and stopped at the door to check that the agents were still in place. All was quiet. After using the restroom, she went into the kitchen and looked out the back window. Where was Sarah? Just then, she emerged from the barn with Dog.

She must have gone to see Jubilee. Satisfied, Julie returned through the swinging door to take her seat in the dining room.

The barn reminded her of Max's talents. "You've sure been handy around here. I know they didn't train you to be a farmhand at the FBI Academy."

Max shook his head. "You're right about that." He laughed. "I never thought I would be cleaning horse stalls again."

"Again?" Julie asked as something shifted in the kitchen. She hadn't heard the door open. "Sarah?"

There was no answer. It must have been her imagination. It was probably something in the music. Julie rose and turned the music off. "Do you guys mind? I want to hear every word."

"You know you can just say her name and 'off' and she will stop," Max said.

Julie nodded. "I know, I know. It's just creepy." Julie returned to her seat, knocking her fork off her plate. Richard bent down to pick it up as a loud shot, followed by breaking glass, sounded.

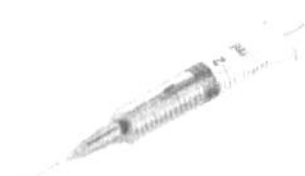

CHAPTER 32

7:00 p.m.

Max's eyes widened as he looked toward the living room. "Get down! Get down!"

He dropped to a stoop as he pulled his gun and scanned the room. Julie got to her knees and headed for the same corner she had huddled in earlier. She couldn't tell where the gunfire had come from. She didn't know which way to go.

Richard came to her side and covered her. "You okay?"

"I think so."

Two more shots rang out as the antique mirror above the buffet exploded into shards of glass.

"Kitchen!" Max shouted.

All three scrambled through the door keeping low to the ground. Once in the kitchen, Max stood, keeping his back to the wall between the dining room and hall doors, gun pointed up by his shoulder. He motioned with his head for them to get behind the island. Richard and Julie scrambled to the other side. Julie huddled with Richard, shaking. They could not see what was going on. The back door opened.

"Run, Sarah!" Julie yelled.

Two more shots.

Max fell to the ground on his back, blood covering his shoulder. The shooter came around the island and pointed his gun at them.

"Grrrrr!" Dog raced in from the open back door toward the shooter and leaped at him.

Bang!

Dog fell to the ground just as two shots rang out from the hallway. The armed man dropped to the ground. He appeared dead. Was this Smitty? Were there others?

The agents entered the room, guns drawn, checking for other shooters. "Clear!" One of the agents looked at them and asked, "You all right?"

Julie looked at Richard and then back at the agent. "I think so." Richard helped her up. Max moaned as he held his blood-saturated right shoulder. Dog was lifeless.

The agents checked Max, Dog, and the shooter. One said, "It's Smitty, all right." The other agent said, "the dog is breathing." He called on his radio. "Two agents down. One man dead. Send paramedics and the medical examiner. Also, get a chopper to recon for other shooters." One of the agents said, "We've got to check the perimeter. Can you handle the triage, Doc?"

Despite Julie's trembling legs and exhaustion, she said "Yes, go ahead." The agents left out the back door.

Julie checked the wound to Max's shoulder, then said "You're going to be fine. Looks like it missed any major arteries. Richard, help me get him up in a chair, get a cloth on the wound, and keep pressure on it. He's going to be fine."

She moved to Dog.

Sarah came in. "The agents told me what happened. What can I do?"

"Help me with Dog. Let's get him to the kitchen table. Then get some towels."

Sarah and Julie lifted the broken hero to the table. With his weakened state from the poisoning, Julie was concerned about his ability to fight through this. Attacked twice in two days.

Please, God, if you're there, keep this poor soul alive.

"Towels," Julie said as she examined their hero's body. Sarah handed Julie some kitchen towels to put pressure on the wound. "Boil some water in the microwave. Get gauze and bandages. Lots of them. And some rubbing alcohol. Hurry!"

"How much water?" Sarah asked.

Julie scanned the kitchen. "Use that microwave dish in the drain rack," Julie said as she examined the wound. He also had a clean shot through his shoulder. He would likely be fine, but he had lost a lot of blood. Sarah returned with the supplies just as the microwave dinged.

Julie pulled Dog's fur back to expose the bullet hole. "He's lost a lot of blood. But it looks clean." Dog raised his head weakly. Sarah rubbed his head. Dog put his head back down. "Hold on, fellow. You can't die. You saved our lives."

"Hold this here," Julie said to Richard so she could retrieve a knife from the cabinet and sterilize it in the boiling water, then with alcohol. Dog whined as she poured alcohol on the dog's skin and removed the bullet. Then she cleaned and dressed the wound, finishing just as other FBI agents, state troopers, and paramedics arrived with two gurneys.

The first paramedics through the door went to Max, who was now sitting up on a chair holding towels over his arm and watching the action. They began to assess his wounds.

The second pair looked around the room. "Where's the other agent?" the blond-headed paramedic said.

"Right here," Julie said, pointing to Dog.

The paramedic looked at her. "That's a dog."

Richard puffed. "That's not just any dog. He's an FBI agent, and he saved our lives."

"That's not a problem for you, is it?" Julie asked.

The two looked at each other. The blond said, "FBI dog? Hero? I'm in."

"I need a saline IV started for him and a ride to my vet clinic. We can take over from there," Julie said.

The bald paramedic nodded at Julie. "I think we can handle that."

They moved Dog to the gurney. Julie hooked up the IV, and the paramedics wheeled Dog out. They shooed away everyone who approached. "This is an FBI agent. Clear a path."

Julie looked at Sarah. "Can you go with them outside? I need to call Angie, and she took my cell phone."

"I wouldn't miss it."

Julie stopped at the hallway phone and dialed Angie at home. Richard walked up behind her, hugged her, and said, "Max's going to be okay. I'm going to go check on Dog."

Julie nodded as Angie answered.

"Doc? What are you doing calling? You're supposed to be a-restin' in your lover's arms."

"Angie, if I told you about my night you wouldn't believe it."

"What happened?"

"I can't talk right now, but I promise to tell you every detail when I see you. Right now, I need for you to get hold of our dads and ask them to meet us at the clinic right away. Dog was shot. He took a bullet that was intended for Richard."

"A *bullet*?"

"Yes. He's a hero." Julie choked up as she said it, realizing just then the full impact of her words.

"I removed the bullet. I conned the paramedics to hook him up to an IV and bring him to the clinic in their truck. He is an FBI agent, after all."

"*What?* That's crazy. I can't believe this," Angie said.

"Listen. We have to go. I'm so tired I can hardly see straight. I need our dads—at least one of them—to be sure I got it all." Julie started to cry thinking about what Dog had been through. "He's been such a hero. He's gotta make it."

"Don't you worry, baby girl. I'm a'comin' too. I'm going to start praying right now."

Julie hung up as they wheeled Max out of the kitchen. She followed them out the front door to the paramedic trucks. Richard joined her.

"You don't look the worst for wear," she said as they loaded Max in the back.

"Well, at least we know where Smitty is. Now you can be rid of me." Max smiled, then winced as the worker locked in the gurney.

"I'm not sure we want to be rid of you. Ready for a career change?" Julie asked.

"I might be after this."

The paramedics closed the doors and drove off.

Julie and Richard headed to the other truck.

"Can you drive to the clinic so I can ride with Dog?" Julie asked Richard.

"Good idea," Richard said as Julie climbed into the paramedic's truck.

A helicopter flew over, shining a spotlight all around. The noise was intense, making her home feel like a war zone. A *war zone*?

"Richard, the windows. We can't leave the house like this." Sarah was answering an FBI agent's questions. Julie looked at Richard. "Would you work it out with Sarah, or call someone?"

"I'll handle it. You just take care of my hero." He blew her a kiss as they closed the door to the most wonderful sight in her life—her husband, alive. How differently this night could have turned out if Dog had not intervened.

Dog looked up at her. She patted his head. She looked at the paramedic across from her and asked, "Are you a praying man?"

"In this business, you have to be."

After all this, Julie should have been. But . . .

"How's he doing?" The paramedic asked.

"I'm pretty sure he's going to be okay. I'm concerned because he was poisoned yesterday, so his ability to fight infection is depressed."

"Who would poison this beautiful animal?"

"Who indeed?" Julie thought back to Cruz and his confession. Cruz had saved her life, but it was hard to believe.

"So what's his prognosis?"

"We'll know more after we get some x-rays. He's in a lot of pain. He needs pain medicine." They discussed what drugs they carried on the truck. Julie calculated the dosage based on his weight. The paramedic administered it through his IV.

He disposed of the syringe and then looked back at Julie, this time focusing on her neck. "What's up with that?"

Julie reached for her turtleneck and pulled it up. "Can you see that?" The bruising must have been spreading. "That was from the first attempt on my life this morning."

"First?"

"You wouldn't believe it if I told you."

"Oh, you have no idea what I see day in and day out riding in the back of this truck. At least you guys smell good."

Julie considered his comment and then said, "You know, before today, I thought we lived in a sweet little town with virtually no crime.

The paramedic shook his head.

"And it's not that I didn't hear stories from my husband. He's the prosecuting attorney here. I guess I've been living in a bubble taking care of man's best friends and other animals that love our souls. We even get the occasional abused animal—which I will never understand—but I had no idea we had such a corruption problem.

"It's not just drugs, but drugs are rampant. We had three heroin overdoses last week, not to mention several gunfights. But even those were drug-related. At the rate things are going, no one will be left to kill themselves or each other."

"It's that bad?" Julie asked.

"And then some," he said, shaking his head. "It's nice to be transporting a hero for a change."

Hero. Julie was married to one who was saved by one. She was blessed indeed.

The truck stopped. The back doors of the truck opened. Her dad and Doc Lawrence stood beside the back door to the clinic with Angie behind them.

Her dad said, "Come on, honey. Update us on his condition so we can take over." With his help, Julie climbed out of the truck. Doc Lawrence followed the gurney into the clinic.

They brought Dog into the surgery room, the place where he had started his adventure with Julie. Eddie was waiting. The paramedics slid Dog onto the table and hung his IV on the rack that was in place. Julie gave the elder vets a rundown of what she had done as they put on their surgical gowns and masks. Julie updated her dad on the poisoning as they examined her work. They cleaned up the wound and added a couple of sutures. They bandaged the wound and checked the rest of his body. There did not appear to be any other damage.

"He's one lucky dog," her dad said.

"No," Julie said, "He's a hero."

Richard peered through the surgery room door.

"Okay," Doc Lawrence said. "I think we can take it from here. I'll keep you posted, but I'm sure he'll be good as new in a few days."

Her dad smiled. "You know, it's been good working with you, Julie. We'd make a great partnership." He winked at her.

Julie grinned. "So, when are you moving here?"

Her dad smiled wryly. "I was going to ask you when you were going to move to DC—I think it's a bit safer where I live."

If her dad had said that two days ago, she would have laughed. How ironic. She lived in a small West Virginia town, and look what she had been through. Corruption. Drugs. Violence. It's how she would have described the D.C. districts before all this.

"I love you, Dad."

Her dad put his arms around her shoulders. She winced when he touched her neck. "Oh, sorry." He didn't speak for a minute, then said, "So, I'm going to be a grandpa. Some way to find out."

Julie snuggled closer. "Well, at least you found out in person." Julie closed her eyes. She was so tired.

She released her dad, caressed Dog's face, pulled down her mask, and kissed her hero. He opened one eye and moaned. "You've got to get better. We're going to adopt you." He lifted his head slightly, then lowered it and closed his eyes. Julie didn't want to leave him, but she knew he was in good hands and she had a date with her man.

Julie looked around the room at her heroes. Doc Lawrence had stepped in the moment she needed him. Her dad had come to her rescue and called Paul Cato to get her out. Dog had saved them all. And Angie, always concerned for her soul. Outside the door, her husband, the town's rescuer.

"I'll see you guys tomorrow."

"Not at the office."

Julie held up her hands in surrender. "You can count on it." She pushed through the surgery room door and removed her facemask and gown. Angie held her arms open. Julie accepted a long-overdue hug from her friend. She stepped back.

Angie said, "You gonna tell me what happened?"

Richard put his arm around Julie's shoulder and said, "Not now, she's not. Let's just say that the bad guys tried to take us out, but our hero,"—Richard pointed with his free hand to the surgery room— "saved the day. That's one bad guy who's not going to give us any more trouble." He kissed Julie's head.

Richard nudged Julie to go. "Sarah's stayed until we could get back. Ready to head home to our hole-y house?"

Angie's face squeezed. "Holy?"

Julie laughed. "Not that kind of holy. This is the kind where windows are shot out."

Angie's eyes grew large. "Are you a-kiddin' me?"

"Nope. Our windows were shot out."

"Well, darlin', my husband just happens to have some plywood in the back of his truck. He'll bring two of the boys and come right over to cover that up. We can't have our lovebirds freezing in their nest."

"No, we couldn't ask—"

"You didn't."

Julie looked at her friend. "You always held hope. You always had faith."

"By God's grace, I always will."

Julie listened. She didn't want to tell Angie she had made God a promise. If no one knew, then she wouldn't have to hear about it.

Angie tilted her head then looked at Richard and said, "Let me borrow her for a minute. Doc will meet you outside when we're done."

There was no point arguing with Angie. Richard nodded once, then headed out.

Angie put her arm around Julie's waist and began to walk her to the front. "I know you're angry with God for a-takin' your mama. I know you miss her, but she's up in heaven, pain-free and singing with the angels. I know it's been hard for you and your sister. God tells us that He works all things together for the good of those who love Him and are called according to His purposes. It's hard to believe that death can be used for his good purpose, but when I look at you, I see the woman God has made ready to be a mama. You would be a different person if your mama had been alive. I don't know all the things God has worked out for you and Richard, but I do see a wonderful woman God is calling to step up and be His. I think your mama is smiling right now and saying "Come on, Julie, let God into your heart."

Julie yearned to agree. Her heart was racing, but she just couldn't let go. She needed to think through this. They stopped when they got to the front door. She turned to Angie. "I guess I have a lot to think about."

"Don't overthink this, baby girl. Your heart knows what's right."

Is that why her heart was pounding? What was she giving up if she let Him in?

Your anger against Me.

My anger? Was that all it was?

She looked at Angie. Her peaceful countenance. Julie wanted that, but her mind was fuzzy and she was tired. Now was not the time.

"Richard's waiting," Julie said. "You sure you want the boys to come over tonight?"

"Changing the subject, I see. Don't worry. I'm a-callin' the boys now."

"Speaking of which, I needed my phone at the house. It's a good thing dad had written your number by the house phone. Hand it over."

Angie retrieved it. "Promise you won't answer it."

"I promise."

CHAPTER 33

Thursday 3:22 a.m.

THE RINGTONE WAS CALLED "ANGEL WINGS." But at 3:22 a.m., it didn't matter if it was a siren or a flutter. The alarm clock's red numbers glared at Julie's one open eye.

Richard reached over Julie, retrieved her phone, and answered like he was a recording. "I'm sorry. Dr. Wheeler is recovering from an illness and will be unable to handle your emergency. Please call the office line for an alternate phone number. Thank you." He hung up, returned the phone to its spot on her bedside table. Then he kissed his bride.

"Who was it?"

"Does it matter?"

She forced the images of breach calves from her mind and turned to Richard. "Not when you're by my side."

Could she get used to life without midnight calls? Maybe she should hire an associate, especially with the baby coming. But for today, it was enough to know that the dads were on call and her heroes were nearby.

***

Friday 10:00 a.m.

JULIE FINISHED PACKING HER BAG as Dog eyed her every move with curious tips and turns of his head. She scanned the bedroom. What was she forgetting? She put her hand to her heart. The pendant.

She entered her closet and retrieved it from the jewelry box. She held it in the palm of her hand. She could not let evil hijack the sweet memory of her precious mother. She watched herself in the mirror as she clasped it on. She touched her stomach and pictured her child reaching for the pendant as she nursed it. The necklace would be evidence to a new generation of her mother's life well-lived.

Richard came to the closet doorway and leaned against the jamb. He looked more handsome than ever. "Are you ready to run away with me?"

Julie lifted her hands to her chin and batted her eyes. "Wherever shall we go?"

"Far, far away—" he said, sweeping his hand outward.

"—To a beach by the ocean where ponies play," Julie said.

"Forget the ponies. I can't wait to get you alone." He winked. "I can't remember the last time we went to your dad's vacation house. How long has it been?"

"Too long ago. I soooo need this." Julie stepped forward. Richard let her pass, but not without a kiss.

"You know it's going to be desolate . . . and cold."

"Yes, but the good news is that this time of year, Chincoteague won't have any mosquitoes, flies, or no-see-ums. Remember the last time?" Julie asked. Richard nodded. "And no tourists. Oh . . . and no *Catherine*. Just you and me."

"Speaking of which"—Richard walked to the bed and poked around her suitcase. She came to him and slapped his roving hand. "So, did you pack that little lacy lavender present I got you?"

"We all know who that present is for. You're the one who gets to look at it." Julie smirked and closed her suitcase. She stood between him and the suitcase then turned to face him. He wrapped her in his arms. Her heart pounded as they kissed for a long moment. She pulled back, caught her breath, and said, "If we don't stop now . . ." She smiled and pointed to her suitcase. "I think that's everything."

Richard released her, took her bag, and headed toward the stairs. He called back. "I'm glad. I don't think there's any more room in the 'Stang."

Richard grinned broadly every time he said "'Stang." Julie didn't know who was more excited about his surprise gift to her—a brand new Mustang convertible—just because. She hadn't even realized that Richard had paid attention when she mentioned her dream car. He even remembered her favorite color—sunshine yellow.

Right now, she hoped the air blowing through her hair might just blow away the pain of the last few days.

Julie looked around the room. She inhaled deeply. The scent of love potions abounded. Sounds and images replayed in her mind of music, candles glowing, and her husband romancing her into motherhood just a few weeks before. Richard was truly the lover of her soul.

Dog watched her every move. "Are you ready for a long ride, boy?" Dog's ears perked. He groaned as he rose. His pain didn't stop his tail from beating the air. "You're such a good boy. I'll be glad when you're all healed up. Come on, boy." He trustingly followed.

Dog took one step at a time, making his way down the staircase. Richard came back in as they reached the bottom, his face serious, his hand full of mail. The top envelope held his attention. He turned into the study. Julie followed.

"What's wrong?"

Richard opened the envelope covered with too many stamps. "It's from Mack." Julie moved to his side as they read it together. "He must have sent it on Tuesday before we met at the mine."

"Wow. I saw him at the Diner that morning. It's no wonder he was so somber."

Richard shook his head. "He thought they were going to kill him. They almost did."

Julie touched her bruises reminding her how far-reaching the Detroit connection was. She, Richard, and Mack could have been killed. Despite the FBI's repeated assurances that they were safe, she was comforted that federal marshals would be keeping watch over them at her dad's beach house and when they returned . . . at least until trial.

She looked back at the letter. "Why isn't Mack going into witness protection? Won't they come after him?"

"He's only dangerous to them until testifies. The feds have seventy days to bring them to trial. The prosecutor said they'll probably set it for thirty unless their defense attorney gets a continuance." Richard shook his head. "I don't see how. The grand jury has already put together a mountain of evidence. And with Cruz's testimony, it should be a done deal. The defense will likely paint Mack as a player, not the victim of blackmail, so he'll likely serve time."

"What about his job? Can you imagine losing your career and pension after all these years when all he was doing was trying to protect Marge?" Julie searched Richard's eyes for a sign of compassion and not his normal "bad choices beget bad consequences" speech.

After a long moment, he said, "A lot of people got hurt—you being one of them." Richard touched her bruised neck. Julie took his hand and kissed it. Richard reread the letter, then folded it and returned it to the envelope. He ran his finger over the stamps and gave a half-laugh. "Honest Abe stamps. How ironic. Bet these are worth some money." He tapped the envelope's corner on his hand and placed it on the desk.

"I wish I had been a better friend. I was too busy to notice them drift off." She paused. "Intentional."

"Huh?"

"That's my new word. Intentional. I remember Angie talking about that with one of the patients. Said her pastor was talking about how we have to be intentional with our marriages or we drift apart. Said we get so busy that we lose sight of each other. That busyness poisons all of our relationships—especially our marriages. I remember thinking how silly that was—that we would never drift apart." Julie shook her head. "That could've been us."

He looked deeply into her eyes. "Let's promise to never get too busy again. Let's take time to love one another." Richard grinned and touched her belly. "And Richard, Jr."

"Or Rosaline, after my mom."

A warm smile graced his face. "Rosie."

"I love you, Richard, Sr., with all my heart."

Sarah emerged from the kitchen with a picnic basket followed by Julie's dad.

Richard took the basket and lifted the corner. "Do I smell your famous cinnamon buns?" He peeked inside. "Oooh, baby."

"You're not kidding," her dad said with a wide grin. "I got to be the taste-tester."

Sarah beamed, then wielded her pointer finger at Richard. "Do not eat those until your wife eats the healthy stuff. And don't forget to stop at that park I told you about. West Virginia parks are the best."

"Yes ma'am." Richard laughed. "Now I just have to find room for the basket in the car. Someone forgot to tell my wife that we are only going away for a couple of weeks. I guess Dog will be sharing his backseat with the basket."

"There are some treats in there for him, too."

"Why am I not surprised?" Richard turned and headed out with his treasure.

Julie's dad put his arm around Sarah and kissed her on the forehead. "If you ever decide to come back to D.C., we've got a kitchen that could use your help."

"Hey, wait a minute," Catherine said as she swept in from the kitchen with a perfectly painted smile. "I heard that." She stopped at her husband's side. Her dad's shoulders stooped and his face dropped as all the joy was sucked from the room. Julie hated the effect Catherine had on him. Why couldn't she have waited until they left to get there? Sarah rolled her eyes and returned to the kitchen. She didn't like Julie's stepmother any better than Julie and Heather. *Let it go, Julie.*

"Promise me you'll call if you hear from Heather," Julie said.

"You know I will." Her dad said. "But you know her pity parties last days, sometimes weeks." He looked up the staircase as if he was remembering something he had seen. "But something feels different this time." He shook his head. "I don't know what it is. I have this feeling I can't shake."

"What is it dear?" Catherine said, pretending to care.

Her dad shook his head. "I don't know." He looked up the staircase again.

Catherine looked up and sighed. "Oh, it's just probably just your indigestion. The good Lord knows Heather's going to be fine." Her dad frowned as Catherine alone laughed. Could she not read her husband after all these years? Oh, wait . . . that would require her to think about somebody else.

Julie had had her own troubling feelings, but with everything happening and her pregnancy fatigue, she had not let the ominous thoughts take rest in her spirit. But now with her dad's revelation, it began to settle back in.

Richard returned with Max who was dressed in a black leather jacket. Somehow the sling detracted from the cool look. He was carrying a couple of yellow and black Mustang ball caps. "Look who I found trying to slip away," Richard said.

"Going somewhere?" Julie asked.

"Yes, ma'am. Right after I deliver your hats for your new ride. I know my sisters would demand color coordination." He handed over the caps. Julie and Richard donned their hats as Max pulled a yellow dog bandana out of his pocket. He held it up. Dog's name was printed on it.

"These are great!" Julie took the bandana from Max and carefully tied it around Dog's neck. "Now we're stylin'."

"Thanks man. These really are great." Richard said. "Let's get a picture with us in our caps and Dog in his bandana." He handed his phone to Julie's dad and asked him to snap a picture that included Max.

"Aren't you going to introduce us?" Catherine said, shaking her head.

Julie wanted to scream, "Run!" Instead, Richard hugged Julie— likely to keep her from saying something ugly. Richard made the proper introductions.

"Nice to meet you," Max said.

If only he knew.

"Your new protective detail has arrived. My job is done here. They already have one set up in Chincoteague. I'm headed off for a few weeks of R&R myself, and then I'm sure they'll reassign me to my next post."

Sarah emerged from the kitchen. "Is that Jake—I mean Max—I hear?"

Max nodded. "Yes, ma'am."

"You wait right here, and don't leave before I get back." Sarah held out her hands as if stopping his progress. "Great hats, by the way," she said as she disappeared back into her lair.

Julie's dad shook Max's hand. "I don't know what would have happened if you hadn't been on the job. Thank you for protecting my little girl."

"Yes, thank you," Catherine said. "She is so precious to us."

Right.

"My pleasure, sir," Max said. "Now I leave her in your hands."

Her dad's face twisted as he looked back up the staircase again, then back to Max. "Son, I know this isn't your job and this is not FBI business, but can you check around for Heather. That girl is a magnet for trouble, and I just have a bad feeling. One I've never had before. I feel like she's in trouble."

"What do you mean?" Max asked.

"Oh, he's exaggerating," Catherine said as she scrunched her plastic face and swept the air with her hand. Her dad withered a bit.

"Catherine. Quit interrupting and let Dad talk!" Julie said.

Catherine's face dropped. "Well, I'm just saying . . ."

"Just stop saying! Go on Dad."

Max looked between them as the awkwardness settled. "Go on, Doc Blanchard."

Julie's dad looked at Catherine as if for permission. Julie hated that look on his face. Catherine must have received a degree in emasculation.

Her dad looked back at Max. "I can't explain it. Yesterday this feeling of dread came over me when I was taking a nap. No, it was more like a nightmare. Heather was running. There was an explosion. Then I woke up sweating. I just don't get dreams like that." His face squeezed. "Well . . ."

"What is it?" Julie asked.

"I haven't had that vivid a dream since your momma got sick. I had a dream then too. It was like I knew she had cancer before the doctors did. We got to the right doctors who helped her to have more time with you girls. Your mama claimed it was the Holy Spirit's work."

That sounded like her mom. "Holy Spirit on not, why didn't you tell me?" Julie asked. "I've been having nightmares about Heather as well. Not as vivid as an explosion. But where Heather is calling for help, and I can't get to her. It was so real."

"Well, we all know that Heather's a nightmare," Catherine said. All mouths fell open.

Richard took Julie into his arms and said, "Babe, why didn't you tell me?"

"I didn't want to worry you. Or anybody. Everybody's already walking on eggshells around me."

Richard looked at Max as if asking without words.

Max looked between Julie and her dad. "You're right, I can't officially do anything, but after all your family has sacrificed for us, the least I can do is check around. I'll see if there's any word on her and let you know."

Her dad shook Max's hand again, forging a man-to-man deal.

Richard released Julie and shook Max's hand as well. "This means a lot to us all." Richard shot a look at Catherine, then looked back at Max. "Thanks, man."

Max nodded. "Thank you all for what you have done. I'll look into this. I hope you'll be able to relax and enjoy yourselves—even with the detail watching you. And I'll do my best to find Heather."

"I feel better already," Julie said. She hugged Max. "Now, go find her."

Sarah came from the kitchen with a wrapped container. "Just you wait a minute." She handed the treats to Max.

"Is this what I think it is?" Max said, with the biggest grin he had ever unleashed.

"Yes, sir. Your favorite—and my specialty—cherry cobbler."

Max received the dish and gave Sarah a long hug. "You have no idea how much this means to me." He released her. "If that husband of yours ever loses his mind and gives you up, I'll marry you in a minute. You are one special woman."

"That's the second offer I've had today." Everyone except Catherine chuckled. "Now go on and get out of here before I decide to run off with you."

Max tipped his head. "Thank you all again for allowing me to share in the richness of this family. You are very special people." He held up his treasure, smiled, and headed out the door.

Julie turned back to her dad, "Well, I guess it's time to go." She searched her dad's pained face. "I love you. Thanks for coming to save me."

"I love you too. And, now that Max is on the job, you had better go enjoy your time together. You deserve it." He embraced Julie for a long moment, then released her to Richard. He gave Richard a man-hug, then said, "Now go forth and take care of my grandchild."

"I will, sir."

Julie forced herself to hug Catherine. "Take care of Dad."

"You know I always do."

Richard scooped Julie in his right arm as he glided her to the door. "Your chariot awaits you. Be warned, either you or Dog will have to sit on top of the picnic basket."

"Ha, ha." Julie patted her leg and Dog heeled as they departed the house. She giggled as she surveyed her sunshine yellow dream.

A honeymoon in the middle of a life that had previously left no time for love. Rice should be pouring over them any moment. Sarah joined Julie's dad and Catherine on the porch as Richard held the car door as his wounded companions mounted Julie's new steed. The day had cooperated with top-down blue skies and unseasonably warm temperatures.

Richard hopped in the front, turned the key, revved the engine, and started her favorite playlist. He eased the car into gear and they drove off to a life of intentional loving.

THE NEW BEGINNING

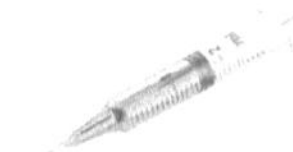

DRUGGED

POISONED SERIES—BOOK 2

Wonder what happened to Heather when she left the Wheeler house too drunk to drive? How can one poor decision lead to being the target of drug gangs and the FBI/DEA? This action-packed story filled with explosions, amnesia, cloak-and-dagger escapes, and drugs leads Heather to the edge of death. Can she survive?

OTHER BOOKS BY PATRICIA HARTMAN

**"A FUNNY THING HAPPENED
ON MY JOURNEY TO HEAVEN"**

Want to know Patricia Hartman better?

Join Patricia Hartman in a *funny* look at life and how the *funny* (amusing, odd, or coincidental) events of life have shaped her. These stories have taken her from a rebellious atheist to the woman of faith that God is still working on today and will work on as she journeys toward heaven's gate. Each funny story reflects upon God's scriptures for the truth, wisdom, and the meaning of God's lessons.

Grab a cup of coffee and a tissue box and join her journey.

"THE CHRISTIAN PRENUPTIAL AGREEMENT: THE POWER OF MARRIAGE UNLEASHED"

Patricia's divorce attorney friends insisted when she got married that she should have a prenup. At first, she explained that Christians don't do prenups. But as she went through her vows, she discovered that we do (or should) have a prenup that expressed the vows we take—they are just oral, instead of written. She went back to her friends and told them, "Yes, and mine will say if I cheat on your or divorce you, I will give you everything."

"Nobody would sign that!" they said.

But isn't that exactly what we sign up for as Christians?

This marriage manual covers examines both God's law and man's law, "love drugs" (chemicals of the brain released when "in love), history of marriage, vows, and the implications of "for worse," agreements (boundaries) with in-laws, and what it means to become like-minded. This is a must-read for all engaged couples and already married couples as well.

Both books are available on Amazon in Paperback or Kindle editions